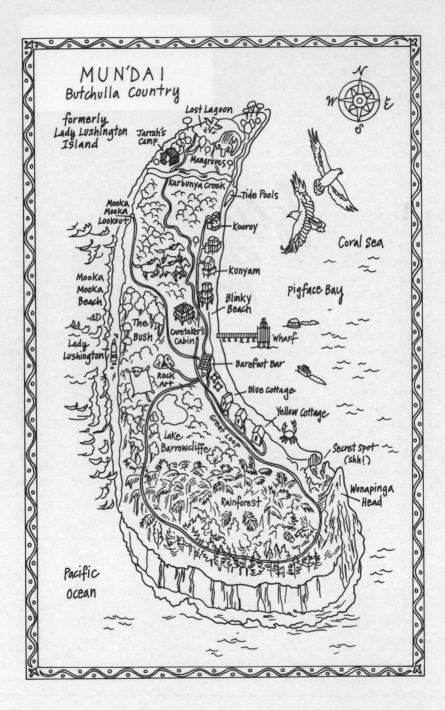

ALSO BY GEORGIA CLARK

It Had to Be You

The Bucket List

The Regulars

Parched

She's with the Band

Island Time

A NOVEL

GEORGIA CLARK

EMILY BESTLER BOOKS

ATRIA

NEW YORK   LONDON   TORONTO   SYDNEY   NEW DELHI

EMILY
BESTLER
BOOKS

ATRIA

An Imprint of Simon & Schuster, Inc.
1230 Avenue of the Americas
New York, NY 10020

First Emily Bestler Books/Atria Paperback edition June 2022

EMILY BESTLER BOOKS/ATRIA PAPERBACK and colophon are trademarks of Simon & Schuster, Inc.

For information about special discounts for bulk purchases, please contact Simon & Schuster Special Sales at 1-866-506-1949 or business@simonandschuster.com.

The Simon & Schuster Speakers Bureau can bring authors to your live event. For more information or to book an event, contact the Simon & Schuster Speakers Bureau at 1-866-248-3049 or visit our website at www.simonspeakers.com.

Interior design by Alexis Minieri

Manufactured in the United States of America

1   3   5   7   9   10   8   6   4   2

Library of Congress Cataloging-in-Publication Data has been applied for.

ISBN 978-1-6680-0124-0
ISBN 978-1-6680-0125-7 (ebook)

For my family

PROLOGUE

Sixty-three miles from the southeastern coast of Queensland, Australia, is an island unlike any other.

Most of it has never been logged or mined or trampled by tourists shoving shells in their pockets. Much of the land is as it was prehuman. Fewer than sixty visitors are permitted at any one time.

The island is so remote, it appears as an afterthought. At roughly six miles long and one-and-a-half miles wide, it isn't particularly large: you can hike from one end to the other in a day. But its modest three thousand acres are home to some of the most astounding biodiversity on the planet.

Like most powerful places, it has more than one name. The first is for the ship whose rusting skeleton can still be found where it wrecked on the western shore in 1803: Lady Lushington (the Aussies shorten this to "Lush").

The second is the island's Indigenous name, in the language of the Butchulla people: Mun'dai, meaning *pretty*.

Two small, uncomfortable ferries service the island daily, crossing the Coral Sea, which is part of the Pacific Ocean. And on this hot morning in mid-March, only one passenger is on board. She scans the endless ocean for so long, she begins to wonder if mysterious Mun'dai is simply the stuff of legend. Surely, there can be no life out here, so far from the mainland. But without warning, the horizon buckles, rising up. An ochre-red cliff soars out of the sea, crowned in a tangle of subtropical rainforest. An ancient world of towering pines and oversized ferns, emerald-green and prehistoric. The southern end: the highest peak.

The ferry circles the head, aiming for Mun'dai's only wharf. A white wedding train of foam trails behind the boat. The cliffs begin to dip, steamy rainforest opening up into airy eucalypt woodland. A sea breeze picks up the scent of lemon and pine. The restless sea quiets into the clear waters of a bay. A crescent-shaped fringe of silica sand, pale as a wishbone, kisses shallows that begin as transparent as glass before deepening into a clear and tender blue.

Not another human being in sight.

Nothing but wheeling seabirds swooping graceful as calligraphy and the triumphant cries of the cicadas ringing out in the sticky, sun-drenched morning.

The ferry lifts over a swell. A bottle of white wine nudges out of the paper bags of groceries at the young woman's feet and rolls across the boat's metal floor. She scoops it up like an errant toddler. There are enough supplies and treats for a week, not a weekend.

The boat bumps against the wooden wharf. A loop of rope thrown, secured.

Amelia Kelly correctly suspects this is where her life will change forever.

But not for the reason she thinks.

PART ONE

PART ONE

I

Stepping over the threshold of the house that faced the ocean felt like entering an abandoned palace: illicit loveliness in a life that wasn't hers. It was so far from what Amelia Kelly understood a rental house to be that her definition of the concept was already evolving.

Press a button, and cream-colored blinds descended from the ceiling like a magic trick. The bathrooms were a sparkling marvel of marble as white as the moon. Ten different types of tea lined the drawer below the needlessly complicated espresso machine, each one organic and elegantly named: *Rich Maple Chai, a love affair of sweet and spicy.* The house hummed with the quiet efficiency of something beautiful and well-made. There was no trace of past tenants; someone had wiped away every fingerprint from the sparkling glass, every crumb from the polished wood floorboards. Like a hostess who greets her guests with immaculate makeup and a tray of cocktails, the house made being ready look easy.

Amelia hefted the three bags of groceries onto the kitchen counter—handsome slate—then slid the balcony door open and stepped outside. On the white sandy beach in front, red-and-white-striped deck chairs and beach umbrellas. A salt-scented breeze moved the soft needles of the casuarina trees. The only sounds were the gentle wash of the tide and the musical lilt of birdsong. Each of the seven rental houses on Lady Lushington Island faced the gumball-blue waters of Pigface Bay.

A thrill fizzed up Amelia's body. The idea of impressing James made her feel slightly giddy, day drunk. She unpacked, ensuring the five new frilly bikinis purchased for her boyfriend's appreciation would be the first things he saw hanging in their closet, like flirty showgirls awaiting their cue. The bright, colorful native flowers—waratahs, banksias, and bottle-brush, purchased at a farmers market on the mainland—were split into two vases. One on the raw-edge dining table for everyone to enjoy, and the other by the double bed she and James would be sharing. She figured out the Wi-Fi and the smart TV and put away a selection of everyone's favorite foods. Surprising and delighting her best-loved people through small, altruistic acts gave Amelia a solid sense of well-being. It was so easy to do, it quietly perplexed her why it wasn't a more widespread practice.

The house—it was called Kunyam—sat on a slight rise overlooking the bay. The ground floor had a small gym and a kid's bedroom, neither of which she assumed her family would be using. An interior flight of wide, lightwood stairs led up to the majestic, open-plan main space on the second floor: kitchen, dining room table and sofa, two bedrooms, plus the balcony, held up on stilts. Another flight of stairs led up to the third-floor master suite.

The door to the suite was constructed from a single slab of red-brown wood. The stainless-steel handle was cool to the touch. Amelia had grown up reading books about plucky girls with big hearts who never met a barrier they didn't surmount. She had no reason to go into the master bedroom except her own curiosity and, perhaps, a dash of self-sabotage. The door opened soundlessly into the most beautiful bedroom she'd ever seen in real life. Wonder and envy made the younger Kelly sister suck in a breath.

The bed was the size of a ship, the tub big enough for a dinner party. Colorful Indigenous art hung above a small desk, a short blurb about the artist neatly stenciled onto the wall. There was even a private deck, which offered the same view as the larger balcony downstairs, but the added elevation expanded the perspective. It felt like something out of *Vogue*, in the travel section that drooled over wildly unattainable lives.

But today, this was her life.

Well, the master suite wasn't her life. The master had never been her life—not once.

But maybe, it would be soon.

The master's earthy linens didn't look like hotel sheets. They looked like normal sheets—normal if you were successful and lived with a spouse, not in a messy Sydney sharehouse with four other roommates. Amelia peeled the top sheet back and hopped in, reveling in the extra space and the titillation of being somewhere she shouldn't.

You could really *do things* in a bed this size.

James Smith was a leading man, not one of the immature boys she'd wasted her love on in the past. He inhabited his life with intention and control. They weren't officially engaged. Yet. But the idea that James seemed to believe his world and hers were at enough of an equilibrium they might have a future together filled Amelia with almost guilty elation. It was a reflection, she hoped, of how even though her life didn't feel like a culmination of hard work and ambitious decisions, like her sister's, it would all turn out for the best.

Her boyfriend was supposed to have traveled up with her, but a last-minute work dinner postponed his plans. Amelia had accepted his sincere apology graciously. Gracious was how she imagined a wife would be about her husband's important work commitments. All Amelia wanted from the three nights on Lady Lush was for her extended family to all love James as much as she did. For James to be impressed by her extra effort and good taste and emotional maturity. For James to be impressed by her, period. For them to get one step closer to her own happily-ever-after.

Amelia Smith. The idea flicked a quick, slightly desperate feeling around her throat.

Maybe by the next family vacation, Mrs. Smith could snag the master.

Amelia remade the bed and trotted back down to the main space on the second floor, settling in the expensive-feeling leather sectional. It wasn't a cheap holiday. Three nights on Mun'dai cost two months' rent, which the sisters were splitting. (James had offered to kick in, which Amelia heroically declined, a move she was vaguely regretting, given the anemic state of her bank account.) But the money was for a good cause.

Lady Lushington Island had always been the traditional land of the Butchulla people, pronounced "*But*-cha-la": one of more than five hundred Indigenous Australian clans. Following an extended native title case a decade before, all three thousand acres were administratively returned to the Butchulla, descendants of the tribe that had lived on the island for thousands of years prior to its "discovery" (read: invasion) by white settlers in the 1800s. In order to protect the geographic integrity and many sacred sites, the Butchulla people sensibly and cleverly decided to allow a small number of yearly visitors to the island, capped by the number of rental houses. A form of ecotourism—the strategy ensured tourists valued the island by allowing a limited number of them to see it and maintain its reputation as a beautiful, worthy place, as well as making enough money from the visitors to preserve it. Amelia had to sign a contract ensuring her family wouldn't take so much as a seedpod with them. Indigenous Australians were allowed to hunt, fish, and camp on the island year-round, and could book the houses at a generous discount. For everyone else, the price of paradise was high. But clearly, worth it. Even the sofa felt like sinking into a marshmallowy dream.

Each house had an informational binder detailing rules, FAQs, and a detailed map. Mun'dai was roughly crescent-shaped, like a C—fat at the bottom and skinny at the top. The seven rental houses were all on the eastern-facing Blinky Beach, which looked onto Pigface Bay, named for the ubiquitous flowering ground creeper whose purple-pink and yellow blooms looked nothing like a swine's snout.

Amelia scanned a handwritten welcome note.

Hello, Amelia & Co!

Welcome to Mun'dai, the traditional land of the Butchulla people. Your house is Kunyam, and you'll find everything you need to know about your stay in the binder. Email, or come by the Caretaker Cabin (indicated on the map), with any questions, requests, or concerns.

Per Butchulla law, "What is good for the land comes first; if you have plenty, you must share; and if it's not yours, you shall not take."

Enjoy your stay in this extraordinary place.

—Liss Chambers

There was more information enclosed: a mention of the Barefoot Bar, a casual beach bar open from 5:00 p.m.; warnings about the brumbies (free-roaming horses, which despite being feral still ignited every visitor's *Black Beauty* dreams) and dingoes (native wild dogs that must not be approached, fed, insulted, looked directly in the eye, referred to by their first name, etc.); tide times and canoe rental hours; a map of the island's Indigenous sites; and details about the food. Each house could indicate the time they wanted their daily meal kit dropped off, a mix of ready-to-eat foods and easy-to-prepare meals. Did she have enough time to meet Caretaker Liss to discuss the menu? It was only listed as "a mouthwatering array of dishes that showcased Australia's best seasonal fare." Matty had mentioned wanting fresh Queensland shellfish in every call since they booked, and Amelia knew from experience her big sister would require a lot of fresh lime on the side.

Just as Amelia's eyes found the time—3:12 p.m.—the ferry horn wailed, as if heralding an arriving army. There, pulling into the long wharf at the other end of Blinky Beach, her sister was here, her family was here!

Amelia threw a kimono cover-up over her cutoffs and bikini and flew down the stairs, out the front door, and onto the beach. She was most comfortable in her body when it was moving, in the air, in the world. She couldn't help but let out a yell of pure joy. The Japanese group waiting to board smiled easily at her as Amelia galloped up the old wooden wharf, as did the gaggle of women about her age who looked sunburned and very hungover.

Matty was first off the ferry. Amelia threw herself into her sister's outstretched arms. "You're here, you're here, you're here!"

The sisters laughed and jumped and squealed, not caring at all about the commotion they were causing. Amelia hadn't seen her mouthy, fabulous, skipped-a-grade sister in person since Matty's wedding last year. And now she was back in Australia *for good*.

"Animal!" Matty laughed, using Amelia's pet name. She pushed her sister back to get a good look at her. "You're so blond. And thin, Jesus, I can feel your ribs. Fuck, it's gorgeous here, look at the water. Where's your lover?"

"Shut up, I had a cheeseburger last Monday. He had a work thing come up, he'll be here tomorrow." Amelia hugged her sister's wife. Only Parker Lee could look so put together and, yes, *fresh*, after a punishing twenty-seven-hour flight halfway around the planet. New York to Brisbane via L.A., and her white button-down was still crisp. "Hi, Parks! It's so good to see you!"

"You too." Parker's hug back was quick but warm. "Wow." She admired the island. "It's even nicer than the pictures. James has a work thing?"

"A dinner," Amelia said. "With clients." That detail was improvised. Amelia didn't want the two women to realize she didn't understand her boyfriend's job: hedge fund something-or-other. James lived in Melbourne, a one-and-a-half-hour flight from Sydney. He came up one or two days a week for work. Amelia's life had revolved around romantic, sex-stuffed hotel stays for almost six months.

Amelia's mum, Jules, was next off the ferry, wrangling overfull tote bags. Her mum's unruly curls were mostly contained under a practical and deeply unfashionable straw hat from Bunnings, the national Home Depot–esque chain. Cargo shorts, well-worn boots: Amelia felt a tap of worry. Her mum had brought nicer clothes than that, right?

"Muffin!" Jules embraced Amelia, as if they hadn't just seen each other for Sunday dinner last week. "You look lovely. Where's James?"

"Work thing," Amelia repeated, grabbing the handle of her sister's carry-on. "He'll be here tomorrow morning, he's really sorry."

"Buggar!" Jules looked crestfallen. "We saved him some of our chips from lunch: he seemed to like them so much at Flying Fish. Glen! Where are those chips?"

"Chips?" With his slightly hunched shoulders and thinning brown hair, Amelia's father always looked a bit like an absentminded physics professor, even though he was a sharply minded, if retired, electrical engineer.

"Yes, the chips we were saving for James!" Jules sounded annoyed.

"James isn't coming till tomorrow." Matty put on a pair of oversized sunglasses that gave her the look of an eccentric celebrity on vacation. "Work thing."

Glen's gaze moved from the wharf's bright *Welcome to Country!* informational placard to a pair of masked boobies, the birds carouseling above the island's thick canopy of trees. "I didn't realize we were saving the chips for James."

"Well, it doesn't matter now, he's not coming till tomorrow!" Jules exclaimed. "Amelia, are you wearing sunscreen? Matty, did you reapply? Do the Lees need a hand with their bags? Gosh, the energy here is incredible. I can't believe we didn't keep those chips!"

"I have the fries." Parker produced the greasy bag seemingly from nowhere and held them at arm's length with the self-possession of someone unlikely to ever sneak a greasy chip.

"Oh good, I'm starving." Matty grabbed a handful of what were clearly soggy, ordinary chips.

For the first time since hearing of James's delay, Amelia was grateful. Imagine giving James Smith, a man who understood the global financial markets and wore the same brand of watch as Ryan Reynolds, a sad bag of cold, crap chips.

"C'mon, Animal." Matty tugged her away from the confusion of suitcases and arriving and departing guests, heading down the wharf. "Let's go for a swim."

2

Matty stood on the balcony of Kunyam's master bedroom and breathed. It was and wasn't home.

When Matty Kelly first left Australia in her late twenties, she couldn't get on the QANTAS flight fast enough. The irritatingly perfect weather and parochial nature of a hometown teeming with ex-girlfriends felt stifling. But after seven years of battling brutal East Coast winters and a truly atrocious health care system, she'd come to appreciate her smaller, safer, sunnier homeland anew.

Even though it was early autumn Down Under, here in the tropics it felt like high summer. Mun'dai's warm air was heavy with the herbaceous scent of the bush and sharp brine of sea salt. Familiar, yet foreign. Matty was a different person now. New York had expanded her, opened her eyes. Still, there was no denying it: "It's fucking paradise."

"It's fucking paradise, mate." Parker mimicked the accent, which made them both laugh.

Their lips met in a kiss, which started steamy, then turned silly, Matty sucking on Parker's lower lip and pretending to eat her. Her wife laughed and pushed her off. When Matty was younger, she imagined marriage as something far more coolly elegant than it was turning out to be. Despite sincerely pledging their eternal love to each other in front of one hundred and twenty-three of their closest friends and family, they still spent hours giggling and mauling each other like puppies. Marriage was smelling your spouse's farts and tweezing their in-grown hairs and realizing that everything Matty found impossibly charming about Parker was also the root cause of her most annoying traits—and vice versa—which all played out in a surprisingly breezy way. Even in tricky moments, Matty could usually get Parker to crack a smile by reminding her *It's just you and me in this two-man show that's playing for the rest of our lives.*

They puttered around the bedroom, unpacking, exploring, an easy ballet. Parker would take the desk facing the ocean; Matty worked in bed. Matty would make a mess in the bathroom with her dozens of testers and samples; Parker would keep the six K-beauty skincare products that she was unflaggingly loyal to in a neat line. They'd mostly given up trying to alter each other. People's circumstances could change. Personalities rarely did.

Parker examined a painted, polished boomerang hung on the wall as art, scanning the short text that explained the cultural significance of the eyebrow-shaped hunting weapon. "Why didn't Amelia take the suite?"

Matty shrugged but she knew why: she'd heavily implied it would be amazing if she and Parker could have the master, considering they'd be getting off such a long flight, and it was basically their babymoon (a term Matty disliked saying out loud). And, after all, they were married. "Dunno. She's obviously planning the full show for this new one."

Parker pulled her MacBook Air out of her carry-on. "Meaning?"

Matty wiped a smudge of Amelia's pink lip gloss off her cheek. "Operation Barbie is in full effect."

If her sister ever embraced the frightening potential of her own beauty, they'd lose her to ego or Los Angeles (or both). Fortunately, Amelia usually treated her good looks as something she was in reluctant possession of; an expensive car she didn't pay for but couldn't not use.

Matty picked up a candle next to the bed, gave it a sniff. Eucalyptus and something spicy. Candles were such a rip-off. Thirty bucks for wax and a bit of essential oil! Matty bought them regularly. "I'm worried I won't like James."

Parker looked up from her laptop. "You don't like James."

The women had met the new boyfriend over FaceTime, after

which Matty declared James to be "up himself." (Parker had to ask: *conceited*.)

"I just want my little sister to be happy! As happy as I am." In the sing-song voice they used when no one else was around, "I love you, boo boo."

"I love you, too, boo boo," Parker sing-sung it back. Matty was particularly proud that Cool Girl Parker Lee was now someone who used the phrase *boo boo* without thinking. "I think you should get on board with James." Parker started typing. "It's what Amelia wants. You've been so excited about seeing her."

Matty glanced at her suitcase, decided to unpack later. Somehow Parker had already unpacked. "Yeah, I'm always excited about seeing my family. Then two days in, I'm reminded why I live in New York."

Parker looked up. "*Lived*, boo boo."

The correction caught Matty by surprise. The reality that they *lived*, past tense, in New York, wasn't settling in Matty's bones. Of course it made sense to start a family in her hometown—free health care and schools without school shootings, being close to family and the beach. Sydney was a highly livable world-class city; everyone knew that! But Matty's brain was still running on a New York operating platform, as if the past few months of logistics and last visits to favorite everythings hadn't happened.

Matty buried her head in a pillow. "You have to save me from Mum's endless baby talk." Jules spent half the ferry ride discussing Matty's fertility levels with a group of British backpackers being dropped at a neighboring island. "I just know she's going to spend the whole trip shoving prenatal vitamins down my throat."

"Are you taking them?"

"Women have been giving birth for centuries without doulas or checkups or bloody prenatal vitamins!"

"Yep, and lots of them died in labor." Parker tossed the jar of prenatal vitamins, displaying the competent athleticism she'd inherited from her father, a compact Chinese health coach prone to exercising anywhere.

Never the athlete, Matty missed the catch. The bottle rolled under the bed. She huffed a sigh. All Matty wanted was to enjoy the weekend with her family—a weekend that didn't involve vitamins or AMH levels or endless discussion of some stranger pumping her full of another stranger's sperm. When they'd first met, Parker was on the fence about kids, and didn't want to carry herself. Over the years, Parker came around to the idea of a family, buoyed by Matty's assuredness. Still, the fast-approaching insemination process made Matty feel strangely uneasy. Normal, surely. What woman didn't feel conflicted about birthing a watermelon through a grape seed (or whatever that absolutely terrifying metaphor was)? Matty figured her excitement over getting pregnant would all kick in soon, like the moment you hear a Christmas carol in November and are suddenly ready for eggnog and stockings. She was Matilda Kelly. She could do anything, and that certainly included conquering motherhood.

Matty briefly considered sex, with Parker or the vibrator that'd accidentally been activated while going through security and unearthed by TSA for everyone to see (*Yes, I have a sexuality! Why is everyone looking so shocked?*) as Parker blushed, fighting a laugh. But an orgasm seemed like too much admin, and her parents were right downstairs. "Let's go for a swim. There's tide pools up the beach."

"You go. I'll catch up."

Matty crawled to the end of the bed to peer over Parker's shoulder. Slack, the messaging platform Parker lived on. Work. "Boo boo, you're on vacation. You're not supposed to start on Sydney time till next week!"

"I know, boo boo." Parker sighed, typing. "But LK's online."

Matty checked the time. "It's almost four. That makes it, what, 6:00 a.m. in New York? What is she even doing up?"

Parker shook her head, still typing. "You know how she is."

Matty did. While she admired the work ethic, Parker's business partner, Lauren-Kate Cutler, possessed the warmth and charm of the iceberg that sank the *Titanic*. But maybe that was gendered. If LK were a man, maybe she'd find *him* efficient and successful. That chunk of frozen water did take out an unsinkable ship, after all.

"Your loss." Matty put on a two-piece because screw it. Every body was a beach body, even—especially!—Rubenesque bodies like hers. She smooched Parker's neck and tweaked her nipple. "Find me when you're done. I'll track down Amelia. Force-feed her a pizza. I love you."

"Love you, too."

A constant daily duet. Matty's father, Glen, called it their mating call.

"Matty?" Parker pointed under the bed. "Vitamins?"

Rolling her eyes, Matty retrieved the jar and made a show of swallowing the oversized multicolored pills with water. At least it was easier than the endless needles and speculums she'd be forced to succumb to in Sydney, going through intrauterine insemination, aka IUI, a form of artificial insemination. "I'm not going to be one of those women who totally subsumes their identity to a child," she said between swigs. "I'm not planning on losing my sense of self."

"Pretty sure no one plans on that. Be nice!" Parker called after her.

"Nice women don't make history!" Matty called back.

"But they do have families who love them!"

Matty let the huge bedroom door swing silently shut behind her, feeling slightly annoyed she was only allowed to have one or the other.

3

The distinctive dot-painting art on Jules and Glen's bedroom wall was by Rover Thomas, a well-known Indigenous artist. Jules felt alarm, not pleasure, at recognizing the work of someone who showed at the National Gallery.

"Good goddess." Jules touched the throw blanket. An expensive-looking fine, light wool. "What do you think they paid for all this?"

Glen assessed the airy bedroom. "Arm and a leg, plus a torso or two."

"But Matty's got moving costs. And Amelia can't afford this on a teacher's wage." Her youngest daughter taught fifth grade at a public school; a job Jules understood far more instinctively than Matty's podcasting career.

"Let's just try to enjoy our children's generosity." Glen rubbed his wife's arms like they were in need of a good spit-polish.

She gave him a look of reproach. "Glen. Don't."

"Right. Sorry."

Jules let out a puff of frustration. "You don't need to apologize. I just think it's easier if we don't . . . Y'know . . ." Touch each other. She put the chichi throw in a drawer: far too nice to have lying around where it might get ruined. Most of the clothes Jules owned were sourced from the local op shop. Thrift stores priced things the way they ought to have been when new.

Glen hauled his suitcase onto the luggage rack, his back to her. "When's James getting here?"

"Tomorrow morning." Jules brightened, even as anxiety kneaded her stomach. "Jeez, I hope he's the one. Animal deserves a break." Her younger daughter had a history of falling in love too fast, too hard, getting her heart broken by a lot of substandard boys. James seemed different. Good job, good head on his shoulders—a head that was pretty good-looking, too. Like Matty and Parker, Jules had met James over a video call, and once in person to surprise their daughter for her birthday. Even though they'd just shown up on her sharehouse doorstep, James barely blinked before taking the whole family out to a seafood dinner at Flying Fish, picking up a considerable tab.

Amelia and James. They just looked right together. They made sense. Jules longed for the sturdy, devoted masculine energy of a son-in-law. Her sister, Marjorie, had a son-in-law who called every Monday to discuss their mutual interests of cricket and what a crap job the government was doing. Her relationship with Parker just wasn't like that. Jules wasn't yet sure what she and James might discuss in a weekly call, but once everything was official, they'd figure it out.

Glen rummaged in his suitcase. "Bit old, isn't he? Forty-two?"

"Just means he's ready for commitment. Ready for kids." The thought brightened Jules further. The need to become a grandmother was powerful: she felt it like a bird's instinct to migrate. As a parent it'd been her responsibility to set the boundaries and protect her daughters' soft bodies. The constant vigilance never relaxed, it just evolved, from choking hazards to spiked drinks. Grandkids, those sweet, worshipful creatures, would allow true indulgence of her love of children without the constant worry. Marjorie's grandchildren waited at the end of the drive every time she visited with signs and balloons, screaming with excitement when the old sedan nosed onto the cul-de-sac. Who else in your life would greet you with such joy and devotion? It made Jules teary just thinking about it, as did poignant commercials or very old people doing just about anything.

"Have they talked about kids?" Glen asked.

"I'm sure they have." Jules took off her hat and shook out her curls. "If Matty gets pregnant in the next few months, and James and Amelia settle down by the end of the year, we could have a grandkid *and* a son-in-law this time next year!"

Glen chuckled. "Don't get ahead of yourself, love."

Irritation barged into Jules's chest. "People are allowed to dream."

"I'm not—I just—" Glen closed his eyes. His voice was an inch off the ground. "I'm trying."

Jules sank onto the end of the bed. "I know."

Glen scratched the back of his neck. "When do you think we should . . . you know?"

Jules stared at him. "Not until after the weekend, obviously."

"It's not better to be honest?"

"No, Glen, it's not." Christ, this was exactly the kind of idiotic thing that made their marriage so unworkable. He never got it. Everything had to be spelled out. "Is that the kind of thing you'd want to hear on a dream holiday?"

"I think I'd want to hear the truth."

"Nobody else is you, Glen. Matty and Parker deserve to be settled— or at least have some peace of mind so she can get pregnant!"

Glen held his hands up. "Okay, okay. Let's keep it friendly, love. Jules," he corrected himself, swearing under his breath. "I'm going for a walk. Give you some space."

For a moment, Jules wondered if she might cry. But she'd already done so much of that. Tears of sadness, of frustration. Of guilt and shame. Tears because she was a woman who put family first, for whom family was everything, and she still couldn't make her own marriage work. It would crush the girls, she knew that. But Jules was tired of feeling like the second-best version of herself. There was no passion, no discovery, nothing left to talk about, let alone laugh about, and she was only sixty! She couldn't bear another thirty years of guessing her husband's feelings and doing all the emotional labor of keeping them afloat. She wanted to dance and dream and have sex—oh, remember *sex*? That thrilling adventure, that ultimate escape? As soon as Jules allowed herself to entertain the frightening, exhilarating possibility that they might separate, she knew, deep down, it would happen. It was only a matter of time.

But not until they'd welcomed James into the family and Matty started IUI. Only then would she disabuse her children of the notion that marriage was forever and their parents were still in love.

Jules opened the window.

The balmy air was honeyed with wattle. Despite having a delicate yellow puff for a flower, it was a surprisingly hardy plant. Coastal communities were harsh places for flora, being constantly exposed to the wind and the tide. Only species that adapted survived. Banksia trees, with their distinctive yellow flowers the size of a corncob, developed leathery leaves to reduce water loss. Ground covers like Knobby Clubrush produced needle-like stems to minimize surface area. Beach grass was salt- and wind-tolerant.

Jules didn't want to become harsh in order to survive. She wanted to stay soft.

The sun was starting to golden.

There was only one figure visible up the far end of Blinky Beach. Randall Lee, jogging at a brisk clip, seemingly immune to the staggering wild beauty that surrounded him.

4

Ludmila Lee was in a standoff with the toilet.

It was her husband's fault. They'd barely put their bags down when Randall shoved a sweatband into his hair and announced he was going for a run. "Then I was thinking we could do the tide pools before sunset," he went on, doing some side lunges. "Breakfast with the Kellys on Saturday, then the hike to Mooka Mooka Beach and back. Lost Lagoon and Lake Barrowcliffe on Sunday. And we should try for two swims a day in the Bay." Randall Lee, the eternal optimizer.

"I'm a maybe." Ludmila stroked the bathroom towels. A thicker, closer-textured cotton than she expected. "On everything."

Randall was almost out the front door when he called back. "Also there's something weird going on with the toilet!"

"Weird how?"

But Randall was gone. Through the wall of windows, she watched him set off at an impressive pace up the beach.

Hence the standoff.

It was Ludmila's first time in Australia, home to the world's deadliest animals. Had a redback spider or eastern brown snake made its way into the bowl? Certainly, and surprisingly, their rental house was stylish and well-appointed; each room boasted several interesting *objets d'art*. A long wooden tube called a didgeridoo was mounted to their bedroom wall, its accompanying description explaining it as a musical instrument. Lovely throws on the bed: baby alpaca, which was not, as many thought, the fur of an infant alpaca, but the finest, silkiest hairs grown by an adult. Softer than cashmere, stronger than wool. She'd request another throw for the seating on their balcony and enquire as to the manufacturer.

Ludmila spent most of her year on the road, sourcing rare vintage textiles and embroideries for Curated by Ludmila, the name of both her creative consultancy and online store full of one-of-a-kind treasures. Her armful of bracelets were from Mexico City, the hand-embroidered silk scarf a lucky find at Istanbul's Grand Bazaar. Her antique emerald brooch was from her home city of Moscow, although just as Randall had no formative memories of his birthplace, Beijing, Ludmila had no recollection of her country of origin, her family having moved to San Francisco before she could walk. Ludmila had agreed to the Australian trip in part because of an industry craft fair in neighboring Indonesia she'd always wanted to visit. At fifty-seven, Ludmila was a seasoned traveler.

But not a scrappy one.

The toilet looked safe enough. The lid was closed, and the entire thing was sparkling clean. But why was there a small basket of what looked like hay next to it? Decoration? An Australian custom she wasn't yet acquainted with?

She'd prefer not to ask the Kellys. No toilet plunger nearby, nothing that could be fashioned as a tool. Or a weapon. To her annoyance—and embarrassment—her heartbeat had risen. She was sweating. *All right, Ludmila. You once told Martha Stewart her throw pillows were tacky. You can open a toilet.*

Ludmila edged her first and middle fingers under the lid. In one swift movement, she flipped it back. An involuntary sound escaped her throat as she half ran, half leapt back across the bathroom, landing in a crouched, defensive position by the marble sink.

Nothing. No fat python, no wet, angry koala.

Ludmila inched back toward the bowl.

And only now she could see what was definitely very wrong about the toilet.

There was no water in the toilet's bowl. Where the water should be was a black, empty hole. Leading—she did *not* want to know where.

What.

The hell.

Was that?

"G'day!"

Ludmila yelped, spinning in the direction of the voice.

Jules stood in the doorway, grinning. "I see you've discovered the drop dunny."

Ludmila placed one bejeweled hand on the bathroom counter. "I know I'm going to regret asking this, but what is a *drop dunny*?"

"A drop toilet. Same as a regular toilet, except instead of water flushing the waste away, it drops into a compost under the house." Jules picked up a small handful from the basket of hay. "You go, and then you—" She released the hay. It floated into the hole, disappearing from sight. "See?" Jules brushed her hands on her shorts. "It's environmentally friendly, low impact."

"Be that as it may, I'd prefer a regular toilet."

"There's no flush toilets on Mun'dai. The showers run on tank water. They'll be full after that cyclone last month but still, best to keep your showers to under a minute."

Ludmila might like to murder the person who invented *drop dunnies* and *showers under a minute*. "I can't use a drop toilet. I'm sorry, but I just can't."

"Hope you can hold it for four days." Even though they were close in age, Jules's skin was considerably more sun-damaged, her eyes crinkling deeply as she laughed. "Honestly, they're not that bad. We have one at home."

"You have one," Ludmila clarified, "voluntarily?"

"Toilets waste a huge amount of water." Jules folded her arms. She clearly wasn't wearing a bra. "And where do you think the runoff would go, on an island?" She pointed to the ocean, visible through the windows. "Look, I'll show you how they work," she added, undoing the top button of her cargo shorts.

"No, no, no!" Ludmila waved her hands in a panic.

Jules burst out laughing. There was something slightly performative about it: the brassy shine of fake gold. "I was kidding! Bloody hell, you're as gullible as a virgin in a fuck truck."

Ludmila found swearing a notch below public urination. "What a colorful expression."

Jules rebuttoned her shorts. "The girls and I are going for a dip in the tide pools. Interested?"

"I think I'll unpack and have a rest. But we'll plan to meet everyone for dinner."

"Righto." Jules headed out. "Hooroo."

The saving grace of this bizarre expression was it presumably meant *goodbye*. Ludmila waited until she heard the front door close before letting out a breath.

Ludmila was not a mean person. In her long working life, she'd dealt with countless annoying clients and colleagues and customers. But try as she might, Ludmila could not connect with her daughter's overly familiar mother-in-law. Even her name was difficult. Ludmila tried using Julia, a lovely, elegant name, but Jules insisted on the nickname with a familial cheer Ludmila found presumptuous.

The Mexican silver circling Ludmila's wrist felt heavier than usual as she left the bathroom.

It was going to be a very long four days.

5

In a precocious tween phase, the Kelly sisters used to play Family. Matty was always Dad, a high-achieving patriarch, inevitably secretly gay. Amelia was Mum, a meek, housebound woman constantly baking while having her period all over "my nice new carpet!" The scenes all took place at home, activated when Matty-as-Dad stormed in, demanding a scotch. Amelia was aware this dynamic still played out between them: the sense that things only got started when her big sister arrived.

Amelia checked no one else was around as she slid the second-floor balcony door shut, sequestering her sister on the outdoor deck.

"What?" Matty asked Amelia. "What's more important than a swim?"

Amelia faced her, positively vibrating. The pleasure of the moment was almost too much to bear. "I wanted you to be the first to know—"

"Are you pregnant?" Matty cut her off with the expression of someone shat on by a seagull.

"Says the woman excited to be starting a family, while looking horrified. Thanks, but no." Amelia smoothed down her kimono with tingling fingers. "James and I are starting to talk about *marriage*."

"What?" Matty squawked. "You've only known him a few months!"

"Almost six," Amelia corrected, slightly annoyed Matty looked more shocked than thrilled. "We're in love. Madly in love."

Matty was wearing her koala-print two-piece, a snorkel mask shoved into her hair. The snorkel waved around like an antenna as she shook her head. "He still lives in Melbourne, right? How often are you seeing him?"

"The same amount of time most couples see each other." It did drive Amelia crazy not being in the same city, but she already knew Matty would hear that in the worst possible way. Her sister didn't know about their exhilarating last conversation in the overpriced hotel room with a partial view of Darling Harbour. The one where James basically asked her to *marry* him.

"Wow." Matty folded her arms. "Well, congratulations, I guess."

"Congratulations, you *guess*?"

"It's just—you always see the best in people, Animal." Matty sounded like she was choosing her words carefully. "And sometimes that means you don't see them very clearly."

Amelia stifled an outraged laugh. No one would call her sister's history with Parker an example of 20/20 vision. "I'm not in my twenties anymore. I'm thirty-three! James is a *man*. With a proper job and a mature perspective and boundaries and he loves me. I don't need your concern. I need you to be happy for me," Amelia added, trying mightily to stop her voice doing the annoying whining thing it sometimes did. "I want you to like James."

"I am. And I'll try. Seriously, I'll be nice."

Amelia had always admired her outspoken big sister. The girl who stood up to bullies, who spoke out about injustices, who loved with a fierce, uncompromising loyalty. Matty was bulletproof, more than most. And part of that strength came from being a bit . . . direct. Matty wasn't the sort of woman who spent a lot of time making other people feel comfortable. She wasn't always "nice."

Amelia gave her sister a doubtful look.

"Fuck off!" Matty said. "I can be nice!"

Amelia snorted in amusement and went back inside, heading for the kitchen. "Not driving your point home, Bratty."

"That nickname has never been funny," Matty huffed, following her. "C'mon, let's go swimming."

"I haven't finished unpacking," Amelia lied.

"What's the Kelly family motto?" Matty answered the rhetorical question, "*You never regret a swim!*"

"I know, but I still have a few things to do and"—Amelia felt herself reddening, knowing she shouldn't tell her sister the truth but compelled to by a morality beyond her control—"James might call, and I don't want to be too far from the Wi-Fi."

As expected, her sister's face went slack with disgust. "James *might* call? It's gorgeous out, and he'll be here tomorrow!"

"I'm not going, okay? Go have fun, and I'll see you in a few hours." Amelia crossed her arms and tried to make herself look stern.

Matty stared back, mouth agape. Then she rolled her eyes and headed down the stairs to the front door. "Suit yourself. We're doing dinner here at seven. Maybe you can make an effigy of James out of sticks and Face-Time him in."

"He's busy tonight, that's why he's not—"

"I was kidding," Matty called back. "Tell him I said hi, if he calls!"

Amelia sagged against the kitchen counter feeling relieved her sister had left and confused that, even though she felt this way, Matty was still her favorite human on earth.

For months, maybe even a year, Matty had displayed similar behavior with Parker, devoted in a way that bordered on obsession. At first, she and Parker were "frenemies," then "actually sort of friends," then "best friends," then "best friends who occasionally snog and touch each other's boobs"—all while Parker had a boyfriend who she *lived* with. In countless stressed, teary phone calls, Amelia indulged Matty's need to dissect every text and loaded moment of eye contact. On one particularly memorable/humiliating weekend, her sister showed up to Parker's upstate work retreat, effectively stalking her. But now that they were happily married, Matty had conveniently forgotten all about the Kelly family's tendency to give too generously of their time and attention when in love.

Amelia let her irritation pass. Now that her sister had left, she could do what she actually wanted, which was bake. A cake. A surprise for James's arrival tomorrow. And not just any cake. Her nan's famous chocolate whiskey cake.

From a tote bag stuffed under the kitchen counter she unloaded sugar, flour, chocolate chips . . . Wait. Where was the whiskey? An image of a bottle of Jack Daniel's on top of her sharehouse fridge flashed into her mind. She'd decided to pack it last, worried it'd leak. Now what? Her family wouldn't have brought hard liquor, and she couldn't ask the Lees for whiskey at five in the afternoon—but what about the bar? Wasn't there a bar, the Barefoot Bar? It opened at five. She could make the batter while the oven was heating, dash over to grab the booze, then pop the cake in the oven and let it cool overnight.

Amelia had never made a batter more quickly in her life and was soon out the door, hurrying—discreetly—in the direction of the bar.

It was a beautiful March afternoon. Insects drowsed from flower to flower in the scrubby bush that grew all the way to the sand. Tiny birds twittered in the trees, like feathery scoops of ice cream. Calm and peaceful, but it almost felt weird that no one else was around. Devoid of tourists and litter and boats in the bay, it was easy to imagine she'd slipped back in time. The sun-flecked sapphire sea rolled to the shore as it would've done for a thousand years.

Amelia jogged past another rental house and the long wooden wharf until she spotted a firepit—unlit and empty—on the beach. Overlooking it, the Barefoot Bar.

Amelia and Matty had spent two weeks backpacking around Bali in their twenties, and the setup here was similar to the more rustic Indonesian beach bars. A small, square building painted white faced the ocean on an angle. Solar panels winked on the roof. Behind the building was a dull green tank for water. Dried palm fronds hung over the counter. The worn wooden bar was about five feet long, four stools tucked under it. Inside was a reasonably stocked bar, its shelves stacked with glasses, bar tools, a blender, a cocktail shaker. A fridge was papered with pictures ripped from magazines. The central one was the dashing cartoon fox from the 1970s *Robin Hood* kids' movie. How funny: Amelia'd harbored a secret crush on charming Robin-the-fox, which she'd forgotten about until this very minute.

Four metal tables, each with four chairs, were scattered on the flat sandy earth in front of the bar. A stripy, sun-bleached cloth was strung up between the screw palms for shade. On a small chalkboard, drinks were handwritten: *Beach, Please. Vacay All Day. Wiiillllsssooonnn!* and simply, *Tequila.*

Ordinarily, the perfect place to soak up a gorgeous view over a cocktail. Except there were no patrons. And there didn't appear to be anyone behind the bar.

"Hello?" Amelia called, approaching the window. "Anyone home?"

A unicorn popped up.

Well, not an actual unicorn, but someone wearing a novelty unicorn head. A rubber one with cartoonish features: flared horsey lips, big starey eyes, and a single rainbow horn protruding from the center of a long white nose.

"*Whatthefuck.*" Amelia gasped, stumbling back. The small shock and complete surrealness of the moment made her bray out a laugh. "Um, hi?"

The person wearing the rubber horse head wove back and forth a few steps, tugging at the mask's neck, as if trying, unsuccessfully, to pull it off. They stopped. Sighed. Faced Amelia. And waved. "Hello."

"Hello," Amelia replied, pleased with this unexpected moment of ridiculousness. "I thought you were the stuff of fairytales." Which— although unpopular for a modern feminist—she wanted badly to believe in.

The unicorn shrugged. Its voice was muffled. "Guess not. So, this is a bit embarrassing . . ."

The unicorn sounded like it might be American. Em*bar*rassing. Amelia took a seat at the bar, her chin propped on one hand. "Whatever do you mean?"

The unicorn huffed a chuckle, then pointed to its head. "I'm stuck." Its thin, delicate fingers flickered in the direction of the houses. "Bachelorette party. Prop. They left it and I . . ."

"Thought you'd never know what it was like to be a magical beast unless you trotted a mile in its hooves?"

"Ha! Yes. Do you think you could . . ." The unicorn pointed again to its head. "Help me?"

Amelia giggled, delighted. She had a soft spot for whimsy. "Come here. And bring that thing of dish soap with you."

The unicorn came out from inside the bar, moving with fawn-like unsteadiness, and handed Amelia the bottle of dish soap.

"Excellent. Prepare to get extremely clean." Amelia squeezed soap around the unicorn's neck, getting large globs of it on its white T-shirt, which felt messy and silly and really rather fun. "Ready?"

Amelia tugged *this* way and the unicorn braced *that* way, until finally—after much laughter and *"Ow!"* and *"My hair!"* and *"No, don't stop!"*—the surprisingly tight neck of the mask slid up, over, and off the person's head. Amelia had it in her hands as it came free, tripping back with the effort.

The person, now unmasked, grabbed her so she didn't fall. Amelia Kelly found herself in the arms of someone elfin and androgynous, with huge hazel eyes and a shaggy pixie cut, dyed blue. "Hi."

"Oh, hello." Amelia felt a shock of recognition, which was strange, as they'd never met. "You're Liss."

The island's solo caretaker, the author of the welcome note. The sun was behind her head, creating a halo effect. "I am."

Amelia realized she was staring. Liss let her go. Sunlight stung her eyes. Amelia was momentarily dazed and unexpectedly flustered. "I'm Animal. Amelia. I mean . . . Animal is my nickname, which is kind of embarrassing, and I wish I hadn't told you."

"We're a perfect pair, then." Liss ran her hand through her soap-sticky blue hair. Interesting little tattoos were sprinkled up both arms, the most distinctive being block-letter text inside her forearm: GIRL VS TRUCK.

There was something soft and vulnerable about Liss's energy—maybe it was the wide, baby-deer eyes—but Amelia still decided this person was eons cooler than her. Liss probably skateboarded or was in a band or something. The mix of shy and chill was a mystery. Amelia's gaze lingered, trying to figure it out.

But Liss didn't meet her eyes. She took one, two steps back and was inside the little bar and switching on the faucet, attempting to stick her head under it. "You're Amelia Kelly, right? You checked into Kunyam today with your boyfriend?"

James. Whom she was supposed to be making a cake for and waiting for a call from! Amelia's act of service returned to the forefront of her concentration. To compensate for the moment of forgetting herself, she added an upgrade. "My fiancé gets in tomorrow morning, but yes, that's why I came by."

"Oh yeah?" Hair rinsed, Liss frowned at her sticky T-shirt. She shucked it over her head like a boy, revealing a simple black bikini top underneath. Small boobs, maybe only an A-cup. Fit and sinewy, though, with a few more tattoos decorating her torso and back. Curious. Cool. But irrelevant. Amelia refocused. "Yes. I need half a cup of whiskey. For a chocolate whiskey cake I'm making."

"Yum. What's the occasion?"

"James is meeting my whole family tomorrow; sort of our first family holiday. I just want it to be special."

Liss's face lifted, even as she continued to wipe off the soap with a wet rag. She had a startlingly pretty smile. "Aw. That's so nice. Congrats."

Offered genuinely, easily. The opposite of Matty's *congratulations, I guess.* "Thank you."

Liss glugged whiskey into a plastic tumbler. "On me. I couldn't have returned to my human form without you."

Their fingertips brushed. A twinge of electricity vibrated up Amelia's arm, floating to the top of her head, and stayed there, fizzing. She backed up toward the beach. "Guess I'll see you later."

"You might not. This is my last day."

Amelia spun back to Liss.

"Yeah, my replacement's starting tomorrow morning." Liss went on, "Don't worry, you'll be in good hands. Just stay away from the Lost Lagoon. Everyone loses their bearings on the way there. Hence the name."

Amelia recalled the Lost Lagoon being located in the swampy mangroves. With only three nights on the island, and not being blessed with a natural sense of direction, she crossed it off her mental to-do list. Hopefully Liss's replacement would be just as helpful. "Well, I'm sorry we didn't get the chance to hang out. You seem like a very cool and interesting person."

Liss appeared amused by her candor. "If you're ever in Montreal, look me up: Liss Chambers."

Amelia knew Montreal was in Canada because Matty spent a weekend there with Parker, when they were still "just friends." It had snowed

(Matty lied to Parker about a deep love of snowshoeing, prompting a four-hour slog through freezing backcounty). Amelia hated the cold. Chances of visiting Montreal in the near future were pretty much zero. Which was a shame. Liss put her instantly at ease, but at the same time, switched on. Maybe it was the hair. "I will. Bye, Liss Chambers."

"Bye, Animal. *Vous êtes très charmante.*"

Ah, *oui*: they spoke French in Montreal. "What does that mean?"

Liss shook her head at herself, just a little. Her smile looked complicated. "Just, *Have a good night.*"

Back at the house, Amelia added the whiskey and put the batter in the oven before rushing to get ready for dinner. While she had plenty to occupy her mind with, for some reason, it kept being tugged away.

To Liss Chambers.

Amelia didn't identify as straight. Which was something only the people she was not identifying as straight with knew about. She'd never told her sister about these people for a whole host of reasons, which had all become irrelevant when she'd met James. James, with his wicked sense of humor and sophisticated palette. There was a solidity about him that made Amelia feel like her longing to be married to a kind, funny, brilliant-in-all-ways person and pregnant with a child was possible. No: probable. Amelia was calmly certain her family would love James just as much as she did.

And yet, over the course of the evening, as hard as Amelia tried to stay present with her family, her imagination kept straying, like a cat at a window, to the girl with the ocean-blue hair. Unable to shake the strangest feeling that they were supposed to meet.

6

A fat orange sun sank into the horizon like a dropped scoop of mango sorbet. The sky was a riot of lavender and peach, deepening to violet then navy blue. Moonlight alchemized the white sand silver. Absent of any light pollution, the night sky came to life with ancient, glittering stars. And, closer to earth, sugar gliders. No bigger than an apple, the small, squirrelly creatures made their home in the tall eucalypts that grew in Moorba's center, emerging each night to go in search of sap and nectar by jumping and gliding. A membrane of skin attached from wrist to ankle turned each marsupial into a tiny paraglider. Everyone else on the island was asleep as Liss watched the sailing sugar gliders from her verandah, drinking the last mouthful of Cup-a-Soup from her favorite Garfield mug.

The Cabin was in a cleared section of the eucalypt woodland, which the Aussies just called *the bush*. A few minutes' walk inland from the beach, far enough from the closest house not to hear the most raucous of parties. A former residence built decades ago, the Cabin was a "Queenslander"-style house: single-story and detached, made from timber with a corrugated iron roof. A verandah wrapped around the front and both sides, and the whole thing was built on stumps, elevating the property five feet off the ground. The area under the Cabin had been converted into storage, its nooks and crannies housing the contents of the meal kits and things that scuttled. It also helped keep the place cool during the sticky summers that kept getting hotter.

Upstairs offered modest accommodation, spread out open-plan, like an extra-large studio. A double bed tucked into one corner. A beat-up blue velvet sofa faced a box television and VHS player. A kitchenette and a bathroom with a shower, no bath. Unlike the beachfront rentals, the Cabin felt more like someone's home, full of mismatched, half-broken things. A hand-knitted knee rug, a collection of cut-glass ashtrays, a bad but somehow charming painting of a chihuahua in a tutu.

It might be the most obvious statement in the world to say that being the solo on-island employee—cleaner, concierge, chef, cocktail maker—was both lovely and lonely.

It wasn't a job that leant itself to longevity. The average turnover was three or four months. Locals didn't want to spend that much time isolated from friends and family, and the recluses who offered to stay indefinitely were not skilled in the art of customer service. The position came to backpacker types drawn to the healing space of the island. After applying through a travel message board, Liss found herself getting used to a tropical hermit life the week before Christmas last year.

Christmas at home would've been unbearable.

Liss rinsed her mug, having used her last Cup-a-Soup for her last night. Tossing the cardboard packaging into the rigorously maintained recycling, she barely missed hitting Max. The bark-brown huntsman spider walked a few inches up the wall, like a disembodied hand.

"Think you'll miss me, Max?"

The spider stayed motionless.

"No, you're not one for sentimentality."

Liss crossed her arms, regarding her hairy housemate. Previously the subject of panicked photos sent to the team on the mainland who had just laughed and told her *Welcome to Australia, mate*. Max was nonvenomous and kept the Cabin free of insects. And her flat-bodied friend had heard a lot of her stories over the months.

"Feel like I've learned a lot from you. Any parting words of wisdom?"

Max didn't move. Liss nodded thoughtfully.

"It's what's unsaid that really matters. Powerful stuff, Max. As always."

Something skittered lightly across the tin roof, probably a glider. Her stomach squeezed. She'd miss the menagerie. Even Max. Maybe more than she'd anticipated.

Liss flipped open her laptop and started another email to Gabe.

The sugar gliders are out in force tonight. Like tiny, furry base jumpers. You'd like them. I'll miss them.

Gabe, I'm sorry. I'm so, so sorry. I know I've already said it a thousand times, but I'll say it a thousand more.

I was stupid and selfish and cruel. You're my best friend—you didn't deserve it.

Please write me back.

Liss paused, wiping a tear with the neck of her T-shirt.

I'm coming home.

Send.

It was the eleventh email she'd sent to Gabe. One a week since she'd arrived. He'd never once replied.

Somewhere on the other side of the island, a dingo howled, slow and plaintive as heartbreak.

She was and wasn't ready to leave. The idea was a minor-key melody, looping endlessly.

Liss's mind drifted to Amelia Kelly.

Beautiful, of course, in the way Sydney women often were: blonde, friendly, able to wear the hell out of a bikini. But what Liss liked most was the soap-and-water earnestness in Amelia's clear blue eyes. The charm she likely didn't know she had. The sensitivity others might mistake as weakness. Baking a cake for her fiancé's arrival struck Liss as meltingly sweet. But she also sensed confidence, always a turn-on in women. There'd been a glint in those eyes, a promise of someone clever and ready to play. Something about the new guest was as familiar and easy as air . . .

Liss thumped her forehead. "Seriously, Max. What is wrong with me?"

Amelia Kelly was a *guest* who was decidedly *not* single. Bad enough she'd attempted to flirt with her—Liss's first attempt at flirting in a very long time.

Flirting, extended romantic fantasies, spending hours crafting then second-guessing a text, scrolling through every single picture on someone's Instagram like a besotted detective—as much as the idea of opening herself up to someone new absolutely terrified Liss, it would have to happen back home. Once she'd done the work. Not here. And definitely not with Amelia "So Excited About My Fiancé I'm Making a Cake!" Kelly.

Her bags were packed. It was all over.

Liss meditated for ten minutes—new habit; helpful—before crawling into bed. But she couldn't get comfortable—recurring problem; unhelpful. It was 2:00 a.m. before a dreamless sleep pinned her to the mattress.

Which meant Liss only got two-and-a-half hours of rest before the explosion that changed everything.

7

The *Courier-Mail* claimed it sounded like a jet engine. The *Fraser Coast Chronicle* went with "as if God hit a strike while bowling." A gunshot, a building collapsing, a giant sonic boom. All were accurate. At 4:48 a.m., Mount Furneaux, one of a long island chain of active and dormant volcanoes to the west of nearby New Caledonia, erupted. It was the most powerful volcano explosion in the region in the last four hundred years.

Matty awoke with a gasp. The room was still quivering with the power of a noise no human alive had ever heard. "Parks!" Matty shook her. "Something just . . . banged."

Parker stirred, groggily asking what time it was, but Matty was already up and heading down the stairs to her parents' bedroom.

Her mother was awake, sitting up next to a loudly snoring Glen, who could sleep through the world ending. Which Matty felt was happening. The air was still buzzing. The noise was not normal: too loud, too unknown.

"Mum!" she whispered. "What the fuck was that?"

"I don't know," Jules whispered back. "Thunder?"

Her mum got out of bed, stumbling over the long edge of her cotton nightie, heading for the door.

Matty felt an old, childlike fear at her parents being apart. "Dad. Dad, wake up!" Panicked, Matty grabbed the glass of water on the nightstand and splashed it in her father's face.

"Wha—Who?" he spluttered, floundering like an upturned turtle.

"Wake up!" Matty repeated, hurrying after her mother and into the main space: kitchen on one side, sectional sofa and dining table on the other, and the second-floor deck beyond.

It was predawn, an hour from sunrise. The ocean was a sheet of silver, the sky just starting to lighten into a soft lemony gray. Cloudless.

Something dark and uncertain unspooled in Matty's stomach.

"Where's Amelia?" Jules asked in a sharp voice.

"I'm here." She came out from the bedroom next to her parents.

Matty stared at her sister's blush-pink silk cami and matching shorts. A far cry from her own raggedy sleep shirt, the one that read: *Hedgehogs: Why Don't They Just Share the Hedge?* "When did you start sleeping in things like that?"

Amelia folded her arms. "What was that noise?"

"What was what noise?" Glen was in the bedroom doorway yawning and toweling off his face. "What'd I miss?"

"Nothing on Twitter yet." Parker strode down the stairs from the master in men's boxers and a black tank top, her face lit by the glow of her phone.

"Nuclear attack?" Matty guessed.

Parker looked up. "If it was a nuclear explosion, that close, we'd already be dead from radiation."

No one could accuse her wife of sugarcoating a situation. Matty recalled the night they were caught in bed by Parker's perfectly nice, perfectly boring boyfriend. In response to his angry *what the hell are you doing?* Parker replied, *Having sex.* "Thanks, babe," Matty said to her now. "Reassuring yet terrifying."

But Parker was staring outside. "Look at the sky."

The previously clear sky was now hazy. Like a film had come over the setting moon, turning the white crescent sepia, the ocean a darker gray.

Matty felt a drip of fear.

Parker was heading down the stairs to the first floor. As one, the Kellys followed her. Instinctively Matty reached for her laptop on the way out, cradling it to her chest maternally.

Outside the air felt too warm for the early hour, like the artificial quality of a greenhouse. Queensland, Matty remembered, the tropics. They were alone on the beach.

"That's weird." Jules gestured at the shoreline. "It should be high tide."

Instead, the water was thirty feet from where it ought to be. Farther, in fact, than the lowest point at low tide. It almost looked as though the water was receding right before their eyes. Matty's heart started to pound, even as her brain failed to understand why.

"Holy fuck," Amelia breathed. "Look at the sky."

Very far away, a dark smudge. Like a column of smoke, rising.

Glen scratched his head. "Maybe an oil tanker exploded?"

The sky was getting hazier by the second. Seagulls were cawing, wheeling, their cries shredded and high.

Parker was gazing at the ocean like a woman possessed. Her words were a disbelieving breath. "Oh my god."

"What?" Matty asked. "Boo, what's wrong?"

Parker pointed at the horizon. The tip of her finger was shaking. "What the hell is that?"

Matty squinted. The ocean was flat gray; nothing but water. Not even a fishing boat. "What the hell is what?"

Next to her, Amelia inhaled.

Something in the atmosphere changed, as if there was less oxygen in the air. Matty's breathing shallowed.

For the five people standing on Blinky Beach, time seemed to slow down. Stop.

The last time Amelia felt the elasticity of time had been with James, in an overpriced hotel room with a partial view of Darling Harbour. The last night before planning to reunite weeks later on a beautiful island vacation. The hotel bed was so big, Amelia could stretch out her limbs and not feel the sides. She liked the feeling of being held by the bed, and the man in it. His mouth on her neck, kissing her jawline and lips. He pulled back to gaze at her. "Good god. I would love to be married to you."

Time paused. She'd swallowed a gasp, unsure what she was hearing. "You would?"

"Of course I would." His kiss was infused with the scotch they'd been drinking. "Life with you would be so easy."

She was too stunned to laugh, rolling on top of him to look him in his face. "Are you serious, baby?"

He lay back on the pillows and admired her body. "You're a goddess, Amelia Kelly. Physically you're perfect, but you're also so *good.*" He skimmed his fingers up her arm, controlled and confident, a playful glint in his mahogany eyes. "You'd be the perfect wife. I'd be a fucking idiot not to marry you."

Amelia pressed her mouth against his again and again so as not to burst into laughter or tears or some other explosion of dizzying, happy emotion. She *would.* She *would* make the perfect wife. Her mum was going to be *so* happy. She'd already imagined a teary mother-of-the-bride speech, delivered in a room filled with lilies and love.

But now she might never get to have that wedding.

At the still-retreating shoreline, a school of whiting lay flipping on the wet sand. The ocean retracted so rapidly that the fish, who had swum inland following the rising tide to feed, found themselves beached amid hunks of pastel coral. There was something deeply shameful, even immoral, about the sight of the exposed ocean floor. It jolted a long-buried memory: Amelia walking in on her grandmother changing out of a swimsuit. The sight of her rolls of flesh and sagging breasts was a disorienting shock. Her kind and generous grandmother, who always smelled deliciously like fruitcake, turned on her, horrified and hissing, *Shoo!*

She wasn't supposed to see that. She wasn't supposed to see this—the gasping fish, the naked ocean floor.

Death was inevitable. It came for us all.

I'd be a fucking idiot not to marry you.

The horizon was tilting. Rising. Racing toward them.

Amelia opened her mouth and she screamed.

Ludmila heard the cry, tossed on the breeze like a rock through a window. "What was *that*?"

Randall, distracted by the shocking information being presented to him by his phone, didn't hear the question.

Still in her silk dressing gown, Ludmila gripped the balcony railing, scanning the beach, the water, the trees on either side. She didn't know what she was looking for. Like the birds and animals all around her—the majority of which Ludmila was wholly oblivious to—she'd instinctively become deeply quiet in order to parse the morning's strangeness. That sound, and now, a scream. Motherhood had sharpened her sense for unseen danger. A parent can hear nothing and know something's up. Parker had retreated in the months—years?—she was falling in love with Matilda, hadn't she?

"Flank collapse." Randall's face was drained of color. He was holding his phone a foot away from his body. "A landslide. Volcano."

He seemed to expect a reply. "What? Where? Here?"

Randall's gaze roved their bedroom, taking inventory. He didn't need to step into the role of alpha male: he was always in it. "Put your shoes on."

All the shoes Ludmila packed had heels. "Why?"

He was back in the suite, pulling on pants. "Now. We're going."

Ludmila's heartbeat quickened. Her grip on the balcony tightened. "Going?" She briefly envisioned leaving on the morning ferry, spending a few forgettable days back on the mainland at a hotel with a kidney-shaped pool before heading off to Indonesia, ice melting in a plastic cup of gin and tonic before wheels up. Even amid the uncertainty, the thought was a relief.

Ludmila would never get on that plane.

"Mila, *now*."

Her husband was afraid. Randall was rarely afraid. He was the kind of man who intimidated other men. Not because of any underlying threat of violence (there was none) or his impressive physical form (although it was a contributing factor, as was his hair). It was his confidence, the kind that made you feel instinctively that this human had figured out the world while you were still bumbling through like an idiot. It was evident ever since he was a teenager. Randall was confident, but not controlling. He wasn't the type to order his wife around.

Ludmila resisted. "And go where? What's happening? What was that noise?"

"We have to get inland."

"Inland?" Ludmila hadn't planned on leaving the house unless it was absolutely necessary. "Shouldn't we check on Parker?"

Eyes angry, Randall inhaled a breath and opened his mouth. Then he froze. Cocked his head. "What's that sound?"

"What sound?"

"That sound, that *sound*?"

A deep, low rumble, like a distant freight train.

An inkblot of fear spread in Ludmila's stomach.

A bird with a red breast slammed into a windowpane. The Lees both started, a small punch of shock. The bird fell to the earth with a broken neck.

A figure in all black was sprinting up the beach, toward the house. Even from one hundred yards away, Ludmila could tell her only child was running for her life.

This would not be the first time a tsunami crashed onto the shores of Mun'dai. The island was more than eight hundred thousand years old. In pivotal moments throughout the centuries, it had been molded like clay. But the pace of change had accelerated over the past few hundred years as the oceans continued to warm and rise. The ozone layer was already wafer-thin in this part of the planet, due to the country's use of chlorofluorocarbons and hydrochlorofluorocarbons in the 1970s. It let in so much UV radiation, two-thirds of Australians would get skin cancer in their lifetime. The carefully laid plans and expectations these people had for their holiday were, in essence, ridiculous. Self-concept nothing more than a shallow scribble on the profound canvas that was Mother Earth. The island was there before any of the humans on it were born. It would be there after they died.

Liss stood on the balcony of the Caretaker Cabin, containing panic at the sight of the birds. Typically, she awoke to their operatic morning chorus, a cacophony of joyful noise. But these calls were different. These movements were different. They were everywhere, swooping, calling. Darwin called birdsong the nearest analogy to language. If birds could talk, right now they were shouting in fear.

Typically Liss could handle a high-stress situation. Prior to landing on Mun'dai, she'd been employed as a social worker and spent half a day a week volunteering for Rainbow Connection, a national LGBTQIA+ teen helpline. Only last night the executive director emailed about it, encouraging her to "log back in and take a call, anytime." When Liss first arrived on Mun'dai, the idea that she might be able to provide guidance and support seemed like a cruel joke. Over the months, those feelings softened into uneasy doubt. She couldn't help kids believe in themselves without first believing in herself. But these were problems to be addressed off-island, after she caught the morning ferry, which would connect her to an afternoon flight to Brisbane, then Montreal. She was going home today, to get back into therapy and right all her wrongs.

In a matter of minutes, the morning ferry, currently moored in Hervey Bay, would be on the ocean floor.

Movement to her left.

A *wongari*, a dingo, one of the island's wild dogs, moving swiftly inland through the scrub. Wiry body. Rust-red fur. Physically similar to a cattle dog, but leaner, with none of the domesticated deference. In all her time on the island, Liss had never seen anything more than a paw print. The small pack of dingoes lived on the western side. Miles away.

"Hey!"

She didn't mean to call out. The dingo pulled up short, front paw raised. Clicked its head to her.

For a long, weird moment, they stared at each other.

Cold intelligence in its eyes, like a jewel thief unafraid to use the gun in their pocket.

You're not supposed to be here, Liss wanted to say, even as she knew she wasn't supposed to be here, either. Humans were tolerated because they paid to keep the island whole and protected. What must this true local think of her and her hair the color of a child's crayon?

The birds were getting louder.

Liss wanted to say, *What's happening?*

She wanted to say, *Help me.*

The dog moved on, melting quickly into the undergrowth.

Liss heard a sound, edging over the sonic wall of birdcalls.

A hiss. A roar.

The birds on Mun'dai, like birds the world over, were descendants of dinosaurs. One of nature's great success stories; they were older than humans. Yet, humanity's dismissal of them was clear. A fool was bird-brained or a goose or a turkey. Humans believed they were smarter than birds. Humans were wrong. Because evolution wasn't about advancement. Evolution had no regard for your app updates or air travel. Evolution wouldn't remember the song of the summer. Evolution was about survival. Dinosaurs didn't make it. Birds did. To say humans were more advanced than birds depended on how you defined that term. Birds might fail humans' intelligence tests. Humans would fail theirs.

Glen stood on the shore of Blinky Beach, mesmerized by the rising horizon. In quiet moments, he'd pondered the apocalypse. Societal collapse, end of days. It was the stuff of thoughtful articles in *The Guardian* or concerned but orderly conversations on Radio Australia between qualified individuals. But now the world was splitting open and he was wholly incapable of comprehending it. Fear held him hostage, every muscle rigid. Fear and awe. Glen knew intellectually that humankind had altered the oceans, but never had he seen such an altered body of water. Not a body: an army. There was something savagely beautiful about the wave. This was true power. It was a baby crowning, an Olympic stadium of fans roaring, the earth glimpsed from outer space. David Bowie, the soundtrack to his youth. *Planet Earth is blue and there's nothing I can do . . .*

"Glen!"

Something struck him across the face. A woman, her eyes ugly and wild. His wife had just slapped him.

Jules screamed, *"Move!"*

Parker ran down Blinky Beach toward her parents' rental house. "You know you could stay with the Kellys," she'd said to her mother over FaceTime, weeks prior. Unimpressed, yet unsurprised. "Jules offered for her and Glen to sleep in the kids' bedroom."

Her mother just looked at her like it was Parker who'd made the disappointing choice.

Parker knew her parents were ambivalent about her and Matty's move to Sydney. New York was six hours on a plane from L.A.; Sydney was fourteen. Yes, it was physically and psychologically further. Ludmila and Randall had never been to Sydney, but understood it to be small, sunny, and full of Australians. The move was a surprise; everything to do with Matty was a surprise. Parker knew Matty was not who her parents imagined her ending up with. She intuited her parents found Matty to be clever and hardworking, but also forthright, maybe even crass. And a woman. It'd taken them a year to refer to Matty as Parker's girlfriend, despite the clear directive: "It's the same as *boy*friend, she's just my *girl*friend." To be fair, the relationship had surprised Parker, too. Unlike Matty, who'd had many girlfriends and one- two- three-night stands, Parker had only dated men, sporadically. She'd assumed all-consuming romance and sexual obsession was the stuff of romantic movies or excitable extroverts. What she had with her boyfriend, Kwan, was like an optimal sales funnel: efficient and logical. And then Matilda Kelly waltzed into that Halloween party dressed like a fried egg and everything Parker thought she knew about love and romance waved goodbye and jumped out the window.

The house came into view.

Parker dared to look to the ocean. It was visible now, the wall of water. Not like a wave that was breaking, more like the ocean as a whole had lifted and was pulsing forward.

"Parker!" Her mother, crying out from the master suite balcony.

"Get—inland!" She tried to yell but she was out of breath, lungs on fire. Instinct urged her toward her parents.

The front door was unlocked. She flung it open, rocketing into a bizarro-world version of their own rental. The same wide wooden steps from the ground floor up to the second floor, where a modern kitchen faced a tan leather sectional, raw-edge dining table, and a deck with a view of the beach. Unlike the Kellys' rental, everything was still neat and orderly, a linen scarf and copy of *Men's Fitness* the only concessions to her parents' presence.

Randall ran down the steps from the third floor. "There's been a volcano—"

"Tsunami," Parker wheezed. Having stopped running, she could feel her face burning, drenched with sweat. "Have to—get inland."

Upstairs, her mother screamed.

Randall and Parker exchanged a glance, then bolted up the stairs to the suite.

On the balcony, Ludmila was staring at the ocean.

The ground started to shake.

"Oh *fuck*." Randall grabbed the two women. "Let's *go*."

Ludmila resisted, pulling Parker from Randall. "No."

A voice from the beach. "Parks!"

Matty, staggering on the sand toward them, still clutching her laptop. Parker thought she was with the Kellys. Her wife wasn't a runner. In a flash Parker realized her plan to sprint with her family into the bush to outrun the water wasn't going to work.

"We're staying here. Find something to hold on to." She was down the steps, heading for Matty. "Get away from the windows!"

Back at Kunyam, Jules was scrambling through the items on the kitchen counter. "Passports! Bags, shoes, *shit*—"

Jules prided herself being the sort of parent who always had a Band-Aid or pen or gluten-free snack. But the part of her brain that was good at being organized was now fat-fingered and useless. Her gaze landed on a yellow spatula; she grabbed it. For one deranged moment she almost laughed, imagining facing a tidal wave with a kitchen utensil.

"Mum!" Amelia was at her elbow. "We can't stay here, we have to get inland!"

"Darling, I just want to get—I just want to make sure we have—"

Amelia yanked her arm so hard Jules yelped. *"We'll drown here!"*

Glen was still on the beach, staring at the water.

"Glen!" Jules yelled.

He didn't move. His hands hung limply at his side. He was paralyzed with fear.

The trio could all see it now. The horizon bearing down on them.

Jules raced for the shoreline, not with the spatula, but toward her dumbstruck husband. How many times had she been forced to collect him, remind him, cater to him? When they had first met, Jules found Glen's shyness sweet, his intellect appealing, so different from the knockabout larrikins and burping footy fans she'd grown up with. She hated they'd come to this impasse. Hated he seemed incapable of the growth and change she wanted for herself. Rage blew like a geyser. Jules slapped Glen hard across the face.

"Move!"

Liss stumbled down the track toward Kunyam. Ordinarily she knew every fallen log, every flowering plant, but now the landscape was alien. The birds were as loud as sirens and something wasn't right with her feet. She was a doll whose legs had been bent backward. Her Cons were on the wrong feet, left for right. She stopped to switch them, hands shaking with adrenaline. A slick brown snake whipped past her, heading inland, away from the beach.

She was going the wrong way. She was going toward danger.

Matty, Parker, Ludmila, and Randall huddled in the master bathroom, bracing together, hearts pounding.

"Govno." Ludmila swore in Russian. *"Govno, govno, govno."*

The windows were rattling. There was a tub of La Mer on the counter. Matty couldn't afford La Mer; she used Acure, a budget vegan skincare line sold at Whole Foods. It struck her that after all the hours she'd spent examining the dark circles under her eyes and googling *what are peptides*, she might die here, in a bathroom, not old or rich enough to use La Mer, clutching a mother-in-law who didn't like her.

Someone was crying. The sharp smell of piss cut through the air.

Amelia ran with her mother around the side of the house, toward the sandy bush track that squiggled inland. She thought her father was with them, but when she looked back, he wasn't there. A jolt of terror. "Where's Dad?"

Jules spun around, smashing her bare foot into one of the large rocks that marked the start of the track. She doubled over. "Oh, *shit!*"

Amelia wasn't used to seeing her mother out of control. Her mum was a force, the first one to welcome a new neighbor, the last one to complain. Amelia still found it shocking when a mother—a friend's parent, a boyfriend's mum—exposed any kind of vulnerability. She looped Jules's arm around her neck, pulling her away from the house. But her mother was heavy and they weren't moving fast enough. They needed to be sprinting. Amelia felt weak, helpless, even as a hot, rough instinct to survive kicked and spat inside her. What time was it? Where was her father? "No," she cried, her face wet with tears. "No!"

The roar of the water was getting louder, the sound of her white noise machine turned to a deafening level.

A snake and then another slid in front of her, heading away from the shore. Lizards skittered up trees. Through the trees, a pack of brown brumbies galloped inland. Their hooves shook the ground like a small earthquake. Amelia'd never seen wild horses before, their fur matted and uneven, their manes overgrown. Horses on an island? The sight of them, powerful and terrified, made her wonder if any of this was actually happening. On an awkward date in the back corner of a bar none of her straight friends went to, a too-smart girl with freckles had told her about block universe theory, wherein every moment of life was happening at the same time. Past, present, future, all layered together like a tiramisu. Amelia indulged this, more interested in the part of the date where someone pressed someone else up against a wall, but a strange, deep part of her understood this as truth. Life was a simulacrum, isn't that what people said?

A figure in a white T-shirt sprinted down the path, her blue hair another streak of unreality in the green-gray bush.

Relief burst inside Amelia like a water balloon. "Liss!" She screamed. "Help us!"

In seconds, Liss had Jules's other arm around her shoulders, and the two of them were half running, half dragging Amelia's mum in a sloppy three-legged-race inland.

The wall of water was visible through the trees, moving fast and relentless. They only had seconds until it reached the shore. No way Parker and Matty would've made it to the Lee's house with time to get Ludmila and Randall out and away. Where was her father? Was he still on the beach? No: her mother had slapped him. Her mother was getting off the ferry in a Bunnings hat. Her mother was using the wrong fork at Flying Fish with James. Her mother. Her mother.

The water hit the house, and everything went dark. Water sprayed like a fire hydrant through cracks between the windows, gushing from the crevices in the ceiling. It stormed the first floor in a crash of things being thrown and coming apart. The air was warm, salty-thick. Someone was pulling Matty's hair so hard there were tears in her eyes, pain spotting her vision. And it *roared*. Water on her cheeks, her arms, the tiles beneath her already wet. No trees or sky outside the third-floor bathroom window, just the dark gray of the ocean raging around the house.

When you're inhabiting a life, it is the size of a planet. That is the human condition. But in this moment, Matty had never been more aware of her smallness. Her utter insignificance. The planet owed her nothing. If the balcony doors didn't hold, if the water reached the third floor, she would likely die with as much fanfare as a slapped mosquito.

The houses on Blinky Beach were underwater. Temporarily on the ocean floor.

———

The bush track forked.

"This way." Liss pulled Amelia and Jules to the right, a direction sloping up. "There." A large red rock shaped like a hamburger bun.

The steady roar came apart into discordant crashes, like someone falling into a set of cymbals: water meeting resistance. The ocean was surging fast through the bush toward them. A beach chair whooshed past, smashed into a tree, exploding into pieces. Fresh adrenaline punched into Amelia's system. She dragged her mother in the direction of the rock without caring if she hurt her.

Liss was up the rock like a spider monkey, helping haul Jules to safety. "Get to the top," Liss gasped before turning back for Amelia's outstretched hand. Their fingers touched. Cold water slammed Amelia's legs, side, shoulders. The shock of it made her scream. She lost her balance. One second she had Liss's hand. The next she was being shot forward like a cannonball, away from the rock.

"Amelia! *Amelia!*"

Her mother's and Liss's screams dived and wove around her. She was underwater, in the ocean, the water stabbing cold. Her limbs pinwheeled. No way to breathe, where was the sky, the air? Something large and spongy bumped against her legs, moving. Something alive, an ocean thing, here in the bush. She popped up, gasping, choking on seawater. In her fingers, something sharp and prickly; a bush, a plant, under the water. Instinct said to grab it. An anchor. The water continued surging forward, but the plant kept her in one place. She kicked her feet, gasped for breath, holding tight, as the surge continued crashing through the undergrowth.

"Amelia!" It was a shock to see Liss, twenty feet in front of her, holding on to a tree. Blue hair plastered to her skull like paint, her face X-ray-white, eyes crazy.

The plant moved underneath Amelia, uprooted by the force of the water.

"It's not holding!" Amelia screamed.

"Grab my hand!" Liss yelled back.

Amelia had no idea how deep the water was, where the rock was, what to do, how to survive. Her limbs were frozen, teeth chattering. She flashed on *Titanic*, Jack sinking to his death when there was plenty of room on Rose's door-boat. The plant lost its grip on the soil. Amelia jerked forward.

Something shot past her—a suitcase?—smashing into a tree with a wet crack.

Human bodies were so fragile. Bones broke so easily.

"My hand!" Liss yelled. A cut on her temple leaked blood into her eyes.

Taken by the water's momentum, Amelia flailed, kicking hard, managing to get close enough to Liss for their fingers to scrabble together. Find purchase. A grip. With surprising strength, Liss pulled Amelia against the current, toward the tree.

"Hold on!" Liss shouted.

Amelia wrapped her arms around the wet, scratchy trunk. Solid, like a lover. The trees on the island were talking to each other in a language the two women would never know.

Liss and Amelia clung together, shivering and speechless, as the bushland around them turned into a lake.

8

Amelia, Jules, and Liss stayed on top of the rock that was shaped like a hamburger until the water stopped pulsing inland, finally quieting. Birds began to call to one another, cautiously, then with increasing confidence. Dead fish floated, along with a beach towel, someone's shoe. Jules had seen a movie about a terrible tsunami in Thailand—something Glen wanted to watch, not really her taste—but this, thankfully, was nowhere near as bad as any of that . . . when it came to the destruction of human-made things. The destruction to the environment would surely be significant.

"The houses." Jules said the thing no one had yet dared to. "Don't you think we would've seen pieces of them if anything had . . ." She couldn't bring herself to say *happened to them*.

There were seven homes available to rent on Lady Lushington Island. Three were cute, if modest, fishermen's cabins—the Yellow Cottage, the Blue Cottage, and the White Cottage—located on the other side of the bar and the wharf. The other four were the bigger, fancier new houses, including Kunyam, which the Kellys were staying in, and the Lees' house.

"I think the big houses will be fine," Liss said. "I know they're earthquake-proof and built to survive cyclones and stuff. The cottages . . ." Her eyes edged with worry as she pushed a hand through her mop of turquoise hair. "At least there was no one in them. You guys are the only guests right now."

Amelia gathered her knees to her chest. "Do you think everyone's okay?"

Matty was the child who refused to be coddled. Amelia required a more indulgent hand.

"Definitely," Jules said, because that's what she was supposed to say. She exchanged a glance with Liss.

Liss sounded equally assured. "I'm sure they're fine."

Jules turned away, afraid Amelia would see her doubt. The girls continued to confer quietly as she scanned the flooded overgrowth. In her lowest moments, she'd fantasized about Glen dying. Nothing violent or painful: a sudden heart attack, in his sleep. But now the idea was horrific. A waterlogged corpse the girls would never unsee? *Please*, Jules prayed to the goddess. *Spare us. We're good people.* In times of crisis, morality was easy to assert.

The sun edged through the trees: the first golden rays of dawn. Jules heard a noise. Something splashing in a strange, rhythmic way.

"There's someone out there." Jules peered in the direction of the noise. "Hello?"

"Dad?" Amelia scrambled to her feet. "Matty?"

"Mr. Lee?" Liss was next to her. "Mrs. Lee? Any Lee at all?"

Something bright red nosed through the trees.

Jules squinted. She'd left her glasses on the bedside table (hopefully, still in their case?): it took a moment to identify the canoe. One of the ones offered for lazy paddles through the estuaries or explorations along the eastern shoreline.

An Indigenous man, with dark brown skin and thick curly hair, was paddling toward them. He was grinning.

Liss's mouth fell open with a laugh. "No freaking way. *Jarrah*?"

"Is that another guest?" Jules asked.

Liss didn't answer, already slip-sliding off the rock to half run, half wade toward the man in the canoe. "Jarrah!" Her arms were around him in a hug, the canoe rocking side to side. "I'm so glad you're here. And safe! What, were you camping?"

"My regular spot at Karbunya." The freshwater Karbunya Creek squiggled horizontally through the island's northern tip. Jarrah's broad

Queensland accent flattened and stretched the vowels, swapping the *r*'s for *ah*'s: *regulah*. *Kahbunya*. "Boat's buggered."

Liss's face fell. "Oh no."

He shrugged. "It was a shit boat." He called to the women on the rock. "You lot missing some of your mob?"

"Yes!" Jules's words came in a desperate tumble. "My daughter and her wife and her parents and my husband, Glen. Have you—Has anything—?"

"Your bloke hung on to a gum tree and the others rode it out on the top floor of their house," Jarrah told them. "Bottom floor's flooded, but everyone's fine."

Amelia let out a cry of delight.

Clear blue relief dissolved the stone in Jules's stomach. "Oh, thank goddess," she breathed, hugging her daughter. "We're okay, darling. We're all okay."

Liss's hand was resting comfortably on Jarrah's shoulder. "Guys." Liss's voice inflected up at the end of the word. "This is my friend, Jarrah Milbi. He is now in charge." It sounded like the biggest relief of her life.

Jarrah lifted a hand in greeting, his grin as big and wide as Australia itself. "Need a ride?"

Jarrah was a Butchulla man. He worked as a ranger on both Mun'dai and K'Gari, the closest island, where he also lived. Unlike the simpler, more remote Mun'dai, K'Gari had multiple resorts and restaurants, and almost two hundred year-round residents. Jarrah was also on the Butchulla council, the board of directors for the nonprofit who owned the houses on Mun'dai. Per the native title agreement, Indigenous people could camp and hunt on the island as they wished, so Jarrah came over on his boat every few weeks or so. "Beach fishing," he explained to the two Kellys, paddling them through the bush in the direction of the shore. "Good time of year for tailor."

Jules recalled how her father used to cook the popular game fish. Grilled whole with lime and chili. Her stomach rumbled.

It was shallow enough to wade, but neither Amelia nor Jules had any shoes: both were still in their nightgowns. Jarrah said it was safer. Jules guessed he was in his mid-fifties. She'd had an Indigenous boyfriend before she met Glen. Confident and good-looking, like this Jarrah bloke. Good to know they weren't in this alone. Liss had relaxed in Jarrah's company, but maybe that was because she hadn't signed up for navigating a natural disaster. Jarrah exuded a solid, capable energy. Instantly comforting. And Jules noted Jarrah hadn't checked out her young, beautiful daughter despite the fact she was in a skimpy pink sleep set. Which meant he was either a total gentleman or gay.

The canoe hit a bump. Jules's foot knocked the side; pain hammered up her calf. It was only a superficial injury—broken skin, not broken toes—but she let out a gasp of discomfort.

Amelia's face was the picture of worry. "Jarrah, is there a first aid kit in the canoe? My mum's hurt her foot."

"I'm fine," Jules protested.

Jarrah pulled a couple of bright green leaves off a plant they were passing. "Chew on those. Don't swallow. Just chew."

Jules frowned at the leaves. "I didn't think Heath Platysace had healing properties."

Jarrah tossed back a surprised look. "Okay, plant lady. Listen to the blackfella. My people have been here for fifty thousand years. How about yours?"

Even though Jules knew this to be true, she felt a snap of anger at his comment. No, it was shame. She often mixed the two emotions up, something Matty once called her out on during her daughter's interminable student activist phase: *You're not angry at me, Mum. You're ashamed because you know I'm right; you have straight privilege, and you always will.* Jules popped the leaves in her mouth. "Ugh." Bitter as citrus. "Oh, that's awful." Still, she dutifully chewed. Jules knew bush medicine was good medicine.

"You're doing great, Mum." Amelia patted her back. "Is that like a general anesthetic, Jarrah?"

"Nah." Jarrah twisted around with an amused grin. "But you're not thinking about your crook foot anymore, are ya?"

It took a second to land. The leaves didn't have healing properties, but how quickly she'd been ready to believe they had! For the first time all morning, Jules felt the light touch of humor. It reminded her that she was a Kelly and she was alive. She spat out the useless leaves, chuckling. "Cheeky bugger." But she was so amused by his joke that for a few seconds, Jules Kelly did indeed forget about her sore foot.

The bottom of the canoe skimmed the earth, coming to a slow stop. Not enough water to keep paddling, which Jarrah pointed out was a good sign: the flooding was already subsiding.

Kunyam was visible through the trees. The wood was wet, all the way to the roof, which was strewn, impossibly, with seaweed. One of the side windows was completely smashed. A large hunk of coral sat nearby like a dumb criminal. Jules wondered how much of the house—and their stuff—had been ruined.

"Everyone out," Jarrah said. "Except plant lady."

"Oh, I can walk," Jules said, as Liss helped Amelia out.

Jarrah leapt out of the canoe and offered his arms. "This is a full-service island. May I?"

The last person to carry her like a damsel in distress had been Glen, on their wedding day. She'd been ten kilos lighter, but he'd still only managed a half dozen steps before dumping her on the bed like a sack of potatoes. "Are you sure?"

Jarrah nodded, grinning in a friendly sort of way.

Only mildly mortified, Jules put an arm around his neck and found herself being lifted, cradled against his chest. "All right, plant lady." He sloshed through the wet sand in the direction of the house. "Off we go."

One arm was across her back, the other under her legs, her feet crossing demurely. She felt weightless and girlish, forty years younger in a matter of seconds. Jules was used to carrying others. "Julia," she said. "My name is Julia." She softened against his chest, releasing her attention to the surroundings.

A hawk floated lifelessly in a puddle of seawater. Next to it, a brown tree snake, its body loose and limp like a discarded piece of rope. A few paces later, a ringtail possum, waterlogged and deathly still.

Jules inhaled a shaky breath, tightening her grip around Jarrah. She was glad she was being carried or the sight of what'd been lost would have brought her to her knees.

9

Jules stood in the middle of the main space of Kunyam, trying to recall what it used to look like. Everything was wet, broken, floating, destroyed: a house dredged up from the ocean floor. Gritty sand underfoot, swirled over the bloated leather sectional, in the bottom of the handmade ceramic mugs. The morning sun cooked a stink of seaweed. There was an orange-and-white clown fish in the full bathroom sink, still alive.

Because their front doors had been left wide open, both Kunyam and the Lees' house had flooded. The residents splashed through the broken plates and upturned furniture, salvaging their clothes and personal items in ill-fitting shoes Liss offered from Lost & Found; the surge was only a foot by the time it sloshed under the Caretaker Cabin. Matty'd had her laptop with her, and Parker and Glen had their phones on them, but Jules's and Matty's phones, and Parker's computer, were either dead or missing. Amelia's phone, which had been in her bedside table drawer, would eventually come good after standing for an hour in a cup of dry rice. Jules's paperback was waterlogged, her toothpaste was fine. Everything in the fridge survived, but Jarrah had switched the power off.

The Lees fared better—the top floor, where most of their belongings were, didn't flood—but one of Ludmila's suitcases with her nicer outfits (for Indonesia) had been by the front door and was now missing.

The Wi-Fi was working, an inappropriate miracle. The news was already reporting the breaking story. As Jules, Parker, Glen, and Amelia lay their clothes on the sand to dry, Matty announced the headlines to the group from Parker's phone: "*Surge from Deadly Volcano Eruption Smashes East Coast of Australia, Once-in-a-Lifetime Disaster, Climate Havoc: Is This the New Normal?*" She seemed energized to be in the middle of a developing global event, but as Jules picked seaweed from her beloved Bunnings hat, she found it difficult for an emotion to settle. Relief, certainly, but also worry and sadness and confusion. Surely, people would've lost their lives, just like the hawk and the snake and the ringtail possum. When she reunited with Glen, she'd accidentally kissed him, an act of decades-old muscle memory, provoking instant regret.

Jarrah and Liss called a collective debrief. Approaching the spot on the beach where everyone was gathered on stripy beach towels, Jules spotted the yellow kitchen spatula stuck in the sand. It made her want to cry. There was no time to fall apart. Jules wasn't sure what her role would be in this unprecedented situation, but it was definitely not one of a woman weeping over a kitchen utensil. That's not what mothers did.

Liss was clapping her hands, trying to command the attention of the adrenalized, chattering group. "Guys? Hey, guys?"

Jules took a seat next to Amelia. Her daughter was cuddled next to Matty, looking worried. "James isn't picking up."

Matty squeezed her sister's knee in sympathy. "He might be stuck at the airport. Parker said flights are grounded in Queensland."

"Guys?" Liss tried again.

"This'll be a story for the unborn," Jules said to Matty, an attempt at softness. There was still a big picture, after all.

Her eldest daughter rolled her eyes. "My womb is still unoccupied, Mum. How's your foot?"

"Surprisingly good." Jules wiggled her toes. Just a dull ache. "Jarrah gave me a few Panadol."

"I heard he carried you back like a superhero." Parker arched a brow. "Way to make Glen jealous, Jules."

Matty and Amelia giggled.

Blood rushed to Jules's cheeks. Not so much at the inference, but at the fact that it—like this entire situation—felt wildly incongruous. "Don't be ridiculous. It was nothing like that."

"Guys!" Liss stuck both pinkies in her mouth and whistled, finally getting the group's attention. "Great. Um, hi. For those of you I didn't meet while escaping a natural disaster, I'm Liss Chambers. First of all, let me say how massively relieved I am that everyone's okay. Awesome job not dying." She gave two thumbs-up.

Jules noted the black-ink tattoos on Liss's forearms. In her white muscle tee with *SAD SACK* embroidered over the pocket, tan shorts, and beat-up Converse sneakers, Liss wasn't dressed very well for the Australian bush. Was that how lesbians dressed in Canada? Jules had no idea. Genderfluid, genderqueer, gender dysphoria, gender bender: Matty had been shoveling these words at her ever since her daughter was elected president of the Gay-Straight Alliance in high school. While Jules tried to keep up, the lexicon kept evolving and the rules kept changing. Jules's "gaydar" was nonexistent, but if she had to guess, she'd pick Liss as not one hundred percent heterosexual. The difference for women of this generation was that difference was good; valued. When Jules was in her twenties and thirties, the best thing you could be was just like everyone else.

Glen was asking about the fact that they couldn't safely stay in a flooded house. "Not till a sparkie's had a proper look."

"Sparkie?" Liss repeated.

"Electrician," the Australians chorused.

"Okay, yeah, your houses," Liss said. "Unfortunately both your rental houses are uninhabitable. Ki'ppa had a bunch of windows break; also a no go."

Amelia raised her hand. "What about the fishermen's cottages?"

Liss inhaled quick, like she'd just gotten a paper cut. "The Blue and White Cottages are in pretty bad shape. The Yellow Cottage we can probably dry out in a few days."

"The Yellow Cottage is so cute." Amelia smiled wistfully.

"But in a few days, we'll be gone," Jules pointed out.

Liss tugged at the neck of her T-shirt. "The very, very good news is Kooroy house made it through the whole thing, high and dry."

"You're kidding," Randall and Glen spoke as one, before exchanging a small, awkward smile.

"Nope," Liss said. "So you all have a very comfortable place to sleep tonight."

A group flicker of surprise. Jules had pictured them camping on the sand, under the stars. She was almost looking forward to it.

"How many bedrooms?" Matty asked.

"Three," Liss said. "It's basically the same as Kunyam, just a bit smaller. The first floor is just the entrance. No gym or kids' bedroom."

"Okay." Matty directed the group. "Parker and me in the master, parentals in the two bedrooms on the second floor, Amelia on the couch. You're okay with that, right Animal?"

Amelia scowled. "What about James? I can't make him sleep on the couch—he's a grown man."

"And considering Randall and I paid for a whole house that we can't stay in, I think we should take the master," Ludmila spoke with authority.

Matty let out a disbelieving breath. Surviving this ordeal together had not brought the two women closer. "Well, considering this trip is to celebrate our marriage, I think the newlyweds should take the master."

"I need privacy," Ludmila said. "So does my husband."

She indicated Randall, who did not look excited about being drawn into a master bedroom pissing match.

Matty bristled. "I also require privacy," she said, equally calmly. "As does my wife."

Jules patted her daughter's leg, attempting peacemaker. Her eldest had always had a problem with authority and all but created opportunities to flex her muscles against it. The last thing they needed was more tension. And, quite frankly, Jules would rather share a bathroom with her daughter and Parker than the Lees. "Sausage, it's only for a few days."

"Exactly," Matty said. "And it's our first trip as a married couple. So, that's sorted."

"Indeed," Ludmila said. "Thank you for seeing it my way, Matilda."

Matty opened her mouth, but Liss cut her off with a loud cough. "Um, so about that . . ."

Everyone stared at her.

"Jarrah Milbi"—she thrust a finger at him—"has important information on *timing*."

The group swiveled to face Jarrah, who rose to his feet, both hands on his hips. Throughout the morning, his attention had been on the island—the poor drowned cormorants, the uprooted plants—not on the tourists who'd have to be handled. It made Jules think of the tiny lines of text stenciled neatly on her bedroom wall at Kunyam, attributed to Galarrwuy Yunupingu: "The land is my backbone . . . I think of land as the history of my nation. It tells us how we came into being and what system we must live . . . my land is my foundation. Without land I am nothing." Jarrah was connected to Mun'dai in a way she would never understand. Sad in a way she would never understand. Even still, he stood as certain and tall as a blue gum.

"I just got off the phone with my mate at the Department of Home Affairs," Jarrah said. "They're about to announce a ten-day travel ban until all this calms down and there's a proper plan in place for rescue and cleanup. That means there's no flights, no ferries."

"Wait, what?" Randall was on his feet. "For how long?"

"The ten-day travel ban is predicted to be"—Jarrah folded his arms—"ten days."

A brief moment of disbelief. Then the group exploded, scrambling to their feet, all talking at once.

"Matty's got her appointment in Sydney on Tuesday!" Panic pounced into Jules's chest. "If we miss it, it'll take weeks to rebook!"

"We have a flight to Jakarta on Monday. I have meetings all week!" Ludmila.

"How's James going to get here if there's a travel ban?" Amelia.

"What if we charter a helicopter?" Randall snapped his fingers. "It can't be that much. The Australian exchange rate is really in our favor; we'll pay for everyone."

"Sorry, but the council will never allow it," Jarrah said. "Too damaging to the environment, and there's nowhere to land, even if it wasn't. And, unfortunately, that's not all." He drew in a careful, possibly irritated, breath. "Look, this was bad. Because of the placement of the other islands around us, and the fact the reef absorbed some of the wave's energy, we actually got off pretty easy. That Kooroy is still standing is honestly a miracle. K'Gari, where I live, wasn't so lucky. My place is okay, but a bloke down the road lost everything. My mate at Home Affairs reckons hundreds of boats have sunk, some with people on board. There have already been nine deaths reported, and there'll definitely be more."

This sobered everyone up, putting their problems in grim perspective. Parker took Matty's hand. Randall put his arm around his wife. It felt like a question answered: the penny Jules had been waiting to drop.

"The ferry that took you here yesterday?" Jarrah went on. "Gone. The whole fleet. Fortunately, because it was early, they were moored; empty. But that means thousands of tourists and locals are stranded. And there's no boats to get 'em. Plus, with the travel ban complicatin' things." He took off his hat to scratch the back of his neck. "There's gonna be a delay."

"What kind of delay?" Jules asked.

"I don't want to sugarcoat it," Jarrah said. "So, here goes. I don't think any of us are getting off this island for the next six weeks."

Everyone's mouths fell open at the same time. *"Six weeks?"*

"Do we have enough food and water for six weeks?" Randall asked.

"Oh goddess," Jules breathed in horror. "We're all going to die." She briefly wondered if she could eat Glen—roast a thigh over an open fire, plenty of tomato sauce?—before dismissing the monstrous idea in embarrassed alarm.

"No, no, no." Liss waved her hands. "No one's dying. We're totally good on water. We keep months' worth under the Caretaker Cabin. Food . . . Well . . ."

"Oh, shit," Matty said. "Hope everyone likes fish."

"I hate fish," said Ludmila.

Parker rolled her eyes. "You never even try it."

"I don't need to try it to know I don't like it," Ludmila replied.

"You should try the Flying Fish," Jules told her, trying to forget her bizarre brush with cannibalism. "Best seafood in Sydney. James took us there for Amelia's birthday."

"We'll definitely have enough food," Liss said. "If we do a tiny bit of rationing."

"How tiny?" Amelia asked.

"Literally bite-sized," Liss deadpanned.

Amelia was the only one to laugh.

Liss smiled in a charmed sort of way at a giggly Amelia before refocusing. "I'll go through our supplies and figure out a daily allowance."

"Do we have to pay for the six weeks?" Jules asked.

Liss looked startled. "No, of course not."

Matty cupped her hands around her mouth. "What about booze?"

"Oh yes." Several people spoke at once: Amelia, Glen, Ludmila. "What about booze?"

"I'm happy to report we have a party-at-Charlie-Sheen's-house amount of alcohol," Liss announced, to relieved sighs and scattered applause. "But yeah, as far as meal kits go, it's just not going to be what you were promised."

"None of this is what we were promised." Ludmila's words could prick a finger. "I have an overnight bag of clothes to last me six weeks."

"You and everyone else, Ludmila," Matty said. "We all only packed for a weekend."

"My daughter'll miss an *extremely important* appointment." Jules emphasized what was certainly most vital. "That's our first step in creating the *future generation*."

"I'll be working nights and sleeping during the days while you're all lying on the beach," Parker said.

"I'm doing all this without James," said Amelia. "Who I won't see for a month and a half."

"I have clients who rely on me," Randall said. "I can't spend six weeks here; I have a business to run. So does Ludmila."

"While we're airing our grievances," Liss piled on, "I'm missing a flight home to Canada. And I'm totally out of Cup-a-Soup."

"I knew I'd regret not bringing my birding vest," said Glen. "It's my best vest."

"Hello!" Matty raised her voice. *"People have died."*

That shut everyone up.

"Lost their homes and livelihoods," Matty continued. "Jarrah lost his boat!"

"It was a shit boat." Jarrah's tone was jocular, but his eyes were cool, watching the group.

"We're safe and healthy and together, with beds to sleep in, and food to eat. And in case you've forgotten"—Matty circled her finger around the beach and bush—"we're in *paradise*. So, *check your privilege* and everyone *shut the hell up*."

Of course it'd be Matty establishing herself as moral barometer and unelected leader of Team Kelly-Lee. Pride and bewilderment twisted through Jules at the sight of her oldest daughter addressing the group of adults like Amelia spoke to her unruly class of schoolkids. Seeing Jules's personality divided into her children was an ongoing psychological experiment, the conclusion to which felt opaque. Matty was bold and fearless, but Jules wasn't sure if she should be the one telling them to check their privilege. (Didn't Matty have a lot of that? Privilege?) Jules wondered if this was who she would've been if she had a mother like herself, saying *You can do anything*, and a father like Glen, saying *Follow your dreams*. And because her parents weren't at all like that, Jules couldn't tell if she was pleased by or even jealous of how her daughter turned out, or vaguely critical of her chutzpah. If only Matty could be a tiny bit more like Amelia.

"I made a cake," Amelia announced, joining her sister. "Chocolate whiskey." Luckily, it'd been in the fridge. "Why don't we move our stuff into the new house, then have a spot of morning tea? Who's up for a cuppa?"

They all were.

Amelia, domestic goddess with a ready-made treat to put into action her big sister's fighting words. Two halves of Jules Kelly split down the middle.

Jarrah addressed the group as they started to rise. "I'm going to organize a cleansing ceremony on Blinky Beach. To pay respect to country; honor the gods and all the lives lost."

He explained it'd take a few days to collect the necessary resources from places of spiritual significance throughout the island. Jules got chills, urged him to let them know how they could help. Jarrah said he would.

Jules wiped some sand off Amelia's cheek. "What'd you make a cake for, love?"

"Oh," Amelia said, folding up her towel. "No reason."

10

The Lees got the master. "What's more important," Parker put it to Matty, "sleeping in a room with a balcony or getting along with my mother?"

Matty cocked her head.

"That was rhetorical," Parker informed her.

"Shh," Matty said. "I'm trying to think."

Parker took their bags into the smallest of the three bedrooms.

Now, Matty sat on Kooroy's sunny second-floor deck, iced coffee in hand, returning a missed FaceTime call to her former work spouse, Levi Jackson, cubicle mate at Spotify. Her phone was MIA; thankfully she had her laptop. Levi picked up, affecting a bad Australian accent. "G'day, mate."

Night in New York. Levi was home in his fifth-floor walk-up in the West Village, reclining on a loveseat overlooking Seventh Avenue: a mess of lights and people and cabs and *life*. Matty's heart scrambled up her throat in an attempt to bungee back to the city. Her response to seeing New York when away was always part-jealousy and part-longing, like seeing a wedding announcement from an ex.

"Matty?" Levi narrowed his eyes, lids licked with a trademark hint of electric-green eyeliner. "Honey, I think you've frozen."

"No, no, I'm here." Matty snapped herself out of it. "You'll never believe what just happened."

Levi crossed his fingers. He still had the mustache he'd grown for Movember, raising awareness for men's health and "my own fuckability." Only Levi could pull off Black Tom Selleck. "Tell me it involves a bottle of tanning oil and a young Russell Crowe."

Matty summarized the morning's events, starting with the explosion, ending with the reveal they were (wait for it) stuck! For six weeks! "It's like something out a movie," Matty said. "The explosion, the surge, the human drama!"

"A movie adapted from a hit podcast." Levi sipped what was likely a Negroni from a rocks glass. "I can hear it now: *Stranded.*"

"Oooh, *Stranded*, yeah, that's good. *Six weeks in heaven? Or hell?* Each week it's about how we survive by making stew out of sand and crabs." Matty picked a bit of fluff off her shirt. "If I was still cranking out pods, which I guess I'm not." Chief marketing officer was Matty's new job in the smaller, more laidback Sydney office; a position that paid triple what she had made in New York. "Is it fucked that my promotion will probably mean less work than being a producer?"

"No." Levi faced Matty with a there's-cake-in-the-kitchen-but-I-accidentally-ate-your-piece expression. "Look, I'm not quite sure how to say this, but . . . I have news."

"You're dating Nate and Jeremiah again." Matty sipped her coffee. "They're not good enough for you, and dating a couple is so complicated."

"That's not it. I mean, yes, I am, and you're probably right, but that's not what I'm talking about. Do you remember that hot divorcé I met at Antoni from *Queer Eye*'s rooftop-party-slash-orgy? Tom Bacon, the guy with the massive . . ."

"Ego?" Matty narrowed her eyes. "Yes."

"We were hanging out and I kind of casually mentioned our dream of starting a little production house of our own—the focus on queer stories, diverse shows—"

"Adventurous, distinctive stories that provoke empathy and curiosity in those who hear them." Matty still knew the pitch by heart. Noisy Brats: the name was her idea. They'd been trying to secure funding for the past two years.

Levi leaned in to the camera. "Matty, he's a partner at River Wolf."

"The venture capital fund? The ones we couldn't get a meeting with?" Matty's heart scrambled back down her throat to begin slamming her rib cage with excited terror.

"Exactly. I know the timing is awful and look, I won't take it without your blessing, but he offered for me to come in and pitch. To *all* the execs."

The world around Matty went sharp and urgent, like the beginning of a scream. For the second time in the call, language escaped her.

"Oh god, look at your face." Levi winced. "I'm not doing it. I'll cancel the pitch. I'll literally text him as soon as we're off."

With all of her might, Matty forced composure. She wasn't going to spend her days making podcasts with Levi in New York City. She wasn't going to be invited to speak on panels or be on the receiving end of a million pitches from audio wannabes or be the name thanked in the credits of *the* hit show everyone was talking about. Matty made her voice firm. "Don't be ridiculous. Of course you should take the meeting."

"Are you sure?"

She wasn't. But she'd made her bed. And, she reminded herself, it was a damn good bed. "Just because it was our dream doesn't mean it can't be your dream."

"Are you *sure*? If I get the funding and you resent me forever, it would not be worth it."

On the beach in front of the house, Jules strolled past, chatting with Jarrah. Her lovely mum was wearing plastic gloves to pick up dead fish to toss into a garbage bag: the sea life needed to be buried or burned. The sight gave Matty a fierce rush of affection. Jules waved. "Hi, sausage! Wanna come help?"

Matty waved back, pointing at her laptop. "In a minute!"

Jules beamed. "Okay. Love you!"

"Love you, too!"

Cofounder. The title appeared like a specter, then faded away.

She refocused on Levi. "Take the meeting."

"Thank you," he breathed. "You're such a better person than I am. I'm already freaking out. They want all these extra facts and figures and *three* 'fleshed-out' show ideas."

"We already have *Fade to Black* and *Baby Talk*." The first was a talk show about race and screen culture hosted by two funny Black film junkies: the guest in the pilot was Ava Duvernay. The second was a moving doc series about two sweet Midwestern gay men trying to adopt a baby—the twist was that both men had been adopted themselves, with radically different experiences. "I'm sure we can come up with a third concept. When's the meeting?"

"Three and a half weeks."

"That's heaps of time! Stranded on a desert island, remember? It'll be good to have something to work on. I can't onboard for my new job in Sydney till I'm actually there."

"Really? You'll help me? That's not weird?"

"I'm a little bit absolutely heartbroken," Matty said. "But I guess this is life. You make the best decision you can with the information you have, and that's what I did."

"And not to be anti–working mom, but it would've been a lot to launch a company and have a baby in the same year," Levi said. "I know the Kardashians make it look easy, but I have sisters, and it's really not."

"You're right." Matty's Sydney job had insane parental leave: twelve months, fully paid. "This doesn't actually change anything." The pep talk was working. Already the shock of Levi's news was fading, replaced by the excitement of helping him nail the pitch. "If I bust a gut, I might be able to cut an entire pilot for *Stranded*."

They chatted for a few more minutes, making a plan. Levi promised to work around Matty's schedule, even if it meant a 3:00 a.m. brainstorming session on his end. By the time Matty hung up, she'd largely managed to absorb the news and see how it could be good for everyone. Jealousy was helpful only insofar as it illuminated one's true desires. And her true desire was to help make progressive shows that changed the cultural conversation. The powerful, rich feeling of doing this work was self-proving, a dynamo that obliterated her lesser emotions.

In the bedroom, the jar of prenatal vitamins was propped up on her pillow, like the world's worst hotel chocolate. Of course it'd survived the surge, unearthed from the bedroom debris by her wife. The sight of it shivered something jangly up Matty's spine.

There was no denying it: the travel delay wasn't an inconvenience. It was a relief. It'd give Matty more time for the idea of having a baby to sink in and start feeling exciting, like it should. While Matty liked the general concept of having a kid (a daughter, obviously, who was very similar to her in myriad ways), she'd been avoiding thinking about the physical and psychological toll that procreation would take. Pregnancy and labor and breastfeeding, oh my. As committed to equal parenting as she and Parker were, it was obviously a thousand times harder for the bio mum: the one actually making the rug rat. When these worries had surfaced in the past, Matty smacked them aside, focusing instead on rushing to the subway or a meeting or drinks with friends. But now, staring at the elephantine vitamin in the palm of her hand, the sound of the ocean replacing the snarl of traffic, her entire body pulsed with unease.

But they'd made a plan. A plan that delighted everyone Matty loved. And surely no one ever felt one hundred percent ready to become a mother.

Dutifully, Matty swallowed the pill with a shallow sip of water. It left an acrid taste on the back of her tongue, a sensation she tried to ignore.

II

Being torn apart by a natural disaster had focused Amelia's enormous reserves of romantic energy squarely back on her boyfriend. "I'm so bummed you can't be here." She gazed at James, rendered in miniature on her phone, memorizing the exact color of his eyes in romantic desperation. When would she see him again? Could she move to Melbourne? What would their children look like? "I really wanted to show you off."

"I know. I really am sorry, baby." He sighed, scrubbing a hand over his face. Bags under his eyes the color of plums. "Truly."

He sounded so genuinely abashed that Amelia reminded him this wasn't his fault.

"Right." He said it as if he only just realized this was true. James was driving, eyes flitting between the screen and the street in front of him. It was overcast in Melbourne. The city tram stops looked crowded. "How long are you stuck out there?"

Amelia traced her fingertip along the sea-softened wooden railing of Kooroy's second-floor balcony. "It might be weeks! I'm so bummed I can't see you till *April*." A small splinter pierced into her flesh, an attack from the world's tiniest sword.

"You could be in a worse spot." James honked the horn, pissed. "Melbourne feels very claustrophobic compared to Lady Lush."

Liss appeared on the beach, coming out from the bush. Amelia sat forward with a start. "Mun'dai."

"Huh?"

Liss was carrying a box of something—tools?—a loop of rope around her body. She was heading toward the fishermen's cottages, away from Kooroy. Amelia went down the stairs after her. "The Indigenous name is Mun'dai, I think that's what you're supposed to call it."

"Mundane?"

"Mun'dai, like *Mun*-day. Hang on, baby. Hey! Liss!"

But Liss kept moving, a determined lope.

"Sorry baby, I'll call you right back." With a small squeeze of guilt, Amelia hung up and set off up Blinky Beach. The sun was hot, relentlessly bright. Amelia leapt over lumps of seaweed and coral to catch up with Liss.

"Amelia. Is everything okay?" Liss looked on edge.

Amelia failed to notice. Despite the morning's drama, she felt enlivened from finally getting through to James and, more so, from the generous offer she was about to make. Like her mother, making others feel welcome asserted her sense of self-worth. "I wanted to see if you and Jarrah would like to have lunch with us."

She expected gratitude, *Sure, that'd be great!* The brief, hot spark she'd felt on meeting Liss had been chalked up to friendship chemistry. Amelia had a fondness for novels set in the nineteenth century, the kind where one was romanced by taking a turn around the garden and all the women wore gloves. A phrase specific to college-aged girls of this era perfectly described what'd happened: getting *smashed* on someone. Like a crush, but platonic and innocent. Maybe she was smashed on Liss, and they could be friends. Because Amelia needed a friend for the next six weeks, especially now that Amelia had been forced to take an unpaid leave of absence from her job, and her sister was working on Levi's pitch. A friend to laugh with, go for a swim with, who could provide occasional respite from her family, as wonderful and nuts as they all were.

But Liss looked slightly miffed, as if Amelia had just told a joke in poor taste. "Oh, thanks, but Jarrah and I have a lot of work to do."

Amelia squinted, shading the sun in an attempt to read Liss's expression. "The sand's already dry. And I'm making sausages and my big Italian salad." A specialty. Whenever she brought it into the teacher's lounge for potluck Fridays, she always went home with an empty bowl. "You can take a lunch break."

Liss's tone was distinctly cool. "The surge killed a lot of animals. Completely disrupted the island's ecosystem. Sand dries, that's what it does." On the empty beach, a wall between them. Clearly, Liss Chambers was not smashed on Amelia Kelly. "If you guys need anything, send me an email."

Liss didn't have time to lunch with the rich, clueless guests whose well-being was an annoying task. She had work to do: real work, created by a tragedy that'd harmed the place she lived in and cared for. Liss was gone without a smile, retreating down the beach.

Shame made Amelia feel stupid and small as she realized just how badly she'd misread the entire situation.

12

Lunch was a testy affair. Jules put her plate next to what she thought was Ludmila's, but after getting sidetracked finding the tomato sauce for Glen, Ludmila had moved. The resulting table configuration had the Kellys on one side, the Lees on the other. Not the interconnectedness Jules had hoped for. She attempted cheery. "Our room's lovely. How's yours, Matty?"

"Small." Someone—probably Parker—kicked her under the table.

"Not as bad as the couch," Amelia muttered, pushing food around her plate.

Matty feigned innocence. "Are you suggesting Parker and I sleep on a sofa?"

"I'm just saying it sucks that I'm paying the single-girl tax yet again," Amelia huffed. "And I'm not even single, for a fucking change."

"Randall." Jules identified Parker's father as the only one not tilting toward the battle, deciding to enlist him an ally. "Tomato sauce?"

Randall scanned the bottle's label with a frown.

"Wouldn't look too closely." Matty scraped her plate clean. "Are there seconds?"

"We can't have seconds, Bratty," Amelia said. "We're rationing."

Liss was still preparing the family's meal kits, but the generous proportions of their first night were now on a diet.

"I need to eat." Matty narrowed her eyes at her sister's half-finished plate. "So do you, Animal. You don't need to take up less space just because the patriarchy wants you to."

Amelia tossed down her fork. "Piss off!"

"Now, girls," Glen reprimanded. "Enough of that or it'll be a very long six weeks."

Tense silence reigned as everyone side-eyed the other humans they'd be sharing a house and, presumably, every single meal with for the next month and a half. Even to Jules, that did seem like a lot.

The Lees excused themselves, ascending the staircase to the master as if returning to Mount Olympus.

"You don't want to come for a walk?" Jules called after Ludmila. "I thought I'd have a look in the bush for injured wildlife."

"I'll come, Mum." Amelia perked up, oddly intense. "We should all be doing something to help. The island isn't a playground, it's an ecosystem."

"Calm down, David Attenborough." Matty pocketed a mandarin. "We're all going to pitch in. Right, Ludmila?"

"Unfortunately I have work to do," Ludmila replied, smooth as butter, closing the door to the master behind her.

Despite her best intentions, Jules felt a swell of relief.

The kids melted off, leaving Jules and Glen to clean up, working side by side with machine efficiency.

Jules met her husband at twenty-four, which was—by the day's standards—flirting with old-maidhood. That Jules hadn't been married off as a teenager like her older sister embarrassed her mother so acutely, she regularly lied about Jules's prospects to the other ladies at bowls. Jules fell pregnant in the wink of an eye—they'd gotten hitched before she started to show. Like many twenty-six-year-old men, Glen wasn't ready to be a father, but it wasn't expected he'd do much more than earn enough to buy a house and take the baby to the park on Sundays.

As a highly competent, often underestimated woman, Jules did better than most with the early years of fatigue and loss of self. She was twenty-five, married to the third man she'd ever slept with. What self was there to lose? Matty was a determined, difficult child. Like Athena, the Greek goddess of wisdom and war, their firstborn emerged fully grown and fully armed. Leaping (as the myth went) from her father's forehead, bow drawn, ready for battle. A "willful" child.

Amelia was a dream, exactly the baby Jules (secretly) hoped she'd have—easily pleased, almost too compliant. A family: a puzzle with its last piece in place, the big picture finally revealed. Jules was needed, respected, and obeyed; motherhood knighted her. Smoothing table linens and fevered foreheads summoned easy pleasure. The unspoken rule that her desires came last after her children's and husband's was as easy to follow as loving her two funny, adorable girls.

But times changed.

One minute she was spooning homemade baby food into her girls' mouths, the next she was watching them apply lipstick in horrendous colors, jostling for a steamy bathroom mirror. Amelia had a boyfriend, then a broken heart, then another boyfriend. Matty announced she was a lesbian in the way she won school captain: with a confidence Jules didn't recognize. She hid her bewilderment by throwing Matty a coming-out party. High school ended. The girls moved to Surry Hills and Newtown, hip, inner-city suburbs, full of young people with pastel hair and terrible tattoos.

Jules insisted on keeping Matty's room as a guest bedroom for when the girls stayed the night, but Glen turned Amelia's into a study without really asking. The first time Jules saw a desk piled with books instead of a bed piled with pillows, she wept.

And just like a house that gets reexamined when the needs of its inhabitants change, Jules was forced to reexamine her marriage. She was forty-five, which as a kid felt prehistoric, but in the modern twenty-first century, was young. She got a degree in horticulture and landed a job for the local council in bush regeneration, cultivating public land to return it to its natural state, pulling out weeds to plant native grasses. A new way to impose her own caring order on the world.

Even though they all lived an hour or so apart, they were still a family. The girls loved their dad's dry sense of humor and nonthreatening masculinity. He was the one they asked about taxes and installing shelves and jazz. She and Glen went on some holidays—Italy, Ireland—always her idea, her itinerary. He went along for the ride but never designed it.

Jules turned fifty, then fifty-five. Her older sister, Marjorie, announced she was getting a divorce, tearily confessing over two bottles of Chardonnay that her marriage was bland, that they hadn't had sex in years. "What I have now," Marjorie had said, "is oatmeal. Oatmeal's fine. But not every day. I want spice! I want flavor! I want . . . ramen! Yes, that's what I want. A big bowl of piping hot *ramen*."

Jules hadn't had sex in years, either. She had oatmeal, too. *Bland* might be one way to put it, but so was *simple*. Oatmeal was cheap and it kept you fed. Switching oatmeal for a complex Japanese soup was beyond her culinary ability. The metaphor was a moot point: she'd never hurt her daughters with the upsetting news of a divorce.

Out of nowhere, Matty announced she was moving to New York City. As believable as relocating to Mars. Jules was supportive, figuring it'd be a year or two before Matty realized how good she had it in Sydney—a world-class city, highly livable—and return.

But Matty stayed.

Jules visited New York but couldn't connect with the dirty, expensive festival of smells that was completely devoid of the natural world. Glen enjoyed it, keen to visit the city's many jazz clubs. Jules never more than tolerated the place that'd stolen her firstborn.

Gradually, Jules started inventing reasons to see Amelia—a new exhibition at an art qallery they must check out. A trendy café a friend recommended in Redfern: Was she free for lunch? Amelia intuited her mother's needs, made herself available. She came home for dinner every Sunday.

Months later, while waiting in line with groceries at the local Woolworths, Jules saw a post on Matty's Instagram. A photo with girlfriend Parker, workmate Levi, and a handful of strangers, all clutching sweaty champagne flutes and grinning, the twinkly lights of a bridge in the background. *Five years in New York! I might never go home (or am I already here?).* The linoleum under Jules's feet bunched and shimmered. Her phone slipped from her hands. In the middle of the supermarket, Jules broke down, heaving guttural, painful sobs. Because even though she'd never told Matty, or anyone, having her eldest daughter live so far away was like living without a limb. The idea her child might never come home, turning the experience of family from physical to theoretical, was a violence Jules Kelly could not endure.

"Mum?" It was Amelia, holding up a pair of gardening gloves. "I found these under the house. Do you think we can borrow them when we go looking for wildlife?"

"Probably," Jules said. "Why don't you ask Liss?"

Amelia half frowned, half flinched. "I'm sure it's fine. I'll see if I can find another pair for you."

She went back downstairs. Jules hunted for the right place to put away a mixing bowl. That the girls would have children of their own was a given. Amelia was naturally maternal, gooey at the sight of anything small and cute, while Matty approached motherhood with practicality and narcissism, demonstrated in their weekly Zoom call when Matty was still in New York. *My future heir*, a typical comment might go, or *someone to indoctrinate*. "Who hopefully doesn't inherit my alcoholic genes. That was a joke, Mum," Matty said once, addressing her mother via the laptop's camera. "I'm not really a drinker."

On the other side of their tiny apartment, Parker laughed.

Jules didn't hear it. The fertility talk had sharpened her senses, like a hunter spotting game—*grandkids: ten o'clock*. She kept her tone breezy. "We don't know how lucky we have it. Amelia said a friend of hers was complaining their daycare costs went up from two hundred dollars to two hundred and fifty."

Matty refilled her wineglass. "Well, per week it's the same here."

"No, sausage: that's monthly."

Matty swung around to stare at her mother on the screen. *"What?"*

"Government subsidies cover most of it," Jules had said. "The public schools are so good in Sydney these days. Amelia says that at Bondi Public"—the primary school Amelia taught at—"when the kids get picked up, their parents take them for a swim."

Matty huffed a breath, which Jules identified—thrillingly—as jealousy. "The beaches here are disgusting. Literally saw a toilet seat at Rockaway last month."

"I guess New York's better when you're childless," Jules said.

Matty chewed her lip, eyebrows drawn. "I suppose we should figure out what it'd look like to be in Sydney for all this." While driven by passion like her mother, Matty was also pragmatic like her father. A rare combination of a dreamer and a doer. "You like Sydney, don't you, babe?"

"Love Sydney." Despite her monochrome aesthetic, Californian Parker was a sun baby.

"You'll get a lot more for your money here. Plus"—Jules indicated her and Glen—"two free babysitters! Three, with your sister. You'd have more time to work, and by spending less on childcare and health care, you wouldn't have to work as hard. I'd really love to have you closer," she added, trying not to let desperation overwhelm her words. "Especially once there's a little one in the mix."

Matty gazed back, the screen momentarily glitching, before reestablishing the connection. "I miss you guys, too."

Jules could tell she meant it. Earlier in the year Matty had gotten a tattoo, presenting it to a horrified Jules like a proud cat with a dead mouse. "See? It's your favorite flower." Two tiny purple Dianellas, a native lily, stenciled in a small black crescent moon on her right forearm. "And golden wattle. So I have you and Australia with me always."

Matty knew Jules didn't like tattoos, yet seemed to expect praise, even gratitude. "The detail is very good," she'd managed, telling herself this choice meant her child was finally homesick.

Glen leaned forward, addressing the two women on the Zoom call thoughtfully. "But you've spent so long setting your life up there."

Jules felt a whack of alarm. "Yes, they've had a good go."

He went on, "New York City seems like one of those places that after you leave, it'd be very hard to—"

Jules snapped the laptop shut.

"Whoa!" He laughed. "What was—"

"*What* is wrong with you? Our *daughter* is thinking about coming *home*. After nearly *seven* years."

Glen paled, turtling back into himself. "I was—I just—want what's best for Matty."

"What's best for Matty, and Amelia, and *me* is having our *family* back *together*. But obviously you don't care about any of that. *Christ*, Glen." The antipathy she felt for this man solidified suddenly, irrevocably, into anger. "If you don't do *everything* in your power to make this happen, I will *never* forgive you."

And so he had. They all had.

It was Glen who'd negotiated the best quote for an international move and made a spreadsheet of everything they'd need to buy once they arrived, down to bin liners and curtain rods.

It was Amelia who'd house-hunted, bewitching real estate agents into calling her first.

It was Jules who'd found the best fertility clinic in Sydney, and figured out Parker's immigration issues, and made herself as available as possible for every single task, while casually mentioning the popular Sydney Podcasting Festival or exactly how hot and beautiful the weather was that day.

It was all theoretical: "Just to help you make up your minds." But as Jules anticipated, once Matty had put her smarts to the task, it snowballed from an idea to a plan. Her eldest had always been the leap-before-you-look type, signing up for a year of hot yoga after taking one class. The weather cooled in New York, and Parker was dreading another six months of winter coats and frozen toes. So, when Amelia flagged the idea of a family vacation so the in-laws could bond and everyone could meet her new boyfriend, Jules suggested March, Down Under. Which might just be the perfect time for Matty and Parker to leave New York, en route to a new year—and a new life—in Sydney.

It worked.

Jules had popped champagne, and when some spilled on the carpet, she didn't even care.

Glen worried. "We weren't *too* encouraging, were we?"

Jules, who could maintain a spirited conversation with a lampshade, was speechless. Finally, she had nothing left to say to him.

As the newlyweds gave up their lease, Glen started sleeping in the guest bedroom. As they started their last trips to the museum/park/best bagel shop, Jules confided in Marjorie that she and Glen were separating. She just couldn't stomach any more oatmeal.

And now they were here. On Mun'dai, all together, just like Jules wanted. She just couldn't have either daughter suspect anything was off between her and Glen.

They finished cleaning Kooroy's kitchen. "Righto," Glen said. "What do you want to do now?"

"I'm going out with Amelia." Jules hung the tea towel up to dry. "What are you going to do?"

Glen stood in the middle of the clean, quiet space, looking left, then right, then left again. "Hmm."

Jules tempered irritation. "Why don't you listen to your audiobook?"

"I finished it last night." Glen looked to her for another suggestion.

She threw her hands up. "I don't know: go bird-watching! I'm not responsible for figuring out what you want anymore, Glen: *you'll* have to do that."

Glen's face unpetaled, flashing through devastation, shame, anger, before closing tight once more. His tone was edged. "Have you thought any more about telling the girls? They'll be upset when they figure out we've been lying to them."

"We're *not* lying to them! We're protecting them! Just like we always have, just like we always will!"

The spouses stared hotly at each other, mirrors of confused annoyance at the other's unreasonable point of view.

As always, Glen backed down first. "Fine." He went into the bedroom, shutting the door behind him.

Jules puffed out a guilty sigh over snapping at him, heading for the steps down to the front door.

Which meant she didn't see Ludmila, paused at the bottom of the stairs from the master. Where she'd overhead the entire conversation.

13

Ludmila returned to the master with the computer charger she'd needed to retrieve, where she found Randall doing his daily set of crunches next to the bed. His movements had a slightly intense energy, as if he were trying to burn off what was percolating throughout the house. She took a seat at the desk facing the balcony, the glass doors closed to keep the bugs out, and plugged in her laptop.

Ludmila had started her career as an assistant at Gensler, a global design and architecture firm. As she worked her way up through the interior design department, she became intrigued by textiles. She befriended one of the reps for textile manufacturer, Maharam (founded by a Russian at the turn of the century), landed a buying job, and started accompanying her boss on trips to China and Paris and India to learn about fabrics and their complex weaving processes. She'd exited the company at the director level eleven years ago to start Curated by Ludmila. Clients flocked from around the world to peruse her meticulous library of textiles, while the online store sold all the handwoven Peruvian blankets and vintage Indian saris she couldn't not buy.

Textiles told a story. In their thread and fabric, the story of its maker. Their culture and taste. Their beliefs and passions. Even cheap, ugly textiles told a story: one of exploitation, perhaps, or the philosophy of capitalism. Textiles mapped the world in a tactile and fascinating way. For

Ludmila, a woman with a bodily consciousness, they were her Braille. To touch was to know.

Only after she'd navigated to her inbox and clicked on the first email did she mention, "I think Jules and Glen are getting a divorce."

"Ninety—What?" Randall sat up, panting. "Why do you think that?"

Ludmila summarized their argument in the same casual tone one used to order a latte.

Randall listened in astonishment while finishing his final few crunches. "*They'll be upset when they figure out we've been lying*—Are you sure that's what he said?"

"Yes."

Randall got to his feet, shucking off his sweaty T-shirt. "Glen's a classic good guy. Bet he's blindsided by all this."

"You think Jules is ending the marriage?"

"Don't you?" Randall asked.

Ludmila thought about it. She was the more intellectual of the pair, but her husband had good instincts. Randall had worked as a personal trainer since his twenties. People tended to get or stay in shape for emotional reasons; the life/success/sex they felt they deserved. His many years of interpreting his clients' unspoken wants and needs resulted in a fairly solid emotional IQ. "Yes," she concluded. "You're right."

Randall went into the en suite, returning with a hand towel to wipe off his face. "Should we say anything to the girls?"

"No." Ludmila looked up from her computer. "It's none of our business."

"Not our time to be the truth tellers." Randall slipped off his workout shorts. Ludmila admired her husband's butt as he rummaged through his clothes to find a clean shirt and pair of shorts. Their sex last night had been particularly good. Different bed, different night sky: vacations invited a bodily renewal. "Glen's a bird-watcher, apparently."

"Are there a lot of birds here?"

Ludmila shrugged, typing a reply to an artist she was supposed to meet in Jakarta the following week. *I'm sorry to inform you that due to a circumstance beyond my control* . . . "They're certainly noisy enough in the mornings."

"You want me to . . . ask Glen about bird-watching?" Randall tried.

"I don't want you to do anything." Ludmila considered herself a good wife and mother. Part of that involved not being excessively involved in her daughter's or husband's lives. Her own mother was a meddler. Freedom to explore one's inner world while expanding one's outer circle was a value Ludmila believed in.

An enormous bird with red-brown wings and a white chest and head landed on the balcony railing outside. Ludmila flinched in alarm. "*Bozhe moi.* What is that? A hawk?"

Talons like twisted wire gripped the railing, its gaze piercing and regal.

"It does look like a predator." Randall folded his arms and chewed his bottom lip, which he only did when he was impressed. "It's a seabird, I guess . . . Oh, it's probably after all the dead fish on the beach."

The bird spread its wings, a giant umbrella unfolding. It swooped off, circled the beach, and dove to scoop up a silver fish.

"See?" Randall sounded equally pleased and surprised. "I was right."

"Well, the body is a system, which makes you a systems expert." They were good at pointing out each other's strengths. It was one of the bedrocks of their long and generally satisfying marriage. "And birds live in an ecosystem, don't they?"

"Yes," Randall said, "I suppose so."

Ludmila tapped out another email. "What are you going to do this afternoon?"

Randall checked the time on his FitBit. "I should touch base with my clients." He cocked his head at his wife, trying to read her. "What, do you think I should check in on Glen and his birds?"

"You do whatever you want to do, *moi sladkiy.* Your life is your own."

Randall opened the balcony door to take a hit from his weed pen. Ludmila didn't smoke herself, and it wasn't something their daughter knew about. "I bet he bikes."

"Who?"

"Glen." Randall exhaled a stream of pale smoke. "He obviously doesn't have a regimen, but his quads are in good shape. If he *is* single again, he's going to want to tone up. Get some muscle definition."

"Well, there's no rush on anything, is there?"

"No. All right, babe, better get this admin done." He put the pen beside the book on his bedside table—*Be the Best YOU YOU Can Be!*—and came to give her a kiss that was unexpectedly passionate for mid-afternoon. The memory of last night flickered in the warmth of her husband's mouth. They were both smiling as he left.

Ludmila suspected she was going to start learning a lot about birds.

At least it was something. After her rescheduling was finished, how was she going to fill the next six weeks?

Her lower stomach pulsed uncomfortably. The surge had pushed everyone out of their comfort zone. Especially Ludmila Lee, who was about to admit defeat to the terrible drop dunny.

14

Beaches were formed from shifting sediment, transported by waves to a place it could accumulate. But the sand particles of a beach never stayed in one place. Thanks to wind and longshore drift, they were in a state of constant flux. Much like the relationship between the two Kelly sisters. Yet even as they careened between bickering and best friendship, some things didn't change. Louise Glück said of two sisters: one is the watcher, one is the dancer. Amelia had been in the front row for Matty ever since she was born.

The shifting sediment of Blinky Beach was crunchy silk beneath their toes as the two sisters walked side by side in the late afternoon. Each grain of sand was exactly how big Matty felt when huddled with Parker and her in-laws as the rushing water swallowed the house. Matty looped her arm through Amelia's, needing to smooth everything between them, and realign. "Sorry for all bitchy comments about your weight," Matty said. "You look like a module in that bikini." (Her slightly sarcastic slang for *model*.)

Amelia tugged at the skimpy top. "Really for James's benefit. On both counts."

"You shouldn't lose weight for a guy, Animal. You should—"

"I know, I know." Amelia cut her off. "You're lucky. Being married. Not having to try as hard."

Matty laughed. "Um, that's not actually how it works. Maybe I don't shave my legs as often. But I have to try a lot harder on a deeper level. Like, not squabbling over petty shit, even though I love squabbling over petty shit: *Babe, can you chew a little less annoyingly, please?*"

Amelia laughed.

Matty went on, "Figuring out how to make myself happy, her happy, and us happy as a couple, which is actually three completely different things."

"You're so wise." The sunset poured over Amelia, making her look like a movie star. With all their power and fragility.

"Are you *sure* he's the right guy, Animal?" Matty asked.

Amelia's expression was heartfelt and sage. "I am. And if James were here right now, you'd see that too. It's so important to me that you give him a chance."

"Then let's FaceTime him tomorrow, as a family."

"That would be lovely." Amelia folded her fingers into her sister's as they strolled, the warm water washing their ankles and feet. "How are you feeling about Levi's news?"

A sneak attack. A carousel of emotion—jealousy, anger, crushing regret—spun hard before Matty grabbed it, and reminded herself how she actually felt. *Happy.* "I'm thrilled for him! He's gonna get the funding, I know it."

Amelia stopped to face her sister. "Matty. It's okay to be sad. I know how much you wanted it."

"I did," Matty admitted. "But Sydney's going to be *great*. I'll be close to you, and Mum and Dad, and it's all happening! It's all already happened. Indecision is the only wrong decision. I made my choice."

Amelia gave her sister's arm a supportive squeeze. "And I'm so glad that you did. But it's okay to be bummed. You were rattled all afternoon."

"The whole thing is rattling." Matty indicated the island they couldn't leave. "But it was weird seeing New York." Being away from home for anything longer than a week made her feel like she was missing a favorite movie one channel over. *Jurassic Park. Star Wars.* New York. "It all happened so quickly. Deciding to leave."

"Well, everything just fell into place."

"Exactly." Matty returned to certainty. "Everything fell into place."

They plopped down on the sand to watch the waves in comfortable silence.

When Amelia was brought home from the hospital, Matty begged to trade the newborn for a Rainbow Brite doll. As much as they squabbled, Amelia was her mirror, her conscience, her sweetest self. Being with her sister, her funny, hopelessly romantic little sister, felt like coming home to a plate of warm brownies after a long, wintry day. Matty wanted to be close to her, especially when starting a family of her own.

Matty tugged a lock of Amelia's hair. "Do blondes have more fun?"

Amelia twirled the piece of dyed hair between her fingers. "I guess. Not sure if I want to stay blonde."

"Why not?"

Her little sister shrugged. "Sometimes I wonder if I actually want to be blonde, or if I've just been told my whole life that blonde is pretty, so that's why I want it. It's actually really bad for my hair."

The words swerved around Matty's head. "Like, what is your true desire versus what you have been told so often is your desire that you mistake it for truth?"

"Good way of putting it. That's why they pay you the big bucks." Amelia got to her feet. "We should head back. The Lees are in charge of dinner, and I'm worried what'll happen when they realize takeout isn't an option."

Matty was only half listening, instead replaying her sister's words. Desire and truth. Her attention snagged on something farther up the beach. Horror chilled her skin. "Jesus. Is that a dead dolphin?"

Amelia followed her gaze to the large dark lump on the sand. "No, honey. It's just a log."

Her sister was right. In the fading light, things weren't as clear.

15

Freud called it the *death drive*. An innate, universal impulse toward self-destruction.

It manifested in different behaviors: overspending, affairs, smoking, addiction. Or, in the case of Liss Chambers on this sultry March evening in the southern end of the Great Barrier Reef, doomscrolling her ex-girlfriend's Instagram.

Sofia Cardenas-Campbell was a Mexican-Canadian actress who'd spent a grueling decade in Toronto playing Murdered Girl and Bored Shopper #2 in soulless police procedurals and earnest indie films. With her caterpillar-thick eyebrows and whip of black hair, Sofia was beautiful and talented. But so were a lot of young women, and sometimes (or really, often), Cute Girlfriend meant Cute *White* Girlfriend. The week after her thirty-seventh birthday, Sofia returned home to Montreal to save her money and her sanity, feeling like a failure.

She'd met Liss while drowning her sorrows at Sad Sack Sundays, a theme night where Liss played melancholic covers of everyone from Elliott Smith to Dolly Parton, at a bar called Black Dog. The Mile End neighborhood fixture was owned by Liss's best friend, Gabriel Martel. Kindhearted Gabe had read that black dogs were the least likely to be adopted from shelters. Always a sucker for the quite literal underdog. Liss and Gabe had known each other since Liss was untattooed Melissa with braces and mousy-brown hair. They'd started a band in high school, Girl vs Truck, gigging locally and doing short, fun tours into their mid-twenties. After Gabe bought the bar, he didn't have time for band practice. But doing covers and occasional originals fed Liss's appetite for music. Playing at Black Dog made her happy, and the mixed crowd of locals and newcomers were a generous audience.

Liss met Sofia on a warm, rainy night in late spring. Liss was bleached blonde back then, and unmoored, embroiled in light romantic drama with an insecure satirist who wrote for a left-leaning newspaper and a woman in her fifties who made sculptures out of garbage. Neither possessed the makings of the great love story Liss was privately hoping to find. During a stripped-bare version of Robyn's "Dancing on My Own," Liss watched Sofia wrinkle her nose at Gabe's first and then second pour, settling with a sigh on the third. Liss dedicated "Lua" by Bright Eyes to "the woman at the bar who makes Eeyore look like a giddy optimist." It made Sofia smile.

The simple, spacious song was painful and pretty and when done right, pure catnip for the brokenhearted.

"*When everything is lonely / I can be my own best friend.*" Liss didn't need to dig around with a needle to tap sadness and ennui; that rich vein was right at the surface.

Black Dog was two-thirds full and transfixed as she got to the first swelling hook.

"*And I know you have a heavy heart / I can feel it when we kiss.*" Liss let her gaze alight on Sofia.

Sofia stared back, captivated. There was power in being the center of attention and choosing where to reflect it back. A small power that Liss enjoyed.

After her set, Liss dispatched tongue-tied younger fans to offer to buy Sofia a drink. Sofia accepted: mezcal. Her eyes were the color of rough-cut emeralds. Liss liked men who were embarrassed by their existence and women who didn't apologize for theirs. Even feeling sorry for herself, Sofia crackled with energy and light. Liss could feel it under her skin, humming like a power line.

"Give me one good reason . . ." Their third round. Sofia's nipples showed though a black silk top, no bra. She was touching the inside of

Liss's wrist, circling the sensitive skin with her thumb. "Give me one good reason why I shouldn't go back to Toronto to give it one more shot."

Liss shifted closer. "One good reason?" They were walking around each other's personal space. Taking a look. "Okay."

The woman with the green eyes tasted of spice and firework smoke. The kiss was sweet but immediately, Liss sensed heat.

She pulled back. Sofia's eyes were closed. Liss worried she'd overplayed her hand.

Sofia's lips curved up. "I might need two reasons."

Liss slid her fingers into Sofia's hair to cup the nape of her elegant neck. This woman was different. This was different. "I am an unlimited number of reasons."

There's an old joke—*What does a lesbian bring to a second date? A U-Haul*—and it's funny because it's absolutely true. The lovers moved in together three months later.

They were happy. Sofia starred in local theater productions, which was more fun and satisfying than she expected. Liss split her hours as a part-time social worker and part-time musician at Black Dog. They hosted dinners for their hilarious, wonderful friends in their tiny courtyard around a folding table piled with pizzas, Liss playing songs by The Cure, everyone getting terrifically drunk on boxed wine. Sofia kept things interesting, her extroversion balancing Liss's introspection. Montreal was cheap. A good place for a young family.

Kids.

Liss had always wanted kids, which seemed to surprise people. She assumed this was because she didn't present as overtly feminine, often a visual shorthand for maternal—another gender-related misconception she tried to be chill about even as it annoyed her. The fact that her sex organs supposedly defined so much of her personality and potential seemed arbitrary and simplistic. Women were like this, men were like that—at best, unimaginative, at worst, dangerous. Biological determinism didn't reflect her lived reality. Liss was interested in nonbinary philosophy and identity; they/them. Plenty of cultures, ancient and modern, had third genders. The Incas worshipped a dual-gendered god known as *chuqui chinchay*. In Indigenous Hawai'i, before colonization, people of the third gender *mahu* were revered as sacred. Liss was friends with nonbinary folk through the social work scene. Not that they'd ever explicitly talked about it; Liss didn't know how to bring it up (*Are you going to that training seminar and also, please explain your personal theory of gender?*). So all this never went further than private thoughts or discussing it with anxious teens in helpline calls. Whenever she'd mused aloud about it to Sofia, her girlfriend was dismissive. "We all don't feel like being a woman sometimes," a typical comment might go. "That doesn't make you some mysterious third sex. That makes you human." Liss would put it aside. But the concept kept coming up.

She may have felt ambivalent about gender, but not about being a parent.

An oddity that her body was built to reproduce even though she had no interest in carrying a child. The fact Liss got a period felt like inheriting a valuable, if ugly, vase from a relative. She couldn't get rid of it, a part of her even respected it, but its ongoing existence in her life was essentially pointless. However, the experience of caring for a child—of putting their needs above her own, of having a tiny newborn fall asleep on her chest—felt deeply, radically sublime. Spiritual. Liss wasn't religious, but deep down, Liss wondered if being a parent would be the closest experience she'd ever have to witnessing god.

Sofia wanted kids, too, and the experience of pregnancy. Liss was thirty-five by now; Sofia was coming up on forty. So Liss started to think about buying her girlfriend a ring. Presenting it while down on one knee. Spotting the vintage emerald on a gold band in an antique store felt like kismet. Liss hid the ring in a shoebox and began noodling on a romantic proposal, able to see down the road of a long, happy life together.

But life took a left turn.

Just as Sofia gave up on her dream, it showed up on their doorstep and let itself in.

Sofia landed the lead role of Nora in a local production of *A Doll's House*, and the early reviews were raves. She secured some modest press as "an actress you might think about keeping an eye on." Her agent, whom she hadn't heard from in so long Sofia had forgotten was still her agent, called. A pilot for Netflix, sci-fi thing. *Earth 3000.*

"Bad name," the agent said, "good script." Perfect for her: Could she send a self-tape?

Sofia shot the audition in their lounge room and emailed it in. Nothing happened. They forgot about it.

The agent called back. There was another self-tape, then a meeting, then a chemistry test with the other lead. In L.A.

"I won't get it." Sofia tossed clothes into an overnight bag. "Even if I do, it won't go."

But she did get it. And it did go. In less than a year, Sofia Cardenas-Campbell went from middling local thespian to bona fide star. At the launch party in downtown L.A., Liss watched an unrecognizably pretty "Captain Natalia Nabarro" lead her motley crew of aliens and humans to victory in a pilot that *Variety* deemed "a surprisingly smart, self-aware space opera that sizzles," and even the *New York Times* admitted it was "out-of-this-world good." The engine of the show was the unresolved sexual tension (TV people called this URST) between Sofia's character and her green-skinned co-captain, Xela Lela, an exceptionally hot Martian, played by another gorgeous, wide-eyed newcomer, Reggie Richards.

Fame came in like a wrecking ball.

When Sofia wasn't filming, she was at meetings and lunches and meetings about the lunches and lunches about the meetings. When Liss visited her in L.A., she'd end up awkwardly hanging out at an actual famous person's house watching Sofia dazzle everyone, or consoling her weeping partner, who was completely overwhelmed by her life's revolution. On her fifth visit Sofia cried in the shower for an hour, then insisted they go to a game night at Lili Reinhart's. When Liss realized Sofia hadn't asked her a thing about how her month had been, she tried a proactive approach. "I'm thinking of pitching a new theme night at Gabe's bar."

They were in the backseat of the car (Sofia had a driver), stuck in the kind of traffic that made *Waiting for Godot* seem pacey.

"Tunes-y Tuesdays: show tunes covers. Very Rodgers & Hammerstein, very gay."

Sofia, scrolling through her phone, gasped. "Mariah Carey just followed me!"

"Or maybe Weedy Wednesdays," Liss improvised. "Stoner anthems. Bob Marley, Weezer. Or songs about . . . weeding? Gardening?" She started humming "Octopus's Garden."

Sofia, examining her face in a hand mirror, grimaced. "I am definitely getting fillers."

Liss expected the fan accounts. Social media fostered troubling parasocial behavior: one-sided relationships wherein complete strangers felt extremely close to her girlfriend, resulting in fan art, marriage proposals, and impassioned DMs that Sofia ignored. They didn't know Sofia. Or Liss. Or that Sofia already had a partner. Sofia said she wanted to keep her private life private, due to the mystery that line invited. Liss expected the tsunami of obsessive fan attention.

She didn't expect the pictures.

Grainy, barely visible photographs of Reggie Richards and Sofia Cardenas-Campbell kissing at a Haim concert at the Hollywood Bowl. By now, the pair had consummated their onscreen URST, in a hot will-they-won't-they have freaky alien sex again (spoiler alert: they will).

"It's acting!" Sofia protested, her eyes flashing like phosphorescence.

But it looked a lot like chemistry and very heaving petting. Sofia made a little whimpering noise when she made out with Reggie on the show. She didn't make that sound with Liss.

"It wasn't a kiss!" Sofia's face was furious on the screen of Liss's phone. Behind her, the cloudless October sky burned a blinding Disney-blue. "We're *friends*. He's the only person who gets what I'm going through!"

"I get it!" Liss exclaimed. Outside the bar in Mile End, it had just started to snow. "It's all we ever talk about!"

That night, Liss had her first panic attack. She was sitting at the bar, replaying the stressful argument while downing whiskey sodas, when her pulse began to race. Stress, she assumed, or misplaced nerves about her upcoming set. But her heart rate kept spiraling, as if she was running for her life, thrashing double-time. Triple. She started hyperventilating. Black Dog was busy. No one even noticed.

In a locked bathroom stall, while patrons pissed and washed their hands, Liss gulped for air, drenched in sweat, unable to cry out or get her phone or do anything except think she was dying. The terror was monstrous, bloodthirsty, and vicious, bigger than the planet and everything she knew to be true about it. She'd never felt more afraid. Or more alone.

When her symptoms subsided, she realized what'd happened. Plenty of people had panic attacks. She wasn't going to die. Even if—every time it happened over the subsequent months, triggered by moments of peak relationship stress—death felt preferable.

As things got worse, the show at Black Dog got better. *Time Out Montreal* reviewed Sad Sack Sundays as "the least fun you'll have on a Sunday night (but that's a good thing)."

Her not-very-good coping strategy was getting messy-drunk after every show, until Gabe finally cut her off, one large hand covering her glass. Concern in his kind, dark eyes. Concern and something deeper. He poured her into a cab. "She doesn't deserve you, Liss."

"What do I deserve?" Liss mumbled, her face in her hands.

"Someone who'll never . . ." His voice was tight. Liss blinked up, glassy-eyed. He was staring at her. "If I—If you and I . . ."

When Liss fell into bed with Gabe, it was to stop herself falling apart. He played it cool, but his feelings were obvious. He knew her better than anyone; they had matching GIRL VS TRUCK tattoos, for Pete's sake. She let it go on too long. When the end came, the week before Christmas, Gabe was blindsided.

"What do you mean, you're going to Australia?"

He followed her around his house, watching her pack.

"I want to try Vegemite. Apparently it's an excellent source of B vitamins."

"Liss. Liss!"

She finally faced him, her cheeks wet. "I can't do this anymore. To you."

"Can't do what? I fucking love you. Isn't this . . . it?"

His lovely face a funhouse mirror of her own months ago. What it looked like when someone detonated your heart. "I'm—so—sorry."

And she left. Neither Gabe or Sofia had spoken to her since.

Now, slouched into the lumpy orange sofa on the balcony of the Caretaker Cabin, Liss's exhausting day of cleanup and unexpected island quarantine derailed her self-control. So Liss was taking Sofia's Instagram for a spin, death drive–style.

A glam shot on a red carpet, chin tilted up. Her new dog, the size of a rat. A thirst trap in a strappy red bikini, and draped around her, Reggie, shirtless with a shit-eating grin. Each picture made Liss feel worse than the last.

"Hi."

Amelia Kelly was at the bottom of the stairs, looking unsure.

"Oh, h-hello." Liss's job did mean she was available to guests 24/7, but it was rarely taken advantage of after sunset.

"Sorry, I know it's late." Amelia climbed one step and paused. Cut-offs, a cream cotton cardigan over a tank top patterned with flowers, blonde hair in two long plaits, all worn with a carelessness that suggested Amelia underestimated her own sex appeal.

Or maybe she knew exactly what she was doing.

"I'm a night owl," Liss said. "What's up?"

Amelia climbed the creaking stairs to the balcony, taking in the tinkling wind chimes, stacks of decades-old magazines, a faded red surfboard. Insects kamikazed around the yellow balcony light. "Is that yours?" She pointed with interest to Liss's acoustic guitar.

It'd been so long since she'd identified herself as a musician, Liss momentarily lost control of the English language. "Mine is the guitar. Yes. Guitar."

"You play?"

Liss made a so-so gesture. "And not really for other people." *Anymore.*

Amelia looked directly at her. "I just wanted to say thank you. I don't know what would've happened if you hadn't come for my mum and me."

Her stark sincerity made Liss feel overly aware of her hands and their proximity to Amelia. "C'mon, it was nothing. Beginner's rock climbing and water sports."

"It wasn't nothing. You saved my life."

"Oh, no. No, you would've handled it without me."

Amelia gave her a *yeah-right* look, reaching into her cardigan pocket. "I have something for you. A gift." She withdrew a box of creamy garden-vegetable Cup-a-Soup. "You mentioned you liked it? On the beach? Guess you have something in common with James: I brought a bunch of everyone's favorite foods over."

It was like being handed back a wallet she didn't realize she'd lost. "Wow. Thank you, Amelia. And I'm happy to have helped. It's my job," Liss added, regretting how cool this sounded.

"Right," Amelia said, with a slightly defeated smile. Her gaze lingered around the balcony, touching every surface.

Liss had been celibate for the past three months. The simple, stoic lifestyle delivered monk-like clarity. Liss didn't want vacation flings or one-sided flirtations, to hurt someone or be hurt herself. Not making a move on Amelia was to protect Amelia as much as it would protect herself. Not that she would make a move because *Amelia was engaged.* Best that they didn't even start up a friendship.

Even if the thought of Amelia walking away made her feel lost and sad in a very strange and specific way.

Amelia hovered. "Well, I guess I should go . . ."

"Night," Liss said.

Amelia turned to leave.

Something small and soft landed on the wooden balcony railing. A sugar glider, blinking its glossy black eyes at Amelia, tiny head tilted to one side.

Amelia sucked in a delighted breath, her expression going wide with wonder. "Hello. Who are you?"

Et tu, Rick? "That's Rick."

A second glider landed next to it.

"And Vyvyan." Liss's gaze swept the treetops, suspecting she was outnumbered by endearing Australian natives. "Which means . . ."

"Neil and Mike are close by?" Amelia guessed with a laugh. "You named them after *The Young Ones.*"

A cult British comedy show Liss had watched a million times grow-ing up. "I did," she replied, amazed Amelia got the reference.

"My family was obsessed with English comedy when I was a kid," Amelia said. "*Ab Fab, Blackadder, Fawlty Towers*—"

"*Monty Python, Ripping Yarns*: yeah, same." Liss smiled at her. "Wait here." She went inside and returned with a few apple slices. "We're not supposed to feed the animals on the island, but these guys are being rehabilitated." She handed Amelia a slice. "Wanna try? Just move slowly and be gentle."

Amelia extended her hand, edging toward tiny Rick, until the glider was close enough to start to nibble. Amelia giggled, breathless. "Reha-bilitated?"

Liss stood next to her, feeding Vyvyan in the same careful way. "They lost their mom. Jarrah and I have been looking after them, but they're still a little weaker than they should be."

The two stood for a few minutes, enjoying the impossibly cute mar-supials. Doing this with Jarrah had been fun, but not intimate. Liss was so close to Amelia, she could feel the gentle heat from her body. She smelled like a mix of clean and sweet: jasmine and soap and coconut sunscreen. An enchanted smile tugged at the corner of her mouth.

"Oh!"

Rick had taken the rest of the slice in his mouth and bounded up the drainpipe. Vyvyan quickly followed.

Liss stepped away from Amelia, putting a normal amount of space between them.

"Well, thank you for the most adorable thing that's ever happened to me." Amelia wiped her hands on her cutoffs. "Are you going to be running the Barefoot Bar while all this is going on? So lucky it wasn't destroyed."

It was physically difficult to look directly at Amelia; too eager, too sincere, too pretty Amelia. Difficult to just look, and not, as Liss wanted, inch forward, closer. "I was just gonna keep it unlocked and use the honor system."

"Really? I know you have a lot on, but it'd be nice to see you."

Liss fiddled with her hair, a nervous habit. *Don't tell her you'll bartend.* "Okay. If I get everything done."

"Yes! And thanks again." Amelia trotted down the steps, her plaits swinging like golden rope ladders. "I know you think you didn't make a difference, but you really did."

Liss let herself hear the words. Even more, accept them. Her cheeks were warm: nerves mixed with something squishy and reckless. Hope, maybe. "Thanks. That really means a lot."

Above her, the night sky spread out, a roll of black velvet powdered with stars. The concept of space had always unnerved Liss, but now she was reminded of its endless possibility.

New energy bounced around her body. Liss knew where to put it.

Her laptop was on the desk inside. She flipped it open and stuck in some earbuds.

"Okay, Max." She addressed the long-legged spider, now above the fridge. "Wish me luck."

Max didn't move.

"You're right," Liss realized. "Luck is a false concept. Dude, you should write a book, seriously."

It'd been months since she'd taken a call for the queer teen helpline. But if someone as good as Amelia Kelly believed that Liss could make a difference, well, maybe she could.

She logged into the backend and hit Accept. A brief bit of static, then she was connected. "Hi, I'm Liss. Who am I speaking to?"

A pause. A hesitant, slightly droll voice spoke. "Well, my birth certificate says Robert, but I've started going by Ro."

"Nice to meet you, Ro." The old training—listen, empathize, validate, support—woke up inside her. The island sounds faded as Liss focused on the voice at the other end of the line. "How can I help?"

16

No one slept well.

The East Coast of Australia and islands like the neighboring K'Gari were in the middle of a crisis. The death count was up to nineteen. Floating cars, sunken boats: it felt alienating to be so helpless, so cut off. Survivor's guilt ribboned through the inhabitants of Kooroy. As much as everyone appealed to their own sense of rationality, their inner voices were hand-wringing and anxious. Sleep proved elusive for all.

Except for Glen.

Glen actually slept pretty great.

He'd always been a solid sleeper, ever since he was a kid. Sleeping allowed him to be quietly out of the way of two strict Catholic parents who treated his existence as an irritating inconvenience. His childhood, like the town it was spent in, was small, harsh, and charmless. While the streets of Paris burned and free love swept the free world, local entertainment in outback Australia consisted of chasing an escaped sheep. Glen's proclivity for the life of the mind was not appreciated by a loveless father. His only child figured out early to fly under the radar, and as a result, Glen Kelly never once soared.

It was an odd recurring fantasy: to soar. To do something extraordinary. To go down in the history books for . . . *something*. A private, slightly embarrassing dream. Glen put it in a box in a cupboard in a basement while doing his duty as a husband and father—trying to meet every need of his powerful wife, whose brazen self-possession bewildered and intrigued him.

A wife who, apparently, didn't love him anymore.

Decades ago, he'd had all four wisdom teeth pulled. Coming to from the anesthesia, he'd momentarily forgotten he had a wife and children, in Sydney, in the suburbs. A quality of that amnesia still permeated his life. He'd done all the right things: worked a job to buy a home that housed his family whom he drove around in a nice-but-not-too-flashy car. Glen was struggling to wake up to the reality that his wife no longer wanted what he'd so dutifully provided.

Even though he'd been sleeping in the guest room at home for months, deep down he assumed that Jules would eventually relent, admitting she'd been a silly goose about the whole thing. She hadn't. She pushed for him to talk to her; when he didn't, she stopped trying. He had feelings, a lot of them, tumbling in his chest like birds caught in a storm. He just didn't know how to let them out, and he didn't know how to soar.

The sky was a morning-cool, milky opal. The waters of Pigface Bay a shifting swathe of silvered gray. Glen slid open the patio door and settled himself into the Adirondack chair, appreciating the warmth of a cuppa soaking into his finger joints as the island's dawn chorus rose.

Ornithologists couldn't agree on the purpose of the collective, communal phenomenon known as the dawn chorus, when birds of all feathers sang more loudly and energetically than any other time of day. Perhaps it was a way to stake out territory. Maybe the dark early hours were impractical for foraging, so why not sing? A way to broadcast one's position to prospective mates. Reaffirm the complex social groups that allowed so many species to comfortably coexist.

Personally, Glen believed the dawn chorus to be an act of triumph. For each species, from the predatorial kookaburra to the acrobatic honeyeater, singing at dawn was a way to declare: *I am here! I am alive!*

And what better place to be alive? Evolutionarily speaking, Australia was where birdsong began. The majority of the world's birds had Australian ancestors. No other continent was as important for bird evolution as Down Under, something Glen felt quietly proud of. The wall of screeches and pings and whistles and trills gave great comfort: like being at a wild party where no one cared if he sat in the corner, alone.

And then he wasn't.

The glass doors slid open, and Randall Lee stepped onto the second-floor balcony. "Morning."

Matty's father-in-law was in short red jogging shorts and a fitted tank top, a sweatband in his full head of hair. Impressive he'd be out this early. The sun had only just edged up over the ocean.

"Morning," Glen parroted, feeling the pinch of anxiety every deep introvert feels upon an unexpected one-on-one encounter. *Don't say anything stupid.*

Randall started stretching, lunging his hips forward. Not an ounce of fat on him, like an exquisitely lean cut of meat. "Good book?" Randall nodded at what was splayed on Glen's lap: *The Last Boobook: Birdlife on Lady Lushington Island.*

"Yes, it is."

"What's it about?" Randall prompted.

"Er, just profiles, mainly. Of the bird species recorded on the island." Three hundred and fifty in total, only one hundred less than Randall's home state of California. Glen tapped the cover. "The author was the last person to see a Lady Lushington Boobook in the wild."

"A Boo . . . book?"

Glen flipped through the pages and held up a photograph of a white owl with a small hooked beak and round yellow eyes. "Little-known subspecies of the common morepork. Endemic to the island, before they went extinct in the seventies."

"Endemic?"

"Only found here. Beautiful creatures. Named for their distinctive two-tone call." Glen attempted to impersonate their low, haunting trill, as evidenced by grainy film clips on YouTube. *"Boobook, boobook. Boobook, boobook."*

Randall checked his FitBit. "Sounds like a fascinating book."

Glen's cheeks warmed. How embarrassing, squawking like a madman to Rambo Randall. *No one's interested in what you've got to say, Glen.* "If you want to have a flick through, you're more than welcome."

Randall adjusted his sweatband. "Oh, thanks."

Glen regretted the offer that Randall clearly wasn't going to take up.

Randall paused, opened his mouth, closed it. "If you ever want to come along . . . For a run."

"Me?" Glen would've laughed if he wasn't so horrified. The idea of staggering next to this action hero of a man made him feel even more ridiculous. "Ah, not much of a runner."

"Anyone can start and stick to a daily wellness routine. A healthy mind starts with a healthy body." Randall winced a little, as if embarrassed to hear himself reciting a well-trod script. "But hey, do you, man."

"Thanks, m-mate." Another stumble, making Glen feel like an even bigger nong. He watched Randall jog up the beach, moving with single-minded athletic purpose.

Of course Glen would like to lose the gut. He'd always been relatively trim, but over the past few years, he'd been biking less, and the belly had bloated. But he'd blown the opportunity—an offer surely made out of pity. Intellectually, he knew he should have close male friends, especially now that his central support system was pulling the plug. But practically he had no idea how to start a friendship with another man. His wife and daughters gathered people to them easily. Glen found the concept unbearably awkward. Like his father once said, *Real men don't need friends. They only need themselves.*

Glen flipped open his book, landing on a page about pied oyster-catchers. He readied to relax into the text, reassuring himself with a bit of snobbery: he was probably much smarter than Rambo Randall, anyway. The fascinating world of birds never made Glen feel inadequate. Everything else around him might, but feathered friends never did.

NOTABLY, PIED OYSTERCATCHERS MATE FOR LIFE, OFTEN
USING THE SAME NESTING AREA YEAR AFTER YEAR.

Everyone around him was mating for life. His own failure to do so flapped in a frantic, painful way.

The sun inched higher into the pink-rimmed sky. The dawn chorus began to quieten. Inside, floorboards creaked. Someone else was up.

Glen Kelly wiped the emotion from his face and rose to say good morning with an accommodating smile.

17

Like her mother, Parker Lee had always worked.

At seven, it was a neighborhood cookie stand. When she realized it was cheaper to bake cookies than reselling store-bought, Parker perfected the homemade chocolate chip. (The secret? A pinch of Maldon sea salt on top.)

At sixteen, it was babysitting. Gone were the days when sitters were paid in pizza and a ride home: she could charge twenty-five dollars an hour in Los Angeles and drive herself home, thanks anyway. The service proved popular. Inspired by a certain middle-school book series, Parker started a network of reliable teen babysitters, splitting the work she procured 70/30 in their favor. By the end of high school, she'd saved twenty-five thousand dollars.

Parker started her first real company at twenty-two, her second at twenty-six. The first, an overly complicated networking app for women of color, and the second, 'Sup, a nonprofit that made ethically produced umbrellas. Most start-ups were nonstarters: these were no exception. But it meant by the time she was graduating from business school (Columbia) in her early thirties, Parker had both the education and experience to get hired as a chief operating officer, right-hand woman to a CEO. She wanted to work for a socially minded company that would explode into the next Bumble or Airbnb. Nothing had. Yet.

Poppe was different. Poppe had true potential. She could see it from the first dinner with LK, five years ago at an Italian restaurant in Tribeca. They'd been friends at Columbia and stayed in touch professionally. Lauren-Kate "LK" Cutler was ambitious, coming from a long line of successful entrepreneurs (although the labor practices of centuries past arguably recast them as robber barons). At thirty-four, she possessed the sort of knife-sharp business acumen that won over clients more often than friends. She always looked the part—ruthlessly blonde and sharky as a Fox News anchor—but her pitch was solid. "The pregnancy products market has exploded." LK's eyes flashed like coins. "But no one's cracked the *it* pregnancy subscription box. If we make something high-end, chic, and modern, we can dominate."

Parker sipped her wine. It was almost two hundred dollars a bottle, which she knew LK was paying for to impress her. It was working. But the job was still a risk: most start-ups failed. And LK was ruthless in a politician-in-an-election-year kind of way. Parker was on the fence.

"I hear you broke up with Kwan and are seeing someone new." LK swirled the ruby liquid in a glass the size of a hat. "Matilda?"

"Matty." Even in a business meeting, Parker couldn't stop a goofy smile from high-kicking onto her face.

LK clocked it. "This is the kind of job that could really set things up for you guys."

"Set things up?"

"Getting married, getting pregnant." LK twinkled. "Putting that kid through college in your dream house in your dream city."

"I don't think so." Parker laughed lightly. Beyond the fact they were a brand-new couple: "Matty has pretty big dreams."

"Me too. Love her already."

LK had a point, and it appealed to the provider in Parker. The idea she could captain a financial future with funny, clever, infuriating Matty Kelly was extremely appealing. "If you raise enough capital in the seed, give me a call."

LK raised two million dollars. Twice what she'd been aiming for. Her origin story of not being able to find a decent subscription box for her pregnant older sister (equally blonde, equally pretty) secured modest press. The company launched with five employees. By year two, they had fifty. The boxes were beautiful: a neon-yellow-and-white modernist design full of clean beauty products, customized supplements, and maternity clothing that was actually cool. Other subscription services looked folksy by comparison. Poppe made being pregnant feel youthful and glamorous. Parker built in a give-back program (for every ten boxes sold, they donated one to a woman in need), but LK was focused on gifting every pregnant It Girl in America a subscription. When Kylie Jenner featured her Poppe box on her Instagram story for less than two seconds, they amassed so many new subscribers their site crashed. LK made *Fortune's* 40 Under 40.

Ever since they'd launched, LK leaned into her identity as a feminist, fashioning her personal success as a triumph for the cause. Her social media featured glam shots with motivational slogans touting "girl bosses get it done" and "ambitious women never give up." The pursuit of money recast as the pursuit of women's empowerment wasn't out of the norm in a capitalist society in love with market-friendly feminism. The SoHo headquarters were stylish and open-plan with bold neon-yellow walls. The sort of place that made young women raised on reruns of *Sex and the City* feel desperate to be a part of it, despite wages a puff over minimum.

But the workplace culture was not as fun as the brand suggested.

Matty once pointed out LK's physical attractiveness was often mistaken for goodness, "and by the time anyone works out she's about as good as a gun, it's too late." Like a gun, LK was brutally effective. She routinely worked a twelve-hour day and over weekends. Even though staff were never explicitly asked to do the same, most did. LK tended to hire twentysomething women whom she referred to in private as "my ducklings." And all of the C-suite, with the exception of Parker, were white men.

LK was oblivious to watercooler rumblings. Parker could smell the tension. She'd been doing everything in her power to create a culture of transparency, accountability, and equity. Part of this strategy involved reminding LK that the company she built also belonged to the people who helped build it. But she needed LK to trust her, and like her, for Parker to do her job.

Which was why their first call since Parker left New York was going so epically badly.

LK was furious. "I agreed to let you work in Australia on the basis you'd be doing it in an office. Not lying on a beach!"

"I'm not lying on a beach." Parker indicated the bedroom behind her. "I'll be starting work after dark. Your 8:00 a.m. is my 10:00 p.m."

"And what about the meeting with Target in April? You promised you'd be back for it!"

"That was before a volcano erupted and left us stranded," Parker said.

LK let out a strangled cry. Even though it was after midnight on a Saturday in New York, she was in the office, pacing. "Do you realize how fucked that is for me? We are months away from selling this company!"

Parker resisted pointing out it wasn't ideal for her, either, deciding not to tell LK she was sharing her wife's laptop after losing her own in the surge. "Everything is fine. This doesn't change anything. I saw the prototypes for the Za'Niyah collab. They look great."

Poppe was experimenting with guest curators. Parker had suggested working with Za'Niyah, a new, incredibly popular Black rapper who'd just announced she was expecting her first child.

LK paused. "Actually, we're not moving forward with that."

Parker dropped her pen. "What?"

To her credit, LK looked abashed. "Ben and Theo and I decided it wasn't the right fit."

Theo was chief technology officer, Ben was chief financial officer. Nonoperational, nonbrand roles. This decision had nothing to do with them. "Why? And why wasn't I looped in?"

"You were on a plane to Australia."

"Za'Niyah is twenty-eight and talented and has ten million followers on Instagram. How is she not a fit?" Parker massaged her forehead. "Jesus, LK. My job is to advise you on decisions like this, not find out about them after the fact."

"I just want us to be associated with more mainstream influencers, okay?" LK snapped. "Our curators have to be aspirational: Ben and Theo agree."

Parker froze.

She knew what LK meant: Za'Niyah was too fat. Too Black. The It Girls LK wanted to be associated with were thin and white. Like Kylie Jenner. Like LK herself.

Parker's heart was racing. She double-checked she was talking to the CEO on her personal cell. Even that was dangerous. "You really can't say things like that."

"Calm down."

"No, seriously, LK. You can't even think things like that. We're built on equality—we have to practice what we preach, or we're screwed."

"Not this again. Half the ducklings are women of color!"

"A third of the *staff*," Parker corrected. "And almost eighty percent of them are entry level." High turnover, low retention: these often-repeated facts washed over Parker as a familiar wave of exhaustion.

LK huffed a sharp sigh, a sign this discussion was over. "Look, I know you're technically meant to be off until Wednesday, but is there any way you could run the All-Hands tomorrow?"

Tomorrow, Parker was planning on lying on a beach, salvaging the scraps of a dream vacation, before shifting to a nocturnal schedule. "I'd be happy to."

It was mid-afternoon. Lizards lay soaking up the sun like prehistoric retirees. The sky was a crisp and vivid blue.

In the kitchen, Parker's mother was placing the tiniest sliver of cheese atop a cracker. Randall was doing squats on the balcony while addressing his phone, propped up on a side table. Parker pulled up a kitchen stool, grabbed the cracker box. "What on earth is Dad doing?"

"Recording a class for a client." Her mother's hair was arranged in a chignon. Her roots were starting to show, dark brown edging out the chic silvery blonde. "Everything okay?"

"Fine. Just not going to see the sun for a while," Parker said, summarizing LK's demands.

"It'll be good practice for once there's a child." Ludmila took a bite of cracker. "You didn't sleep through the night for almost a year. I was running on three hours' sleep for what felt like forever. Once I was so tired I drove all the way to the supermarket without you in the backseat."

"Yeah, and didn't you still do the entire shop?"

"I knew you'd just watch television the entire time. And I was right."

"I was six!"

Ludmila had started her small business when Parker was three weeks old. Parker couldn't imagine working full-time in the way she currently was and being a good parent.

Randall slid the balcony door open, shining with sweat. "Whew! Not sure why, but that's a lot harder to do over the phone."

"Tell me about it." Parker tossed her father the cracker box.

He scanned the ingredients, then shook out a few. "Where are the Kellys?"

"A walk," Ludmila replied. "To one of the lakes."

The trio eyed one other.

"Which one?" Parker tried.

"Not sure," Ludmila replied.

They exhaled. Off the hook.

Randall pulled up a stool next to Parker. "Remember that trip we did to Lake Okoboji?"

Parker snorted laughter. "The one where Mom found a squirrel the size of a Buick in the tub and terrorized that poor manager into giving us an upgrade?"

Ludmila's left eyebrow quirked. "And a free breakfast."

"That was Lake Tahoe," Randall corrected. "I meant the time we went out in the canoe."

"Oh," the women chorused, "the canoe."

The three of them, dressed for dinner with the Royals, in the middle of a featureless lake, completely lost. Ludmila refused to paddle for fear of wetting her vintage silk blouse.

Randall mimed frantic paddling. *It's this way! No, honey, it's this way!*

Parker laughed. "And then we saw that *eel*."

Ludmila shuddered, smiling. "Hideous."

"Those things are seriously gross," Randall agreed.

"How did we get back in the end?" Parker tried to remember.

Randall replied, "This little fishing boat full of—how should I put it—*mountain men* comes by and I'm waving them over, trying to understand their *flavorful* accents—"

"They were hicks," Ludmila supplied, slicing off more cheese.

"—while your mother says nothing until right at the end, she asks if there's anywhere in town where she can get a *cappuccino*. To the cast of *Deliverance*."

All three Lees broke into laughter.

"Oh god, Mom." Parker giggled. "You're such a snob."

"Your mother has standards," Randall corrected. "And we've all benefited from that."

Ludmila stroked her wrap wistfully. "I never did get that cappuccino."

"So for our next family trip," Randall said. "Rome. Remember?"

A week of pasta eaten alfresco served by indifferent waiters with thin mustaches. Astonishing, ancient architecture at every turn, ignored by the locals. Thin alleyways opening up to piazzas with fountains and fluttering pigeons. The air was sweet with red sauce and flaky pastry. Tiny cars. Enormous doors.

"I got pickpocketed," Parker recalled in mild outrage. Not at the thieves: at her parents for putting her in such a position. "They stole my Hello Kitty purse, do you remember?"

Ludmila shut the fridge. "And you never left your bag on a chair again."

Parker sat back, absorbing this. She'd understood this moment as an anomaly, not a catalyst.

"But afterward," Randall said, "we let you have some wine with lunch. Watered down, like the Italians kids drink it."

"I remember," Parker said. The height of grown-up-ness.

Ludmila leaned forward to stroke the soft skin on the back of Parker's hand. "You said, *It tastes like something you'd have in a fairytale,* and I said, *That's exactly what it is.* Something you'd drink in a fairytale." Her mother sighed. "I love Rome. Very good cappuccino."

There was something so comforting about being in her insular family unit and their humor that bordered on black. Matty had a wicked streak, but Jules took her role as moral gatekeeper very seriously. Amelia didn't quite have the palette for a dark take. Glen—who knew? People seemed to feel sorry for only children, but Parker liked that she didn't have to share her parents with anyone. Didn't have a sibling against whom her own behavior and choices could be judged. The Lees worked best as a trio.

Parker went to the fridge for cold water. Under a magnet—*Always Was, Always Will Be, Aboriginal Land*—a note, in Jules's cheerfully determined scrawl. *Gone to Lake Barrowcliffe. Join us! :)*

"Mom!" Parker held up the evidence. "Lake Barrowcliffe!"

But her mother was already floating back up to the master. "I have work to do."

Parker groaned. This would surely be seen as further proof of her parents' coldness. "She's not even pretending," Parker complained to her father. "They're family."

"Give her time." Randall was on his phone, getting sucked back into virtual fitness land. "This isn't your mother's comfort zone."

"It's not anyone's comfort zone! I'm talking about making an effort." Parker grabbed her sunglasses. "I'll try to find them. You coming?"

Randall hesitated. He was about as good a liar as Amelia. "I better, uh, go check on your mother."

Parker understood she'd gained a new family through marriage: her in-laws. What she didn't anticipate was her own parents' failure to likewise evolve. Frustration and betrayal surged up her throat, sharpening her words. "An effort, Dad. Family effort. It's important to me."

"Next time, honey," he promised, already halfway upstairs. "We've got six weeks!"

Parker exhaled her irritation, pocketing the paper map on her way out. If only there could be as clear a set of instructions as to how to get her two families to actually like each other.

*

Like her daughter, Ludmila Lee had always worked.

Her parents had emigrated from Russia when she was just a baby, following the death of her older brother, not even a year old—complications relating to pneumonia. It was the height of the Cold War, but Ludmila's father worked for the government. She had no memories of her ghostly sibling, but his legacy was such that her parents approached life as if it were a Dostoyevsky novel: sure to end badly. Despite being raised in leafy, laidback San Francisco, Ludmila embodied a fierce work ethic, excelling at anything she put her mind to. She couldn't recall not working. Her efficiency was one of the things of which she was proudest. That, and her family. She'd raised her daughter to be an equally hardworking, independent young woman. Parker's choice of romantic partner was perhaps questionable (personality more than gender), but Ludmila's design career had taught her there was no accounting for taste. Despite that one count against her, Parker possessed a work ethic that marked her as Ludmila's actual and moral kin.

So now, stranded on an island in the middle of the South Pacific, Ludmila Lee was staring down the barrel of a surprise six-week vacation with apprehension. There were no interesting markets to sift through, no art museums to meander. Just all this . . . nature. Sand that ended up in one's bed. An ocean full of creatures that bit and stung. Ludmila didn't *get* nature, in the way some people don't *get* art. She understood the point from a technical perspective—photosynthesis, carbon dioxide, etcetera—but what were you supposed to *do* with nature? Look at it? For how long? What were you looking for?

Certainly, she was the person most ill-equipped to deal with being stranded. Already she was feeling a growing claustrophobia at being cooped up in the master, but the solution eluded her. Work was usually the solution. And now, she didn't have work.

Who was she if she wasn't working?

Who was she without her work?

There was a time, long ago, when that question had a very different answer to whatever it would be right now. A time she tried not to think about. A time that no one in her orbit today knew about, except her husband. A time she'd promised herself never to tell her daughter about.

She heard the shower turn off, Randall whistling as he dried himself. With a flick of her wrist, Ludmila tugged her cashmere wrap tighter around her body, taking comfort in its softness, its willingness to yield.

18

Liss spent the next few days cleaning out the Yellow Cottage to give the Kelly-Lees more housing options, and making a spreadsheet of the entire food supply, and helping the tech team on the mainland reschedule the next month's guests, and doing everything she could think of not to work at the Barefoot Bar and see Amelia Kelly. Liss was an emotional, compassionate Pisces, the symbol for which was two fish swimming in opposite directions, in constant conflict between fantasy and reality. Her head warned against a crush on an unavailable stranger. But by late Tuesday afternoon, her heart—and a sense of responsibility to the island's guests—won out.

The youngest Kelly was at one of the metal tables, staring at the ocean. Flaxen blonde hair pulled into a messy topknot. Fringed kimono thrown over a tank top and cutoffs. The sight of her made Liss's chest bunch like a fist, which was embarrassing and dumb.

"Oh, hey!" Amelia called. "If it isn't the unmasked unicorn."

Liss chuckled, mostly to hide her sudden nerves. The anxiety that accompanied interest in another person was back, hyped-up and jittery, snaking around her ear: *Did you miss me?* "What's up, Animal?"

"My sister is more interested in a work presentation than me, and her wife is dead asleep because she's working nights. Randall is exercising, Ludmila is working, Dad is bird-watching, and Mum said something about trying to track down Jarrah. So, in answer to your question: not much."

Her tone was a little too light.

Liss resisted the impulse to squeeze her shoulder. "Can I buy you a drink?"

Amelia examined the cocktail menu on the chalkboard. *Beach, Please. Vacay All Day. Wiiilllllsssooonnn! Tequila.* "Your concoctions?"

"Yup." Liss wanted Amelia to think these were funny and was pleased to see the suggestion of a smile. "People seem to like Vacay All Day."

"One of those and the Wi-Fi password, please."

"It's an open network. Any allergies?"

Amelia shook her head, her gaze on her phone.

Inside the bar, Liss turned on the router and put on a mix by Cali Conscious, relaxed surf-reggae vibes. She picked a pineapple from a small orchard of fruit trees planted nearby, cut it up, and tossed it in a blender with ice, coconut juice, Bundaberg rum, a good squeeze of lime, and a few drops of lemon myrtle oil, harvested from the native plants on the island. The blender buzzed like industrial machinery. Liss garnished the cocktails with a maraschino cherry and wedge of sticky-sweet pineapple.

Amelia was still staring at her phone, annoyed. "If you and I were together, how often would you call me?"

Liss almost spilled the cocktails. "I'm not, um, looking for a—" *It's rhetorical, you idiot!* "All the time. Constant calls."

Amelia dropped her phone on the table, seeming not to have noticed the fumble. "I know he has a stressful job, but he hasn't even replied to my texts. I feel like I'm going crazy!"

"Your fiancé." Liss put Amelia's Vacay All Day in front of her. "James, right?"

"Boyfriend. This was supposed to be his big Meet the Family weekend! And now—radio silence. While I'm literally *stranded* on a *desert island*!" Amelia stabbed the metal straw into her cocktail and sucked.

So, they weren't engaged? The revelation was a welcome one. It did not feel natural to stick up for James. But it did feel natural to give Amelia some assurance. Instead of going back inside, Liss leaned against the wooden bar, nursing her cocktail. "When did you last hear from him?"

"Saturday morning."

It was Tuesday afternoon. "He's probably planning on calling tonight after work."

"Have you ever been waiting for someone to get back to you in a way that feels like every *second* they don't, a part of your sanity dies?"

Liss recalled the way it'd felt with Sofia in the death throes of their relationship. The eleven unreturned emails she'd sent to Gabe. "Welcome to my life. Look, there's some saying about a watched pot never boiling, which is nuts because science, but anyway, why don't you take your mind off your phone for a bit?"

Amelia indicated her cocktail. "Why d'you think I'm drinking at five in the afternoon?"

"Because it's five in the afternoon. Which means it's time for . . ." Liss reached behind the bar, feeling around for the old rectangular box. She presented it to Amelia like the winner of a lucky door prize.

Amelia's eyebrows slanted. "*Guess Who?* I'm fairly sure that's a game for the little kids I don't have because my boyfriend won't call me back, let alone impregnate me."

"I love games. I'm into games. You're learning something new about me. Lucky you." Liss took a seat across from her and flipped open her board. Twenty-four cartoon faces and names, which Amelia couldn't see, but had on her identical board. Something about this moment recalled performing: stepping into a public-facing persona to engage and charm an audience. Liss hadn't really missed it until now. "We're about to play the greatest game of all time—actually one of my own invention— *Highly Subjective Guess Who?* Pick a card."

The hint of amusement on her mouth, Amelia did as she was told.

A flock of pelicans skimmed the blue-green ocean, wingtips soft as paintbrushes. Unseen cicadas buzzed from the bush, their high, hypnotic chorus the only sound scoring the hot, peaceful afternoon. Between check-ins and check-outs, preparing the meal kits, and endless admin and customer service, Liss was usually busy from sunup to sundown. As she'd mentioned to Jarrah a few times, when fully booked, it was a job for two people. Being able to drink a cocktail over a board game with someone warm and interesting felt luxurious.

Liss picked her card: Claire, a woman with surprisingly on-trend eyeglasses and bold hat choice. "I'll go first. Does your person . . . smoke weed?"

Amelia let out a laugh. An understanding smile spread across her face, lighting her from the inside. The Amelia that Liss liked best was back: happy, at ease, ready for fun. She made a show of considering the person on the card. "I'm going to say . . . yes."

Liss flipped down everyone on her board who didn't look like they hit the wacky tobaccy: Anita, George, Bill.

"Wait a sec," Amelia said. "This is never going to come off—What if we don't think the same highly subjective things?"

"That," Liss said, "is the magic of *Highly Subjective Guess Who?*" Her lyrical Canadian accent lengthened the first vowel of *maaagic*. "We have to mind meld for it to work. Which, to be honest, it usually doesn't. But when it does, trust me when I say there is nothing more exciting. Your turn."

Amelia was grinning. She narrowed her eyes in concentration. "Does your person . . . have a cat?"

Liss considered Claire. Definitely cat-lady vibes. "I can't believe there isn't a cat *in* this picture."

As the cocktails disappeared the questions became more risqué: *Do they watch internet porn?* (Basically everyone, they agreed.) *Have they ever punched someone in the face?* (Not always the obvious contenders.) *Have they ever masturbated on a plane?*

Amelia almost choked on her cocktail. "Have you ever masturbated on a plane?"

"It was a long flight!" Liss protested. "And otherwise I'll just get drunk and watch *A Dog's Purpose* while weeping."

Amelia laughed. "I lost it watching *Bend It Like Beckham*. And that's not even a sad movie."

Liss examined her remaining players. "David Beckham is fit."

Amelia's eyes met hers. Liss could see her understanding the comment as a deliberate indication of heterosexuality. "Totally," Amelia said, a bit too breezily. "He can kick my goal anytime."

As carefully as she guarded her heart, Liss was still the kind of person who liked others knowing she was an equal-opportunity dater. "I always had—have?—a bit of a crush on Keira Knightley."

Amelia's eyes flashed to hers, then away. "Not really my type."

Liss couldn't tell if Keira wasn't her type of girl or if girls weren't Amelia's type at all. She leaned back in her chair, stretching her legs out. "Who is?"

Amelia's cheeks colored. She focused on the game. "My turn, right? Have you ever . . . played in a band?"

"Good one." Liss studied Claire. "No, I think."

Amelia began flipping down her non-band players.

"I used to play in a band," Liss offered. "A few, over the years."

Amelia's eyes lit like a match. "Really?"

Liss pointed to the tattoo on her forearm: GIRL VS TRUCK.

"That was one of your bands?"

Liss nodded, testing what it was like to share this. Amazed that she wanted to. "Me and my best friend. Gabe."

"A duo?"

"Yeah, very White Stripes meets, um, Hall & Oates."

Amelia giggled, looking impressed. "So cool."

Liss sucked up the last mouthful of cocktail, feeling bashful and un-burdened. "Ah, you never heard us play."

"What were you—"

"Awful."

Amelia laughed.

God, it felt good to make her laugh. It felt good making anyone laugh, but it felt especially good to make Amelia Kelly laugh. Liss felt weightless and energized to show off, like someone bounding on the moon. "My turn. Have you ever found a turtle in the middle of the street and taken it home and, like, tried to find the owners and couldn't, so you named it Bob the Turtle and every night, you play Bob the Turtle jazz records?"

Amelia looked absolutely delighted by this. "I'm going to say *yes*."

Liss flipped down all her icons except for Sam, the human hard-boiled egg, who to her mind looked like someone who smoked dope and had a pet turtle named Bob. "Let me reiterate, this game usually does not work, which is actually an interesting comment about our assump-tions, and if we go back to where we went—"

"Oh shut up and tell me who you have!" Amelia was close to bursting.

"Can I get a drumroll?"

Amelia pattered her fingers on the metal table.

Liss made her voice dramatic. "Are . . . you . . . Sam?"

Amelia's eyes shot wide. She grabbed her card, thrust it at Liss. "Yes! Yes, I'm Sam!"

Liss was genuinely shocked. "No way!"

"Yes way, I'm Sam!"

"We did it!" Liss sat back, amazed. "We mind melded!"

Amelia was giggling. "I can't believe it!"

"Neither can I: that has *never* happened with someone first go!"

They were both laughing, buzzing from the rum and the win and the pure pleasure of it all. The air was warm and the bar was open and there was absolutely nothing to do except hang out. Liss indulged in the simple pleasure of looking at the woman across from her. Her clear, laughing-bright eyes. Her complete lack of pretension. Yes, she was beautiful, just like Sofia, but sweeter, less critical of the world, less intense. She seemed like someone who was typically, naturally, happy.

The sun was beginning to dip down over the trees, streaking the sky with pink and honey-gold.

Amelia gazed back at her, smiling.

Liss wanted to kiss her. She could imagine it clearly: the gaze that softened then sharpened the space between them. Leaning toward each other over the metal table, desire taking control of her anxious brain. Sinking into Amelia, her lips hot and light. Nothing crazy. Just a kiss. Sweet and simple: a first kiss. Amelia would taste like rum and pine-apple and summer afternoon—

Amelia's phone dinged. She picked it up, still smiling. "You were right, I totally forgot about—James! He finally texted!"

And just like that, the moment went flat.

This wasn't a date. Amelia had a boyfriend who was probably a nice guy, a normal guy, a guy-guy. Shame slithered up Liss's neck.

The inside of the bar was dim; it took a moment to adjust to the sudden darkness. Liss rinsed her cocktail glass with a sour exhale. Liking Amelia was a bad idea and she'd let it happen anyway. *Idiot.*

When Liss came back out, she was expecting to see Amelia texting back, a look of pleased concentration on her face, or already halfway up the beach to Kooroy to make a more private call. But the pretty Austra-lian wasn't doing either of those things.

"Weird," she muttered, holding the phone out. "Does this make any sense to you?"

James's text was under three of Amelia's: *My afternoon was just me trying to build a radio out of coconuts, how about you?* Then *Waking up alone is not as fun as the alternative. Miss my Jamie-baby. How are you?* Then *Will send bikini selfie in exchange for smoke signal. Act now, limited time offer.*

Cute. Liss appreciated good text game.

James's reply to his girlfriend was four rather cryptic words.

Can you pu Lucas

"What's *pu*?" Liss asked.

Amelia shrugged. "Don't know."

"Who's Lucas?"

Amelia shrugged again. "Don't know again."

Liss reread the text. "Could be a butt dial. Or he just meant to send it to someone else. Maybe *pu* is a typo."

"Can you . . . ping Lucas?" Amelia tried.

"Exactly." Liss was impressed she'd cracked it so quick. "It's probably a work text."

"Right," Amelia said. "I'll just call."

She did. It rang out. She dialed again. It rang out again.

Which to Liss's mind seemed to prove the point. "It's a work text, that's why he didn't pick up because he's at work."

Amelia shook her head as if trying to get water out of her ear. She swung around. "Right, he's probably—" but her elbow caught her glass and knocked it the ground, splashing Liss's legs with the dregs. "Crap, I'm so unco." Australian for *klutz*. She fumbled for the glass. "I better go. Thanks for . . . everything."

"No worries." Liss grabbed a bar towel. "Let me know if you're up for a rematch."

But Amelia was already retreating in the direction of the house.

The sun sank over the tree line. The breeze cooled. Liss dried her legs, talking herself out of feeling crestfallen, and began to pack up the abandoned game.

19

As beautiful as the island was, Jules could feel its sadness.

It was tempting to refer to the land as "empty." "Untouched wilderness." Which was dangerously close to "undiscovered," as had been the logic of the crew of the Lady Lushington, when their vessel wrecked on the island's western surf beach more than two centuries before. When they encountered the people who lived here, naked but for necklaces of shells and kangaroo teeth, they deemed them primitive. The Aborigines of the island had no permanent structures. No written language. No churches, and thus, no religion. Not really human, then. They had, to the small, hard minds of the white settlers, no claim to the land.

The land they lived in harmony with.

The land that was their religion.

The land that was their home, and had been for tens of thousands of years.

The history of Mun'dai was one of attempted genocide. Family separation. Death, disease, slavery, poverty. An iteration of the story of all of Australia and its violent dispossession from its Indigenous population. Its discovery was its theft—a crime that was, in many ways, ongoing. Indigenous Australians were the earth's oldest civilization. They were also poorer, sicker, and had shorter life expectancies than non–Indigenous Australians. Jules had many criticisms of the current administration: a greedy old-boys' club, embarrassing in their devotion to industry and power. But the thing that hurt her heart the most was the way in which this young, brash country of hers continued to fail the people it truly belonged to. The white settlers of this island hadn't listened. Jules didn't intend to make that same mistake.

Jules knew from years of reading the *Sydney Morning Herald* or watching various programs on the telly that reclamation of traditional land was a key issue for Aboriginal and Torres Strait Islander people. It allowed tribes to protect the land they maintained a strong connection to for future generations, as well as preserve the natural resources and sacred sites. Native title had only been recognized since a milestone court case in 1992 called Mabo, which enabled many Indigenous communities to reclaim land lost following colonial settlement. Native title could be claimed by any tribe who could prove their ancestors lived on the land before the waves of brutal displacement, beginning with Captain James Cook's claiming possession of the east coast of Australia in 1770. The year Jules was taught at school that "Australian history" began.

Jules tucked her curls into her Bunnings hat and laced up her boots. Being stranded on Mun'dai was worrisome (what if someone got sick or hurt? Would her neighbor back in Sydney keep her veggie garden going?), but it also presented opportunities. The bush tucker cooking class she'd booked had, of course, been canceled. Jules was disappointed but unexpectedly a little relieved. Official classes for hapless tourists had their own limitations. Jules liked to learn by experiencing things in a less rigid way. Like the cleansing ceremony Jarrah had organized a few days after the surge. Truly one of the most impactful and impressive experiences Jules had ever witnessed. The fires of dried debris, sending smoke up to the heavens as the sun sank into the west. The intricate colored sand art interweaving between them. The sight of Jarrah, painted in red-and-white ochre, naked but for his underwear and a headdress of bird feathers, singing and dancing and communing with the creator spirits, gave her chills. He was so confident. So connected to the land. *If Glen had been a man more like Jarrah,* Jules thought, *I'd never be able to get over him.*

Setting out from Kooroy, she followed the track west to Mooka Mooka Beach.

While Jules lived in Sydney, her heart was in her home state of Queensland. She craved the heat. The laidback humor of the locals. The fact that a juicy pineapple or a buttery avocado only ever cost a dollar. She'd grown up in Hervey Bay, the port from which the ferry that'd dropped them on the island departed, until she left for Sydney at age twenty. They'd come back for school holidays when her parents were still alive, but Glen hated the heat and preferred the energy of a bustling, cosmopolitan city, the opposite of his Podunk hometown, and eventually the girls wanted to spend holidays with their friends, not mucking about in the mangroves or playing pirate ship in the casuarinas. Her parents passed, and their house wasn't worth much, so she and her sister renamed it the Shack and kept it as a budget Airbnb/family holiday house. But without her kids and husband in tow, it'd faded from importance. As Jules walked through the familiar, thick heat, she calculated that she hadn't holidayed at the Shack in four years. She made a mental note to suggest to Matty they all go up after her grandchild was born. She'd love an excuse to spend more time there.

The coastal vegetation gave way to the tall eucalypt forest. Eucalypts were true Aussie icons, and what most foreigners tended to imagine when picturing "the bush." Eucalypt was a collective term, referring to several groups of closely related woody plants. Blackbutts and scribbly gums and the Moreton Bay ash. Huge, strong trees, the kind of thing used to build a solid deck. Her favorite was the Queensland blue gum, whose smooth, cream-colored trunk was singular and straight for over half its height before branching into an impressive tree up to fifty meters tall. Almost all of the roughly nine hundred species of Australian eucalypt were found nowhere else in the world.

Because of the oil glands in their leaves, eucalypts were highly combustible. But fire was part of their survival, allowing the trees to release the seeds inside their woody pods. Beneath the scarred bark, sap flowed. Under the scorched earth, roots anchored the tall trees. Sometimes, a cleansing fire was needed. To burn everything down and start again.

After a while, the eucalypt forest morphed back into coastal vegetation. Over the birdcalls, Jules could hear the pounding of waves.

The western side of Mun'dai was exposed to the elements and currents, unlike the east, which was protected by the island itself. A rolling surf beach reached miles in either direction. Jules made her way down the sloping dunes toward the shore. Gulls circled above; their piercing cries lost to the wind that tried to push her hat from her head.

In the distance, a lone figure cast a line with a long beach rod into the frothing ocean.

Maybe this was a silly idea, an inconvenient request. But Jarrah had spotted her, and turning back would be ridiculous, so Jules barreled on through the fresh, whipping wind until eventually she could make out the gleaming white of his smile.

"You're a hard man to find," she told him, when she was finally close enough for him to hear.

Jarrah cast out, flicking his rod in a quick, graceful motion. A gang hook baited with a whole pilchard splashed silently beyond the break. "Should be easy. Only blackfella on the beach."

She chuckled. "Still chasing tailor?"

"Yeah. Some blokes'll tell you they're a winter fish, but out here they bite all year round. You fish?"

"Not really. My father was mad for it. Used to take my sister and me out in a little tinnie every morning before school. Before the trawlers came," she added, meaning the huge commercial fishing boats that now scraped Hervey Bay clean. When Jules was a kid, they'd get a hundred whiting in a few hours. These days, you'd be lucky to get a dozen all day.

"You local?"

"Born in the Bay, moved to Sydney in my twenties. I love it here, though." She gazed at the sky, a glorious unrolled sheet of blue. "Sort of a spiritual home, I guess."

"Yeah." He grinned. "Know what you mean."

Jules flushed. It wasn't her spiritual home. It was his. She considered tossing out a cheery farewell and heading back toward the house. But that wasn't what she wanted. "I have a favor to ask."

"Anything for you, plant lady."

"Would you be interested in taking me to some of the Indigenous sites on the island? I know there's a quite a few. If you have time. You can say no."

Jarrah chuckled. The salt breeze made his curls extra springy, falling over his forehead in a charming sort of way. "I have time, plant lady. But you don't need me to take you. All the places you whitefellas are allowed to visit are marked on the map."

"Oh, I know," Jules said, rushing to add she didn't mean *sacred* sites, she meant the more general sites of significance marked on the map. "I just thought it would be interesting to hear about them. From you."

Jarrah reeled his line in a touch, the movement designed to make the bait seem lifelike to an unsuspecting fish. "Mun'dai is a pretty magical place."

"I can feel it, I think." Jules hoped that didn't sound absurd. More than anything else, she didn't want to seem foolish. "I dunno, I do a bit of energetic healing."

"With crystals?" Jarrah didn't sound dismissive. He sounded interested.

Jules nodded, still vacillating between shy and friendly confidence. "Wish I'd brought some with me."

"Sacred stones. I like sacred stones." He cocked his head to the side, deep brown eyes resting on her curiously. "I'd be happy to take you. Saturday? Eleven a.m. at the Barefoot Bar?"

"It's a date! I mean—I don't mean it's an actual date," she hurried to add.

He scratched the back of his neck. "I wouldn't think so. You're married."

"Separated, actually." Jules hadn't spoken those words out loud to anyone other than her sister. The world spun as a rush of adrenaline caught her unawares.

Separated meant *single*.

When she was younger, Jules heard about older women being erased from society. As a natural optimist, she'd assumed this was an exaggeration. It wasn't. Sometime in her mid-fifties, people began to look right though her. If she was walking down the street with Amelia, passers-by would see her daughter. But if Jules was walking down the street alone, they'd see no one. Shop attendants and bus drivers stopped saying hello, making her feel like a ghost who hadn't got the memo that no one cared she was still hanging around. She joked to her sister she was going to take up shoplifting: the cameras literally wouldn't pick her up.

Jules didn't want to disappear. She was still here.

Jarrah reeled in his line. "You okay?"

"Yep, yep. Right as rain." She straightened, clearing her head. "Okay. Saturday at eleven. I'll bring lunch."

He cast out again, sun catching droplets of water on the line. "For our non-date." His grin was cheeky, but a kindness beneath Jarrah's gaze caressed her cheeks, featherlight.

It made her aware of her skin. How much she missed being touched. "Hooroo, Jarrah."

"See ya, Julia."

Jules had forgotten she'd introduced herself by her full name. She hadn't been Julia for decades.

Striding back up the beach, the tide crashed around her shins, soaking her shorts. A delicious shock. She wanted to leap in the air, yell *Wahoo!* But in order not to look silly, Jules kept moving forward.

20

Dusk, and the possums were trying to get into the compost again. Of the island's forty-eight species of mammals, the confident possum was the one most determined to stuff its belly with guests' leftovers. The council had tried three different versions of possum-proof compost. From the balcony of Kooroy, the Kellys and Lees watched a pair of stocky fuzz-balls push and pull at the large plastic tub by the side of the house.

"They're so cute!" Jules cooed.

"They're pests," Glen addressed the Lees. "They'll nest in your roof, spend all night making a ruckus."

"Well, we—people—chopped down their homes to make room for ours," Matty pointed out. "Would you prefer they just die out?"

No one noticed Amelia slipping out of Kooroy, quiet as a ghost. Branches snagged the hem of her white housedress; she'd been so distracted she hadn't thought about changing. The moon was waning, just a fingernail tossed in the sky. The blackness of the bush and its secrets pressed in, elevating her already racing heartbeat, until the warm light of the Cabin appeared through the trees. Thank god Liss was still awake.

She answered the door in black terry-cloth shorts and a loose cotton tank top with *Oui, Oui!* printed in a curly seventies font. If Amelia had been paying attention, she'd have noticed side boob.

Amelia spoke before Liss could. "Hi. I know it's late, I'm so sorry. Were you asleep?"

Liss pushed a hand through her highlighter-blue hair, looking slightly dazed. "No, I was just catching up on some *Buffy*. Come in."

Ordinarily Amelia would delight at such an eclectic, eccentric home, wanting to know the origin story of every single object. But her gaze only swept the double bed, sofa, old TV, and kitchenette, before spinning back to an increasingly concerned-looking Liss.

"Amelia, what's wrong? Is everything okay at the house?"

"I have a theory. About the text. Before I tell you what it is, there is a chance I am *completely losing my mind*. Maybe I'm just stressed or stupid and my brain is playing tricks on me. So, please, just tell me if I'm nuts. Okay?"

"Okay." The way Liss was staring made Amelia feel like she really must look unglued. "Why don't you sit down? Can I get you anything?"

"No, no: just hear me out." Amelia started pacing, her words coming in a tumble. "James lives in Melbourne, I live in Sydney, we're long distance. We met at a hotel bar, he bought me a drink, I'm always a sucker for stuff like that. We talked about work—I'm a primary school teacher."

"Is that like elementary school?" Liss was leaning against the back of the sofa facing the TV, which was paused on Buffy herself, mid-stake. Amelia hadn't watched the show since it first came out.

"Yeah, I'm at Bondi Public." Unlike her sister, Amelia had always felt like she'd fallen into her career rather than pursued it. It was a quiet source of shame she kept buried in the part of herself she didn't like looking at. The part that was starting to bubble up. "James is a hedge fund blah blah. I don't speak money."

"Me neither."

"He's an amazing guy." It wasn't hard to remember their early days. The giddy intoxication of feeling like a sunflower drawn to him, the sun. "I still have butterflies around him. Nerves. I always thought I was excited to see him. But I'm starting to think that feeling is . . ."

Intuition.

Worry.

Liss sounded confused. "Did you hear from him?"

Amelia backed toward the end of the double bed, sinking onto it. Her voice was barely a whisper. "It's just I've never met any of his friends.

Never visited him in Melbourne—he says he's at work all the time there and Sydney is where he gets to relax. I don't know anything about his family—he said his parents passed but I've never even seen a picture. And you said this thing before, and something just clicked in this really weird, awful way."

"What'd I say?"

"*It's a work text, that's why he didn't pick up,*" Amelia recited.

"Yeah." Liss vaguely remembered saying this hours earlier. "So?"

"Pick up—*pu*. What if the text meant *Can you pick up Lucas*?" A tear snaked down Amelia's cheek. "And he was sending it to his *wife*?"

"Oh, no. No, I don't think so." Liss sat next to Amelia on the bed, touching her shoulder. "Animal, no. I think you'd know, wouldn't you?"

Amelia's teeth were chattering. Having pried off the lid to these nightmarish fears, they were seething and multiplying. "I believed everything he told me. Like, he's not on social media, at all. Of course I've googled him, but James Smith is like the most popular name in the whole world. It's so good when we're together—he says all the right things but . . ."

"But what?"

"I just have a feeling. That he's not who he says he is." The self-loathing she didn't even try to contain boiled over, making her words drip with hatred. "Because I'm a gullible fool."

"Hey." Liss brushed a tear away with her thumb, her finger warm and soft. "You're not a fool. You need to figure out if this is actually happening. I assume you've called and texted."

Amelia held up her phone, showing Liss the four texts she'd sent in as many hours: *Babe? What does this mean? Was this meant for me? Who is Lucas?*

"You need to talk to him," Liss said. "Have an honest conversation. Not just about this but the reason why you'd come to this conclusion in the first place."

"I have an idea." Amelia started typing.

"I would definitely not recommend texting while you're upset."

Amelia read her text. "*Was this meant for me or your wife?* If I'm wrong, I'll say it was a joke."

"It's risky," Liss said. "He might deny a direct accusation, especially if you have no proof. Why don't you wait till morning?"

"I sent it."

A hot, eerie silence filled the Cabin. It reminded Amelia of standing on the beach in the gray predawn, watching Parker stare at the unnatural horizon. The fear on her face. The moment before everything changed.

A onetime therapist (engaged purely because of her sister's urging) suggested Amelia trusted people as a way of showing them love. People needed to earn trust. Amelia left the session confused if she should trust the therapist.

Liss shifted closer. Her hazel eyes were shimmering with empathy as she slowly threaded her fingers into Amelia's, squeezing her hand.

Amelia squeezed back, needing every ounce of strength this kind human was willing to give.

She trusted Liss. But maybe that was just another mistake.

Her phone vibrated.

Jamie-Baby 😄 *calling.*

21

Glen lingered on the balcony after dinner under the pretense of reading, but really wanting to give Jules space to shower and get into bed on her own. Some of their tension appeared to have dissipated—Jules seemed happy and light. But Glen wasn't so naive to think she was happy and light because of him.

When the balcony doors opened, he assumed it was Matty, coming to run one more line past him: *What do you think's better, Dad: "Stories That Challenge You" or "Stories That Make You Think?"*

But it wasn't his daughter. It was Randall Lee. Despite the fact they'd all just eaten dinner together, here came that familiar pinch of nerves. He sat up straighter, sucking in the gut. "G'day Randall."

"Hey, Glen." Randall shut the doors behind him. A peculiar look crossed his face. "I wanted to ask you about something. Earlier this evening, on my run, I saw a bird."

Pleased surprise relaxed Glen's shoulders. "Oh, that's fantastic. Which one?"

"Well, I'm seeing a lot of birds actually. Started noticing them ever since we talked the other morning. But I was right up the north end of the beach, past the tide pools, just after sunset. And I saw a—a *white bird*."

"Pelican?" Glen guessed. "Seagull? Egret?"

"No!" Randall sat in the other Adirondack chair, pulling it closer until their knees were almost touching. His voice was low: that of a spy.

"I think I saw—I'm almost certain I saw . . . a Boobook. Like the one in the picture."

Glen flipped open *The Last Boobook* to the photograph he'd shown Randall.

"Yes!" Randall exclaimed. "That's it! It was in some trees near the shore. And I heard the cry." He impersonated the haunting call. *"Boobook, boobook. Boobook, boobook."*

Was Randall making fun of him? *Of course he is! You're so stupid, you can't even tell.*

"Fascinating." Glen shut the book. "I'm not sure what bird you actually saw, but it sounds like a beauty. Possibly a sulphur-crested cockatoo or a white-bellied sea eagle—"

"I think it was the Boobook. No, I'm sure of it." Randall sounded absolutely convinced. And dead serious.

"Randall." Glen used a tone from when the girls were small, unreasonable creatures. "The Lady Lushington Boobook has been extinct for almost fifty years. If it were still alive, someone would've seen it."

"I'm telling you, Glen: it was a Boobook."

Bloody hell. You're going to listen to Rambo Randall about some silly, long-dead bird?

Yes, he was. Randall seemed genuine and enthusiastic about something that gave Glen pleasure and satisfaction, even if it was typically a solo activity. With great effort, Glen drowned out his taunting inner voice and focused on the man sitting next to him. "What were its feet like?"

"Its feet?" Randall frowned, thinking. "Maybe they were talons. Sort of pinky-red."

True surprise leapt into Glen's chest. He was so shocked, he couldn't speak.

"What?" Randall asked. "What is it?"

"Dark pink feet are a defining characteristic of the subspecies! And they weren't visible in the photo—"

"So I'd have no way of knowing!" Randall finished.

When Glen was a boy, an old mentor called Dr. Gunter Hamburg discovered a rare species of tree frog on an expedition in a remote Queensland rainforest. Quite simply, it was the most exciting thing that'd ever happened to Glen at that age. The memory still evoked an expansive thrill at the endless possibilities of the universe and its many complex mysteries.

He didn't want to get ahead of himself—most likely Randall had seen a cockatoo—but there was an undeniable excitement in allowing himself the *possibility* that a Lady Lushington Boobook was still on this very island. "Tell ya what: Why don't we go to the same place you think you saw it, at the same time of day, and have a look?"

"Yes!" Randall punched the air.

A boyish sense of adventure made Glen feel like giggling.

Randall rose to his feet. "It's probably a one-hour walk. We should leave at, say, five tomorrow."

Glen got up, too, his lower back pinching. He tried to make his question casual. "How long would it take to run?"

Randall's eyebrows shot up. "For a beginner? Forty minutes."

Run? You can't run!

"Maybe we could run part of the way," Glen suggested. "Kind of a kill-two-birds-with-one-stone thing, if you'll excuse the inappropriate metaphor."

"Yeah, yes! Good for you, man. Okay, we're going to start you on something easy," Randall said, adding something about partial reps and drop sets.

"Sure." Glen nodded, not following a word. He'd always pooh-poohed gym bunnies, but now he was looking forward to trying a workout. Randall was clearly an expert. Glen reminded himself that bird intelligence was measured by the creature's ability to *try something new.* Behavioral flexibility—seeking a creative solution or an inventive approach to a problem—separated the cunning crow from the sweetly dumb tern. In the animal kingdom, novel or unusual behavior was often intelligent behavior. "But we should probably keep all this"—the workout, the extinct bird hunt—"to ourselves," Glen added. "Don't want to get anyone's hopes up." Or for their family to think they were idiots.

Randall nodded. Possibly, he seemed pleased to have a shared secret. "Good idea."

"And we should both have cameras tomorrow," Glen said. "In case we see the . . ."

He trailed off for the sake of discretion, but the two men caught each other's eye. They couldn't help but finish it together, voices lowered like the coconspirators that they were.

"Boobook."

22

Amelia stood alone on the balcony of the Caretaker Cabin, the vibrating phone in her hand. Her cheeks were wet, her head was throbbing, her mouth felt like she swallowed a fistful of sand. She didn't know how she'd maintain a shred of normalcy.

Please, she prayed. *Please, let me be wrong.*

She answered James's call. "H-Hi."

"Hi. Hey, baby. Your text was hilarious. How's Gilligan's Island?"

So, he was denying it. Her boyfriend sounded like he always did: suave, smooth. Totally at ease. A path opened up before her. The path where she pretended she'd never gotten his message about Lucas and instead volleyed back a joke about making a dress out of palm fronds. The typical path. The wrong path. As much as she hated looking at dark things, Amelia knew she had to.

She pressed the sweaty glass of the phone screen to her face. "What was that text about? Who's Lucas?"

"Baby, it wasn't for you. Don't worry about it." A light laugh, ice tinkling in a glass. Probably whiskey on the rocks. James's voice deepened, becoming rakish. "So does that count as a smoke signal? Because I am front row for the smoke show. What are you wearing right now?"

She'd always found his flirtatious side sexy, but now it sounded almost sleazy.

Liss had been right: he'd likely deny a direct accusation, and she didn't have any proof. So Amelia improvised. "I've decided to come see you as soon as we're off the island. Which is going to be sooner than we thought: we were able to, um, charter a helicopter. Tonight. So I'll be able to get to you by . . . very soon." She tried to sound breezy, but it felt like she was speaking with a knife between her teeth. "What's your address? I'll arrive with kisses and croissants."

I want to be wrong, let me be wrong.

A long pause. Then her future husband was back, his voice blithe and apologetic. "Oh, baby, that sounds great, but I'm away right now."

Her life left her body. Poof: gone.

"I'm at a conference in Adelaide. And the city of churches is kind of yawnsville."

"I don't care, I'll come to Adelaide." She couldn't hold it together much longer. Her eyes were filling with tears. Her next words were a choked whisper. "You said you wanted to marry me."

"Wait, what?"

"You said you'd love to be married to me. That I'd look hot in a white dress."

"You would. And yeah, I would love to be married to you. I think a lot of guys would." Impatience edged his tone. "But I can't marry you, baby."

"Why, because you're already married?" She didn't mean to say it. Amelia waited for James to laugh or get angry or *something*. But he didn't. He was silent. "Are you?" She was holding the phone so tight her hand was cramping.

Still nothing. She was right. *She was right.* He didn't love her. He just wanted to fuck her.

Amelia started crying, silently. "How could you?"

He was back, sounding contrite. "I've been meaning to tell you, there was just never a good time: I'm in an *open* marriage, Amelia, we're not monogamous. My wife knows about you—she found out about you— she wants to meet you." He sounded like he was making a generous, if furtive, offer: cutting her in on a haul of blood diamonds.

For the second time that week, the world folded in on itself in thick, messy layers, distinctly unreal. Later, Amelia would fantasize about shooting back a sharp, cool line: *It's not an open marriage if I don't know about it.* But in the hot, frantic moment, her words were less refined. "Oh, fuck off." She yanked the phone from her ear. "Fuck no." She held it right to her mouth. *"Fuck you!"* She threw the phone as hard as she could into the bush.

Humiliation sucked her under. Her knees buckled, and she wound up curling forward to the floor.

Amelia broke down, heaving sobs of anger and sadness and shame, so much shame. Another failed romance. Because she was impossible to love. She was only barely conscious of Liss's arms around her, guiding her to the lumpy orange sofa. Holding her as she wept, her heart in pieces in her chest.

23

The trees on Mun'dai, like trees the world over, knew to not grow too close to one another. They were thoughtful neighbors, occupying their own piece of land while sharing resources under the soil through invisible networks powered by fungi. Ample space helped the collective flourish.

Back in New York, Matty and Parker had rented an apartment so small they sidestepped around the bed. The dishwasher door didn't open all the way and one of their views was of a brick wall, four feet away. Yet Matty's memories of life there felt luxuriantly spacious compared to Kooroy.

Her mother never locked the door to the bathroom they shared: Matty'd walked in on her at least a dozen times. *Just go about your business, darling, I'm only doing a wee!* Someone was always somewhere—on the balcony, in the kitchen, on the sofa, in her face. Food she was saving disappeared. Nothing was private. Her family kept offering opinions about things she'd been discussing privately with Parker, as if it were an open group discussion: *You're probably not drinking enough water, Matty, that's why you're constipated.*

"It would just be nice," Matty muttered to her wife, tossing out the empty carton of shelf-stable milk someone had irritatingly put back into the fridge, "to have a little *space*."

She shut the fridge door hard.

Glen was standing behind it. "Sorry, pet." He smiled apologetically, reaching past her. "Just making a cuppa."

And now, Matty's sweet and predictable sister was in a serious funk. Amelia had been morose and prickly for days. When Matty suggested a Friday night Games Night, it was partly because Games Night was a beloved Kelly family tradition, partly because everyone would be hanging around so she may as well wrangle them with a group activity, and partly to cheer up Amelia. "Have you and James had a fight?" Matty tried that evening, after everyone had been roped into Games Night.

"No," Amelia replied, sawing a defrosted baguette like it'd wronged her. She didn't meet Matty's eye.

Matty was fairly sure she was lying.

The game was set up on the huge polished granite coffee table. Glen, Randall, and Ludmila sat in armchairs on one side, while Amelia, Liss (whom Amelia invited), Jules, Matty, and Parker spread out on the tan leather sectional.

Americans played with a Monopoly board different from the English version used in Australia and on offer in Kooroy: Matty was pleased to see the game she'd grown up with, not the version she'd played in America on weekends away with friends. What Americans knew as St. Charles Place was, in the Aussie-English version, middle-class Pall Mall. Mediterranean Avenue was crappy Old Kent Road, while North Carolina Avenue was fancy Oxford Street. The crown jewel, Boardwalk, was, in the Commonwealth version, Mayfair. Ocean views were expensive in any language. Luckily they didn't have to pay for the view of the Pacific tonight. The balcony doors were open to a balmy evening. Glen put Thelonious Monk—tricky jazz—on the Sonos. There were two bottles of wine on the table, plus some roughly chopped baguette on a platter with cheese, veggies, and homemade dips. But despite the affectation of being relaxed, the atmosphere was strained.

Amelia landed on Oxford Street, where her father already had a hotel.

"Ha!" Glen rubbed his hands together. "Pay up, Animal."

"I'm basically bankrupt," Amelia muttered, tossing him some money.

Glen scanned everyone's piles of cash. "Yep, you're officially in eighth place," he announced with a grin. Her father was good at games, bad at reading the room. "Too much avocado toast, not enough investments, eh, Ms. Millennial?"

Randall laughed and offered Glen a high five.

Matty watched the two men slap hands with bemusement. She'd never seen her dad high-five anyone.

Amelia slumped back into the sofa, cradling a very full wineglass. "Okay, boomer."

Her tone was bitchy, but Matty decided not to reproach a comment she'd have probably made herself. Glen and Randall were being weirdly bro-y. "Your turn, Mum."

Jules, a passionate, invested player, landed on the currently unowned Pall Mall, and whooped. "I'll buy it! Although it is morally reprehensible to *own* land."

Ludmila looked up from filing her nails. "What do you mean?"

"You own a house," Matty said, "and you and Auntie Marj co-own the Shack."

"Well, the Indigenous caretakers of this land never *owned* it. Not in the way we do," Jules replied, counting her money. "Or think we do."

"You'll have to excuse my wife," Glen said to a perplexed Ludmila. "Never found a bleeding-heart cause she didn't like. Pretty sure I've been to a rally for saving homeless vegan whales."

Matty winced. He didn't mean to be insensitive. But Matty had not inherited her passion for social justice from her father.

"Piss off, Glen." Jules spoke casually, as if answering a mundane question. But a ripple of tension passed through the group and, for a moment, no one knew what to say.

Liss shifted forward from her position on the end of the sectional, next to Amelia. "Guys? I have good news." She was wearing tight black jeans and a loose white tee, more suited to a dive bar than a tropical island. Somehow, Canadian Smurf pulled it off. "Jarrah and I, and Amelia, finished cleaning out the Yellow Cottage." She looked to Amelia. "So it's now available."

"Fantastic!" Matty sat up so quickly she splashed wine on her dress. Finally, some good news! "Parker and I can move there, and Animal gets her own bedroom."

"Yes, that worked out nicely." Even Jules, mother superior, looked relieved. "Thank you, Liss. I'll have to send you some of my jam when we're off the island."

Liss was still looking at Amelia in a strangely expectant way. Amelia could befriend a potted plant, so it was unsurprising that she'd commandeered the gamine bartender. But the vibe between them seemed both overly familiar and weirdly tense.

Amelia cleared her throat. "Actually, I'd like to stay in the Yellow Cottage."

Matty scooped up the dice. "Right, but we're married, and Parker has to work nights. The Yellow Cottage is bigger than our bedroom here: she'll have more space and I won't have to wear earplugs when she's on calls." Unlike the sleek, modern houses, the one-bedroom beachfront cottages had a cozy, lost-in-time feel. Brightly patterned vintage curtains and a porch that faced the ocean. Matty rolled a six, moving her token to: "Electric Company. I'm buying!" More good news. "Animal, want to sell me Water Works? I'll pay three hundred."

"No," said Amelia. "Matty—"

"That's double what you paid for it!" Matty interrupted. "And you're basically out of cash!"

"Matty," Amelia repeated, firmer. "I want to stay in the Yellow Cottage."

"Well, we don't always get what we want." Matty swallowed a mouthful of wine. "That's a fact of life."

"Don't you always get what you want?" Amelia's tone was distinctly baiting.

Matty's hackles rose. "Considering I'm spending all my time helping my best friend start a company we dreamed of together," she said, "no, I don't. Your turn, boo." Matty turned to Parker, who was fast asleep, her body clock completely off.

"Girls, settle," Jules said. "By the way, Jarrah's taking me to see some Indigenous sites tomorrow morning. I'll be gone most of the day."

"That sounds cool," Matty said, since Amelia seemed to need some alone time. "I'll come with."

"He really only invited me." Jules rearranged the cards she "owned" with a studied casualness.

Which sounded like the impossible: maternal deflection. "I thought you invited yourself," Matty said. "I don't think he'll mind if I tag along."

"I mind," Jules said.

No doubt about it: her mother didn't want her to come. Her mother had never not wanted her to come.

The rejection tipped Matty off-center, furthering the impression that every family member was playing a different role tonight. An image of the prenatal vitamins, still on her bedside table, crested into Matty's mind on a wave of guilt and uncertainty. She hadn't taken another one since the day of the surge. Discombobulated, she addressed her mother-in-law. "How's your week been, Ludmila?"

"Dull," replied Ludmila, gathering the dice. "There's nothing to do."

"There's plenty to do!" Jules exclaimed. "You can canoe or hike or fish off the beach. Try something new. You might just surprise yourself."

"Seeing you fish off the beach would be the very definition of a surprise." Randall sipped a seltzer. "I'd give anything to see that."

Glen chuckled in agreement, reaching for his beer, then switching course for a seltzer.

"Yes," Jules amended, "I guess that was a silly thing to say. It's actually quite difficult and not for a first-timer."

"I'm sure I could fish off the beach if I wanted to." Ludmila shook the dice in her palm.

Matty's mother-in-law was draped in a vintage Chinese robe and a heavy rope of freshwater pearls. Her manicure was still, impossibly, flawless. Jules frowned. "It's not for a first-timer."

Ludmila pursed her lips and rolled a seven, moving her token to a railroad Parker had purchased before she passed out.

"Twenty-five dollars," Matty read the rent off Parker's card.

Ludmila took the last piece of cheese from the platter. "She's asleep."

"Well, considering I legally co-own the property—thank you gay marriage—I'm collecting on her behalf." Matty held out her hand until Ludmila reluctantly counted out the bills.

Randall landed on Community Chest and read off the card. "Second prize in a beauty contest."

"Second? You were robbed, mate," Glen quipped, arms flung gregariously behind his head.

Randall laughed.

"What were you guys doing together last night?" Matty asked the double act. "Sleeping beauty over here said she saw you when she went for her morning run. Which is at, like, 6:00 p.m."

The two fathers exchanged a glance. *A glance.* "Nothing," said Glen. At the same time Randall said, "Going for a run."

"You were running," Matty addressed her father. "Mr. Cryptic Crossword."

"People can change." Glen lobbed a look at Jules.

Who stiffened. In a distinctly odd way.

Matty opened her mouth to demand *what* was going on with basically *everyone* when Jules piped up, "Let's FaceTime James!"

"What?" Amelia, who'd been muttering something to Liss, jerked back into the conversation. "Why?"

"That's a great idea, Mum." Matty gave Amelia her most supportive smile. She did want to like her sister's new boyfriend, even if Amelia was being as amenable as a wet cat. "Even though he can't be here, it's important James knows he's part of the family."

"That's right," Jules said. "We are a family and we will always be a family, no matter what."

"Exactly," Matty said, a little puzzled by her mother's choice of words. "Maybe he can take Parker's turn."

Amelia's face was reddening. "No, it's not a good time. It's too late."

"It's not even nine." Glen scooped up the dice. "I'll roll for him after my turn."

"He has something tonight." Amelia looked to Liss, as if she alone knew what this was.

"Um, yeah." Liss fiddled with her hair. "You said he had to drive . . ."

". . . his dentist . . ." Amelia supplied.

". . . to a . . . ballroom-dancing class," Liss finished.

The rest of the group frowned, the bizarre image settling in their minds.

"Why is he driving his dentist to a ballroom-dancing class at nine o'clock on a Friday?" Matty asked.

"You haven't met James in person," Jules addressed Matty. "But he is absolutely the kind of man who would drive his dentist to a ballroom-dancing class. He'd drive anyone to a ballroom-dancing class, he's very generous! I told you he paid for our meal at Flying Fish, didn't I?"

"Only a hundred times," Matty replied. "You know Parker and I have paid for way more of your meals, right?"

"Oh darling, shush." Jules addressed Amelia, "Is James waiting for the dentist to finish the class?"

"Why don't we just call him and see where he is?" Matty said. "If he's driving the dentist, we can call back. If the dentist is already dancing, maybe James can talk."

"I don't want to call James," Amelia said.

"What if *we* want to call James?" Matty said. God, her sister could be a brat sometimes!

"I don't want to call James," Amelia repeated, more insistent.

"You've had a fight," Matty decided. "I knew it."

"It's getting late," Liss announced. "And I have a lot of *Buffy* to catch up on. Maybe we should pick this up tomorrow."

"Have you had a fight?" Jules looked to Amelia, stricken. "Muffin, no."

"We haven't had a fight," Amelia snapped. "I just don't want to talk to him right now, okay?"

Jules paled. "What was the fight about?"

"Here's a question." Glen tented his fingers. "Is the dentist a man or woman?"

"My future son-in-law is not having an affair with a *dentist*!" hissed Jules. "Not when he has a perfectly good teacher in his life!"

A sharp expression slashed across Amelia's face.

"Dentists can be very good-looking," Randall offered. "Several of my past clients have been dentists. Beautiful smiles."

"I've never met a good-looking dentist," said Ludmila. "Not once."

Ludmila, Randall, and Glen began discussing the relative attractiveness of dentists, while Matty and Jules attempted to parse whether James would be waiting in his car or watching the dentist's dance class. (Do they allow that? Would that be something James would enjoy?) Matty pointed out they didn't know if James was giving the dentist a lift home or not.

"How else would the dentist get home?" Jules asked.

"A cab, the tram, a lift from someone else!" Matty turned back to her sister and Liss. "I think we just call, even if he's with the dentist and can't pick up. Getting a missed call will show that we care."

Liss and Amelia traded another loaded look. Liss hedged, "I think maybe wait."

Glen piped up, "What time do dentists open for business?"

"Late," Ludmila said.

"No, early!" Matty could tell her sister wanted everyone to shut up, but quite frankly she was having too much fun. The cacophonic push-pull felt like a raucous New York dinner party at the stage where everyone was screeching with laughter and fantastically drunk and not at all worried about babies or the future. "Why aren't we talking about *that*? If the dentist has to open early, he's probably—"

"I don't want to talk to James tonight." Amelia's eyes were thunderous.

"You *have* had a fight," Jules declared. "Darling, you *must* make up before you go to bed! Just say it was all your fault and apologize!"

"Dentists make a lot of money," Ludmila announced, apropos of nothing.

"Why don't we just call him?" Matty raised her voice. "Even if you've been in a fight!!"

"Oh for fuck's sake!" Amelia shot to her feet. "We broke up! Okay? James and I are through." She grabbed the empty platter and stormed into the kitchen.

The noise woke up Parker, who came to with a gasp. *"I have those numbers right here!"*

Glen froze with discomfort.

Jules trailed Amelia, mouth opening and closing like a guppy. "What? How? When? Why?"

Matty was just as blindsided. The shock of the revelation transformed into anger. She was off the couch, marching toward her sister. "You broke up? With the guy you were talking about *marriage* with?"

"What?!" Jules shrieked.

"Thanks a lot, Matty," Amelia hissed, hurling the platter scraps into the compost.

"Animal, why don't we take a walk?" Liss was at her elbow, hand on the small of her back.

Matty was momentarily distracted by the familiarity. When had they become such good friends?

"You were talking about getting married?" Jules's hysteria was rising like a boiling teakettle. "To James? Why did you break up with someone who wanted to marry you? Amelia? Amelia!"

Amelia threw the empty platter into the sink, smashing it to pieces. "Because he's already married, Mum! He took me for a ride, okay? *He lied to me.* And I believed every word because I'm a *fucking moron.*"

It wasn't the volume that stunned everyone into silence. It was the self-hatred.

Amelia wiped her runny nose with the back of her hand. "So now it's *allll* out in the open. I'm single. *Again.* And probably will be for the rest of my fucking life!"

"Oh, honey." Jules opened her arms, coming in for a hug.

"Don't, Mum." Amelia batted her away. "I want to be alone. In the Yellow Cottage. Which I am taking, Matty. *I* booked this holiday. *I* did all the work. I'm sick of being treated like second-best because *I'm not married like you.*"

"But I need—" The words formed automatically in Matty's mouth, her thoughts a churn of personal requirements, work demands, and her wife's wishes.

Amelia whirled on her sister, eyes blazing with rage and grief. Each word was a threat. "It's. Mine."

Matty had never seen Amelia look so powerful. So frighteningly assured. Matty raised her hands in surrender.

Amelia grabbed her already-packed suitcase and stormed out of Kooroy. Liss scooped up her cardigan and a book from the couch, on her tail. Pausing in the doorway, Liss spun back. "Just for the record, there was never any dentist."

And they were gone, leaving the rest of the family dazed and dumbfounded.

Glen broke the silence, reaching for the dice. "Can anyone remember whose go it is?"

PART TWO

24

The ocean was different every day, charted by whoever was on a Kooroy balcony, watching the tide.

Dawn, and the water was calm, the pale pink of the inside of a seashell. By unrelenting noon, it became an unsubtle denim-blue, crashing to the shore with cheerful athleticism. As the air cooled in the late afternoon, the bay took on a mysterious quality, delicate as tissue paper. The ocean at dusk was a pretty girl with secrets, bats flickering around her like quicksilver. By the balmy, star-freckled evenings, a colossus moon painted the black water silver, like chromosomes uniting and dividing and uniting again. Once, they saw a pod of snubfin dolphins rollercoastering in the moonlight.

It was difficult to savor such loveliness. The instinct was to wolf it down and fall asleep sunstruck, already anticipating the delicate bloom of another dawn.

Of course, there were inconveniences. A lack of things—contact lens solution, tampons, T-shirts. A lack of people—neighbors, friends, a barista to make a perfect flat white. An overabundance of bugs and housemates taking too long in the drop dunnies. But soon all the inhabitants began to surrender themselves to the island's timeless spell.

Except Amelia.

Amelia locked herself in the Yellow Cottage, yanked the cheery curtains shut, and gave everyone a master class in breakup breakdown.

She wept, alternating between stunned, sad whimpers and wronged-woman howls. She ate an entire pint of mint-chip ice cream, a highly prized grocery item; no one dared try to stop her. She refused all visitors with the exception of Liss, who dropped off home-cooked meals and emptied her trash cans of tissues. Even the gentlest attempts at small talk ended with the jilted Kelly sister descending into tears and stating a desire to be *alone*.

On Sunday evening, Liss found five half-burned bikinis outside Amelia's door, the flirty showgirls irrevocably disfigured. "Guess I just won't go swimming for the rest of the trip," Amelia muttered to Liss.

Liss unearthed a navy Speedo one-piece from the Lost & Found and gave it a wash in the sink. Amelia accepted the swimsuit as one receives a ballgown. It instantly made her recall being in Nippers—junior lifesavers—as a tween. Amelia reminisced to Liss about cold mornings on the beach, squealing as she ran into the water with a gaggle of girls. An innocent time, before puberty and the understanding that her body was a sexual thing men had an opinion about. Amelia said she wasn't ready to get out of bed, but Liss saw her fold the swimsuit carefully before putting it away.

The following evening, a sunset of neon orange and pink swirled the sky, like a giant bag of melting candy. The rest of the family were outside, gobbling it up. Liss arrived to find Amelia in bed in a robe in the dark, on her phone, which Liss had retrieved from the bush for her. The Yellow Cottage smelled like BO and sadness.

Liss stepped past a stack of empty tissue boxes by the door. "Well, this is feeling very At Home with Howard Hughes."

Amelia's gaze snapped up. A distinctly manic glint in her eyes. "You know how Mum keeps going on about that dinner at Flying Fish? He paid with *a credit card*."

It took Liss a second to catch up: James had treated the Kellys at an often-referenced seafood restaurant for Amelia's thirty-third birthday. "Okay. So?"

"I called them. Said I was his girlfriend, that I'd just been in for my birthday dinner, but my boyfriend paid with the wrong card. He paid with his *brother's*, and we didn't keep the receipt." Amelia impersonated herself on the phone, making her voice syrupy. *"So I'm just calling to find out the total so we can pay him back. Please."*

Liss felt equally intrigued and alarmed. "And?"

"Five hundred and thirteen dollars," Amelia said, repeating her earlier conversation on the phone *"And that was on James's card, right?"* Then, the response: *"Actually it says here* Dale Spencer." She showed Liss her phone screen. "Dale Spencer owns a chain of car washes." Amelia swiped to a Facebook page. "Here's his wife. And his kid. At a zoo-themed birthday party, I think. He's dressed as a panda. He lied about everything."

"Amelia, whoa." Where to begin on this episode of *The Catfished Who Catfish?* "Wow—so many thoughts." Liss sank onto the end of Amelia's messy bed. "Okay, first: congrats on what sounds like a well-executed scam. Impressive and frightening."

Amelia went back to scrolling. "Thank you."

Liss held her hand out for the phone.

Reluctantly, Amelia handed it over.

On the screen was a straight couple with a kid who looked about ten. She could see how James-Dale could be considered attractive, even as the sight of his smug face filled Liss with disgusted anger. "Obviously this is the most tempting rabbit hole in the world to go down. But this guy, Animal: he was a bad guy. He doesn't deserve any more of your time or attention. Seriously."

"Don't tell me I have to go for a swim or something." Amelia groaned, pulling the covers around her. "Honestly, I just can't."

"I'm not going to tell you to do anything. I'm inviting you to something."

"If it's another Games Night, I am swimming back to the mainland."

Liss reached for the bag she'd left by the door to present a box set of VHS tapes.

Amelia read the cover. "*Buffy?* I know you're into it, but I don't really remember it."

"Then you've never *seen* it." Liss didn't need to affect her enthusiasm. "*Buffy* isn't just a show. It's a religion wrapped in a parable wrapped in a nineties pop-culture phenomenon. Buffy Summers is so many things—

friend, fighter, die-hard fan of the butterfly clip—but first and foremost, she's a *survivor*. And Slaygal's superhot like"—Liss stopped herself swerving into *you*, awkwardly rerouting to—"for, um, a teenager." She winced. "Yeah, that came out wrong."

Amelia gestured for the videos, examining the photos with mild skepticism. "You think she's superhot?"

"Of course. She's the Chosen One, and she's a cheerleader."

Amelia looked unimpressed.

"Angel is also a walking chef's kiss," Liss tried. "If you like the undead, and I do."

Amelia blew her nose on a piece of toilet paper. "Weird pitch. But okay."

Liss convinced Amelia to shower and put on clean sweats. With the promise of whiskey and a frozen cheese pizza back at the Caretaker Cabin, she successfully got Amelia to leave the Yellow Cottage for the first time in seventy-two hours.

The twilight air was elegant as lace. Liss encouraged Amelia to smell the salt breeze. Hear the butcher birds warble their lyrical looping song. Notice the swirls of pink and citrus clouds. Amelia glanced at them as if there were buzzing mosquitoes. At the Cabin, she beelined for the beat-up blue velvet sofa in front of the TV, wrapping herself in the crocheted blanket. "I should've worn my nightie-gown."

"Nightie-gown?" Liss repeated, charmed by the Aussie instinct to add an *ie* to just about anything. "Tell me that's not a word you actually use."

Amelia was busy getting comfortable. "Got any choccie bickies?"

"Ha. Sorry, mate. Fresh outta bickies." Liss opened the *Buffy* boxset. "Now, this is not the best season—that honor goes to two or three. But what season one does so effectively is invert the helpless-blonde-killed-in-every-horror-movie trope, over a background of high school teen drama and good jokes and fun premises *as well as—*"

"Liss," Amelia interrupted as the cheesy opening montage faded in. "Shut up."

Liss had already rewatched the first season, since the Wi-Fi at the Cabin was not strong enough to stream new shows. She still enjoyed the pilot, wherein Buffy, a miniskirted SoCal high school student wearing a startling amount of makeup, resists her duty as the latest in a long line of vampire slayers. What Liss liked more, however, was watching Amelia get sucked into the story, even managing a tiny smile at Cordelia's classic burn, "*What* is your childhood *trauma*?"

At the end of the episode, Liss looked over at the woman next to her, eyebrows raised.

Amelia reached for another slice of now-cold pizza. "When does Faith get there?"

"I believe rogue slayer Faith makes her first appearance early in season three?"

Amelia made a face, speaking with her mouth full. "That's ages away. Wasn't Faith the coolest one?"

"No argument here. We could skip straight there," Liss suggested, moving to get a different tape.

"No." Amelia stopped her, offended. "My boyfriend might be a cheater, but I'm not. I'll do the work. C'mon, keep going."

Liss let out a soft laugh. Not only was Amelia's stubborn side pretty endearing, but Liss saw a spark of the old, un-heartbroken Amelia. Maybe this was working. "Ex."

"Huh?"

"He's your ex-boyfriend." Liss pressed Play.

With one intermission to feed the sugar gliders, they finished half the first season by midnight. Amelia shuffled out the door with the blanket wrapped around her shoulders, and Liss assumed they were done with *Buffy*. She awoke the next morning to find Amelia back on the sofa, her expression hopeful. "Morning." Amelia waved the remote in greeting. "By the way, there is a massive fucking huntsman above your recycling. I hope you're okay with spiders."

Liss was rocketed back to living with a partner. The creation of a shared life in a shared space, and all the joys and frustrations that go along with it. It was comforting to find Amelia in arm's reach.

"That's Max. He's friendly." Liss sat up, careful not to reveal she wasn't wearing pants. "You know, technically, this is breaking and entering."

"Why don't you call the cops? They'll be here in six weeks."

Liss laughed. Amelia looked away as she swung herself out of bed to pull on her most flattering pair of shorts. She padded into the kitchenette to pour herself a cup of coffee (another girlfriend benefit: someone else makes coffee). "Maybe we can start around sunset?"

"Maybe we can start around now?"

"I have to work." Liss took a sip from her favorite mug (Garfield embracing his teddy bear, Pooky, under a rainbow. The text read *Have you hugged your boss today?*). The brew was exactly the right sort of bitter. "Mmm, great coffee."

"Oh good, we like the same kind. You can blow off work for a day, right? Just take the meal kits over. Email can wait."

Liss would typically get a day off every ten days, covered by a local Butchulla woman who lived in the Bay. She hadn't taken an official "day off" since the surge. There was less to do with only seven guests, but still: "I don't want it to seem like I'm doing something I'm not supposed to."

"Your job is customer service. I'm a customer! I need service, specifically a TV buddy to take on the Hellmouth. Please?" Amelia puppy-dogged her eyes. "Being with you is literally the only thing that makes me feel good."

Pure catnip.

Liss dropped off the day's food to Kooroy, updating the concerned Kellys that she was helping Amelia with the magic power of television and treats. Jules reacted to this as if Liss were in scrubs announcing a patient on the brink would pull through. Amelia's mother had put her entire life on hold in case her daughter needed so much as a tissue. Which closely resembled Amelia's commitment to being on call for James-Dale. Evidently, Amelia's apple had not fallen far from her mother's tree when it came to being in devoted, selfless relationships.

They were into season two by mid-afternoon, but Willow's one-sided crush on Xander turned Amelia maudlin. When Liss suggested they take a walk to the tide pools, Amelia groaned, burrowing deeper into the blanket. "No. I'll run into Mum or Matty or perfect Parker and I just can't take their pity. The way they'll look at me, like I'm an idiot who'll believe absolutely anything." Her eyes were leaking. "God, I'm such a loser."

The social worker in Liss noted Amelia's grief seemed centered around her humiliation and the shattering of an illusion over the loss of someone she truly cared about.

"Animal." Liss touched Amelia's shoulder, her thumb circling. "You're not a loser. You're actually my favorite person on this entire island."

Amelia wiped her nose with her sleeve, gaze raw. "I am?"

Her topknot was an oily, unwashed mess. Her skin was breaking out and she smelled like old sweat. Amelia Kelly didn't seem like someone who regularly abandoned the work of feminine presentation: Liss almost felt flattered she was seeing this side of her. Liss nodded.

"That's so nice." Amelia's chin trembled. "You're such a good friend."

"I guess I speak fluent breakup." Liss reached for the remote. "Plenty of practice."

Amelia's tears were replaced with curiosity. "Meaning?"

Liss hadn't meant to let this slip. "Meaning things ended pretty badly with Max." She indicated the spider with a rueful wave of her hand. "I'd like to be friends, but he still isn't speaking to me."

Amelia smiled but her gaze stayed questioning. Liss pressed Play before Amelia could ask what she really meant.

The next morning, Amelia was back. Again, Liss capitulated. But as another sunset came and went in a whirl of stakes and werewolves and love spells gone wrong, and Amelia started talking about "picking this up again tomorrow," Liss realized she'd created a monster, not unlike Adam in season four, which she definitely wasn't planning on getting to. Just before midnight, Liss plucked the remote from Amelia's grip and switched off the TV, leaving the space lamp-lit.

"What are you doing?" Amelia whined. "They're about to go slay."

"Oh-kay." Liss turned to face her friend. "Hi."

"Hi?"

"Amelia," Liss said. "Don't get me wrong: I'm a wallower, too. Love a good wallow. Some might say too much. But I'm starting to suspect we are cruising through the wallow stage and into the this-is-how-I-live-now stage."

"So?" Amelia tucked herself in tighter. "Maybe this is how I live now."

Liss shook her head. "You can't. Firstly, I blew off work the last two days, but I have stuff to do." Including the hotline, whose volunteer shifts she kept rescheduling. "And secondly, there's a whole island to explore! Have you even seen any of it, apart from Blinky Beach?"

"I've explored the bar."

Her petulance almost irritated Liss. Almost. "We're going for a hike. Tomorrow afternoon. I'll pick you up after I finish my day."

Amelia whimpered. "Hiking sounds hard."

"It won't be hard. It'll be good for you. Fresh air. Endorphins. And till then, I need to sleep. So . . ." Liss pointed in the direction of the Yellow Cottage.

"You're kicking me out?" Amelia pouted. "Can't I just sleep here?"

"No." Liss chuckled, opening her front door. Outside, a chorus of frogs shouted joyfully at the moon.

"Why not?"

Not the real reason: "You need a change of clothes."

Amelia sniffed her armpit. "Ooh. That's ripe."

"Good night, Animal. See you tomorrow."

She shuffled down the path, the blanket trailing behind her. A queen's robe gathering sticks and leaves.

Liss showered and got into bed. The house was quiet without Amelia. Empty, in a way it hadn't been before.

And so Liss did something she hadn't done in months. She slipped her hand under the band of her underwear and touched herself. She was wet. Of course she was. Because even while whining over a breakup with a trash guy, Liss found Amelia Kelly unbearably attractive.

Liss circled her fingertips around this forgotten part of herself, exploring in the way she would a new city: aimless meandering propelled by curiosity. When she first arrived on Mun'dai in December, she'd masturbated to thinking about fucking Sofia, and Gabe fucking her, and, weirdly, herself fucking Reggie, but it always left her feeling hollow and sad. It was easier to be celibate, and as a result her sex drive had been left in park, the battery run flat. But now . . . Now when she ran her finger over the nub of her clit, her entire body vibrated with pleasure.

Just don't think about Amelia.

Liss closed her eyes, moving her hand in a familiar rhythm.

Anyone but her.

The nighttime noises of the bush faded away.

A club. Kreuzberg. Thirteen years ago. One of the spank bank's most lucrative investments.

Her name was Katarina. A grad student (photography?) living at the sprawling punky squat Baby Liss was crashing at for a week of schnitzel and adventure in Berlin. Septum piercing, blunt white-blonde bangs, pencil-thin eyebrows: Katarina was reading Anaïs Nin and could blow a perfect smoke ring. Liss kept getting tongue-tied around her.

On her last night, Liss wanted to go dancing. "I'll take you," Katarina had said, and it ended up being just the two of them, getting quickly, deliberately drunk. On the dance floor, everyone was sweating through neon-mesh singlets and glittery makeup. They bopped around to European pop. Slowly getting closer in a way that looked casual, but which Liss was executing with chess-champion strategy. Finally, Katarina curled one hand around Liss's neck, snaking her hips, smiling like she knew a secret. Liss's mouth pooled, everything sharpening fast into need.

Robyn's "Dancing on My Own" blasting, the drum break in the third chorus. Katarina laughing as Liss pushed her into a dark corner. Their mouths on each other, desperate and hungry. "*I'm in the corner, watching you kiss her, oh-ooh-oh.*" Hands in hair, lips on skin, the oblivion of uncontrolled desire. Kissing without guilt, kissing because she was twenty-two and had just come out and wanted to taste the entire world. This girl's neck was salty and sweet; *skin*, that luscious carpet, that soft, living thing. Liss felt a pulse point under her tongue, she wanted to bite down like a vampire. The air was hot and smelled like cigarettes, everything loud and dark and sticky. Liss pushed her knee between Katarina's legs and they ground against each other, sending thick waves of giddy heat. Around them, other couples pawed at each other. Boys with boys, boys with girls, girls with girls: *Berlin*. Katarina held her gaze, wicked, and undid the top button of Liss's jeans. Slid her hand all the way down until Liss felt a lightning bolt of pleasure slam up her spine. Her pussy was open, wet, so sensitive. She'd never done this in public. But this was Berlin, where she knew no one and everything felt permissive. A city open to everything, open to life. "*I'm right over here, why can't you see me, oh-ooh-oh.*" Liss cupped Katarina's heavy tits breathlessly, running her thumb back and forth over each nipple, still kissing, moaning into each other's mouths, unchecked, undone. Katarina's hand started pumping in and out and over her clit, gaining momentum. Liss could barely hold herself up. Jesus, she was gonna come, here, in public, in this dark corner of the world's best club on the world's best night. Liss wanted to see Katarina's face when she did. The lights strobed, illuminating the girl whose fingers were inside her.

Amelia, arched and groaning, "God, you feel *so good*."

It was too late to stop herself climaxing: even those with hearts as walled as Liss have their limits. The peak and release made her cry out so loud, even the sugar gliders paused, curious.

Sweat cooled on her skin, bringing her back to the present. That would be the first and last time, Liss swore to herself. Hands above the top sheet, she squeezed her eyes shut, summoning sleep as one calls for a misbehaving dog. But all she could see in her mind's eye was gold hair slipping over suntanned shoulders and lips like crushed summer strawberries parted in a smile.

25

Come twilight, and the showy beauty of the island folded inward. The quiet rhythms of the night were a mystery all of their own.

The small native mouse emerged from its burrow, nose twitching to gather the story of its surroundings. It planned to go in search of food for its blind, hairless babies, each the size of a cashew. It did not see the watchful owl. Did not hear the whisper of its wings as the bird dove through the branches. The mouse would barely register the sensation of flight, now eye-level with the top of a shrub, a tree branch. The small world of this mouse cracked all the way open for a single, majestic moment before it was eaten alive. A death witnessed with grim fascination by Parker Lee.

Three a.m. in Mun'dai, 1:00 p.m. in New York. Parker was waiting on a reply to her last DM in Slack, her bare feet propped up on the second-floor balcony.

LK to PARKER
you see the ROI on the facebook spot!?? that 30s vid is killing. the retargeting worked. pump it up—3x, 4x, 5x. we need more subs!

PARKER to LK
I've seen it. We're studying the analytics to understand the real LTV lift here and how the spike might impact churn down the line. The

goal is to triple ARR and decrease CAC. This ad is working now but if cancellations skyrocket we're just feeding a leaky funnel. That's an expensive proposition. Plus, we need to diversify. We can't rely on FB for all of our growth.

Being fluent in this form of business jargon used to comfort Parker in the way an expat returning home feels an instant sense of belonging at being surrounded by their native tongue. But tonight this language felt sort of silly. Like they were playing with Monopoly money, pretending to be adults.

Parker wasn't sure if any of it really mattered.

Her laptop was hot against her bare thighs: even at night, it was warm enough for shorts. She closed her computer and tiptoed back inside to refill her water bottle, rereading the black stenciled text above the sink like she always did.

Corroboree: An assembly of a sacred or festive character.
Mob: Kin or family.
Deadly: Slang, meaning awesome or great.

That language felt important. Corroboree. Mob. Deadly.

Parker returned to the balcony, leaning against it, scanning the trees for the hidden nocturnal world.

How would she describe the owl and the mouse to a child?

The cycle of life, she supposed. Some animals (predators?) ate other animals, while some ate seeds and plants (herbivores? Or were those dinosaurs?).

Parker imagined the high voice of a child, her brown eyes worried. *Did the mouse hurt, Mommy?*

Only for a second, she'd say, because that was likely the truth, and Parker had a vague instinct it was best to be honest when possible.

Mommy. Even this close to becoming a parent, Parker had never imagined a child calling her this name. In years past, she felt vaguely embarrassed by how her smart and powerful female friends—women who ran companies or marathons—devolved into Mommy. She'd decided to be Mom. Short, powerful, less sentimental.

But now, the only human awake on the island, listening to the friendly menace of its nighttime noises, Parker felt a wet, urgent tugging in her chest.

Mommy.

She wanted to be a mommy.

26

It's a terrible thing to want something.

These words had been spoken to Matty by the head of podcasting at the Australian Sound Academy, the year before Matty moved to New York. ASA was boutique and prestigious, specializing in long-form audio-based storytelling. Matty applied twice; once right after high school (even though ASA was explicitly a graduate center) and again four years later. Both rejections destroyed her. She'd given up on the idea when she was invited to interview; her radio work had caught the new director's ear. On a fresh winter's day, clouds scudding west as if on the run, Matty felt oddly equivocal about discussing a position in a program that'd been her life's ambition for half a decade. She was twenty-eight, and like Jim Carrey's Truman, starting to knock up against the claustrophobic limits of her pretty hometown.

It's a terrible thing to want something.

Ambition had always ruled Matilda Kelly's life. She'd wanted to be a storyteller since she was a child: first an actor, then a filmmaker, like her hero, Woody Allen (bummer, right?). She'd grown up watching his movies taped from the television, fast-forwarding through Aussie-accented commercials for Chicken Tonight to black-and-white films full of jokes about Freud and existentialism and New York Jews. Things far beyond her understanding as a kid in the Sydney suburbs, and yet, not. Matty recognized something in these films of what she wanted. Who she could be. Her favorite was *Manhattan*. In it, a forty-two-year-old comedy writer (Allen) worried about dating a seventeen-year-old high school girl (Mariel Hemingway), set against a backdrop of Gershwin and trips to the Met and dinners on the Upper East Side. It took Matty longer to realize she wanted to visit, not just watch films about, New York than it did to parse the inappropriateness of her favorite film's central relationship. These days, she completely omitted Allen from her creative origin story. Sometimes it seemed like all her idols were revealing themselves as creeps or crooks.

Stories were a way to claim cultural territory. Matty's professional philosophy was part of a larger mission to center the experiences of women and queer people, but Matty also wanted to make money and get invited to fun parties by cool people eager to know her. Ego and altruism braided together. In her twenties, she doggedly rose through the radio ranks to become a popular on-air journo for the ABC, the national broadcaster. By everyone else's markers, successful. But all Matty could see was the book proposal that didn't sell, the screenplay no one bought, the women's networking group that petered out after just a few months. And each time, when an idea was on its deathbed, and Matty was wondering why the hell she'd ever thought it was any good, a new concept would spark, and she'd balloon with a belief bordering on religious that *this* idea was *the one*.

This pattern, of Sisyphean effort fueled by imagined super-success, preceded by an underwhelming reception or, worse, gut-wrenching failure, had repeated itself so often that Matty had never not known it. When she saw Greta Gerwig's *Little Women*, Jo March made her weep. She recognized a fellow traveler. One whose happiness was precipitated on all but impossible markers she alone set. Whose greatest foe wasn't lack of talent or drive but lack of perception and patience. Ambition as a hot, harrowing fever dream that pushed and punished, exhausting and unrelenting: oh yes, Matty knew Jo March. Matty Kelly knew ambition.

It was impossible to imagine life without it.

"It's a terrible thing to want something."

As Catherine Miller, head of podcasting spoke the words to Matty, back at ASA almost eight years ago, she recognized them as equally true and terrifying.

Catherine went on, "I want to win an Academy Award."

Matty smiled but felt vaguely embarrassed. Why wasn't the comment inspiring? Perhaps the answer was confidence: it was more a confession than an assertion. Catherine was a striking woman, attractive and powerful, but at the time, Matty thought of her as old. Her voice had a smoker's edge, each vowel elongated. "I want you, Matty. I want you at ASA."

The moment should've been a victory. In language akin to a seduction, the head of podcasting—at a school Matty once coveted so badly it had robbed her of happiness—was offering her a place. Perhaps it was this simple fact that left her inexplicably ambivalent. Her spot was offered, not hard-won. Ambition was vicious. It preferred a fight to a handout. Or maybe Matty was already sensing the limits of her well-worn hometown, the horizon just part of the set. In the following year, she'd move to New York, a city fueled by ambition, to become a tiny fish—krill—in the world's biggest pond.

Matty told Catherine she'd think about it. But the only thing she thought about, and still did, as she walked down Blinky Beach to the Yellow Cottage the next morning, were those words.

It's a terrible thing to want something.

Amelia answered the door with a smile that dropped: she'd been expecting someone else.

"Morning! I made muffins." Matty offered a plate.

Amelia looked doubtful. "You baked?"

"Well, Mum helped." Matty inhaled the overripe stench of her sister's quarters. "Oof, it stinks in here. Open a window." She yanked back the curtains. Sunlight crashed inside.

The sisters sat on the porch facing the ocean, picking at the not-very-good muffins. Matty stumbled through an apology. *Sorry I was a brat about the room. And James. And whatever else.*

Amelia let her babble for a minute before cutting her off. "Matty, it's fine. Apology accepted."

"You sure?"

Amelia raised one shoulder. "Of course. We're in each other's lives forever. Auntie Amelia, remember? And one day, if there is a goddess, you'll be Auntie Matty."

If ambition ruled her own life, the quest for true love, which included the relentless search for a co-parent, defined her sister's. They shared a desire for something just beyond their fingertips, fueled by passion, and quite possibly, a dose of delusion.

It's a terrible thing to want something.

Matty studied Amelia's profile. Her cute-kitten nose compared to Matty's horsey schnoz. Plump, pillowy lips and the sort of spun-gold hair that made Rumpelstiltskin look like amateur hour. Matty used to be jealous of her sister's good looks. Now she saw it as a double-edged sword. She believed beauty diminished ego in women. "I keep thinking about what you said on the beach last week, when you were talking about your hair. The thing about not being sure why you want to be blonde." The idea that Matty rephrased as *What is your true desire versus what you have been told so often is your desire that you mistake it for truth.*

Amelia furrowed her brow. "You . . . want to change your hair?"

Matty chuckled. "No. It's an interesting concept: Where do our desires come from? Nature? Nurture? Are we even capable of independent thought, or are we just prisms reflecting back society's needs and demands? Like the 'need' for women to raise children so men have time to self-express and consolidate power and do . . . sport."

Suspicion lit behind Amelia's eyes. "What are you saying?"

"I'm just pontificating over—"

"You don't want kids? You don't want to be a mum?"

"No! No, I'm not saying that. I do want kids, I think."

"You *think*?" Her sister sat ramrod-straight, speculation sharpening into fear. "Well, you better get sure, because in a parallel reality, you're already pregnant."

"*What?*"

"If there wasn't the volcano—" Her sister's chest started to rise and fall. "Have you and Parker been talking? Are you backing out? Does Mum know? What the hell, Matty—"

"Amelia, stop! Nothing's changed! God forbid I share an unfiltered thought with my sister." In an attempt to appeal to her sibling's boundless empathy, Matty admitted, "This stuff scares me. And I'm not as crystal clear on it as you. Becoming a parent means I have to give up a lot of things that are important to me."

"Like what?"

"Like ambition," Matty replied honestly.

"Um, I'm pretty sure you can be ambitious and a parent."

"I mean the time. The focus. The dream-chasing."

Amelia stared back uncomprehendingly. Matty's sister had never been ambitious, unless you counted the pursuit of romance as ambition. Their parents weren't overly ambitious, either. A therapist once intimated that Matty used ambition as a way to define herself against her family. Another reason why New York felt so much like home. Ambition was the fuel that kept the city alive.

"Well, maybe it'll be a nice break from all that." Amelia's tone was gentle. "You can focus on something that really matters: a baby."

Anger caught Matty unawares. She readied to launch into a cutthroat defense of her life and choices before realizing it'd be a waste of breath. She'd never be able to convince her sister that her ambition was as important as motherhood. Matty wasn't sure if she could convince herself of that. Her family saw someone who ran into brick walls again and again and again. They were proud of her accomplishments, but Matty also suspected they thought she was nuts. While ambition was an effective motivator and laser-focused guide, it could also be powerfully self-destructive.

The tension between her and her sister had ebbed. Matty wanted to keep it that way. "You're right," she said. "Becoming a parent could be a welcome respite from what goes on in my brain."

"Thank god." Amelia exhaled loudly, sagging with relief. "I could not survive losing my boyfriend and the chance to be an aunt."

And Matty couldn't hurt her sister or her mother or, of course, her wife: the three women she loved most. She wasn't really considering a change of plan. Cold feet were normal: surely every prospective parent got them. "What are you doing today?"

Amelia said something nebulous about going for a hike, which Matty clearly wasn't invited on. So Matty updated her on all the news from Kooroy: Randall had become their father's personal trainer, the pair disappearing for absurdly long stretches of time; Ludmila was running out of things to color coordinate; Jules had spent the morning making chutney from native bush tomatoes. The gossip dovetailed into a suggestion for the *Stranded* podcast idea. If motherhood was on her mind, Amelia proposed, why not interview Jules and Ludmila about their takes on being mothers? If only because Matty was sure to get two radically different philosophies.

"That's actually a good idea," Matty mused.

"You're actually welcome."

It'd be good to have a reason to ask her mother-in-law directly about Parker's origin story. Doing the math, fifty-seven-year-old Ludmila got pregnant at eighteen. Surely, Parker must've been a mistake. And talking about motherhood with actual mothers might help channel the enthusiasm and joy she should be feeling. "I'd only been thinking about it from my perspective."

Amelia let out an unsurprised laugh, quickly muted into a blithe smile. "Happy to help."

Matty left her sister looking more content than someone who'd been epically dumped deserved to be, curled up on the porch with a romance novel. No doubt something with a lot of claptrap about soulmates, refueling Amelia's heart for Attempt #604. At least no one on the island could hurt her sister's delicate heart.

27

Jules heard from Matty that Amelia was well enough to be going on a hike that afternoon. "So, why don't you go on that walk with Jarrah?" Matty suggested. "The one you wanted to go on alone?"

Jules focused very hard on cleaning an invisible spot off the kitchen counter. Blood heated her cheeks. "Maybe I should stay close by. Bring her some tea?"

"Mum! Do something for yourself!" her daughter insisted. "But I'll take a cuppa if you're popping the jug on."

A few minutes later, Liss dropped off the meal kits, mentioning Jarrah was at the Caretaker Cabin helping with some minor repairs. Jules arranged to meet him at the Barefoot Bar. He was already there when she arrived just after eleven, his gaze skimming the surf and bush. Nice to see someone simply sitting, observing the world, without their head in their phone. Jules felt a flutter in her chest, like tiny birds bathing in a creek. "Morning, Jarrah."

"Morning, Julia." He was on his feet, adjusting his hat. He almost always had a hat on. Just like she did. "Ready?"

He led the way on a track due west. He explained he'd done bushwalks like this many times. As part of his job as a ranger, he'd take tourists on bush tucker or flora and fauna walks. Other responsibilities included protecting and managing cultural sites, natural resource management like weed and fire control, and community liaison. Jules asked what he loved most. "Being on country—connecting with country. Working with the community, learning from the Elders. Being a role model for the next generation."

His reply was more earnest than Jules was expecting. It felt like a balm.

It was a hot day. Rivulets of sweat ran between her breasts. Jules had stopped wearing a bra years ago. The heat felt good: thick and familiar. The cicadas filled the morning with the deafening chorus of their wings. Somewhere nearby, a kookaburra laughed—*coo-coo-coo-CAH-CAH-CAH*!

"In Butchulla language we call kookaburras *Koogarka*," Jarrah said, handing her a berry pulled from a bush. "And this is a midyim berry, bush tucker."

The small white, purple-speckled berry was sweet and tangy on her tongue, tasting of cinnamon. "Delicious."

Jarrah nodded, grabbing a few for himself. His gaze slid to something near the base of the bush. "Oh, g'day, Yindingie."

He was talking to an enormous olive and brown snake, curled into a tight spiral.

Jules was pretty good with reptiles, but it still gave her a start. "Friend of yours?"

"Yindingie is a messenger god who can travel between worlds," Jarrah said, plucking another midyim berry off the plant. "Yindingie taught the birds and animals and first men and women the things they had to do. It's said when he comes down to earth, traveling on a rainbow, he takes the form of a carpet python."

Jules regarded the likely sleeping snake with renewed interest. "Fascinating."

They set off again. No rubbish on the path, no other tourists. Just her own body propelling her forward under a burnished blue sky, a handsome man leading the way. A man with strong calves and a pretty nice bum.

Jules blushed at where her mind had wandered, turning her attention back to the plants.

"Here we are." Jarrah came to a stop in a small clearing marked with various signage and warnings. He checked the position of the sun, wiping sweat off his brow. "We're a little early."

"For what?"

He led her to a small cave, a space as big as a fridge between two rocks. Inside it was dark. "Rock art is the oldest surviving art form and a vital part of Indigenous culture," Jarrah explained. "It offers a rare and unique window into how our ancestors lived. Our story is the land and the land is our story."

It sounded a little rehearsed—he'd likely said this many times—but they were still powerful, beautiful words.

There were two types of rock art. Petroglyphs, or rock engravings, were created by removing stone through pecking, hammering, or abrading in order to leave a negative impression. Pictographs, or drawings, were made by applying pigments to the rock. "We told stories about everything from our creator ancestors and creation stories, to plants and animals, to the white man's arrival." Jarrah gestured for Jules to come closer to the cave's opening. His warm breath tickled her cheek. "This is one of my favorites."

The sun moved to light up a series of drawings inside the cave. Rendered in deep, reddish ochre were the outlines of several large sea creatures. "Mooka mooka," Jarrah said. "Whales. And this fella." He pointed to the skinnier one underneath the three whales. "Crocodile."

So unexpected, this beauty in the darkness. The crocodile in particular was stunning, viewed from above, with four distinct limbs, long tail, and a powerful jaw.

"No crocs on Mun'dai these days," Jarrah added, "but we still have the whales coming up each year to breed. The story goes that way back in the First Time, Yindingie was telling the birds who they were, what they would eat, whether they were day or night birds, when he noticed a swordfish and a baby whale arguing in the sea."

A creation story. Jules hadn't heard this one.

"So Yindingie picked up the little whale," Jarrah went on, "and put him in a lake. But the whale didn't like that. When he scrambled out to get back to the sea, his tail knocked Yindingie over. Yindingie got angry and said to all the whales, *From now on, you may only come once a year to play.* And that's why the whales only come to the waters of Mun'dai once every year."

Jules smiled, enamored by both the story and its storyteller. "How old are these drawings?"

Jarrah stepped back to allow her a better look. "Couple thousand years."

Jules pictured someone standing close to where she was right now, centuries ago, creating this artwork, recording their culture. Not for money or ambition or self-conceit. Art that didn't hang on display for shuffling crowds on the white walls of a gallery, but art that was held close by the natural contours of the earth. Art that told the story of the planet. Could this long-dead painter ever imagine that she, Julia Kelly, would be bearing witness to it, in the early years of the twenty-first century? Perhaps not: the ancient artist probably didn't imagine how cruel and unnatural things would get. The world had changed beyond recognition, but not this spot. Not most of this island. A wave of fierce gratitude and respect washed over her for how the Butchulla people fought to keep this part of their culture. It was all so moving, Jules was embarrassed to find a knot in her throat and tears in her eyes.

The sun shifted. The cave wall went dark.

"Beautiful." She stepped back. "Just spectacular."

Jarrah's eyes were damp, too. "Still gets me," he said, unembarrassed by his emotion. "Especially when it gets someone else."

Jules set out lunch under the shade of a Queensland gum. Cheese, ham, and tomato sandwiches: all thick cut, big as a man's hand, slathered with homemade chutney that Jarrah said was the best he'd ever tried. They ate in comfortable silence, listening to the tinkly twittering of the rose robins darting about the banksia. The gentle murmur of native stingless bees winging pollen from flower to flower.

Jarrah nudged Jules's foot, nodding at something. "Swampie."

Through the undergrowth, a rust-brown swamp wallaby blinked back at them. The stocky marsupial was half the size of a kangaroo, balanced on its hind legs by a long tail. As they all regarded each other, a baby stuck its nose out of the pouch. Jules and Jarrah traded a grin. The simple movement was enough to startle the swampie, its tail thumping as it bounded off through the bush.

When the sandwiches were gone, Jules unveiled the big treat: two cold bottles of beer. To her surprise, Jarrah declined. "Oh, go on," she said. "It's a very nice pale ale."

"Actually, I'm sober."

Jules flushed with shame, instantly mortified. "Oh shit, I'm so sorry."

"No need to be sorry. Please, feel free." He gestured for her to drink.

"Oh, no. Not on my own." She put the bottles back in her backpack, trying not to feel disheartened while floundering around for a conversation starter that wasn't *So, why don't you drink?*

To her relief, he got it started. "How's everything going with your ex?"

"Glen?"

"Is there another ex?"

"No." She chuckled, settling against the tree trunk behind her to answer his first question: "Complicated."

"Yeah?" He pushed up the brim of his hat to flick her a smile. "I'm good with complicated."

She loved that he said that. Not all men would. Jules found herself painting the broad brushstrokes of her marriage and family—Matty and Parker's move, Amelia's recent breakup, two reasons why it wasn't a good idea for the kids to know about their parents' pending divorce.

Jarrah was a good listener, sympathetic and nonjudgmental. He didn't offer advice she didn't ask for.

"Is it hard?" he asked. "Having to share a house with your ex and your in-laws?"

"I wouldn't say it's easy. But in the scheme of things, we're lucky to have a roof over our heads and food in our bellies. And it's not like Glen and I fight. We've just . . . run our course."

"Yeah. That happens."

What did that mean? Had he left a marriage? Was he single, was he straight, what was his history? "What about you?" Jules aimed for light. "Anything, um, complicated in your life?"

His laugh was apprehensive. He didn't quite meet her eye. "I think everyone's pretty complicated." Jarrah was on his feet, brushing off the dirt. "Better head back."

Jules took the hint. But she wasn't going to ruin the special day by being disappointed. Sixty years on the planet taught her to tally in bounty, not lack.

28

Liss considered canceling the hike with Amelia but figured that would create more drama than maintaining simple boundaries. She reminded herself friendships were meaningful and generally longer-lasting than relationships, as long as you didn't end up accidentally porking.

Liss came by the Yellow Cottage in the late afternoon. Amelia was showered and fresh, her hair washed and braided under a wide-brimmed hat. Liss ignored the observation that wholesome looked very sexy on her, and they set off.

The best hikes on the island meandered through the rainforest in the south—full-day hikes, with significant elevation. But it was already getting on, so Liss took Amelia west to Mooka Mooka Beach, aiming for the main lookout above the colored dunes. Only an hour or so there and back. If they were lucky, they'd see brumbies galloping up the beach.

What Canadians and Americans called hiking, Australians called a bushwalk. Liss led the way, tapping the ground with a stick to scare off snakes, like Jarrah had showed her when she first arrived. The heat of the day was starting to relax, the promise of a balmy evening ahead. Liss kept the conversation light. No personal stuff, definitely no flirting. Beer or wine? (Wine, they agreed). Day or night? (Amelia, day; Liss, night). Dogs or cats?

"Dogs," Amelia replied, certain.

"Correct. Big dog or small dog?"

"Small dog."

"Ooh: incorrect."

"According to who?" Amelia giggled. "I want a doggie I can carry around like a baby."

"I want a dog that can protect me, and that my future toddler can ride around like a horse."

"No, dogs like that do huge poos."

"What?" Liss guffawed. "A small dog will also poo."

"Ugh, don't say poo! I hate talking about poo!"

"You brought it up!"

They paused for water in the shade of a brush box tree. Liss pointed out a ball of sticks in its branches—a ringtail possum's nest, known as a drey. "Fun fact about possums: they're the only marsupials who love close-hand magic. Can't get enough of it."

Amelia's eyes were wide. "Is that true?"

"No. Wow, you are so gullible," Liss teased.

"Shut up." Amelia's cheeks were pink as she sipped from the water bottle.

Liss realized she'd embarrassed her. "I think it's a good thing to be trusting. You're open to magic of the universe. Just like a possum is open to the magic of a disappearing coin."

Amelia splashed water in Liss's face and stomped off.

They made it to Mooka Mooka Lookout in time for sunset. Crashing surf stretched for miles in each direction. In the distance, the rusting skeleton of Lady Lushington sat forever shipwrecked on the shore. Unquestioningly romantic, so Liss didn't sit too close to Amelia as they waited for the fat orange sun to kiss the horizon, chatting idly about high school, then elementary school, then favorite movies in elementary school. "*Neverending Story*, definitely," Liss said.

Amelia nodded, tossing a pebble off the edge. "All I wanted to be for Halloween for, like, four years was the princess at the end with the thingy on her forehead."

"Oh yeah," Liss agreed, remembering. "The thingy."

Amelia sighed. "She was so beautiful and sophisticated."

"And sad," Liss said. "She was so sad. I was obsessed with her sadness. '*Why don't you do what you dreamed, Bastian! Call my name.*'"

"What was her name?" Amelia wondered, and they both thought for a moment.

"Sharon," Liss landed on, which—satisfyingly—made Amelia laugh. "But watch that film now," Liss added, "and Sharon is a literal child. She's like six, or fifteen. I don't understand children."

Amelia glanced over, eyes narrowed in curiosity.

Liss sensed a question about kids. Far too intimate. She scrambled for another film. "Um . . . *The Goonies.*"

Amelia looked back at the water. "Never saw *The Goonies.*" She nodded at the setting sun. "We should get going or we'll be hiking back in the dark."

Liss dropped Amelia home in the purpling dusk. Amelia invited her to the family dinner, but Liss declined, and Amelia didn't push. She seemed grateful for Liss's time, even polite. In fact, Amelia had been different all afternoon. Slightly more guarded, a little less goofy and overly familiar. Perhaps the red-hot center of her breakup was starting to cool, and the codependency of the past few days was an anomaly already ending. Which was what she wanted, Liss reminded herself.

She didn't see Amelia the next day or the next: she wasn't home when Liss left the meal kits, and Liss didn't want to ask the Kellys about it, because what business was it of hers what their younger daughter was up to?

Under the bright, waxing moon, Liss fed the sugar gliders, trying not to feel lonely. "I hope this is platonic," she told Rick, as the tiny marsupial shared an apple slice with Neil. "For your sake."

That night, she drank her first Cup-a-Soup from the box Amelia gifted her. Even that didn't deliver the comfort she sought.

Amelia's unexpected absence bled into Liss's volunteering with Rainbow Connection. Able to make a regular shift, she'd spoken with Ro a few more times—fifteen, pansexual, genderqueer—they'd call when Liss tended to pick up. She'd never seen them in person, but vaguely matched the droll voice to someone colorful and expressive, maybe olive-skinned, dark-eyed (was there a hint of a South American accent?). After helping Ro make a plan to come out to their well-meaning but conservative family, their conversations had become more and more casual.

"I have a crush," Ro announced early one evening. "On a guy at school. I think he's bi? Very cool. And hot. A true temperature paradox."

"I don't know, dude." Liss sighed, swigging a beer. "Love complicates everything. It's all fun and games until one night you find yourself at some terrible Irish bar in West Hollywood doing Jägerbombs with the screenwriter for *Sharknado 2*, about to place a significant bet on live eel racing while your girlfriend is at a Golden Globes afterparty with *him*, and you're like, *What happened to my life?* And the answer is love. Love happened, and it *destroyed* you."

"Good gravy," Ro said. "One: you win the Very Very Sad Award. And two: we are definitely talking about you and not me."

"Sorry," Liss caught herself. "You're right, we were."

"What's happening with Amelia?"

Liss choked on her beer. She usually saved her monologues for Max. How often had she been discussing Amelia with this teenager? "Yeah, I should probably stop talking about my personal life with you."

Ro sighed, low-key drama. "What's going on?"

"Okay, so I *finally* ran into her on Blinky Beach yesterday and she said she'd been going on lots of long walks and swims to *process everything*"—admirable, Liss felt, even surprising—"but then she asked if I'd do the Great Loop with her, all the way to the south end of the island—she has zero sense of direction and y'know I'm Canadian, I spent every summer avoiding bears in woodland settings—but the Great Loop is a full-day hike! Obviously I can't spend a *whole day* with her."

"Because you're in love with her."

"Because she's straight!" Liss exploded. Max moved one of his eight legs: the huntsman version of shook. "*And* a guest, *and* I'm going back to Montreal when all this is over, alone, without *another* broken heart! Jesus, we've both been dumped by people we thought we were going to *marry*."

Ro made an unconvinced noise. "So, when are you going on the hike?"

Liss grimaced, recalling the way the plan just fell out of her mouth. "Day after tomorrow. But just as friends."

Ro started laughing, which only strengthened Liss's resolve.

After finishing the call, Liss grabbed her guitar and flopped onto the orange sofa, letting her fingers take a walk over the strings. It was the tail end of dusk, the last of a deep red sunset disappearing in the west. The cooling air smelled like eucalypt and salt.

The song arrived unannounced: *"I was friendly with this girl, who insisted on touching my face . . ."*

"Untogether" by Belly, a regular on rotation at Sad Sack Sundays. The elegantly simple, bittersweet song was one of Liss's favorites. To her, it was about not the impossibility of love, but the inevitably of its end. The color of heartbreak. The poetry of the lyrics and gently soaring melody offered understanding. *"You can dry your eyes,"* Liss used to sing to the damp-eyed patrons of the bar in Mile End. *"You can't hold the impossibly untogether."* But tonight, there was no crowd of sad sacks, no line at the bar, no honking traffic outside. Just Liss, alone, singing to her fellow night creatures. When the last note faded, there was no applause. Liss's entire being softened, reaching a new level of peace. It was transcendent to play music for so much love, an audience wasn't required. She was playing for the trees that shaded her. For the wildflowers whose scent carried on the evening breeze. For the ocean, that great god, whose waves she could hear crashing and receding and crashing again. Liss was playing for the island and that was enough.

29

Matty didn't exactly ask Jules and Ludmila if she could interview them for her new podcast pilot—she told them. "It's just an audio interview, and it won't take long. I could do you now, Mum, if you're free?"

Jules's eyes darted around the sunny kitchen she'd just finished cleaning. Like Amelia, Matty's mother felt nervous being in the spotlight.

But, like her mother, Matty tended to get her way. "You both look free to me," she decided. "Ludmila, I'll come get you when we're done."

"I'm a maybe," Ludmila said, ascending the stairs to the master. "On everything."

Matty had never had an easy relationship with her mother-in-law. The Kellys connected through humor; Ludmila apparently had none. After Matty stopped trying to play the perfect wife, revealing more of the behavior that'd earned her the Bratty nickname, they'd become even less interested in each other. Parker once confessed that Ludmila pulled her aside on their wedding day to ask in all seriousness if getting married was really something she wanted. "It's not that she's a woman, you know I don't care about that," Ludmila had said to a disbelieving Parker-in-a-tux. "It's that she's just so . . . *Australian.*"

On their *wedding day*.

Matty set up on the dining room table, with the balcony doors open for the sea breeze. Jules started shy, speaking too close to Amelia's phone, before realizing the topic was one she enjoyed as an expert. "I remember"—she smiled, folding her fingers around a teacup—"when you were first born. I'd come in every morning with a big smile and say, '*Hello, darling! Hello, Baby Matty!*' and you'd just stare at me, unblinking." Jules snorted in amusement. "It was so creepy! You barely cried. You just spent all day looking at your father and me like, *Is this it? I'm just stuck with you two dingbats?*" Jules was really laughing now.

"Hilarious." It wasn't. Matty knew the story. "And when Amelia was born—"

"And when Amelia was born, everything changed! She was always crying or giggling or wanting to play or be held. It was like the penny dropped for you, like, *Oh, is that what I'm supposed to be doing?*" Jules patted Matty's hand. "Animal taught you how to feel and express emotion. And, of course, she worshipped you: her brave big sister. It was so lovely to see."

In the end, Matty could barely shut her mother up.

Ludmila was different. It took Matty several hours to bulldoze her mother-in-law into finally sitting down together. When she did, her spine was as straight and stiff as the eucalypts outside. Matty started recording, pretending this was all very normal when, in reality, she was squirming with emotional discomfort. Yet it didn't cross her mind to pull the pin. Ambition was a dogged and resilient copilot.

"I thought we could start with time line," Matty said. "You had Parker at nineteen, correct?"

Ludmila twisted her fingers into the fringe of a silk scarf, eyes narrowing. "I suppose."

She *supposed*? "Well, you're fifty-seven now, and Parks is thirty-eight, so you must've delivered at nineteen. How long had you known Randall?"

"I thought you wanted to talk about motherhood."

Her mother-in-law was being cagier than a cat. Why? Matty tried not to sound as befuddled as she felt. "We are."

Surely, Parker had been an accident; Ludmila would've been eighteen when Parker was conceived. Even Parker seemed vague on the exact details, but maybe knowing every gruesome particular of your own birth was abnormal, not vice versa.

Matty checked her notes. "Parker once told me you met Randall at a gym."

"Yes."

"In San Francisco?" Where Parker was born, before the family moved to L.A.

"Yes."

"Impressive that you were at the gym as a teenager," Matty said, trying for light. "Still yet to make that leap myself, at the tender age of thirty-six."

Ludmila's gaze could turn water to ice. "Obviously, Matilda," she said, "we are very different people."

30

She was cute. That's all. Liss was cute.

Typically after a breakup, Amelia would distract herself by planning a complex class project involving dissecting frogs or revisiting *Gilmore Girls* over a bottle of something cheap and sweet. With none of her usual diversions on offer, she'd been forced to reckon with having fallen in love with a car wash king *she didn't even know*. Over the past few days of solo hikes and swims and attempts at journaling (*Does anyone know the real me? Mum, I suppose. And Matty. Dad? Most of my friends and exes: hmm, maybe too many people know the real me.*), Amelia had inched past anger into resignation. Carving out this perspective helped her see the relationship in a blinding new light. At the time, never knowing when James was going to call or how long they could spend together felt exciting and romantic—two lovers, snatching time. Now Amelia realized she was playing a part she didn't know she'd been cast for. They were in two separate movies. Hers, a swoony romance. His, a twisted Lifetime movie starring C-list actors.

When Amelia asked Liss to do the Great Loop with her, she wasn't planning anything more than a day of outdoorsy exploration with someone interesting and witty and, yes okay, cute. She was curious about Liss's past and what'd jettisoned her from Montreal to Mun'dai. Maybe, over the expansive course of an entire day, she might get some answers. Amelia knew they had chemistry, but in her mind it was platonic and the furthest things might go was mild flirting. A hand or gaze that lingered for a second too long. Amelia awoke the morning of the hike with a resolution to enjoy their connection while practicing a healthy boundary. "A new me!" she declared to her reflection in the bathroom mirror, while dabbing her neck with jasmine perfume.

They set off early, the island still dewy, mist-wrapped. As they started moving south, the vegetation changed. The airy eucalypt woodland became denser and lusher. The canopy closed above them. Trickling streams underfoot turned the earth muddy. The light became filtered, almost viridescent.

Rainforest: the lungs of the earth.

Low-growing bracken fern tickled their calves. Every fallen log was blanketed with liverworts. Hanging vines festooned tree branches. The forest smelled like damp moss, cool and green. But while the air was still, it was far from quiet. Everywhere, the liquid, rich sound of birdcalls— soft churrs, operatic trills, tiny peeps, and whistles. The crack of the whipbird. The croak of a frog. They passed under ancient, seven-feet-high tree ferns in comfortable silence listening to the soundtrack of the rainforest, sweating through their cotton T-shirts, muscles beginning to ache.

The old-growth forest covering almost half of Mun'dai had never been logged. Amelia's mind drifted to block theory—past, present, future, all folded together, happening at once. It was easy to imagine glimpsing a dinosaur or dodo through the curtains of green. The way Liss fit into that felt entirely normal. Maybe they existed in time together, always.

The pair reached the end of the island just before one. The vegetation thinned, ocean sounds filtered in, and they were there. Wonapinga Head: the highest point on Mun'dai. Blinky Beach and all of Pigface Bay rendered in miniature like an oil painting. The smooth muscle of the rolling, opalescent sea. The sand, white as tusks. Sea eagles circled on the breeze.

"There's my house!" Amelia pointed at the distant smudge of yellow. "And Kooroy would be . . . there, right?"

Liss looked down Amelia's arm and adjusted her fingertip. "There."

"God," Amelia breathed, looking at her with a smile. "It's so beautiful."

Liss smiled back. That shy, startlingly pretty smile.

She was cute. That's all. Liss was cute.

On a plaid picnic blanket, a shared lunch: pasta salad, buttered bread rolls, cheese and fruit, a bar of chocolate. A bottle of white wine, not quite cold. They finished a plastic cup each then topped up, eating lustily, lolling in the sun. Amelia could sense Liss's armor loosening as the wine sharpened her own intense fascination with this person. Amelia reached over to run her fingertip over the words stenciled on Liss's inner forearm: GIRL VS TRUCK, the name of Liss's band. "So, you were the girl, he was the truck?"

Liss laughed lightly, rubbing where Amelia had touched her. "Wasn't really a gendered thing. More like a . . . vibe."

"Mmm, yeah. A vibe." Amelia nodded. "Do you miss him?"

Liss was bad at playing dumb. "Who?"

"Gabe. You said he was your best friend."

Liss tucked her knees to her chest, curling up like something missing its shell. "Yeah, I miss him. But as you Aussies say, I sort of stuffed it up."

A door edging open. Before Amelia could figure out how to push through, Liss asked, "Do you think you'll tell James's wife?"

Clearly a dodge. But at least they weren't talking about the weather. Amelia rolled onto her back and sighed. "I'm still deciding. I don't want to ruin her life, too. I just can't believe I'm single *again*. It's just *exhausting*: always being the third wheel. Smiling through baby showers that I've organized while I'm dying inside. Losing all my girlfriends to their *loyal* boyfriends and husbands. I've been a bridesmaid nine times. Nine!"

"One more and you might win a stuffed toy."

Amelia snorted. "Everyone says I'll 'meet someone when I least expect it,' which is the least helpful advice *ever*. By that logic, I'll lock eyes with someone while going to the toilet."

Liss choked on a mouthful of wine, laughing.

Amelia let her laugh become a groan. "I know I'm an optimist. I like that about myself! But my sister thinks that's why I can't make something work: I'm not enough of a realist. But I think if you love someone, truly *love* them, things will find a way of working themselves out."

She expected Liss to nod in wholehearted agreement, but her friend looked doubtful, and Amelia felt a splash of embarrassment. Perhaps her theory sounded naive. She tried to explain. "I just want what Mum and Dad have. They're practically the only parents of all my friends still married. Thirty-six years."

"That's amazing." But something had happened in Liss's face that reminded Amelia of clouds passing in front of the sun.

"Are your parents still together?" Amelia asked.

"No."

Amelia waited. But that was all: *no*. Irritation bubbled, even as Amelia reminded herself that Liss owed her nothing. That was how people with good boundaries conducted friendships. "Maybe we should head back."

Liss seemed surprised. "Now?"

"It's just . . . you know so much about me and I feel like I know nothing about you! Which is fine, totally fine, I'm obviously being a stickybeak."

Liss let out a laugh. "A sticky—what?"

"Stickybeak." In spite of herself, Amelia giggled. It was a ridiculous slang. "Someone nosy. I'm just interested in you. What made you come here, what happened with Gabe, and your band."

Liss chewed her bottom lip, thinking.

The silence became uncomfortable. Obviously Liss's boundary didn't allow for any real personal information, at all. "Forget it." Amelia reached for her shoes.

"I slept with Gabe and kind of broke his heart."

To Amelia's surprise and pleasure, Liss stumbled out a stop-start version of what'd landed her on Mun'dai. Black Dog and Sad Sack Sundays, Gabe and Gabe's bed. *Earth 3000* and Reggie Richards and her mercurial, unfaithful, exciting ex. How it felt to be cheated on and have her heart ripped from her chest. How it felt to do that to Gabe, her oldest friend. The Catholic-level guilt she felt, and she wasn't even Catholic. "And the nuts thing is, sometimes I don't know if I should've left," Liss thought aloud. "Gabe is incredible. We probably could've made it work."

Amelia listened closely, her vision swimming a little. Getting so much deeply personal information made her feel high, like the fuzzy-brain tickles from ASMR. "But Gabe wasn't the one?"

"No, but isn't that just dangerous fairytale rhetoric? Does any sane adult believe in stuff like that?"

Amelia blushed.

"You believe in stuff like that," Liss concluded.

She shrugged, toying with her fork. "Maybe there's more than one "one." But I think it's nice to believe in soulmates. Don't you?"

"I guess I'd like to," Liss admitted. "It does sound pretty romantic."

Amelia was a native in the land of big emotions: Liss's confession was the most at-home she'd felt all day. "I knew you were a secret romantic," she teased.

"Don't tell anyone." Liss smiled back, holding her gaze.

Amelia resisted the urge to purr.

She. Was. *Cute*.

They finished their second cup of wine. Amelia held up the bottle hopefully. The booze felt key to the close, warm space they'd created.

Liss held out her cup. When Amelia leaned forward to top her up, she was pretty sure Liss checked out her boobs. Amelia leaned a little farther than necessary to make sure Liss got a good look. They toasted their cups and sipped without breaking eye contact.

When Liss spoke, her voice sounded odd. Like she was trying very hard to sound casual. "So, this search for a soulmate that you're on. What are your . . . parameters?"

"Parameters?"

"Guys . . . Girls . . . ?"

Amelia's heart started to pound. Not so much at the question. At the way Liss was staring at her, more direct than she'd been all week. Amelia knew they had a connection, but she didn't know how Liss felt about her, not really. This was the first real inkling that Liss might see her as more than a friend. "Not even my sister knows, um . . ." Sharing this felt like handing Liss something unbearably precious. "I've been with men, and women, and someone who didn't identify as either, actually. I'm . . . bi."

An alarming flash flood of emotions bombarded Liss's face, whooshing frantically behind her hazel eyes. Amelia hoped she wasn't having a cardiac event: the chances of carrying Liss back through miles of rain-forest like a superhero were absolutely zero.

Liss wrestled her face into neutral and nodded as if Amelia had stated a preference for apples over oranges. "Cool."

It sounded like she didn't believe her. Which, halfway to drunk, made Amelia pissed. Sure, she didn't look as obviously queer as Liss did. But it didn't make her any less so. "Yeah, thanks."

Evidently, they'd both forgotten how to have a conversation.

"Who's, um, your type?" Liss asked.

Even before the question left her mouth, Liss winced, but Amelia heard it as a challenge. Like she didn't expect Amelia would be able to answer. "My type?"

"Of course you don't have a type. I don't have a type."

"You don't think I have a type?" This was probably how her sister would react: doubtful questioning resulting in flat-out denial. Bi erasure—wasn't that a thing?

Liss fiddled with her hair, looking increasingly mortified. "Of course you don't! It's not like people have a checklist!"

"They don't?" Amelia ticked off her fingers defiantly. "Girls who kinda look like boys but are also really hot. Musicians. Accents. Funny. Kind." All five fingers were open. She shut her hand, dropped it, and gave Liss a triumphant look. She *did* have a type, thank you very much!

And that type was Liss Chambers. Only now did Amelia put that together.

Liss sat up unevenly. "Sorry, are you . . . are you joking?"

All at once, the full picture of the situation crashed around Amelia like a second surge.

She liked Liss. *Liked* her. Even though Liss was different from the handful of girls she'd been with in the past, in some ways, she wasn't. Androgynous, clever, soft-hearted: check, check, check. Amelia pressed her fingers to her lips, wishing she could push the tipsy confession back inside her mouth. Heat flamed her cheeks and neck. "Wow, I really shouldn't day-drink."

"Me?" Liss pointed to herself to clarify the *me* she was referring to. "You're into girls . . . like me?"

"You're what I'd build for myself in a lab." Amelia tried to make it sound like a joke. "I just didn't mean to . . . say that. To you."

"Because it's not true?"

"No." Amelia felt like someone being given a cheeseburger and realizing they were, in fact, absolutely starving. She had a crush on Liss Chambers. Sexy, mysterious, gorgeous Liss Chambers. "It's true."

They were both breathing hard, staring at each other.

Amelia was certain Liss was about to kiss her. Touch her. The idea sent another wild wave of heat through her body, pulsing hard between her legs. Amelia's heart was beating so fast and hard she could barely hear herself.

But Liss looked away. Wiped her palms on her shorts. "That's really flattering. So, should we go back or, um . . ."

In the language of abrupt topic switches, it sounded like a refusal. Amelia had just told her, albeit accidentally, that she liked her, and Liss was saying *no*? Embarrassment and regret seared her chest, making it hard to breathe. Amelia started packing up the lunch, speaking more to herself than Liss. "*Why* did I just tell you that, *what* is wrong with me? I'm obviously *nothing* like your ex."

Liss looked startled. "Um, what?"

"I'm not mercurial, or unfaithful, or exciting, or an actress." In fact, she was the opposite. "Why did I ever think you'd be into me?"

Liss's eyes were wide, watching Amelia unravel in fascinated fear. "Most of those weren't good things. And you are exciting. In a totally different way."

Amelia tossed the last Tupperware into the backpack. Like love, rage consumed her too easily. "*So* embarrassing."

"You're my type, too," Liss blathered. "Obviously! You're everyone's type!"

Amelia paused, staring at her. "Ouch."

"Jesus, you're beautiful. You're one of the most beautiful people I've ever seen in real life."

"Beyond the fact commenting on my physicality isn't a real compliment, don't bother. I get that you don't want to date someone like me: message received."

"Date you?" Liss ran both hands through her hair, thrown. "I don't think dating is a good idea for either of us, no."

Infuriating. "Why not?"

Liss choked out a laugh. "Why shouldn't we start dating? On the island we're stuck on? With no one except your family? Who you're not out to?"

"Obviously my family wouldn't care if I dated a woman."

Liss looked pained. She moved closer to pick up Amelia's hand, pressing it to her lips, not quite a kiss. The sensation rocketed up Amelia's back. It was all she could do not to fall into Liss's arms, suction their mouths together. Liss held her gaze, her words soft and sincere. "It's not that I'm not attracted to you, Amelia. I am, trust me. It's just that . . ."

Her beautiful face contorted; a universe of thoughts unspooling in her tortured brain.

Let me in, Amelia wanted to scream. *Talk to me!*

Liss let Amelia's hand drop. "The timing isn't right for me. I'm sorry."

Something in Amelia's chest disintegrated. She was close to sobbing, further embarrassment. With every ounce of strength she possessed, she made her voice as cold as the ocean crashing far below. "You're right. I wasn't thinking. Forget I said anything." She shouldered the backpack, swiveled around, and started walking off.

"Animal!"

"Don't come with me. And don't call me that!"

Eyes blurring with tears, Amelia started the interminably long hike back, humiliated. Alone. Again.

31

Later that night, Parker sat in bed with Matty, intrigued to hear the rough edit of the two interviews her wife had recorded with Jules and Ludmila. On the question of what makes a good mum:

Jules: *Someone who's always there, always available. You have to put your kids first!*

Ludmila: *A woman with a strong sense of self. You can't meet anyone else's needs until you're meeting your own.*

What was the best thing you ever gave your children?

Jules: *Unconditional love. I also handmade all your party dresses until you told me not to.*

Ludmila: *Independence.*

Is it morally reprehensible to have a child in this day and age?

Jules: *What do you mean, sausage? Being a mum is the best thing I ever did! Gosh, I can't wait to be a grandma, I'm getting all teary just thinking about it.*

Ludmila: *Probably.*

Parker snorted in amusement. She'd always found her mother's dark take to be funny, even if Parker's own sense of humor wasn't nearly as black. "I really like your edits, boo boo. Feels like neither of them is right or wrong, just different."

For someone who cherished compliments, Matty seemed preoccupied. "Thanks, boo boo. That's what I was going for."

Parker wondered if Matty planned on interviewing her. Far from a chore, the prospect was intriguing: a place to share her emerging new feelings on parenthood. But now wasn't the time to bring it up. There were only a few minutes left before her first Zoom call of seven. Parker slid off the bed to go put on a bra. The physical restriction helped delineate work from not-work. "Have you started recording your own tape yet?"

"Mmm, sort of."

"What's the angle? Of the whole thing? How does the island figure in?"

Her wife closed her laptop. "Not sure. Hey, did you notice how weird Animal was at dinner tonight? She barely said a word."

Parker suspected this was a redirect but figured it was still too early in the creative process for Matty to sum up her vision. Perhaps the fact that neither Jules nor Ludmila embodied a model of motherhood Matty related to was confusing or disheartening. But whose mother did? Generations were always carving new normals. Case in point, Parker would become a parent *two decades* later than her own mom. They'd make it up as they went along, and there'd be a kid, a funny, awesome, adorable kid in the picture. The idea made Parker's seven Zooms feel like a walk on the beach. Compared to being a parent, this was probably peanuts.

They spent a minute or so discussing gloomy Amelia, Matty getting ready for bed as Parker slicked on some mascara and tidied up her brows. Parker could tell Matty was done talking about the interviews. But something about them nagged her. Only as she was just about to leave did she figure out what it was. "How do you think the kid's going to feel?" she asked. "Listening to this?"

"The kid?"

"Our kid."

Matty looked surprised, even alarmed, as if Parker had just found said kid in the walk-in closet. Her wife took an unusually long moment to lasso a pithy reply. "Obviously they're going to be impressed I spent six weeks on an island working so hard."

Not what Parker was expecting or meant. "Say this podcast ends up on the internet, and in seven or eight years' time, Matty Jr. is listening back to their grandmothers, and you, presumably, discussing their existence. How will they feel?"

"Seven or eight *years*?! Parks, I don't know what's happening in seven or eight *days*!"

"Calm down. I'm just saying—"

"I can't think about making something for a fictional audience of one, that's absolutely insane!"

"Future," Parker said. "Not fictional. I'm not trying to restrict you, sweetie, I'm just trying to help you see the full picture. Think of things you're not thinking of."

Matty stared at her, close to aghast. Her reaction seemed out of proportion to what Parker felt was a helpful note.

Marriage was part love story, part power play. Who was offended or needed comfort, who got their way, whose needs were prioritized rolled back and forth like the endless tide. Matty was a powerful woman, born of a powerful woman. It'd taken Parker years to figure out how best to move in synchronicity with her, in a way that kept them both sated. And some scrapes just weren't worth having.

"Or not," Parker said with a shrug. "Maybe in seven or eight years' time we'll all be living on Mars. Night."

"Night," Matty echoed, switching off the bedside light.

Parker closed the bedroom door behind her.

The house was dark and quiet, everyone already in their respective bedrooms. It was usually so full of people it felt odd when it was empty, like a blank canvas hanging on a wall.

32

The following morning Ludmila was waiting by the front door of Kooroy when Jarrah approached carrying two fishing rods, an old canvas bag slung over one shoulder. "G'day," he greeted her. "Heard someone's after a lesson."

Ludmila nodded. "I can offer fifty dollars an hour."

Jarrah chuckled. "You don't need to pay me. I like teaching people to fish. But you can make a donation to the council. Funds go toward educational and community development programs."

She nodded again, committing to this. "Let's go."

He squinted at her outfit: a white linen T-shirt tucked into the tailored pants she'd worn on the plane, a silk scarf knotted at her neck. Currently, her most casual outfit. "It's a pretty messy business."

"I'm ready."

They walked along the foreshore, sand getting into Ludmila's sandals until she slipped them off. The warm sand felt surprisingly good underfoot, crunchy, like a natural exfoliant.

Jarrah explained that the best time of day to fish was early morning or late afternoon; fish preferred low light, ideally on a rising tide, which brought the food the fish were after onto the beach. "It's better over on Mooka, but there's still a few spots here." He scanned the ocean.

"What are you looking for?"

"See how the waves are washing over those sandbars? Fish like to feed in the gutters between them. You can tell by the color of the water—the deeper it is, the bluer the water looks. See that bit there?" He pointed to a patch of lapis lazuli ocean. "That's our spot."

Jarrah handed Ludmila the shorter of the two rods, showing how to rest it against her hip, the best place for each of her fingers. It was heavier than she was expecting, and longer. "Reel. Line. Rod." He pointed to each part of the apparatus. "Sinker, kept in place by a swivel, to keep the bait on the ocean floor. Too heavy, you won't feel the nibbles; too light, it'll get washed around. Bait to lure the fish. We're after whiting, so we're using yabbies."

"Yabbies?"

"Like little prawns. And the hook's to catch the fish." He demonstrated with his finger, hooking it into the corner of his mouth.

Ludmila memorized each word.

"First step: casting."

They spent a few minutes practicing the deceptively difficult act of getting the baited hook into the water: flicking the tip of the rod to cast the line far ahead of them, letting it sink, and reeling it in slowly until the tension on the line settled. A delicate, technical act. Ludmila tried a half dozen times before she got it right. Jarrah whistled in appreciation as her hook arced all the way to the edge of the sand bank, settling into the deeper water. "That looks pretty good."

"Now what?"

"Now," he said, casting next to her. "We fish."

He showed her where to place her dominant fingertip on the line to feel the gentle tug of a fish biting, at which point the line should be jerked back to hook the fish. "Pull too hard or fast and you'll pull the hook right out of its mouth. Wait too long, and the fish has his feed and you're fishin' with no bait."

It'd been weeks since Ludmila focused on her sense of touch, such a pivotal part of her professional life. This honed sensitivity was coming alive in the way it did when being presented with a new textile, one that didn't feel like it looked. She felt a nudge and yanked the line back.

"Got something?"

"I don't know."

He put his finger on her line, feeling the odd, tapping pulse she could feel. "That's just the sinker bumpin' on the ocean floor."

"How can I tell the difference between a bite and the sinker?"

He shrugged, grinning. "Practice. The sea has a rhythm. Look: waves moving in, and out. In, and out. Like breath."

"Like breath," Ludmila repeated.

Jarrah indicated her rod. "Let's check your bait."

Obediently, she reeled the line in. The hook was bare. "I didn't feel a thing."

He rebaited her hook for her. "They say there's a fine line between fishing and standing on the shore like an idiot. At least in a boat, you can easily move if they're not bitin'," he added.

"Do you miss it?" Ludmila asked. "Fishing in your boat?"

"More than I should, mate. More than I should."

They fished without success for another half hour. Jarrah decided to head back to camp before it got dark. "You comin'?" he asked, reeling his line in.

"I'll stay a few more minutes," she said. "If you don't mind lending me the rod."

"All yours."

Ludmila fished on the beach for another hour. She'd assumed she'd be able to catch at least one fish on her first try. As she stood casting and waiting and jerking the line, her impatience melted away.

A fresh sea breeze lifted the tiny hairs on her arms even as the last rays of the sun warmed her skin. Warmth and coolness, mixing in the clean, salt-thick air. The tide splashed about her ankles, the cold water a pleasant shock every time. Standing with the heavy rod pressed to her hip, her fingers monitoring the sensitive line, Ludmila felt simultaneously connected to the beach and the ocean and the sky and herself. How deeply meditative, to simply stand, and feel all the elements of this strange and beautiful place. A wonderfully rich mix of pure sensation.

She closed her eyes.

She could still smell it. The unique combination of sweat, Tiger Balm, and hairspray.

She could still hear it. The sound of collective breath.

Something pulled the line under her fingertip, a deliberate yank. The tip of the rod tugged toward the water. Jarrah hadn't talked through what would happen if she actually caught a fish. In a panic, she started reeling in, her heart racing. The line kept pulling, until—*bozhe moi!*—a silver fish emerged from the ocean, twisting at the end of her line. "Ha!" In triumph she pulled the rod back hard. The too-quick motion flipped the fish free. It fell back toward the water, disappearing into the ocean.

Ludmila exhaled in disbelief. A mistake—a costly one. And yet it did not deter her. She had learned long ago that the only thing standing between the beginner and the master was ego.

It was dusk. The cooler air was more richly scented with the smell of the bush, the sea. The inhabitants of Kooroy would be wondering where she was. Ludmila reeled in the wet line, securing the hook like Jarrah showed her. Scooping up her sandals, she started in the direction of home, already certain that she would request another lesson tomorrow.

33

The first thing Jules had been focused on missing while stranded on Mun'dai was Matty's IUI appointment. The second was her own birthday, the coming Friday. She'd be turning sixty-one on Mun'dai, which, all things considered, wasn't a bad place to celebrate another trip around the sun.

"It'll be a full moon on Friday," Ludmila remarked. "And high tide at just after 7:00 p.m."

Mildly confused as to why Ludmila knew the tide times for a date days away, Jules asked what she meant.

Ludmila looked at her like she was a bit slow. "Maybe a good night for a party?"

A party! A moonlit swim, dinner outside, firepit at the Barefoot Bar. It'd be nice to do something as a family, considering the last time they did was the infamous ballroom-dancing-dentist Games Night.

And it'd be a good thing to invite Jarrah to.

He was still camping by Karbunya, the freshwater creek that flowed through the northern tip of the island from Blinky to Mooka. Floating the creek and meandering back along the bordered pathway that ran alongside it was one of the island's key attractions; both Matty and Amelia had come back raving. On Friday afternoon, Jules slipped a long-sleeved shirt over her swimsuit, grabbed a donut-shaped floatie, and followed the map up the beach to the mouth of the creek. After a slightly awkward struggle to get herself situated in the floatie, she was off.

Karbunya was a tidal creek, affected by the ebb and flow of the ocean. Jules had checked that the tide would be coming in, the current taking her to Jarrah's spot. The creek moved slowly, carrying her west. The water was cold and clear enough to see every moss-edged rock on the bottom. The gentle murmur of insects and twittering peeps of tiny birds wove a dreamlike spell as she passed under the shade of the casuarina trees. She almost started to drift off, before the creek rounded a bend, and there was Jarrah's camp.

A large army-green tent, its entrance unzipped, faced the creek. A folding chair and a few books were positioned under a large shade cloth. Towels and shirts flapped on a clothesline, drying in the sun. There was a campfire, unlit, and a large cooler. The ability to camp was an attractive talent. It indicated a certain ruggedness and self-sufficiency Jules admired.

She'd just pulled the floatie onto the bank when Jarrah appeared, post-swim: hair wet, towel over one shoulder, in a pair of red swimming trunks. Her heart belly-flopped into the creek.

"G'day!" she called, picking her way up the bank.

"Julia," he greeted her with a surprised smile.

"Sorry to just drop by. Or float by, I guess." She was suddenly conscious of her bikini line—unwaxed since the nineties—on full display. She tugged the edge of her shirt around the tops of her thighs.

"No worries. Just had a swim at Mooka." He toweled his hair, his biceps cresting and receding. His chest was broad, his back strong as hardwood.

"A swim is actually what I'm here about. It's my birthday, and we're all getting together tonight for a moonlit dip and a fire at the Barefoot Bar. We'll have food and drink—nonalcoholic options, of course. Just very casual."

"Sounds lovely," he said. "Did you need my help with something?"

"Oh no, I'm inviting you!" Jules chuckled. "Sorry—what a goose I am. I'd love you to come."

She expected him to accept, happily. Instead, his face turned unsure. "I dunno. Sounds like a family thing."

"Liss is coming," Jules said. "She's as much family as you are."

His uncertainty flipped to disbelief.

Some people—people like Jules—like being included in other families. Jarrah, evidently, found it presumptuous.

"It's not just a family thing," Jules amended. "It's a birthday thing that quite literally everyone on the island is invited to."

"Yeah—better not." He hung his towel over the clothesline and gave her an apologetic smile.

Jules was radically unprepared for Jarrah to decline. After their lunch at the rock art, they'd bumped into each other on Blinky Beach days later. They'd got to chatting, mostly about a mentor program Jarrah ran for young rangers, "youngfellas," over on K'Gari. "Sort of like a big brother thing," he'd said, which had impressed Jules greatly. She admired anyone who volunteered, especially with kids. They'd talked for hours. She thought they were friends.

No: she had a crush. Her dusty old heart had a crush and only now, in the moment her feelings were unequivocally not returned, was she able to admit it.

"Oh." She grasped for the right thing to say. "Oh, um . . . okay. No worries."

"But happy birthday. Hope it's a great night." He turned to pull a dry shirt off the line.

"Thanks," she managed, gathering her wits enough to turn in the direction of the floatie and begin making her way to the water.

Why didn't she enlist Liss to ask, to have mitigated this disappointment? Jules had definitely been planning on doing more things with Jarrah—seeing more rock art, maybe, or feeding him more thick-cut sandwiches. Sharing more of her past. She wanted to tell him that she made her own paper out of garlic skin and artichoke leaves and about the willy wagtails who visited her birdbath back home in Sydney and that once, when she was fifteen, she'd shoplifted a pink plastic bracelet and took it back the next day expecting trouble, but the shopkeeper just laughed and said, "Darlin', you keep it."

But he wasn't interested in her. She was a soon-to-be-separated mother of two in her sixties, so far past the flush of youth she could

barely remember it. The slight embarrassment she felt at her hairy bikini
line bloomed into full-fledged mortification: at her saggy boobs and
dimpled thighs. All the monstrous thoughts about herself and her body
that she worked so hard—*so hard*—to keep at bay attacked like angry
wasps.

Her body would never be desired by a man like Jarrah, ever again.
Her body was old, a failed version of her younger self, like something left
outside overnight and ruined. She was an old woman. No one wanted
an old woman. They wanted them to shut up and go away. Women mattered when they were young and beautiful, and once they weren't, they
were just an unattractive inconvenience. Shame filled her like brackish
water, turning everything ugly.

Jules nudged the floatie back into the creek. With every ounce of
inner strength she possessed, she gave Jarrah a friendly wave, a smile
slapped on so hard it made her eyes water. If either of her daughters felt
this way when they were her age, it would break her heart. "Hooroo!"

But Jarrah wasn't looking at her. He was looking past her, to the creek.
His mouth was slightly ajar. "What the bloody hell are you doing here?"

There, in the clear water, not more than six feet from where she
stood, was an enormous sea turtle.

Its shell was the size of a tire, its flippers and head tiled in rust-red
and cream. Its eyes were almond-shaped, moonless-black. The eyes of
someone much older and wiser than she.

Jarrah was gesturing for her to come back up the bank. "Slowly," he
murmured. "Don't want to scare the poor bugger any more than he already is."

Jules picked her way back up the bank, rejoining Jarrah on the grass.
"I take it you don't usually see turtles that big in this creek?"

"Don't see turtles like that in this creek at all." A light went off behind his eyes. "The surge. Must've washed it in. Poor thing's too big to
get out on its own."

"Can it live in freshwater?"

"Not permanently."

"You look so rattled." Jules touched his arm in sympathy. "I'm sure we
can help get it back to sea."

"We can, we can," he said. "It's just . . ." His face took on the expression of an awed little boy.

"What?"

"Sea turtles are my totem animal."

"What's a totem animal?"

"Sorta like a spiritual emblem," he hedged. "All Aboriginal people have one, inherited through family. A descendant of the Dreaming. Connected to our spirituality. They have special meaning."

He held her gaze.

Something sweet and warm passed between them in the honeyed afternoon light.

The turtle didn't think of itself as old or ugly. The ancient mariner swam. It ate. It lived. Jules was reminded that our greatest teachers were all around us. We just had to pay attention to their lessons.

"Tide's already turning," Jarrah said. "We've got about three hours to dig this poor fella out."

Jules rolled up her sleeves.

They spent twenty sweaty minutes trying to gently move the enormous sea creature beyond the mouth of the creek, into the ocean. But the turtle was too heavy, easily three hundred pounds, and the mouth of the creek was too narrow: it'd need to be dug out.

"Let's call for backup," Jules suggested. "As long as I have time to shower before tonight." She indicted her straggly hair and mud-streaked skin with a wry smile. "Not the birthday look I was going for."

Jarrah laughed. The physical effort had softened things between them. "What time's your shindig kicking off?"

"Seven?"

He nodded, his expression turning almost sheepish. "I'll be there."

Happiness flowed through her, pooling in the dark places.

34

Of all the unusual native animals on Mun'dai, one of the quirkiest was the echidna. This football-shaped loner had spines like a porcupine, a beak like a bird, a pouch like a kangaroo, and laid eggs like a reptile. Baby echidnas, called puggles, fed on their mother's milk through a patch of her skin, fine pores secreting milk through specialized hair follicles. Once the puggle started growing spikes, the mother left the baby in a burrow to go forage, returning every four to six days to feed her offspring. When the puggle was about six months old, mum dug her progeny out of the burrow, fed it one last time, and toddled off. She wouldn't return to the burrow or have any further contact with her young. The echidna was the oldest surviving mammal on the planet.

Matty Kelly didn't notice the one snuffling for ants on her morning bushwalk; she was busy monologuing aloud, scribbling notes for her podcast. "Is parenthood an essential component of the human experience? Or is there just a powerful cultural fiction that says being normal or fulfilled means having kids, which obviously isn't true?"

Matty was sweating, and not just from the muggy morning heat.

The extended time on the island, and the motherhood podcast project she'd elected to pursue, was making it increasingly difficult for Matilda Kelly not to confront marrow-deep fears that the chaotic pace of life in New York made it easy to ignore. Stories had a way of surfacing even the most well-buried hopes and fears. The pilot wasn't exploring what it meant to have kids. Almost of its own accord, the podcast pilot for *Stranded* was explicitly forming around the question of whether or not to have children *at all*.

If she was brutally honest with herself, the domestic life seemed at best banal, at worst, frightening. Matty didn't have the urge to look inward. She wanted to look out, at the world, and at her role in it. Maybe a new part of her heart would unlock as she became #blessed with her #littleangel. Or maybe she'd find herself chained to a diaper change-table, covered in baby poo, wondering if it would've been easier to get a dog. She'd secretly read *HuffPost*'s "Funniest Tweets from Parents This Week" as terrifying warnings from people whose lives were being run by tiny unpredictable dictators. Yes, she wanted someone to look after her when she was old, but no one could predict the future. Case in point: she was stuck on an island in the middle of the Coral Sea. Maybe by the year 2070, her iBrain would be uploaded to the cloud and her body would be stored in a box under the bed. Who knew?

Being a queer parent, specifically, was a significant part of Matty's concerns. She couldn't, nor did she want to, sink into heteronormative parenthood. Parenting with a woman definitely made the whole prospect more appealing—beyond the fact she loved Parker, Matty wouldn't be the only one relegated to domestic duties and emotional labor in the way so many of her married straight friends inevitably were, no matter how feminist their husbands claimed to be. But the idea she'd have to keep coming out again and again and again on the playground and at PTA meetings, navigating Father's Day and *yer-mum's-a-lez* bullying and explaining why almost every movie starred a "mum and dad" felt exhausting. Trailblazing was fine when it was a choice. But she didn't want to *have* to trailblaze every time some moron asked about the rug rat's father. Sexuality was weird in this way—in some ways it was the least significant part of her personality; in others, defining. Like it or not, she would always be a Gay Mum. That was *very* annoying.

More annoying still was the fact she couldn't just make a baby with Parker. They were using a Chinese donor so the baby might look like their theoretical spawn. But it wouldn't have Parker's excellent genes—her cool intelligence and endless patience and big heart. It'd have a *stranger's* DNA and honestly, wasn't that just a bit *weird*? Weirder still was pregnancy. Every time Matty imagined growing another human inside her she imagined *that* scene from *Alien*, followed by *that* scene from *Spaceballs*. Far from a profound rite of passage every woman should experience, giving birth was starting to feel like an abject horror show every sane person should avoid.

Publicly, Matty would usually never express any of this. Publicly, the conversation was still about creating and defending the right for the LGBTQ+ community to parent, period. But for the purpose of the podcast pilot, this was where Matty Kelly was at. Art worked best when you were uncomfortably honest. When what you said would ruffle some feathers.

The fact that all of her files were password protected so her family wouldn't accidentally hear them was something Matty tried not to focus on.

When Matty arrived home to Kooroy, Amelia was making a cup of tea in the kitchen. "Where is everyone?" Amelia asked, giving Matty a hug.

"Ludmila's somewhere, no idea actually, and everyone else is helping dig a turtle out of the creek with Jarrah," Matty said, downing a glass of cold water. "Y'know, island stuff. You should've seen how excited Dad and Randall were. They got so intense about it, looking for shovels, then running up the beach like a couple of aging action heroes."

Amelia poured two cups of tea. "Is Liss with them?"

"She was the one who texted, so I assume so. Go help if you want."

"I'm good." Amelia handed her the tea. "How are you?"

A half hour later, out on the balcony, Matty wrapped up a TED Talk on gay parenting, tempering her words as a bloodletting on the *inevitability* of being a gay mum, not, as was more accurate, an investigation of it. She recorded the conversation on her phone as possible tape for the podcast without mentioning to her sister the explosive question at the heart of the show. "Of course I'd like to be talking to my wife about all this, but she's out cold." Matty gestured toward the bedroom. "And honestly, I don't want to stress or upset her. Poppe's a bit of a nightmare, and I think she's sparing me the worst of it. And neither of us planned to be starting our marriage while living with the rellies. There's never a good time to bring any of this up."

"Poor Parker," Amelia murmured. Her voice pitched higher. "How did you win her over in the end?"

"What d'you mean?"

"Well, there was all that drama for so long— What happened in the end? I don't know if I ever got the full story."

Matty shrugged, feeling facetious. "She realized she couldn't be happy without me."

"Aw." Amelia's smile became a question. "And how did she realize that?"

"Wasn't like there was one moment or anything." Matty thought back. "Although, I guess, if there was one moment, it would've been Levi's thirtieth."

Amelia sat forward, looking the most engaged she'd been all afternoon. "What happened at Levi's thirtieth?"

"We were broken up, again, and I'd kind of been a dramatic mess about it, threatening to skip the party. Levi got so mad, going on about how I had to '*Kate Middleton circa 2007 this shit. No more Waity Katie—you have to show up looking hot as fuck and show her what she's missing. Just like Kate did to Wills when they were broken up: that's how she landed her prince.*' So I did. I Middleton-ed her." Matty chuckled, remembering the epic night. "I wore this amazing metallic-gold jumpsuit—totally extra—I got a blowout and a mani and was just the right amount of buzzed. I brought a date, this comedian friend of mine, and Parker followed me around all night like a lost puppy. By midnight she was attacking me in the bathroom, and yada yada yada, we're married." Matty laughed. Of course, it'd been more complicated than that—she could write a thesis on the art of partnership and barely scratch the surface—but there was no denying that night had been a turning point.

"So 'hard to get' works with women," Amelia said, sounding surprised. "And dressing sexy and stuff."

"We're all just human beings," Matty said, relishing the chance for a mini-lecture. "Gender's a construct, and so is gendered behavior. We all get jealous; we all get horny. Most women want sex just as much as most men. Anything else is just blah blah blah patriarchy."

Amelia sat back in her chair, thinking. Always satisfying to see her absorbing Matty's words of wisdom. "Well, thanks for that," she said, getting up. "Better start getting ready for the party."

"Yeah, I need to finish these notes," Matty said, feeling apprehensive about her developing subject, but also, undeniably, excited. Uncomfortable personal truths made for good art. "I'll talk to Parker after the party."

"Does she have a swimsuit I can borrow?"

Matty pointed to her spouse's light blue string bikini, drying on the balcony. "Might be a bit small on you." Amelia's butt and boobs were twice the size of Parker's.

Amelia scooped up the scraps of material. "This'll work."

"Animal?" Matty called after her. "I just wanna say: it's really nice when you take an interest in my relationship, and gender stuff. I really like sharing with you."

Amelia stared back, her cheeks a tiny bit pink.

Why she was wearing blush on the island was totally beyond Matty. Who was she trying to impress?

35

It took Glen, Randall, Liss, Jules, and Jarrah all afternoon to get the giant turtle safely back into the sea. Digging out the mouth of the creek was sweaty, high-stakes work. The turtle was an endangered species in distress, but the sudden rescue mission was also undeniably fun. It reminded Glen of being a young man living in Sydney, out with friends on some harebrained mission, when the world felt fresh and full of potential. It was bonding; it meant something. The five worked well as a team, utilizing Jarrah's and Jules's combined knowledge about turtles and plants and water systems. And Glen was impressed with how his body held up, a result of his training sessions with Randall. After receiving the text that help was needed, he and Randall jogged up Blinky Beach to the mouth of Karbunya Creek, paddled a two-man canoe to Jarrah's camp, *then* spent two-and-a-half hours digging wet sand. Finally, in a Herculean effort, all five of them carried the turtle over a final shallow bit, setting it free. As they stood shoulder to shoulder on Mooka Mooka Beach, watching a wild creature swim home as the sun set over the Pacific, Glen had tears in his eyes. He'd never experienced such a beautiful sense of accomplishment.

After canoeing back up the creek to Blinky Beach, he and Randall were taking a breather before heading the couple miles back to Kooroy to get ready for Jules's party. The sun had just set. The bay was a pink-

and-silver mirror. They sat on the sand, exhausted yet energized, delving into a play-by-play of everything that'd just happened.

"I had no idea turtles got that big," Randall said, wiping his brow with the edge of his shirt.

"I know, bloody enormous!" Glen said. "There was a moment, right at the end, when I didn't think we'd make it."

"When Jules got caught on that tree branch." Randall laughed. "But you know who saved the day?"

"Liss," they answered together. It felt like remembering a favored colleague or notable party guest. A warm, expansive generosity settled over the two men.

"Liss is great." Glen leaned back on his elbows. "So funny."

"Very funny, very good sense of humor," Randall agreed.

"Dry sense of humor."

"Very dry. Very quick."

"Is that a Canadian thing?" Glen pondered.

"Probably," Randall said. "Probably a Canadian thing. And what about Jarrah?"

"Oh, good bloke." Glen shook his head in admiration. "Great bloke."

"In great shape," Randall said. "Excellent triceps."

"Smart guy."

"Very smart. Knew exactly what to do."

Which brought them to Jules. She'd elected to head back with Liss to the Caretaker Cabin to pick up some ice for the party, which, to Glen's ears, sounded like an excuse not to travel back with him. It'd been fine working together, of course: there were five of them, and things between the couple remained civil. But Glen wondered if Randall picked up on the tension between him and his wife.

"Jules knows how to handle herself." Randall sounded diplomatic.

Glen pulled a piece of spinifex out of the sand, tossing it away. "Yeah. Always been an outdoors girl."

They sat in silence for a moment, watching two pied oystercatchers scurry around the shoreline. The name was a misnomer. The black-and-white birds seldom ate oysters, instead prizing apart mollusks with their bright orange bills. The two birds ran daintily around the edge of the tide, as if afraid of getting their knees wet. A pair for life.

"Should we get going?" asked Randall at the same time Glen said, "Jules and I are separated."

"Ah, shit." Randall shook his head in sympathy. "I'm sorry, man. That's tough."

Glen hadn't told a soul about his separation. He didn't know what else to say. He gave Randall a slightly helpless look.

"Do the kids know yet?" Randall asked.

"No. Jules wants to wait until Matty and Parker are settled in Sydney."

"How do you think they'll take it?"

"Not well, I don't think. They're adults, but y'know . . ."

"Every kid wants to think their parents are in love."

"Yeah," Glen said. "Guess so."

A seagull landed near them. They were always bigger than they looked in the sky: beer-belly barrel chest and cold blue eyes. It reminded Glen of his father. He flicked his hand to shoo it off. The bird lunged for his fingers. Glen flinched, cowering back.

Go on, take a swing. Would that make ya feel better?

"Should we head back?" Randall asked.

"Righto." Glen got to his feet. He assumed that was The Talk With Randall About His Divorce. But he'd forgotten a key factor. Matty's father-in-law was an American. And Americans liked to talk about feelings. Even Rambo Randall.

"So," Randall said. "What happened with Jules?"

Glen attempted to condense his entire marriage into a couple minutes. Which became ten minutes. Fifteen. It wasn't simple to explain the feeling of coasting through life thanks to his wife's unfaltering momentum and his own desire to be a good guy who didn't ruffle anyone's feathers. Having never related to Australian machoism, he'd always felt like a bit of an outsider. His family provided shelter, and a role, and rules. But with that shelter soon gone, he was starting to feel lost. Anxious and confused about what was supposed to happen next.

When they passed the Barefoot Bar, Glen realized he'd been mono-loguing for almost the entire beach. He pulled up short with a hot, embarrassed laugh. "I've been yakking on for way too long about this, I'm sorry."

"I asked," Randall said. "And it's good to share."

The topic was heavy. Unloading a bit of it onto Randall made Glen feel lighter. "Yeah. It is good. Ah, I just wish we could tell the kids. I don't like it's a secret. I'm worried they're gonna hate me for it. I don't know what I'd do without my girls."

"Sounds like you're a great father," Randall said.

He'd tried to be a good dad, kind and accommodating. Did it matter his girls never confided in him like he was confiding in Randall? Jules was the steward of their emotional inner lives; he'd never been invited to play that role. Or taken the initiative himself. The insight was a blurry one, glimpsed as if through fog. He was missing a point, but he wasn't sure what.

"Try to be," Glen said. "A good father. Not good enough to pick up that James-the-Shithead was married." A burst of angry remorse. "I can't believe I didn't figure it out. I met him!"

"I didn't know my daughter was gay." Randall puffed out a breath, staring at the roll and curl of the waves.

A great-winged petrel sailed past them over the ocean. Fast flight with a flexed wrist, heavy head angled downward. Deep-sea specialist. Adept at being alone. "It's not easy, is it?"

"What isn't easy?"

"Being alive, I guess."

"Better than the alternative."

Glen chuckled. He was really glad Randall was on this trip. And he wanted to believe Randall felt the same way. Maybe that was the piece of the puzzle he was missing: something to do with intimacy and honesty and opening up to other human beings. "Thanks for listening, mate. Not used to 'talking it out,' like you Americans."

Randall grinned, and put a hand on Glen's shoulder, leaning into his accent. "Happy to help."

Warm and sincere. Genuine.

And then, out of nowhere, came a sound. *The* sound. The low, haunting cry.

"Boobook, boobook. Boobook, boobook."

Both men went stock-still. Stared at each other. Inhaled a clipped breath. Glen spun clockwise. Randall spun counterclockwise. Scanning the trees, the beach, the air.

"That was it, that was it, that was it," Randall whispered, eyes wide.

"I heard it, I heard it, I heard it!" Glen whispered back, punchy with adrenaline.

"Where's your phone?"

"It's dead. Where's yours?"

"Didn't bring it."

"Shit!"

Randall ran north up the beach. Glen ran south down the beach. Randall ran south down the beach. Glen ran north up the beach. They searched. And listened. And looked. And waited.

Minutes passed. Nothing. Not even an egret. But it still felt like a victory.

"That was it, that was definitely it," Glen said, pumped.

"I told you. I told you!" Randall said, equally pumped.

"Randall." Glen looked him right in the eye. "We are one step closer to proving the Lady Lushington Boobook is no longer extinct."

"Glen," Randall said. "We *will* prove the Lady Lushington Boobook is no longer extinct. I know we will." He clapped his hands together. "Right. I'm going to put together a thorough plan of attack for us. Consistency and a targeted approach is key."

The two men high-fived, so full of excitement they were bouncing on their toes.

A full moon was rising over the ocean. The sky was dusky-blue, daubed with fat clouds and white terns sailing home for the night.

"We better get going," Glen said. "But we can pick this up again tomorrow. Or later tonight."

"Roger that." Randall fell into step with Glen as they began striding toward Kooroy. "Hey, should we make up a secret Boobook handshake?"

"Definitely," said Glen, dead serious. "We should definitely make up a secret Boobook handshake."

36

Amelia dressed for her mother's party as carefully as an assassin preparing for a kill.

It'd been an excruciating week. Telling Liss exactly how attractive she found her was the single most humiliating event of Amelia's entire thirty-three years. That night she'd laid in bed for hours, praying for early dementia to wipe her memory, *Eternal Sunshine*–style. Instead, a hideously heightened version of their lunch played on loop. By 2:00 a.m., all Amelia could picture was herself pinning a petrified Liss to the ground to scream in her face, "I LOVE HOT MUSICIANS WITH ACCENTS, WHICH MEANS I LOVE YOU!!"

As a serial monogamist and die-hard romantic, Amelia was unaccustomed to concepts like rebound sex or one-night stands. Deep down, she didn't really believe "casual" sex existed—the idea that you could have sex with someone without exchanging a piece of your soul was foreign. But everyone else her age seemed to be hooking up all the time. Wasn't this the perfect time to try it? And wasn't Liss the perfect person to be trying it with? No-strings-attached sexiness was something adults in full control of their bodies and emotions did all the time. Amelia Kelly decided it was about time she grew up and gave it a red-hot go.

She'd obviously freaked Liss out with her carnal Christmas list and hadn't made things better by chucking a tanty then storming off like a child. But at least she'd successfully avoided her all week, maybe, hopefully, giving Liss a chance to miss her. Obviously, they had a connection; Liss said she was attracted to her, too. There weren't any real reasons why they couldn't hook up, not now they were both single.

On the night of her mother's birthday, a full moon the size of a whale hung over Pigface Bay, its brilliance bleaching the beach as if for a film shoot.

Amelia spent most of the afternoon baking and decorating and setting everything up. Now, she swiveled in front of the mirror in the Yellow Cottage, assessing every inch of her golden curves. Parker's light blue string bikini left only the best bits to the imagination. The tiny bottom was high cut and tied at her hipbones while the triangle halter top clung to her C-cups. Her freshly blown-out hair waterfalled down her back. Gloss glistened on her lips. The combined effect would hopefully eliminate all memories of Amelia being weepy or stinky or hopelessly desperate. Admittedly, a long shot. But one worth taking aim at. Amelia slipped on her fringed kimono and blew herself a kiss. Having a bangin' bod was not a personal achievement, but she could work it. And if Matty was right, and queer women were just as attracted to a chick in a bikini as straight guys were, Liss Chambers didn't know what the hell was about to hit her.

Amelia arrived late, assuming Liss, who didn't really know anyone except Jarrah, would be sitting alone, adorably awkward and eager for her company. Amelia was wrong. Evidently this turtle mission had bonded the group. Amelia approached the spot of activity on the warm, moon-bright beach to find Liss chatting with her father and Randall like they were all best friends, calling out some inside joke to Jules and Jarrah as the pair headed in for a swim. Ludmila was sipping wine in an Adirondack chair. Parker and Matty were trying to get the fire going, fiddling with the kindling. Her sister didn't even look up. "Animal, find me some matches."

Amelia put the lemon layer cake she'd made on a folding table piled with drinks and snacks, and cut her eyes at Liss, assuming she'd notice her arrival.

But Liss, Randall, and Glen were all miming carrying something heavy, animated and oblivious.

Why had she bothered shaving her legs?

She tossed Matty the matches, trying not to feel huffy. The moon-light bounced off the water, and in the near-distance, the long wooden wharf. It was already April: this would all come to an end in a manner of weeks. The surge was long gone from the news cycle, the travel ban was over. Thankfully far-flung Mun'dai with its tiny population of healthy tourists was last on the pickup list. Jarrah had confirmed his initial esti-mate, with R-Day—Rescue Day—scheduled for the last week of April. Amelia didn't want to leave the island with any regrets. Or feeling like she hadn't done everything she wanted—with increasing intensity—to do.

"Amelia, darling, come in!" Jules called from the water, waving. *"You never regret a swim!"*

Thank goddess for her mum. "Okay!" she yelled back, a little louder than necessary. Hoping it'd been enough to get Liss's attention, Amelia let her kimono slip off her shoulders.

It fell onto Matty's head, who batted it off. "Jesus, those swimmers are way too small for you. I can basically see your labia."

"I think they fit really well."

"Why are you so dressed up?" Matty looked in the direction Amelia was deliberately not. Her sister frowned and shook her head, as if having misheard something.

"What?" Amelia asked.

Matty's tone sounded oddly light. "For a ridiculous second, I thought you were Middleton-ing Liss."

The bull's-eye rendered Amelia dumb. If Matty knew, everyone else would in about five minutes, scaring Liss off forever.

Matty did a double take at the expression on Amelia's face and raised her hands. "Calm down, my mistake. For the record, you'd make a super-hot couple."

Her sister's assumptions were impossible to dismantle. For once, they worked in Amelia's favor. She resumed her role of the heterosexual sister, affecting a dismissive snort. "Don't be insane."

"You'd be happier with a woman. Deep down, everyone's bisexual. *Everyone.*"

Amelia arched her back to pull her hair into a high pony. She was dying to know if Liss was watching. Too soon to check. "I'll keep that in mind."

Matty went back to the fire with a satisfied grunt.

Pony secured, Amelia pretended to adjust her top, sliding the light blue scrap of stretchy fabric around her nipple. Sensation tingled hard through her body, all the way across her back. The peep-show-for-one was turning herself on, heartbeat quickening, mouth getting dry. She wanted Liss to be doing these things. Touching her in this way. Was she watching? Amelia scooped up a smidge of cream cheese icing with her fingertip and put it in her mouth, sucking as she snuck a peek in Liss's direction.

Liss was staring.

Her fingers were pressed to her open mouth. On catching Amelia's eye, she dropped her hand and snapped away, pretending to reengage with Randall and Glen. But even with twenty feet between them, Amelia could see Liss was starting to blush. She couldn't focus on the banter. As if against her own will, her gaze was tugged back to Amelia. Tracing slowly up her legs. Caressing her boobs. Landing on her mouth.

They locked eyes.

Even as her blood pounded hot, Amelia kept her expression ice-cool.

Liss looked like someone had just punched her in the face.

Amelia spun on her toes to give Liss a good perve at her ass. "Coming, Mum!" she called, doing her best *Baywatch* jog into the warm waters of Pigface Bay. Feeling Liss's gaze all over her, every slo-mo step of the way.

37

The family sat around the fire under a sweep of impossibly bright stars, listening to Jarrah share stories about the Dreaming.

"There are over five hundred Indigenous clans in Australia," he said. "All with their own language and myths. So when I talk about the Dreaming, it might be different from how another Aboriginal person might talk about it."

The fire hissed and popped, jumping light around Jarrah's face. He always had a natural, easy confidence. But tonight, Jules thought he looked like a king.

"The Dreaming is not a time in the past. It is the past, the present, and the future. It is the living world itself. It belongs to every Aboriginal person. It's our stories, our guides, our spirituality," Jarrah said. "The most famous creation myth is that of the Rainbow Serpent. One of the oldest continuing religious beliefs in the world."

Jules squeezed her girls closer. She'd read this story to them when they were little.

"The way it was told to me," Jarrah went on. "Was in the beginning, the world was flat and barren; asleep. The Rainbow Serpent awoke from where she'd been sleeping under the ground. She began traveling far and wide. The movement of her body created winding tracks, shaping the flat earth. She called to awake the frogs. They awoke with bellies full of water. The Rainbow Serpent tickled their stomachs and when the frogs laughed, water spilled out all over the earth to fill the tracks of the Rainbow Serpent. This is how the lakes and the rivers were first formed."

Jules pictured Karbunya Creek gushing with water, springing to life.

"Now, when we see a shooting star, it's the Rainbow Serpent, still watching over us. Watching over you, Julia." Jarrah raised his seltzer in a toast. "On your birthday."

The family clapped and raised their glasses, chorusing a mix of "Happy birthday, Mum-Jules."

"Thank you Jarrah. Thanks, everyone," Jules said. "I'm just so happy to be here with my girls."

"And Dad," Amelia prompted.

"And Dad," Jules hurried to add. "The love of my life."

Glen gave her an *oh, c'mon* look. Jules accepted it guiltily, shoving it out of sight. Not a lie, per se. Just not exactly the truth.

Matty started handing out forks and the aluminum-foil packets that'd been cooking in the fire's embers. Each contained a steaming fish, the tender white flesh stuffed with preserved lemon and garlic. Jarrah must've brought them. As everyone dug into dinner, Jules moved from her position between her daughters to sit next to him on the other side of the fire. "That was one of the best birthday presents I've ever received."

"My pleasure, Julia," he said. "And sorry about saying no, earlier. Wasn't anything personal."

Jules waved it off. "Of course."

"It's just, considering you and your husband are still, y'know . . ."

Jules glanced over at Glen, who for some unknown reason, was staring intensely at the treetops with Randall. She'd never understand that man. She didn't need to, anymore. She looked into Jarrah's warm brown eyes. "I'm just glad we're friends," she said, laying her hand briefly on his.

"Yeah." He smiled, not moving away. "I'm glad for that, too."

"God, this fish is amazing!" Matty forked half a fillet into her mouth. "Thanks, Jarrah. Dinner and a show: you're officially MVP."

"It's very good," Jarrah said, taking a bite himself. "But I didn't bring the fish."

Matty looked at Liss, who shook her head, then at Parker, who shrugged. "Wait, so where did this come from?"

"Me." Ludmila's expression was smug. "I caught the fish."

"What?" Parker almost screamed, twisting to face her mother. "You?"

"You're joking." Matty's jaw was loose. "There're ten fish here."

"You caught ten fish," Amelia said, "By yourself?"

"Did you pay off the fish somehow?" Liss asked. "I have heard they work for scale."

Amelia muted her laugh with a frown, as if hiding her amusement.

Ludmila looked exceedingly pleased with herself. "Not bad for a beginner."

Jarrah grinned. Jules tipped her head back and laughed.

Once they'd finished their meal, Amelia presented a cake with flickering candles.

"Make a wish, Mum."

Jules was a woman hungry for wishes: more laughter, more love, more *life*. But on this balmy April evening, her desire was motionless. The Dreaming as a past-present-future space swirled around her.

Jules wanted a present and future informed by integrity. A clarity of purpose, a commitment to growth. Her past was a complex place, full of bright spots of happiness threaded with a longing for something she didn't have words for. In thinking about the future, this night was what Jules wanted more of: connection and community. Things that surprised her. Generosity and joy. Jules felt an affinity with Jarrah, but she didn't yet know if it was with him as an individual or what he represented— someone living in closer harmony with the natural world. Someone with passion and opinions. Someone open to everything she couldn't explain about the universe, comfortable in the nonlinear, in a world where the past, present, and future might exist in synchronicity.

The candles went out in a breath.

Above her, a shooting star arced, burning a trail of silver fire. She gasped and looked again to Jarrah. He'd seen the star, too. They traded a smile, flicked in secret over the dancing orange flames.

38

Amelia dangled herself like a yabbie on a hook all night long, whisking herself away as soon as Liss attempted to talk to her. At first Liss seemed confused: maybe it was a coincidence Amelia had to use the bathroom or get another drink every time she approached. But as the full moon sailed overhead like a clock with no numbers, Amelia could see her antics landing as deliberate. She couldn't tell if Liss was amused or irritated or pained. Maybe all three. Whatever the effect, Amelia could feel Liss tracking her with increasing intensity. Waiting for an opportunity to pin her down and do . . . what?

Time to find out.

Everyone except Ludmila was dancing to Janis Joplin, Jules's favorite. Amelia made sure Liss noticed her slip toward the Barefoot Bar, under the pretense of getting more wine.

The bar was unlocked. Amelia switched on the single bulb overhead, illuminating the shelves of mismatched glasses and bottles of clear and brown booze. There was a cracked mirror over the sink. Stuck into the bottom of the frame was Sam, their joint winning card from *Highly Subjective Guess Who?* The fact Liss kept it, a memento to look at every day, gave Amelia a giddy thrust of confidence. She fluffed up her hair, channeling a 1960s sex kitten. *You can do this*, she instructed her reflection. *It's just sex, that's casual. What's so hard about that?*

Footsteps outside.

Amelia opened the fridge to grab the closest bottle of white.

Liss came in via the back door and closed it behind her. "Hi."

The two of them, in this tight space. The air between them became thicker, hotter.

"Oh, hello." Amelia pretended to examine the wine.

Liss stood in front of the fridge, arms folded. A bemused expression on her face.

Amelia put the wine on the sink, gesturing at the fridge. "Sorry, do you mind?"

Liss stepped aside, watching Amelia select another bottle. "What, are you playing hard-to-get?"

"No. Maybe." Amelia peeked over her shoulder, coquettish. "Is it working?"

Liss let out a laugh. She had three distinct laughs: a polite, low chortle when she wasn't actually amused; a hearty, punchy guffaw when she was; and a shy, nervous chuckle when she felt awkward or awed. This laugh was that last one. "Nice outfit."

"This old thing?" Amelia gave her a spin for the full effect.

Liss laughed again, the guffaw that dissolved into the self-conscious chuckle. She rubbed the back of her neck. "Is this how you're going to punish me? Parading around in things like that?"

"Why would that be a punishment? You're not into me."

"I never said that."

Amelia quoted her. *The timing isn't right.*

"The timing isn't right."

Amelia huffed in exasperation. "Who cares about timing? You know what they say: the best way to get over someone is to get under someone else." Horniness was making her hungry. She padded toward Liss. "Maybe we can help each other get over our exes."

Liss moved out of her path. "It can't be like that with you."

"Why not?"

"It can't be casual with you."

"Why not?"

"Jesus, Amelia! I like you." Liss met her gaze, held it. Color in her cheeks blooming like a sunrise. "I like you. A lot."

The words were a release. The hot-girl pretense Amelia had been working so hard to mimic washed away. Liss liked her. They liked each other, for real. She was suddenly so *happy*. "I like you, too."

Liss laughed: the nervous one. "I'm starting to get that impression." She took a step back, tearing her eyes away. "I have to close down the bar."

"Now?"

"Yep."

"Okay." Amelia hopped up onto the low freezer, taking the wine with her. Placing the cold bottle between her spread legs, she leant forward, supersizing her cleavage, and started uncorking the wine. Slowly.

Liss watched every move, one hand twisting into her faded-blue hair. "What are you doing?"

"You have to ask?" Amelia pulled the cork out with a *pop*. "I'm seducing you." She made a display of drinking from the bottle, letting rivulets of wine spill down her chin. Between her breasts.

Liss's chest was rising and falling with increasing speed. "And that usually works on people?"

"It's working on you." Amelia slid off the freezer, sidling closer, impish. "You're looking a little flushed, Liss." With the bottle still in one hand, she began stroking the swell of her wine-soaked boobs, running her fingers up and down, up and down, summoning trails of goose bumps. Beneath her bikini top, her nipples were hardening, brushing up against the tight fabric, deliciously sensitive. Aching to be touched by the person who looked like she was about to pass out.

"Are you trying to give me a heart attack?" Liss was attempting glib, but Amelia could see she was losing control. Her pupils were huge. She was clenching the edge of the sink behind her. "How will you explain my dead body?"

Amelia put the bottle down and moved closer. Close enough to smell her. Closer than they'd been all night. Liss was close to breaking. Amelia couldn't keep this up much longer, either. Desire was taking over, controlling her body, her words, obliterating logic. She needed Liss. Needed to feel her tongue in her mouth, her hands on her tits. She needed Liss to push her up against a wall and just *take* her. Her words were a pant. "Don't you want to kiss me?"

Liss let out a pained groan.

Amelia went to circle her arms around Liss's neck. Liss caught her wrists. For a moment, they just stood there, breathless. Liss holding Amelia, their eyes fixed on each other. Liss was stronger than Amelia imagined. Amelia waited for her to drop her arms and back up again, continuing this sexy game of cat-and-mouse. But Liss didn't let go. Instead, without breaking eye contact, she squeezed Amelia's wrists. Just a pulse of pressure. Slow. But deliberate. The feeling pushed Amelia over the edge. All the desire that'd been building in her body rushed fast and hard between her legs. She felt herself thicken, getting wet and slippery. Becoming hot and sensitive. Needing contact. Needing release. She was so turned on it hurt, a deep, painful ache in her core.

Liss was teetering. She dipped her mouth closer to Amelia's before stopping, refocusing. Her voice was low. She looked honest. "I want to do a lot more than just kiss you, Amelia."

Amelia almost fell apart.

She needed Liss to take both wrists in one hand and slide her fingers under Amelia's bikini bottom, down between her legs. Now. She needed Liss to touch her swollen clit, right here in the backroom of the bar. She needed Liss's fingers inside her, sliding in and out, getting faster and deeper, finding her G-spot. She needed Liss to fuck her with her hand until in about ten seconds she'd pulse uncontrollably around her fingers, and Liss would have to hold her up as tsunamis of pleasure crashed and smashed and destroyed her and she would collapse in Liss's arms. Then one minute later, do it all again, to Liss.

Now.

Amelia could barely get the words out. "You could make me come so hard right now."

Liss exhaled and the smell of her breath made Amelia swoon. She closed her eyes and parted her lips, waiting for Liss's mouth to claim hers.

But Liss let her go.

Amelia's eyes flew open.

Liss was switching things off. Readying to leave.

How did *anyone* have that much control?

Liss moved past her. "I'm going to bed."

"What the fuck?"

"This is actually for both our benefits." Liss flipped off the light.

Amelia followed her out, watching in disbelief as Liss began heading in the direction of the Caretaker Cabin. "Don't do anything on my behalf! I'm an adult, I can make my own choices."

"So can I," Liss said. "And I'm choosing to say good night."

Amelia could *not* believe it. She had her fair share of failed relationships. But she'd *never* not successfully seduced someone. Her disappointment sharpened into anger. "I'm really mad at you!"

"Good!" Liss called back, disappearing up the path and into the moon-limned night.

39

Because Parker was on New York time, midnight felt like the middle of the day. When Matty suggested they head home, Parker resisted, enjoying a bluesy beach boogey to "Piece of My Heart." But then her wife gave her *that* look, and Parker understood.

The pair had similar sex drives: not especially high, not especially low, easily aroused, familiar with each other's turn-ons and shortcuts. Their sex life was good—they almost always came, and Matty would tell anyone willing to listen she'd never faked an orgasm. But the heat and boundary-pushing of the sex from their first few years together was now a fond memory, as opposed to the norm.

Parker gave Matty head, then used the vibrator until her wife started tensing up, squirming with pleasure, free-falling toward climax. When Matty regained her breath, it was Parker's turn to jump off the cliff. Parker had only slept with two women; Matty, and someone to make Matty jealous when they were in an "off-again" part of their courtship. Sex with women was revelatory, like those viral videos where deaf kids get cochlear implants for the first time. A new world permanently obliterating the old one.

Afterward, Parker brushed her teeth, her focus getting tugged toward work. LK's assistant had just given her notice in a fairly terse email; Parker wanted to make sure there wasn't any bad blood. She picked up her phone on the nightstand.

"Hey, boo? Can we talk?"

Parker put the phone down. "Of course."

Standing in the bathroom doorway, Matty looked atypically unsure. "Just wanted to check in, I guess. About Sydney and babies and having babies in Sydney."

Matty was acting vague. Never a good sign. "Did you get an update from the clinic?"

"Um, no, I haven't been able to reschedule," she said, adding something about the clinic's strict cancellation policy. "I mean more big picture."

"Okay." Parker took a seat on the end of the bed.

"I know we've talked about this, but we've never really nailed down *all* the logistics. All the what-ifs."

Because Matty kept avoiding these finer-detail conversations. Parker had assumed that, like everything else, her capable wife had the future on lock.

"Like, say we move to Sydney," Matty went on, "and I get up the duff and crap out a kid but then something amazing comes up, like an awesome job in a different country. Would we move again? What if both our jobs get really full-on: would one of us have to scale back? Or quit? I've never not worked—I seriously can't even picture it." Matty was pacing back and forth, her words coming in free fall. "I read that a baby leaves your body with a fifth of your brain power. I need *all* my brain; it's my most prized possession! Also, the sleep thing is really freaking me out. They say you don't get a full night for *years*. We *have* to sleep train. You know I'm a basket case if I don't get, like, fourteen hours a night."

"When are you ever even awake?" Parker quipped, internally replaying the first words of her wife's monologue. *Like say we move to Sydney.* They were in the middle of moving to Sydney.

"Right? I always thought *can women have it all* was sexist bullshit, but maybe we can't have it all. We can be a good mum *or* have a good career, but I want both, no compromises."

Where was Matty going with this? Parker focused on not getting tripped up. "I want that, too."

"It's just . . ." Matty sank onto the end of the bed next to Parker, looking unnervingly terrified. "Do you really want kids? Like, really?"

A trapdoor opened in Parker's stomach. "We have been through this. Quite a few times. I was ambivalent about kids but now I'm not."

"I wore you down," Matty interpreted.

"I changed my mind," Parker corrected, giving Matty's shoulder a reassuring squeeze. "I'm really excited for us to start a family."

But her wife stayed worried. "I just . . . I thought by now I'd be feeling differently. I'd be more excited, more ready. But honestly, Parks, I just feel kind of . . . scared. And I don't feel ready, at all."

Parker took Matty's hand, not used to seeing her confident wife so uncertain. "Sweetie. I know this is a lot"—she indicated the island—"but don't let it rattle you. It's all going to work out."

Matty didn't look convinced. "It's just so weird being stuck out here. Everything on hold. So much time to think. I was going along in my life and everything was fine. And now I'm like, wait, was every decision I've ever made completely wrong?"

Parker gave her a wry smile. "Thanks a lot."

"Not you, boo. I mean, am I really doing what I want to be doing? Am I on the right path?" Matty crawled into Parker's lap, putting her head on her thigh. Her voice was thin and worried, on the edge of tears. "I miss New York. I miss our friends. I miss our *life*."

"Shh." Parker stroked her hair in the way she liked. "Shh." Even as Parker consoled her wife, it felt like she was falling. It was a struggle to keep her voice calm. "Is this about Noisy Brats?"

"I don't know. Maybe."

"When's the pitch?"

"Next week."

Parker had the most uncharitable thought in recent memory. She hoped Levi didn't get the money. She hoped they bombed. Because there was no way Matty could truly be happy for him and not resent the fact he was doing it without her. She'd always feel like her life in Sydney was second-best to what was happening in New York. Parker was excited for Sydney. A new city to explore, one defined by sunny beauty and an easygoing population who found her Americanness flatteringly fascinating.

Like her mother, Parker believed individual freedom in marriage was essential to its success. She wanted to build a partnership that allowed for different opinions and agendas and ways of moving through the world. But they still had to operate as a team. They needed a shared vision of the future.

Parker regained control, stabilizing her emotions. "I want you to picture something. It's Christmas morning in Sydney. Hot and sunny. We wake up and two of the cutest little kids you've ever seen run into our bedroom and start jumping on the bed."

"I assume these are our kids," Matty said, "not neighborhood delinquents."

"Yes, these are our kids. We all go downstairs in our matching PJs—"

"Very Norman Rockwell," Matty said. "Weirdly into it."

"And there's a huge Christmas tree with a massive stack of presents underneath."

Matty rolled onto her back to look up at Parker. "I love presents."

Parker laughed. "I know you do, you nut. So do our kids. We make coffee and OJ and toast some banana bread—that's one of our Christmas traditions: homemade banana bread—and start opening our presents. Our kids are so cute and so happy, and we all get exactly what we want."

"I want a new phone. Like, that's actually what I want."

Parker poked her, and they both giggled. "Your parents and Amelia come over for lunch—"

"And we stuff ourselves with prawns and potato bake and pavlova—"

"Then go for a swim at Coogee."

"With wine. White wine." Matty sat up. "Then that night we all snuggle up and watch a Christmas movie!"

"Yeah, like *Home Alone*."

"More like *Gremlins* or *Die Hard*."

Parker chuckled. "Sure, babe. Whatever you want." She lay down next to Matty, so they were gazing at each other. "I want all that." Parker touched her wife's face, the sweet, funny face of the woman she loved so much. "I know it's easy to think about what we'll lose: sleep, energy, money, sanity. We don't spend enough time focused on what we'll gain."

Matty returned her gaze. "A family."

"Exactly." Parker squeezed her hand. "Memories. Traditions. People we love and who'll always love us, no matter what. That's what I'm working so hard for: that life. Our life. We're on our way, boo boo. We're so close."

They wiggled toward each other, lips meeting in a kiss.

"You really want this," Matty whispered. "Don't you?"

"Yes," Parker said, with all the sincerity she could muster. "I do."

A stern, determined look took control of her wife's face, obliterating all previous doubt. "Then forget everything I just said."

Relief and uncertainly battled for control in Parker's brain. "Are you sure?"

"*Yes.*" Matty's expression was fierce. "I'm just tired. You're the most important person in the world to me, Parks. And then there's Mum, and Dad, and Amelia, and I want what we have! I want a family, too. I'm just getting lost in the details. I'm sorry if I scared you."

"It's okay. Just be honest with me. We're in this together."

"I know. I will be." Matty yawned, exhaustion relaxing the muscles in her face. "I love you, boo boo."

"I love you, too. So much."

A few minutes later, they were tucked into bed, the light off. Matty's breathing slowed as she slipped into unconsciousness.

Parker lay next to her, watching the rise and fall of her wife's throat in the moonlight.

40

Could you rub your own clitoris off? Liss Chambers was certainly giving the concept a run for its money.

She was fast losing her grip on this entire situation. It was one thing to keep Amelia at arm's length when she was ostensibly straight and in a relationship. It was another to resist a simpering sex goddess begging Liss to make her come. Liss had been close, she'd been *this close* to doing a thousand different dirty things to Amelia in the Barefoot Bar. Scenarios she'd been playing out all night and all morning, in extremely graphic detail. But now, well past the time she typically dropped off the meal kits for lunch, she'd forced herself out of bed and into a cold shower. As cliché as it sounded, they had to talk. Liss had to explain to Amelia—well, she wasn't even sure what anymore. Something to do with heartbreak and Amelia and how her breasts would feel in the palm of her hand— Liss jolted back into reality, thumping her forehead with a groan.

No one was at the Yellow Cottage, so Liss jogged up to Kooroy. The parents were all still in bed—it'd been a late one—so there was only Matty to ask, subtly, about her sister's whereabouts.

"Oooh, yum." Matty inspected lunch: grilled shrimp tacos with avocado and a pineapple salsa made from the fruit trees by the bar. "She said something about going to the Lost Lagoon."

Liss tempered a flash of alarm. "On her own?"

"Think so. Hey, are there more limes?"

"Um, I can check. Sorry—Did she take a map or anything?"

"Who, my sister? I doubt it. Why, what's wrong?"

"She's just not great with directions, and it's one of those places where it's easy to get lost on the way. Hence the name."

"I'm sure she'll be fine." Matty waved all this off. "About those limes? They really make fresh shrimp taste amazing."

"On it," said Liss, already knowing two things. One, Amelia would be lost, and scared, alone in the mangrove mudflats. It was overcast, the sky an iron sheet of gray, and Amelia couldn't tell north when the sun was out. The thought of her turning in circles, realizing she didn't know how to get home, made Liss feel panicky. So, the second thing Liss knew was that Matty wasn't getting those limes.

The Lost Lagoon was an hour from Kooroy. The track started in the bush, curving north, the opposite direction from the rainforest. There, the landscape turned dank and swampy like the rotting contents of a broken fridge. Although plant nerds liked to wax lyrical about the essential function of mangroves—helping stabilize coastline ecosystems, preventing erosion, absorbing storm surges—there was something creepy about this part of the island. It was prehistoric. Reptilian. The plants' dark roots stuck out of the sand in order to breathe, but they reminded Liss of fingers. As if something was trying to claw its way out after being buried alive. A tough old Queenslander with a face like a leather boot once told her mangroves were where they used to "dump dead bodies." He was joking, she assumed, but as Liss traveled deeper into the muddy mangroves, she could see his point. It was a good place to dispose of, or commit, a crime.

"Amelia?" Liss called as she walked. "Amelia!"

Nothing. Maybe Amelia decided not to go. Maybe she was never going to, maybe she'd just told her sister that. Maybe she was at the Caretaker Cabin, peering in the windows in her light blue bikini. That thought wedged itself so hard in Liss's mind she almost about-faced.

A rustle, close by.

Liss paused, her senses sharpening. Everything looked the same in each direction: low mangrove trees, dark, silty mud, the occasional crab scuttling across the sand. Liss's heartbeat picked up.

"Amelia?"

Sudden movement to her left jerked her around. Two herons took flight, wings flat as palms slapping the humid air.

Liss let out a nervous chuckle, embarrassed by her edginess, and kept going.

Liss hadn't figured out what to do if Amelia wasn't at the Lost Lagoon. But she didn't need to. Because as Liss rounded the last bend, there was Amelia Kelly, source of and solution to all her problems, floating in repose in the middle of the peaceful watering hole, surrounded by a tangle of jungly trees. She was wearing her sensible navy one-piece and enjoying her afternoon.

And Liss felt like a total fool.

Amelia did a double take and flipped from her back to tread water. "What are you doing here?"

From where Liss stood on a little strip of white sand, it was only one hundred feet to the huge log on the far side of the muddy bank behind Amelia. A kingfisher dove quick into the water, wings flashing a brilliant blue. The sun was breaking through the heavy cloud, sending out delicate fingers of light. The water was clear in the shallows, deepening to a spectacular emerald green. The same green as the engagement ring Liss bought for Sofia, still shoved in the inside pocket of her duffel. Which, surreally, made it seem like Amelia was splashing around in a giant version of that former piece of her heart.

Liss twisted her fingers into her hair. "Matty said you were coming here. I worried you'd get lost."

Amelia cocked her head, still expertly treading water. "So you came after me?"

It sounded insane. Worse: patronizing. But Liss's mortification was undercut by Amelia's growing smile.

"Aw. That's cute." Amelia ran her hands through her wet hair. It spilled behind her like a puddle of gold. "But I'm still mad at you."

Liss guffawed, more relieved than amused. Maybe she'd go in for a swim, too. Maybe they'd keep up this play-fighting for hours. Maybe Amelia would make her laugh and turn her on and tell her things like how much she wanted Liss to—

Liss's giddy train of thought hit a bump, her reality glitching a millimeter off course. For a moment, she couldn't figure out why.

Then it happened again, and this time, she understood what was happening.

The log behind Amelia on the far bank moved.

It was something massive and thick, the trunk of a dead gum.

But logs don't move.

That was because the log behind Amelia on the far bank wasn't a log at all.

It was a crocodile.

Fifteen feet long, its ridged tail twitching. Looking at them both.

"Liss? I said I'm still mad at you."

But there were no crocodiles on Mun'dai.

Until this. Until now. Terror crashed into Liss's consciousness like space debris making landfall.

"Liss? Hello? I said I'm still mad at you."

The surge must've washed it up, just like it washed up that turtle, which meant it'd been on the island for the past three weeks, a stranger in a strange land until a girl went swimming in its new home, a girl who was splashing around and calling out right now. A girl who would do god-knows-what if she saw the prehistoric killer that'd survived a millennia right behind her.

A girl she might watch die.

Hot, spreading horror. Liss couldn't feel her hands. Her entire world narrowed to the human in the lagoon and the dinosaur thirty feet behind her. As part of her counselor training, Liss had studied the fear response. From deep in her brain, a message had been sent to her adrenal glands for a burst of adrenaline, the action hormone. It was making her breathe faster and deeper, see sharper, hear better. The fight or flight response. Flight was impossible. Fight was the only option. Liss had to stay on top of her own fear. When she spoke, her voice sounded wonky and distant.

"Hey, Amelia, why don't you come here and we'll . . . go."

"Why would I want to do that?"

Tears edged Liss's eyes. She tried to keep her voice even. "I want to talk to you. Come here now, please?"

Amelia laughed.

The croc's tail snapped. Its teeth were an uneven jumble curving up a three-foot jaw. It could close the distance in seconds. Which meant Liss was going to watch Amelia Kelly die. The green water of the lagoon would turn red and Liss would watch her get taken into a death roll or worse, eaten alive, limbs torn from torso, all from a helpless vantage on the bank.

Liss's heartbeat was slamming so much blood into her ears, she couldn't hear herself. "Come out, and we'll watch some *B—Buffy*."

"Hmm, I would, but the timing isn't right for me." Amelia ducked under the water, splashing as she came up.

"Amelia, shhh." Liss's teeth started to chatter. "Please trust me. Please come here." A tear escaped down her cheek.

Amelia squinted at her. Frowning, she kicked to twirl herself in a circle, looking behind her.

She saw it.

She understood what she saw.

She stopped moving.

Amelia's body started to sink. She started treading water, just enough to keep her chin above the lagoon's surface. She was facing the crocodile. Liss could barely hear her. "Omigod. Omigod. Omigod."

"Amelia, baby, swim to me." Liss risked opening her arms, taking a step forward. "Swim to me."

"Omigod, I'm gonna die. I'm gonna die. I'm gonna die."

"No, Amelia, look at me. Look at me."

"I'm gonna die."

"No, baby, you're not."

"I'm gonna die. I don't want to die. I don't. I can't."

"Amelia, look at me. Look over here. Please, baby. Please look at me."

Finally, Amelia looked over her shoulder at Liss. Her face was skull-white. She was sipping air, hyperventilating.

Liss tried to smile, freezing and sweating. "Swim to me, baby. You can do it."

Amelia shook her head. "I can't."

"Yes, you can."

Amelia looked tiny: a floating head in the middle of the lagoon. Her voice was so small. "Liss, I can't."

The crocodile blinked. It switched its tail hard like a whip, hitting the mud with a *thwack*.

Amelia flinched badly, her muted cry barely audible.

"Then I'm coming in to get you." Liss started slipping off her shoes.

"No, don't do that. Don't do that. Don't come here. I'm coming. I'm coming." As if trying to make the least amount of movement possible, Amelia began dog-paddling back to shore.

"That's good, baby, that's good."

But she wasn't moving quickly enough.

The croc began opening its mouth.

Horror clamped around Liss's chest. "Quick as you can, Amelia. You're doing so good."

Amelia was panting with fear, gulping air. She got a mouthful of water and coughed, spluttering.

The too-loud sound almost made Liss yell in fright.

Amelia was over halfway to shore. "Is it still there?"

The croc took a step forward, its jaw still creepily unhinged.

"It's not moving," Liss said, edging into the shallows, ready to help haul her out. "Just keep going."

The croc took another step forward.

The world spun. Liss was losing what little control she had. "You gotta come quicker."

Amelia started doing freestyle, her arms slicing through the water, her feet kicking behind her. She was a good swimmer—now she was really moving. Almost to the shore. But she was also making a lot more noise. The croc snapped its jaw shut.

Liss almost screamed. "Great, baby, fast as you can!"

The croc pushed off and slithered into the water, disappearing from sight.

Liss bolted into the shallows, yelling, "It's coming, it's coming, go, go, go!"

Amelia thrashed so hard that for one nightmarish second, Liss thought it had her. She braced for Amelia to scream, to get sucked under, readying herself to dive in and fight. But Amelia was just swimming for her life, a powerful, assured athlete. In three smooth strokes she was close enough for Liss to grab her arm. Liss pulled her into the shallows, both panting in terror.

They sprinted ahead, off the track, into the mangroves. Jumping rocks, crashing though bushes, sharp things slashing their shins. Liss shot a look over her shoulder.

Through the mangroves, the enormous crocodile bolted out of the lagoon and raced toward them with shocking speed. Amelia screamed. A fresh burst of adrenaline punched them forward. They careened through the mud and low scrub. Liss waited for something to slam her from behind, drag her back, anticipating pain. Praying it would be her and not Amelia. The reptile was faster than they were. She could hear it, behind them, crashing and snapping, about to catch up to them. It was seconds away—

They tore into a line of mangrove trees and found themselves in the air. Falling. Slip-sliding down the gentle slope of a sand dune, toward the beach not far below. The sky arced wide overhead. The ocean crashed in front of them.

They were at the northern-most tip of Mooka Mooka Beach. The point where the mangroves met the sea.

Liss grabbed Amelia's hand, pulling her up, as they tumbled and waded through the dry sand to the beach.

They ran. They ran for what felt like miles, until their legs were burning and lungs might explode. The shore was wide and empty at low tide, the wind tossing off white caps on the distant surf. Eventually, they paused, spinning in circles, half expecting the nightmare beast to charge out of the ocean at them. Nothing. They'd escaped.

Liss grabbed Amelia's shoulders, examining the scratches on her face and body. "Are you okay?"

Amelia nodded, hiccupping tears, panting hard. "You're bleeding."

Liss touched her cheek. It came away wet with red. She couldn't even feel it. "Are you sure you're okay?"

Amelia nodded again, her eyes wild and wide. Gulls whirled overhead. "God, Liss. If you hadn't come for me, I'd be dead."

Liss's instinct was to deny it. But Amelia was right. If Liss had ignored her instinctual worry, this afternoon might not have been an extremely close call. It could've been a tragedy. Amelia's family could've lost her. Before Liss had the chance to say, or do, anything.

"I know." Liss ran her thumbs over the mud and scratches on Amelia's face. It hurt to see she'd been hurt. "But I did come. I always will, I promise."

Amelia threw her arms around her neck and hugged her. Liss let herself soften into it. Let herself feel the exquisite, almost unbearable pleasure of holding someone she cared about so deeply.

They held each other until they stopped panting, breath returning to normal, adrenaline flushing out of their bloodstream. But they didn't calm completely. Something blistering and huge was unfurling in Liss's belly at the feeling of Amelia in her arms. Liss wouldn't be able to let her go if she tried.

Amelia's voice was deliciously low in her ear, teasing. "You called me baby."

Liss glanced at Amelia in surprise. "I did?"

Amelia nodded. "Back there. *Swim to me, baby.*"

Liss hadn't meant to. It just felt natural.

"I liked it," Amelia whispered.

Liss rested her forehand on Amelia's, overwhelmed with gratitude that this girl was safe and in her arms. "I don't know how much longer I can resist it, Animal."

"Resist what?"

Liss lifted her head to look deep into Amelia's eyes. The color of the forever sky. "You," Liss said. "Us."

Amelia smiled, and it was the kind of thing that inspired skyscrapers and space travel and great works of art. "So stop resisting."

Liss ran her hands down the gentle curve of Amelia's back. Touching her felt like singing in harmony, a song that was so simple, so sweet. "Aren't you afraid? Of getting your heart broken?"

"No, Liss. I'm not afraid. I'm . . . a believer. I believe in it."

"Believe in what?" Hands moving of their own accord, Liss touched her chin with her thumb and forefinger.

"You," Amelia whispered. "Us."

That there could be an *us* with Amelia Kelly was like being handed the keys to her own personal utopia. Liss was out of excuses. The walls she'd built around herself revealed themselves to be nothing more than a trick of the light. Liss let herself do what she'd wanted to do, for every minute of every day, since she'd first met Amelia Kelly while wearing a novelty unicorn mask. She cupped Amelia's face in both hands, and she kissed her.

Amelia kissed her back. It was urgent. Galactic. The kiss of two people given a second chance at life. A second chance at love. Amelia's hands were on her cheeks, in her hair, kissing her over and over and over again. Desperate and loving, intense and sweet. All Liss's fear and trepidation were incinerated by the hot, sweet pleasure of Amelia's mouth. Emotion and want fountained through Liss, making her feel weightless with desire and conscious of nothing but Amelia's breath and lips and tongue moving in rhythm with her own. There was no beach, no island, no ocean, no air—there was only this, this kiss, this breathless, electric, intensifying kiss.

A noise escaped the back of Amelia's throat, a moan of need and relief. The sound unlocked a new level of need in Liss, kissing Amelia so intensely that for a moment they stumbled on the sand. Liss was barely aware of it. She never wanted to stop, never wanted this moment to end. She wanted to keep kissing Amelia Kelly until the stars went out and the sun exploded.

"Amelia," Liss managed to choke out, wanting to say so much— *I think about you all the time. I want you: I need you*—but no words came.

Amelia's tongue ran over her bottom lip, biting down gently and sucking, enough to make Liss giddy. "I know," she whispered back, pulling Liss close, then closer still. "Me too."

The ground underfoot started to shake. A low hum sounded down the beach. Liss and Amelia broke apart, twisting in the direction of the noise.

Amelia gasped, her face lighting in astonishment.

A dozen brindled brumbies were galloping up the beach toward them. Liss had only ever seen them from afar, never this close. The beach was wide enough that when the horses saw them, they veered toward the shoreline, enough distance away to feel safe.

Wild horses weren't a threat. They were beautiful. They were free.

Their bodies were sleek, hot muscle. Their manes and tails snapped behind them like banners. Amelia spun back to Liss, laughing in delight as the horses started to pass. She tipped her mouth up so their lips could meet again. Liss kissed her, pouring every happy and hurt and healing part of herself into it. She wanted to give Amelia all of her and she never wanted to let her go. Ever. What a fool she'd been to fight this. The thought alighted with the weight and innocence of a fairy wren.

Amelia Kelly is the one.

As Liss kissed Amelia's lips and cheeks and the tips of her fingers, the concept didn't feel frightening or overwhelming. It didn't feel hard.

It simply felt true.

41

Lemon-scented tea tree. An evergreen, whose narrow, bright green leaves were rich in citronella oil, giving an astonishing lemon scent when crushed. Jules had been doing some light weeding out the back of the house, pausing on her haunches to enjoy the distinctive natural smell. When the girls became teenagers, they drenched themselves in chemical-smelling sprays from The Body Shop, sickly sweet waterberry or vanilla, womanhood with training wheels. A heartbreaking time for a mother: the clear, collective disgust for their own bodies. She wanted to freeze the descent into female self-criticism, unable to explain *it would never stop*. Now, as Jules lifted the tea tree leaves under her nose, letting the fragrant oil seep into her skin, a flick of dread cut through the warm afternoon. Strangely familiar, from the years when the girls and their fake smells would miss curfew, screen her calls.

Something was wrong.

"Mum!" Matty's scream upset a trio of black cockatoos, swooping off with screeches so loud they could tear through the sky.

It took a few disorientating minutes for the sight of a bloodied and bruised Amelia and Liss to sink in. Her daughter had almost been eaten alive by a saltwater crocodile. The absurd horror flushed afresh all the fear from the surge. Jules started to cry. Glen became angry. Matty needed to hear the story again and again, unable to process the grisly reality that her only sibling nearly died. Randall shook Liss's hand, his face

serious and fatherly, then everyone wanted to shake Liss's hand in a serious, fatherly sort of way. A tattooed, blue-haired Canadian as knight-in-
shining-armor wasn't how Jules understood the world worked. But Liss
had rescued her daughter not once but *twice*, so obviously, Jules understood nothing. "You saved my baby!" Jules wailed, embracing a surprised
Liss. "You're getting jam for life!"

"So you coaxed Animal out of the water"—Matty pushed her mother
aside—"even though you could *see* the croc *coming* for her? Who are you,
Crocodile Dundee?"

After the survivors had showered and had their cuts tended to by a
weepy Jules and a practical Ludmila, the family gathered on the sectional for a croc-related summit. Liss settled on the far end, wrapped in
a blanket. Jules pulled Amelia in to sit between her and Matty, flanked
by Parker and Glen, everyone clutching each other and looking to Jarrah
for what to do next. Bewildering to have her family and the man she had
an illicit crush on all navigating this stressful moment as one.

There was no need to panic, Jarrah said, but certain parts of the island, such as all significant waterways and the entire mangroves, were
now off-limits. If there was just the one croc, it wouldn't stray too far
from the Lost Lagoon, but if there were others, they'd have found a
warm, brackish creek or stream to hunt in, near the coast. The sunny
beach coves and shallow tide pools were likely safe, being so exposed.
Likewise, anywhere flowing with cold ocean currents. The reptiles were
warm-blooded and would avoid very cold water. But just to be sure,
no more swims at dusk or dawn, when they tended to hunt, and no
more moonlit dips. It was statistically unlikely there'd be more than
one, Jarrah reckoned, given the sheer distance the surge had to carry the
reptile—the closest island was many miles away—and what a dangerous journey that was to start with. But they must be vigilant. This was
Queensland, after all.

"Then you can't keep camping by Karbunya Creek," Jules said.

"No," Jarrah agreed, "I can't."

"I don't like the idea of you camping anywhere," Jules went on. "Not
with this giant bloody killer on the loose."

"It's not *on the loos*e." Matty frowned. "Wait, is it?"

"I'm thinking the best thing would be to move into one of the empty fishermen's cottages," Jarrah said. "There's no electricity"—none of the empty houses had it until a sparkie could rewire the properties—"but I've got a camping stove and candles."

"We can help move you tomorrow," Jules said. "Tonight, you'll sleep on the sofa here. No, no, no," she spoke over him. "I am not taking no for an answer. We have to keep each other *safe*." She shifted so close to Amelia she was practically sitting in her lap.

"Mum!" Amelia protested, wiggling out of the family sandwich. "I'm fine. Liss saved my life, remember?"

The two glanced at each other and smiled.

"I'm beat," Amelia announced, cheeks flushed pink. "I'm going to turn in."

"It's seven," Matty said.

"Oh muffin, you have to stay here tonight." Jules clutched an arm. "With me, in the bed. Dad can sleep on the floor."

"I can what?" Glen asked, but Amelia was already up and shaking her head.

"As much as I want to sleep in the bed with you, Mum, I'd much rather sleep with . . . um, myself."

"Are you sure?" Parker asked her. "I can sleep on the couch if you want to share a bed with Matty."

"And be treated to her chronic nocturnal farting?" Matty snorted. "What's the opposite of a blessing in disguise?"

"Matty!" Amelia looked mortified.

Jules recalled the girls as infants, burping and farting with abandon. Of the two, Matty had emerged more confident of her body, less embarrassed by its functions. She was also more careful with it: less heartbreak, less hazardous situations. If only Amelia could be a tiny bit more like Matty.

"Randall and I will walk you home," Glen announced gallantly. "Won't we, mate?"

"Absolutely," Randall said, reaching, inexplicably, for a pair of binoculars.

"Matty and I will come, too!" Jules scrambled up, determined to make this a family affair.

"Yeah, I've already had a shower and I'd rather not get my feet sandy." Matty helped herself to a glass of wine. "Plus, I'm pretty sure Animal can walk five minutes on her own."

"No, she can't." Jules's horror was akin to Matty suggesting this course of action for a toddler.

"Liss can walk me home," Amelia said. "Like Jarrah said, we're completely fine on Blinky Beach. I'm fine. What I really need now is to, um, meditate."

Was that something Liss had gotten her into? Jules examined her daughter's face. "I didn't know you meditated."

"Yeah, I follow this guru, Matta Hatta—" Amelia grabbed Liss's hand, pulling her down the steps to the front door. "Batta . . . Up."

Jules made a mental note to google Matta Hatta Batta Up.

"Night, Team Croc!" Matty called, snuggling into Parker, whispering something that made her wife laugh.

They seemed closer these past few days. Even more loving and attentive than usual.

Glen put on some jazz. Ludmila helped Jarrah locate some clean sheets. Randall proposed a stir-fry. The evening appeared to be settling into yet another new normal, the one where their children barely escaped man-eating predators. Jules watched Amelia and Liss from the balcony, wondering if she was the only one who wanted to run after her daughter with the excuse of pressing some Rescue Remedy into her palm. *Aren't they delicious?* A fellow new mum had cooed at the girls when they were still just chunks at her hip. *Don't you want to just eat them up?*

It had never gone away: the desire to swallow her children whole.

Jules raised her fingers to her nose. The sharp scent of lemon brought her back to her body. Amelia and Liss were gone now, disappeared by the pale purple dusk. "Stir-fry sounds great, Randall." Jules headed back inside to the brightly lit kitchen. "I'll give you a hand."

42

In her previous life, Ludmila was someone for whom a penny-sized coffee stain triggered hot irritation that could linger all day. So she had to laugh when she caught sight of herself after returning home from a morning fishing trip: someone not just messy, but wholly deconstructed. Her pants were covered in so many fish scales, they glittered in the sun.

She showered and changed, then knocked on Jules's door, a little amused at the request she was about to make. "Can I borrow some clothes?"

Jules pushed her glasses into her hair, putting aside the romance novel Amelia had left lying around. "You want to borrow clothes . . . from me?"

Ludmila nodded, leaning her head against the doorframe. The bedroom was smaller than the master, but no less thoughtfully appointed. The windows were hung with gauzy, ivory-colored linen adding to the luxe, airy feel of the space. "To fish."

"Ah." Jules's face cleared up. "Of course." She sorted through the few pairs of shorts and T-shirts she'd packed. "You're really getting into it."

Ludmila made a small noise of affirmation, not quite able to articulate the deep and peaceful state the practice lulled her into. The way she was mapping the island through the way it felt on her skin.

Jules handed over some clean if well-worn items. "Hope they keep biting for you. That fish pie last week was so scrummy."

Scrummy was most likely a compliment. "Thank you."

"Oh, what a stunning necklace." Jules admired the polished red stones on a rope of knotted black silk. "Garnet?"

"Ruby. I got it in Paris, years ago."

"Paris." Jules sighed. "I've always wanted to go."

"Avoid the Fourth arrondissement. Too many tourists."

"No idea what you're talking about, but okay, sure. You travel a lot for work, don't you?"

"New York and Mexico City three times a year. Europe and India once or twice a year."

"Holy Dooley." Jules appeared impressed, although it looked more like embarrassment. "Well, you're obviously good at your job. You have fabulous taste, Ludmila."

Ludmila blinked, feeling surprised. Then pleased. She didn't think Jules liked her taste. An impulse to be generous overcame her. "You may borrow it." She unclasped the necklace.

"Oh, no." Jules flapped her hands in alarm. "No, I was just saying—"

"Please." Ludmila pushed the jewelry into her hands. "I'm borrowing from you."

"It's too pretty for me." Jules held the necklace like an unwanted if adorable puppy.

Ludmila knew she could take the necklace back and leave it at that. But the desire to step emotionally closer to Jules flushed into her chest, filling her with warmth. Ludmila's voice turned teasing. "Perhaps not too pretty for Jarrah?"

Jules's face went slack with horror. She shut the bedroom door behind them. "I haven't—" she stuttered. "I mean, nothing's . . . Nothing's happened."

Ludmila took a seat on the end of the bed and crossed one leg over the other. "Go on."

"There's nothing to go on about!" Jules caught herself. "Do you know that Glen and I—Do the girls know that Glen and I—"

"Julia—Jules, please. Relax. Glen told Randall a week ago," Ludmila said, deciding to omit the fact she'd overhead Glen and Jules arguing the first day they were stranded—it would only embarrass Matty's mother.

"But your business is your own and we would never share news that's not ours to share. As for Jarrah"—Ludmila shrugged—"I'm a woman. And men are not very complex."

"I don't know if that's true." Jules plopped down next to her. "Obviously this is all so new for me. I'm not even legally divorced."

"But it's over?"

Jules slumped, looking like a soggy sandwich. "It's over."

"I'm sorry." Ludmila patted her leg. The intimacy surprised them both.

Jules shot her a shy, cautious smile. "Thank you, Ludmila."

"And . . . Jarrah?"

A tiny smile tickled the corner of Jules's mouth. "Oh, it's nothing. Silly schoolgirl crush. That I'm far too old to have."

"But a crush that is, at least, two-way?" Jarrah kept his guard up around all the guests—even with Ludmila during their fishing lessons—but Ludmila noticed that it was most pliant around Jules. She recalled the way the pair exchanged little glances and jokes all morning, while packing up his camp for the move to the Blue Cottage. The others, distracted by crocodile-fueled logistics, didn't seem to notice.

Jules looked sweetly hopeful. "You think?"

Ludmila nodded. "Why not? You have things in common. You're in the same place. You're attracted to each other." She shrugged, embodying the decisiveness she'd imparted to her daughter. Case closed.

Jules glanced over at the mirror and winced. "Seems so hard to believe. Never wore enough sunscreen when I was younger."

Ludmila waved this off. "Attraction has more to do with a feeling than the physical." She looked around the room, her gaze landing on a bright throw pillow with a complex geometric pattern. "What do you think of that cushion?"

"It's all right." Jules shrugged. "Not my favorite."

"Interesting." Ludmila rose to collect it, stroking the bold, colorful design. "This is a Phulkari pattern, first invented by the dressmaker of a Punjabi princess in the fifteenth century. The dressmaker used the design to send secret messages to the princess's lover, indicating when and where they should meet. A secret love affair, hidden in the stitches.

Once the affair was discovered, the design became so popular it traveled through generations and across continents, until today it is this very pattern I hold in my hands."

"Gosh. That's incredible," Jules stared with renewed wonder at the cushion. "Is that true?"

"Not one bit." Ludmila flipped the cushion over to show her the label. "This is from Target. But the story made you feel differently about it, no?"

Jules let out a loud bark of a laugh.

While the story Ludmila had told Jules about the cushion had been made up, Phulkari embroidery was real, defined by stitching the rough side of coarse cotton cloth with silk thread. The rough side—typically, the wrong side—was made beautiful by the intricate silk. Ludmila had always seen Parker's mother-in-law as crass. But Jules was actually just bold. Ludmila liked bold textiles and bold women.

"You are the weaver of your own story, Jules." Ludmila took the ruby necklace and placed it around Jules's neck. It brought out the hidden red hues in her irrepressible curls. "What story are you going to create?"

43

There wasn't anything about Liss Chambers that Amelia Kelly didn't like. She liked her shy, excited smile when Amelia flew up the steps of the Caretaker Cabin and into her arms. She liked the little quirk in her eye when she was about to say something funny. She liked her white T-shirt collection, which, despite all looking more or less the same to Amelia, was a careful curation of sacred items, each with their own mood and story (Liss's detailed show-and-tell took two hours). She liked her small, sensitive breasts. Her silences and the sadness lingering under her skin.

And Amelia really, *really* liked kissing her.

No one was as good a kisser as Liss Chambers. Hours disappeared in sultry, love-drunk stretches. On the beat-up blue velvet sofa. In the kitchenette. On the sandy trail to the Cabin, pressed against the hard, creamy trunk of a eucalypt.

It was a living, layered thing, a kiss. Sweet and sincere could become as wild as a summer storm. Intensity could lighten to something as delicate as a butterfly wing. It was a conversation Amelia never wanted to end. They kissed until their lips were swollen and their bellies were growling like companionable dogs. They kissed until it was night then day then night again.

"I love kissing you," Amelia whispered. "I feel like I can't stop."

"Don't," Liss murmured back, her eyes dreamy and soft. "Promise me you'll never stop."

Amelia was a freight train of love hurtling forward. A train whose power and speed tended to frighten the people it was aimed at.

But she sensed Liss could be a freight train, too. And it felt like she'd taken her foot off the brakes.

Liss said they shouldn't have sex right away. That lasted forty minutes. The first time Liss touched her, Amelia came fast and hard, just as she'd predicted at the Barefoot Bar. Her climax had her screaming into a pillow, feral with pleasure. Some people resisted being untamed. Amelia sank her teeth into it. The second time, minutes after the first, was just as intense.

"Jesus, you're like an orgasm machine," Liss said, as Amelia lay panting, her chest jumping like a puppet on a string.

Amelia had slept with women before. But they were women like herself: excited but inexperienced. At best clueless and coy, at worst squeamish and full of shame.

Liss knew what she was doing.

"Again," Amelia said, pulling her close. "Again."

Now, three days into what felt like three years or three minutes of being together, the afternoon sun slanted over their naked bodies. The Caretaker Cabin was a mess of dirty plates and discarded clothes. Dust motes floated in the air. In the unmade bed, Liss slid her fingers around Amelia's body, learning to play it like an instrument. Teasing, stroking, engrossed in the way her movements made Amelia writhe and whimper. Amelia let herself drown, never wanting to come up for air. She wanted to live in this intoxicating feeling. The feeling of being with Liss Chambers.

Liss trailed her fingers down the slope of Amelia's back, up over her ass. Unguarded and dopey with desire. "God, I feel like I want to write a song about your body. I am officially that guy."

"Please write a song about my body," Amelia said. "I would love that."

Liss propped her head up with her hand, letting her fingers keep playing, exploring. They were rarely not touching. "What kind of music do you like?"

"Jazz, all kinds, and Taylor Swift."

Liss chuckled, seeming charmed. Amelia guessed her list would be longer, full of bands she'd never heard of. "Jazz and Taylor Swift, right on. Who got you into jazz?"

"Dad."

Liss nodded. "Glen's into jazz, cool." She picked up Amelia's hand to nibble at her fingertips. "So you're a Swiftie? Favorite song?"

"Oof, that's hard. So many epic jams. I always think of the last song I liked when I think of my favorite song." She sorted through the mixtape in her mind. "I really had a moment with "August" off *Folklore*. It's beautiful and sad and delicate and I love it."

"Beautiful and sad are the bricks of my wheelhouse. How does it go?"

Amelia shrank back. "I can't sing."

Liss kissed her shoulder. "Just the melody."

Amelia shook her head, feeling genuinely scared. "Singing in public is one hundred percent my worst nightmare."

"You're not in public! C'mon."

Groaning, Amelia tried to hum the melody without completely butchering it.

Liss picked it up, somehow pulling the first few lines out of the back of her brain. "'*Salt air, and the rust on your door / I never needed anything more.*' Yeah, I remember it, I think."

"It's not actually a love song—more a love lost song. There's a bit at the end that goes, "*You weren't mine to lose.*" I always thought it was you *were* mine to lose. I got it totally wrong. As per usual."

Liss lifted her head from kissing Amelia's collarbone. "Hey, that's one of my favorite people you're dissing. You, not TayTay."

Amelia snuggled on top of Liss, settling her head on the pillow next to her. She liked it when as much of their naked flesh was touching as possible. "What's your favorite song?"

Liss turned her head, mirroring Amelia. Her nervous edge was as malleable as wet sand. "You'll find it."

"You'll find it," Amelia repeated. "What does that mean?"

"You'll find it." Liss shrugged, smiling the shy smile that made Amelia feel like her body was full of flowers opening on fast-forward.

Amelia sat up, wriggling down between Liss's legs. "Better start looking." She kept eye contact as she lowered her tongue to Liss's clit. Amelia was still fairly inexperienced when it came to oral sex. But she did not have to fake her enthusiasm. Vaginas were such exquisite, delicate things. Soft as a scallop, as pretty and private as a secret garden. She liked the taste, the salty-sweet scent that made her instantly horny. But most of all, she liked the way the lightest touch could make Liss's eyes roll back in her head, her muscles tensing with pleasure, fists bunching the sheets.

There wasn't anything about Liss Chambers that Amelia Kelly didn't like.

Her family had a dinner at Kooroy she couldn't get out of, so Liss planned to take a few calls for the volunteer helpline. The idea of time apart was agonizing, but Amelia loved that Liss volunteered, and wanted to give her space for it. Amelia regularly spent her own money on school supplies and working unpaid overtime: she was accustomed to doing more than was strictly necessary in order to please and be helpful. But the concept of teaching felt very far away now, as if her Sydney life was already dissolving into rumor. Work was a means to an end. A paycheck, not a passion. Amelia was in no hurry to reconnect with her real life.

But what was real life? Her father once said that the world humans experienced was radically constrained by their cognitive, biological, and cultural limitations. Birds, he explained, could smell the shape of an entire landscape. Hear sounds inaudible to human ears. See unimaginable explosions of color and pattern: literally, a bird's-eye view of the world. This was how being with Liss made Amelia feel. Like she could see colors she never knew existed. Speak a language she didn't know before. She couldn't unknow this new way of being. It changed her in a way that felt wonderful and a little frightening and, above all, permanent.

Now that Amelia knew Liss Chambers existed, she couldn't not be with her.

Amelia was late to dinner, sliding into the last open seat as her mum served up fish and chips. Excruciating to sit through her sister nattering about the Noisy Brats pitch tomorrow and her mother's wondering if Amelia should do therapy for PTSD after her run-in with the croc. "You look underslept." Jules peered at her. "Have you been getting enough rest?"

"Tons," Amelia lied. "I mean, not enough. I might be coming down with something. I think it'll take me a few more days to recover."

"You're never sick." Jules tried to touch her forehead.

Amelia wriggled away. What else was she never supposed to be? Queer? Selfish? Adventurous, unexpected?

"How's the podcast pilot going?" Amelia asked her sister.

Everyone looked at Matty, allowing Amelia to finally exhale.

"Really good," Matty enthused. "Mum and Ludmila's interviews turned out really well—thanks again, guys—so now I'm shaping it around, like, my fork in the road."

Ludmila sipped her wine, sounding curious. "What kind of fork, Matilda?"

Her sister appeared to catch herself, doubling back. "Not a fork, a sort of, um—Oh wow, look at the sunset!"

Evenings were slow, unhurried things at Kooroy, focused around the fading of the light and onset of stars. Amelia offered to clean up, edging toward the front door as soon as the last plate was put away, mumbling something about needing to rest.

"But we were going to play canasta!" Matty called, but she was already out the door.

Liss and Amelia fell into each other's arms like a couple reuniting after war, aware of the silliness but both admitting how much they missed each other the ninety minutes they were apart.

Then, after brushing their teeth and getting into bed, Amelia found the song.

They were listening to an indie band from Montreal. Half Moon something-or-other: moody, percussive, sad-people music. Not typically Amelia's taste, but because Liss liked it, she was paying attention. But she was also paying attention to Liss's body. Her boobs. The shape of her fingers, the tiny freckle on her palm. There, on the pinkie side of her left wrist, a tiny tattoo. Four words, in delicate cursive: *you, strange as angels.*

Liss had one arm behind her head, the other around Amelia. She twisted her wrist around to read the tattoo. Her smile was like a mild morning. "See? You found it."

"This is your favorite song?"

Liss nodded. "It's from a song by The Cure. 'Just Like Heaven.'" She sang the lyrics in a low, musical voice. "*Yo-o-ou, soft and only / yo-o-ou, lost and lonely / yo-o-ou* strange as angels."

Amelia recognized it. "Ooh, I love that song." Upbeat eighties, glittery and dizzy and fun.

"Great pop song. And a love song. Robert Smith wrote it about his childhood sweetheart, Mary. They met when he was fourteen. They've been married for thirty-three years."

"Aw. Should we put it on next?" Amelia reached for Liss's phone.

"Ah, no." Liss stopped her hand, instead bringing it to her mouth to gently bite Amelia's thumb. "That's one of the songs Sof got in our breakup."

"But it's your song," Amelia said, tracing Liss's lips, touching her cheek. "It's your tattoo."

"It was a tactical error," Liss allowed.

"How did you make it hers?"

Liss looked up at the ceiling, blowing out a breath. "We used to have these dinner parties, and when I sang that song, she'd sing backup and do this cute dance, and, I don't know, it was hers."

Amelia was unable to hide her disbelief. "She sang and danced around, that's it?"

"It was very charming!" Liss protested.

"You have to get that song back. It's yours! Why are you giving it to her?"

"I don't know." Liss rolled on top of her to kiss her neck, her jaw, her mouth. "You're very wise."

"Am I?" Amelia kissed her back.

"Mm-hmm." Liss nodded. "Wise, and sweet, and funny, and brave. And, of course, you're outrageously sexy."

"Ooh: outrageously?"

"Shamelessly sexy," Liss kissed her. "Swashbuckingly."

"I happen to think you're swashbuckingly sexy, too." Amelia flipped on top of Liss to admire her. The delicate tattoos inking her peaches-and-cream skin. Her mystery and her magic. Over the weeks, her lover's hair had faded from deeper indigo to an ethereal, gas-flame-blue. Impossibly pretty. "You're like every bi girl's fantasy, ever. And the guys, I mean, they must just . . ."

Liss's expression became incredulous. "No, please, assess my fuckability with men." They both started to laugh, Liss circling Amelia's wrists. "Um, why are we fighting?"

Amelia giggled. "We're not. I'm obviously just jealous of all the other guests you've found swashbucklingly sexy."

Liss kissed her again. Her hazel eyes were honest and completely clear. "You're the first person I've kissed on this island."

Because that's what Amelia wanted to know. Even before she knew it herself. "Phew," she said, tracing the *you, strange as angels* tattoo with the tip of her tongue. Wondering how to get this song back for the person who was, to her love-soaked mind, just like heaven.

44

Like two different species of birds living in the same territory, Glen and Jules went about their business as if the other did not exist (not unlike how it typically was at home, Glen noted) until one afternoon he finally bumped into Jules in the kitchen, on his way out to meet Randall for a training session/secret bird-watching mission. "Oh, Jules, I got an email about the car rego. We need to renew by the end of the month."

Jules wiped down a jar of homemade chutney, cooling on the kitchen counter. "There should be money in the joint account."

The joint account. The car, the car registration. The house, their superannuation, their wills, one thousand other things. The sheer magnitude of extracting himself from life with his wife felt like being on a ship in high seas. He could still remember their wedding day. His mother dabbing her eyes with a lace handkerchief and smudging her mascara. A work colleague getting drunk before the ceremony and throwing up behind a rosebush. Jules, in a puffy-sleeved short silk dress, dancing down the aisle toward him to a round of whoops and cheers.

To have and to hold, to love and to cherish, as long as they both shall live.

No one else was around. "What does it mean to you," he asked, quietly and without venom, "that we're breaking our wedding vows?"

Jules met his gaze in astonishment. She looked truly thrown. "It means—I don't know—that we both . . . changed."

Glen nodded, conscious of the red running shorts and tank top he was wearing.

Jules came closer, her expression empathetic. "It doesn't make us bad people, hon. Christ, we were just kids. And we did our best. Don't you think?"

"I don't know," he said. "I don't know if I did do my best."

When Matty mentioned she was seeing a therapist in New York (*Everyone sees one here—it's like having a MetroCard*), he thought it was ridiculous. But his daughter had a dialogue with herself that was worlds more sophisticated than his own internal narrative. Should he have seen a therapist? A marriage counselor? Opened up to more friends? Made friends to start with? Was that what it meant to be a man, in this modern age? Or was that a lot of woo-woo nonsense? Woo-woo was Jules's territory; Glen had long armored himself against anything self-helpy.

Possibly, that was shortsighted.

"Making some chutney?" He nodded at the jar.

Jules's expression blanked, a familiar reaction when he turned something serious into something meaningless. "I was just going to drop it round to Jarrah."

"Righto." He turned to leave. "Didn't you drop off some to him yesterday?"

His wife busied herself with wiping the bench. "Did I?"

"Didn't you?"

"Well, I guess he likes it." She was using the voice she affected when telling a waiter she loved something she'd just been complaining about.

How much chutney could one man eat?

The idea swerved at him like a car running a red light. "Is something going on with you and Jarrah?"

"No!" His wife looked appropriately shocked.

See? Ya got it wrong again, idiot.

Then she lowered her head, mumbling like a teenager. "I mean, not yet."

The car made impact, throwing him ten feet. Bones broken, punctured lungs. "*Yet?* So—So there is something going on?!"

"I don't need to keep you abreast of my personal life, Glen!" Jules had the audacity to look affronted.

Glen held the edge of the kitchen counter to avoid wobbling to the floor. Deep in his gut, he truly expected their marital woes to work themselves out: a deus ex machina of relationship resolution. It wasn't something he necessarily wanted to happen—he just believed it would.

But his wife had already moved on.

Which filled him with a feeling Glen hadn't experienced in a long time. An unimpeachable sense of righteousness. Pushing past the shrinking fear in his limbs, he let go of the kitchen counter and raised himself to his full height. "Then we absolutely must tell the girls."

Jules scoffed. "I said *not yet*. There's nothing to tell."

"Untrue." Glen used his deepest voice. "We don't need to tell them about Jarrah. But we do need to tell them about us."

Jules pointed at a tea towel. "Pass me that?"

"Jules." Glen folded his arms. "I insist."

Jules met his eye with dark amusement. "You insist?"

Was that too threatening? He dropped his arms. "Being honest is the right thing to do."

"Okay." Jules's light tone was instantly unsettling. "Say we do, and they fall apart, out here, a million miles from anywhere. Who's going to pick up the pieces?"

He assumed he wasn't supposed to say Jules. "Matty has Parker."

"And Amelia has no one," Jules finished. "So you're saying you'll be there for her?"

Glen tried to imagine soothing his songbird-delicate daughter: saying exactly the right things, comforting Amelia in her hour of need. It was like searching for a light source in an entirely dark room.

"We're not telling them now, Glen. We're doing it at home, in the family room, early on a Friday evening. I'm going to make my chicken casserole and some mint tea; I've already figured it all out." She was irritated.

Glen knew breaking the news was up to him as well, that it was a joint decision. He wanted to say this out loud but it was difficult to articulate it over the cold, hard voice in his head: *Stop upsetting your wife! Christ, boy, can't you do anything right?*

"Trust me, hon." Jules gave him a sympathetic look. "This is the best way. So can you just hand me that tea towel, please?"

He didn't believe her. He did hand her the tea towel.

Tossing off a curt farewell, Glen jogged down the stairs toward Randall on the beach, finishing his crunches.

They did their Boobook handshake—fingers flat, crossed to make an *X*, the knuckle of the little finger of one hand against the knuckle of the pointer finger on the other to resemble a bird's wing. They "flapped the wings" two times by bending the ends of their fingers, then slapped their open palms twice in quick succession.

Since hearing the Boobook's call near the Barefoot Bar, they'd been doing a regular loop past it. Generally, they chatted as they jogged, but Glen was silent, stuck on his conversation with Jules.

He didn't want to bother Randall. But Randall was his friend. He wouldn't mind being bothered. He'd probably be interested.

Glen stopped short. "Something's going on with Jules and Jarrah."

Randall shot past him, then doubled back. "What?"

Catching his breath, Glen told Randall everything. "But nothing could actually *happen* between them. Right?"

Randall wiped his forehead with the crook of his elbow. Sandpipers danced daintily around the water's edge. "I don't know for sure. But look—it's not out of the realm."

The air in Glen's lungs hissed out like a popped balloon. He dropped to the sand. Randall sat next to him. Both men stared at the gentle wash of the tide. The sky was heavy: rain on the way.

"I guess, in a way, I'm not surprised," Glen said. "She's been different lately. Distracted and . . . happy."

"She's not usually happy?"

Glen tossed a piece of driftwood into the ocean. "I guess neither of us has been happy for a while."

"So, with the caveat nothing might actually happen: How would you feel if it did?"

"Pissed off!" Glen exclaimed. "My wife—ex-bloody-wife—shagging another bloke? *Pissed off* is how I'd feel!"

"Why?"

"Why? Whaddya mean why? Because she's moved on! Because it's really over! Because she's sorting herself out and I'm left behind, as usual!"

"What do you mean?"

Glen tried to explain: Jules was an extrovert whose big personality and big dreams created the life she wanted, and he just went along with it. Having someone tell him what to do and say and wear and cook made things easy. As long as he could pursue his interests—bird-watching, jazz, reading—he thought that was enough. But as things began to sour, he'd started to wonder if the relationship was truly equal. If he was getting what he wanted in the same way she was.

"And what's that?" Randall asked.

"What's what?"

"What do you want?"

The question caught Glen off guard. "It's just . . . Jules has a habit of bulldozing over things if they stand in her way—"

"Sure," Randall interrupted. "But you didn't answer my question, man. Look, you've got a long road ahead of you—divorce isn't easy, or quick, or painless. But my point is: it's your turn. Who will you be and what will you do, free of all responsibilities? Your girls are out of the house and your wife wants to move on. What do *you* want?"

An albatross soared overhead. A magnificent, kingly bird. Oh, to see what it sees. Go where it goes. Sensation built in Glen, surging and billowing to the extraordinary height of the albatross.

Desire. Courage. Determination.

Glen shifted to face Randall, feeling clearer than he'd ever been. "I want to soar."

Randall's eyebrows flicked down, his head tipping to one side in question.

"I want to soar, Randall." He let himself speak, without second-guessing, each word a tap against the shell that surrounded him. "I want to move to Sydney and live in the city and go to jazz clubs and bird-watch in Centennial Park and maybe have sex with someone else and I want to discover the Boobook! I want to discover this bloody Boobook!"

"Yeah!" Randall popped to his feet, hauling Glen up. "Say it again!"

"I want to find the Boobook!" Glen yelled.

"Again!"

Glen faced the ocean and shouted. "I want to find the Boobook! *I want to find the Boobook!*"

The shell surrounding Glen Kelly finally cracked. Not all the way; Glen's fragile wings weren't yet ready for flight. But progress had been made.

"Let's go!" Randall cried. They did their handshake again then set off up the beach, eyes on the treetops, a fresh urgency in every step.

45

Liss stood at the edge of the mangroves, watching Amelia slip-slide down the sand dune where they'd escaped the crocodile. It seemed to go on forever, endlessly sloping. "C'mon," Amelia called, holding out a hand. "Come here!"

Liss's sneakers pushed a shower of sand off the edge. She couldn't do it. Couldn't jump.

She woke with a start. The metaphor was so stupidly obvious, she groaned, laughing under her breath.

The rainstorm that'd been looming all afternoon drummed on the Cabin's tin roof. Water slid down the windows in snaky rivulets. In the kitchenette, Amelia was making dinner. She was wearing one of Liss's T-shirts knotted at her hip and a pink, lacy thong. Jaunty jazz bopped from her phone speaker.

Liss stretched and sat up, enjoying the view. "Hi."

"Oh, hello." Amelia splashed hoisin sauce into a sizzling frying pan. "I'm making noodles."

Liss's mouth flooded. When had they last eaten? "I love noodles."

"I know. That's why I'm making them." Amelia skipped over to kiss her, tasting like garlic and salt. "By the way, Max moved. He must like you."

The spider the size of a goddamn dinner plate was right next to her head. "Je*sus*." Liss scrambled out of bed. "Seriously, Max: your dance space, my dance space."

"*Dirty Dancing.*" Amelia got the reference, shimmying.

Liss loved that Amelia always wanted to be touching. Always wanted to make out, no matter where they were or what they were doing. The building could be on fire, but Amelia would happily linger inside if it meant another chance to press their mouths together.

"I like how affectionate you are," Liss said, as they did the dishes after dinner, finally cleaning up a bit.

Her hands in the soapy water, Amelia leaned over to kiss her. "I'm very affectionate."

"I like that," Liss said, drying a plate. "I'm pretty affectionate, too, I think. Not always in public, though."

"I am in public, too," Amelia said, matter-of-fact.

Liss laughed. "Okay, cool." She put a stack of clean dishes in the cupboard. Being domestic with Amelia was fun—she even made *cleaning* enjoyable. The Cabin used to feel lost and nostalgic, like an old photo album forgotten under a bed. Now, with the lamps on, jazz playing, and a cute girl in cute underwear doing dishes while it poured outside, it felt cozy. Homey. "I always thought this was a good place to, like, brood and be alone like a total weirdo," Liss said, "but having you here all the time makes it feel lighter."

"This space is amazing," Amelia said. "I love it. I love everything about it. And I really love everything about you." She kissed her again.

Liss felt so happy she was giddy. Smitten. That was the word: she was smitten. "Have you ever had a girlfriend?"

The question came out before she could filter it.

Amelia paused for a microsecond before meeting Liss's gaze. "No."

It was and wasn't a surprise. Liss had been with until-I-met-you straight girls before, including Sofia, but they'd never been as confident with their feelings. As into sex. Part of that was explained by Matty having done the heavy lifting of introducing same-sex coupledom to the Kelly family. But part of that was just Amelia. Eager, affectionate, loving Amelia. Still, Liss was curious. How would the Kellys take the news if it ever came out? "Have you ever dated someone who surprised your family?"

Amelia put the pan on the drying rack. "I went on a few dates with a runner-up on *Australian Idol.*"

Even to her own ears, Liss's chuckle sounded nervous. "Right."

"What?"

"Nothing." Liss told herself to drop it, then in the same breath, "Do you think you'd come out to your family?"

"Totally. I would one hundred percent do that. I mean, not right now. It's too soon—right?" Amelia looked to Liss for confirmation.

Liss got the impression if she replied, *Too soon? No way! Let's go tell everyone we're a couple!* Amelia would grab her hand and run through the rain to Kooroy, excited to share the wonderful news. "Well, we've only been sleeping together for five days."

"Five days?" Amelia looked shocked. "Feels like a *lot* longer. But yeah, I will come out to them. To everyone." She stood between Liss's legs, curling warm, soapy hands around the back of her neck. "Because the more I think about it, the more I want to be with someone exactly"— *kiss*—"like"—*kiss*—"you."

"You've got me," Liss murmured, dropping the tea towel to kiss her back.

Later, Amelia lay drowsing on Liss's chest, tracing and retracing the *you, strange as angels* tattoo on her wrist with a sleepy fingertip.

Liss was wide awake. Usually, she felt on edge in new relationships. She and Sofia played a stupid text game for weeks before they started to relax and trust each other's feelings. Amelia opened up right away. Day one, minute one. Liss wanted to be like that, too. Just *choosing* happiness. Choosing love, choosing trust. Could it be that easy? "Hey?"

"Mmm?"

"You know how you said I was who you'd build in a lab for yourself?"

Amelia looked up, half laughing, half groaning. "It's only branded on my memory for all time—so, unfortunately, yes."

"If I could create a sentient being with my own hands—if I was comfortable bridging that moral-ethical divide—you're who I'd build in a lab, too."

Her lover's lips curled into a smile. "Really?"

"But y'know, that's not entirely true," Liss second-guessed herself. "I'd probably build someone less good, because I wouldn't think I could be with someone as amazing as you."

"Aw. You're so sweet." Amelia frowned. "Or you have very low self-esteem."

Liss smiled hopefully. "Can both be true?"

Amelia propped her chin up. "I feel that way, too, about you. Sometimes I think I made you up, that this is all in my head and I'm actually locked up in a mental hospital in the year 2050."

"Weirdly specific."

Amelia gazed at her, melting, as if overpowered by just how fucking *cute* she was. "Ugh, you're like this *perfect* person."

"Wow." Liss laughed. "I am not perfect."

Amelia sat up, sitting cross-legged. "Prove it."

Liss sat up, too. "Okay: I have a bit of an anxious brain and I'm pretty particular about things. Sometimes I get jealous or moody or cheap? Yeah, money issues, for sure. If left to my own devices, all I'll eat is cheese and Cup-a-Soup, so I have some minor digestive issues, but I do not like going to the doctor. I do a lot of WebMD-type self-diagnosis, and—"

"Okay, okay," Amelia stopped her, somewhere between amused and alarmed. "Message received."

"What are your flaws? Apart from being really bad at lagoon selection?"

Amelia laughed uneasily. "I have flaws."

"Prove it." Liss folded their fingers together, expecting banter.

"Well, I'm a chronic people-pleaser. Bad with directions. Gullible, as we all know. I can run a teensy bit hot—"

"You? Haven't noticed."

But Amelia didn't laugh and shove her as Liss was expecting. Instead, her gaze turned inward. She pulled her hand away, back into her lap. "And . . . well . . . deep down . . . I'm unlovable."

Amelia didn't say it like a joke. She said it like it was true.

Before becoming a counselor, Liss would've spluttered out something like, *What? You're crazy! That's crazy!* Now, her intuition told her to give Amelia space to open up. "Can you tell me more about that?"

Amelia shrugged, her face hard. "Everyone I've ever cared about has dumped me or disappointed me. And that's because deep down there's just something about me that is fundamentally unlovable. I'm not as smart as my sister; I've basically been told that every day of my entire life. Not as accomplished, not as brave, not as special." She was tearing up. "I make terrible choices all the time—like James. And Huon. And Oscar, god, *Oscar*. I paid for him to enroll in a TAFE course and the *day* he started, he broke up with me. Still did the *entire* course."

Liss didn't know what a TAFE course was but understood this had been a poor decision.

Amelia's eyes were flooding. "I'm just—a lot. A lot for someone to take on."

"Amelia—"

"I'm too much. I've always been too much. I'm too emotional, too intense, too needy, *too much*—"

"Amelia, Amelia." Liss took her hand again, meeting her gaze. She made her voice as honest and direct as she could. "You are none of those things. You are not unlovable."

"Of course you have to say that, but—"

"No, Amelia, please, listen to me. You are not unlovable. You are extremely lovable and whoever put that idea in your head, they are wrong. Because you are lovable. You have a family who loves you." Liss wiped a tear away with her thumb. "I'm not sure if you've noticed, but I am pretty into you. You are not too much. You are not unlovable."

Amelia frowned, biting her bottom lip. Her voice was as small as a sugar glider. "What if I put that idea in my head?"

Liss nodded in understanding. "I get it. I put ideas in my head, too. Like, stories I tell myself about why I'm in the situation I'm in." And only as she was saying it out loud did Liss realize how true it was. And what exactly she meant. "One of my stories is I'm going to hurt the people I love or who love me."

Amelia curled closer. "Because of what happened with Gabe and Sofia?"

"Yeah. And my parents, too, maybe." Liss hated talking about it, but it was only fair after what Amelia had shared. "They split up when I was fifteen. Messily. I was kind of a bad kid—skipping class to play music with Gabe or hang around record stores and stuff. I ended up almost getting kicked out of school, then my parents split up and I definitely equated the two—thought it was all my fault. They told me it wasn't, but I didn't listen to them."

"That must've been so awful."

"Yeah, I was devastated. I was a kid, an only child. No one to lean on." Liss remembered her parents yelling at each other, night after night, while she played Pink Floyd to drown out the sound. She must've listened to *Dark Side of the Moon* one hundred times that summer. "I guess, deep down, I've always worried that I'm going to hurt the people I love or be the cause of some horrible separation drama. But that's actually a really dangerous idea. Because it means . . . Because it means I can't ever be close to anyone. And I don't want that."

"You weren't the reason your parents split up."

"And you're not unlovable." Liss looked back at the sweet, sensitive woman in bed with her. Amelia's impulse for perfectionism made more sense now: often a way those with internal struggles exerted external control. "So I have a proposal for you."

Even while damp, Amelia's eyes lit up. She held up her left hand and wiggled her fourth finger.

Only Amelia could make a joke about the two of them getting married—after five days—and somehow come off cute and charming. Liss laughed, her head in her hands. "Not that kind of proposal, you lunatic, unless we're on *Gay Bachelor in Paradise* and no one's told me."

"For the record, I would say yes." She said it fast, like a joke. "What's your second-best proposal?"

"I'm going to stop believing that I'm going to hurt the people who love me if you stop believing that you are unlovable. Because I actually think we both have the power to make those stories, that fake news, untrue."

Amelia nodded. Her eyes were so full of love and trust, Liss almost couldn't handle it. "I'll try. If you try, I'll try." She took Liss's face in her hands. "I'm so crazy about you."

"I'm crazy about you, too."

They sank into a deep, tender, thought-obliterating kiss. The kind of kiss that made Liss feel both desired and cared for. Her body was too small for the oceans of feeling that kept finding new depths. She was trying to keep things in perspective. This intense honeymoon phase wasn't real life or sustainable. The euphoria was dopamine, and her obsession with Amelia a combination of norepinephrine and adrenaline. There was so much they hadn't talked about, so much they didn't know.

But those concerns felt like paper dolls. What felt important, what was above the fold, was what Liss *really* wanted to say to Amelia Kelly. A thought as quixotic as it was dangerous.

I'd say yes, too.

The rain eased up. Insects began millioning around the lone balcony light. The tiny flying creatures evolved to navigate by the light of the moon; by keeping it at a constant angle, they could maintain a steady course. Artificial light radiated in all directions. In attempting a straight course, the helpless bugs were caught in an endless, hopeless spiral dance around the wrong source of light.

46

Matty organized to borrow the Yellow Cottage for the Noisy Brats pitch, after Amelia offered to sleep on Liss's couch. (*I don't mind! It's way more comfortable than Kooroy was.*) Which did not help her sister's I'm-not-Middleton-ing-Liss case, but Matty had bigger fish to fry, and unlike her little sister, she was not a natural cook.

The meeting was set for 10:00 a.m. in New York, midnight in Queensland.

"There's something exciting about starting work after dark!" Matty said to Parker, as they both got dressed after dinner.

"Be thankful you're only doing it once," Parker replied with a wry smile. "Here." She handed her a thermos.

Matty unscrewed the lid and took a sip. Coffee. "With half-and-half! I thought we were out."

"I wrangled some more off Liss. That stuff has a disturbingly long shelf life."

"Aw, thank you, boo boo." Matty stepped back to admire her wife's crisp button-down and flawlessly neat hair. Parker had a Zoom with the Target team and was looking especially polished. "Oof. You look hot, babe. Very boss bitch."

Parker laughed. "Thanks, boo boo. Would you buy a company off me?"

"Absolutely." Matty kissed her, then kissed her again. "I really would."

A few hours later, Matty touched up her lipstick in Amelia's tiny bathroom mirror with a thumping heart, and not just due to coffee-fueled nerves. Strangely, she felt like she was about to do something illicit. Something bad.

Matty'd claimed she didn't need to practice her part of the pitch for anyone, that running it with Levi was enough. "It's honestly not that interesting," she'd told her family. The truth was, her half of the thirty-minute pitch finished with the line: *So, do my wife and I end up having kids? Help make Noisy Brats a reality and find out.* She'd been explained to the River Wolf execs as a consultant. But her involvement in the potential company was understood to be . . . flexible.

Matty FaceTimed Levi. He was in the foyer of River Wolf's offices in downtown Manhattan. White marble walls, black leather sofa; so different from the beach. Everything about him was stylish: lick of electric-green eyeliner, quiff with a number-two fade, floral print button-up under a black cashmere sweater.

"Are you nervous?" Matty asked.

"Depends."

"On?"

"No, I'm telling you I'm wearing Depends because, yes, I am nervous."

"Ha. Right there with you." Matty forced her jittery brain to focus. "We should mention that new Supreme Court ruling when we're on Baby Talk."

"Definitely. And I'll humble brag about being on that Vulture list profiling Black rising stars in the media. Also, I'm going to play v3 of the *Stranded* trailers; it's the most personally invasive and therefore the best."

Matty let a wallop of guilt pass. It was her truth, and hers to give. Right?

She heard someone tell Levi they were ready for him.

"See you in there." Her friend was glittering with energy. "We got this."

"It's ours and I won't give it back."

Matty hung up and hovered her mouse over the Zoom link that would connect her virtually to the pitch.

There was a moment, before hitting record or starting an edit or striding into a busy New York restaurant for an important work lunch, that Matty was in love with. The moment of pure potential. The moment before everything could change.

Matty clicked the link. The green light in her laptop illuminated, like a traffic light switching to Go. A conference room of faces lit up her screen, turning to look at her. She watched her own face change on the Zoom screen into someone in full possession of their own identity.

*

In their bedroom at Kooroy, Parker was on a considerably less enjoyable Zoom: the weekly All-Hands, every staff member jammed into the largest conference room at Poppe HQ. Parker created and ran this meeting, designed to ensure each employee felt connected to the business and its mission through understanding operations and priorities. Her theory was, if Product knew what Sales was doing and Design knew what Partnerships were up to, everyone would feel more invested. And studies showed employees liked their bosses more when they were able to be in the same room, face-to-face. Even though LK pushed back on it, Parker insisted the All-Hands were essential.

Now, she was wishing she hadn't. Even through layers of makeup and brassy new highlights, Parker could tell LK was hungover. There'd been a Young Women in Power dinner last night; LK had obviously gotten drunk on her own young woman power and the open bar. Parker skidded through the team leader updates, hoping to get through the meeting before LK took her bad mood out on the "ducklings." Everyone was working harder and later than usual as the acquisition by Target loomed ever larger.

It was almost done. Almost through.

And then it happened.

"Finally, we are hiring." Parker addressed the last action item. "Shelley, our amazing performance marketing director, is on maternity leave, and we're hoping to fill her shoes ASAP."

LK, Theo, and Ben traded glances. The unamazing Shelley had only held the position for two months before taking advantage of Poppe's six-months-paid parental leave. A policy LK had never been in favor of. "Most companies offer half that or less," she'd whined, when Parker first pitched the idea, years before. "Legally we only have to offer eight weeks."

"Most companies aren't in the pregnancy business," Parker had countered. "These are our values. It's important they're borne out in policy."

LK grumbled that employees would get hired just to get pregnant and get paid. Parker dismissed this. Unfortunately, Shelley, who'd interviewed in a shift dress to hide her baby bump, proved her wrong. She'd been the fourth senior staff member in as many months to take maternity leave—not an insignificant staffing and budgetary issue. This was the flipside of having a young, mostly female staff. They had a terrible habit of occasionally propagating the species.

Bhavani, a current member of Shelley's team, spoke up. "Are we still hiring from within?"

"Yes," Parker said. "Anyone is free to apply—"

"Actually"—Ben spoke over her, deepening his voice in a way that felt deliberately authoritative—"we already have several candidates in mind."

Another sidebar conversation Parker had been excluded from. The meeting-after-the-meeting, roll call LK, Theo, and Ben. "Great." Parker kept her voice neutral. "Thanks for the update, Ben."

Bhavani addressed Parker. She had rings on every finger, and this week, her hair was lime-green. "I was hoping to apply for that role. Shelley's written me a reference. I already know the job inside out."

Theo said, "We have a solid shortlist. A few from my alma mater, actually. Harvard grads."

Kill me, Parker thought. "Fantastic," she said. "That's it from me. Thanks, everyone."

The meeting started to wrap up. Bhavani stayed seated. "But Shelley said when she took maternity leave, I'd be the best person to cover her."

But it wasn't Shelley's call to make. "Bhavani," Parker said, "why don't you and I continue this in private?"

Bhavani rolled her eyes, muttering something to the young women sitting around her. But the exec team were signaling the conversation was closed.

And that's when it happened.

The projector behind the exec team was still showing the final slide from a marketing presentation, mirroring from Theo's laptop. Which meant that when LK privately Slacked Theo, it popped up on the giant screen as a notification.

LK 11.01 a.m: Have to hire a dude for this or we'll go broke paying for everyone's fucking mat leave.

An ax swung into Parker's chest.

LK, Theo, and Ben were oblivious, already circling up.

No one else seemed to notice.

Except Bhavani. Her phone was in her hand, aimed at the projector.

The message faded—it couldn't have been there for more than a second. Had she managed to take a photo in time?

Parker's heart was slamming against her ribs.

The assistant slipped her phone in her pocket and joined the other young women streaming out of the conference room.

How would I explain this to my own daughter? was the intrusive thought Parker kept trying to quash.

It took an excruciating hour to get LK, alone, on the phone. The CEO was dismissive. "It was a private message and a joke. That no one even saw."

"Bhavani might have a photo. You definitely have to interview her."

"I'm not hiring her—she just got married. She's probably knocked up like Shelley was. This isn't a charity, Parker, I can't keep paying for—"

"LK, shut the fuck up." Maybe it was the toll of working nights or being shut out of things or the knowledge that Matty was on the troublesome Noisy Brats pitch, but Parker couldn't control her anger. No— her fear. "This is the kind of shit that takes companies down."

"*No one even saw it.* God, Parks, chill out. I'm the dramatic one, not you."

The barb pushed Parker even further. She was almost shouting. "Title seven of the Civil Rights Act makes it *illegal* to discriminate on the basis of sex! You just broadcast a message to our entire staff you intended on *breaking federal law* by hiring a man instead of a woman. At a *pregnancy* company."

"I was joking!"

"Well, I didn't see Bhavani laughing. I saw her taking a picture. Did you know she has ten thousand followers on Instagram? People lose their entire careers over tweets less offensive than that." And if LK went down, she'd drag Parker with her. Five years of work. Three months from acquisition. No one would touch a company that was the latest lightning rod for workplace sexism. Parker was at her laptop, scheduling a meeting. "I'm setting up an interview with you and Bhavani, today."

LK was silent.

"LK? I'm serious. *Today*."

"Parks, I just got an email." LK's voice was strained. "Looks like Bhavani filed an official complaint for discrimination with HR. I guess she got that picture."

Parker got full body chills.

Have to hire a dude for this or we'll go broke paying for everyone's fucking mat leave.

The room undulated. Parker struggled to focus. "I need to talk to our lawyers. And we need to hire crisis management PR right now."

For the first time all morning, LK sounded unsure. "Wouldn't that send a bad message?"

"That ship has sailed. We need everything buttoned up. Everything aboveboard. Don't talk, don't Slack, don't even *think* a word about any of this unless a lawyer and a publicist are present."

Parker hung up and stared out the bedroom window, chest heaving, pulse racing.

No moon tonight. The ocean was vast, inky nothingness.

47

Despite its ubiquity, one of Jules's favorite coastal plants was beach spinifex. A stout, dioecious perennial grass—one of the most common and important species on coastal foreshores. Not only did the straggly, sage-green grass possess a wild, hardy beauty, it was also a pioneer sand-stabilizing species. Being salt- and wind-tolerant, spinifex anchored and protected sand dunes, the backbone of the beach. It kept the whole thing together.

This was a role Jules was familiar with. Being a woman with a secret crush? Not so much.

After dropping round her third jar of chutney, Jarrah asked Jules if she'd like to help with some weeding. Jules accepted as if he'd proposed a Michelin-starred dinner and a moonlit stroll: "That'd be absolutely *lovely*, Jarrah!"

As part of his job as a ranger, Jarrah kept an eye on invasive species, such as the pretty but pernicious asparagus fern. The chance to spend a few afternoons together, crowning and bagging the fern, felt like an excellent use of her time. In her boots and Bunnings hat, Jules slipped back into the role of bush regenerator, effective and sexless. They chatted as they worked, mostly about the plants and the island. "People think this place is perfect," Jarrah commented, "but we have our fair share of problems."

"Like what?"

Jarrah hefted his weight onto the shovel. "Like the ferry service. It's a private company and they charge a fortune, as you know. I've been trying for years to get a discount for Indigenous people. They won't budge. The island belongs to our mob. We just can't get 'em over."

On their third afternoon, Jarrah all but shook her hand as they said goodbye. Jules wondered if this was what her daughters meant by the "friend zone." But then Jarrah's body language softened, and he asked what she was doing Sunday morning. They made a plan to meet at Mooka Mooka Lookout.

Jules sensed this wasn't going to be another weeding session. On Sunday morning, she ironed her nicest T-shirt and shorts, and took some extra time wrangling her curls. At the last minute, she slipped on Ludmila's ruby necklace. The idea of picking up vintage jewelry at a fabulous Parisian market made her feel stretched out with longing. She'd been waiting for the right time to wear the necklace for Jarrah. Her gut told her this was it.

Rubies had many properties. One was offering encouragement to follow one's bliss.

Jules had been to the lookout for a sunset or two and was already anticipating the rush from the panoramic view. What she wasn't anticipating was Jarrah in ceremonial dress. White paint striped his bare torso and face. Such a stunning, unexpected sight, Jules stopped short, speechless. She worried she'd stumbled into something she wasn't supposed to: the last time she'd seen Jarrah dressed this way they'd been expressly invited to the cleansing ceremony. But then he raised a hand in greeting. "Morning, Julia."

"Morning, Jarrah," she managed. Beyond them, the Pacific rolled blue and endless. "You look *fantastic*."

He grinned proudly. "I'd thought you'd like to see this."

Jules tried not to let her gaze linger on Jarrah's burnished brown biceps—that probably wasn't what he meant.

"Every year," he went on, "thousands of humpback whales make the five-thousand-kilometer journey from Antarctica back to north Australia to mate, calve, and nurture their offspring."

Jules knew this: Hervey Bay was world-famous for whale watching, and she still remembered the creation story Jarrah had told her about them at the rock art. It'd slipped her mind that the world's longest mammal migration was soon to begin.

"But for Indigenous people, it's more than a breeding cycle. We are connected to the whales through ancient songlines—long-held traditions that guide people through country, share our spirit, and create a safe journey." Jarrah faced the ocean. "We welcome these majestic Elders back, as family. We do it by practicing a tradition that's been lost for decades, but that people in my community, and other clans up and down the coast, are starting to practice. We sing in the whales."

Prickles of emotion caressed Jules's skin. She wouldn't be able to speak if she tried.

"I sing Gurrin-ina-narmee," Jarrah said, "a corroboree song that welcomes the spirits of my ancestors and greets the Elders of the sea. A blessing that brings balance." Jarrah pointed north, past the break. "It's early, but I've seen a couple already this week. If we're lucky, we'll see more."

He encouraged Jules to get comfortable in the shade of a blue gum, then picked up two short, whittled sticks. Tapping them to create a rhythmic percussive beat, Jarrah started shifting his weight from foot to foot, stamping his feet in a dance. He started to sing, *"Buma Romi Joonu Myun Mye Marunyu . . ."*

Jules couldn't understand the words in his native tongue, but it didn't take away from the raw beauty of the moment. She knew intellectually that First Australians were connected to country. Seeing Jarrah sing in the whales made the idea come alive. Jules couldn't take her eyes off him.

Jarrah's voice swelled, his attention focusing on something in the distance.

There, just a few miles out, a column of water shot up in the air. The dark body of a creature as big as a train carriage broke the surface.

Jules sucked in a breath. Her eyes filled with tears.

A humpback whale, graceful and ancient, on a journey its kind had been making for thousands of years.

Hello, old friend. Welcome home.

They spotted three more whales in the sun-sparkled Coral Sea. It dazzled her soul, giving Jules a thrilling kind of vertigo. The only way she knew that three hours had passed was from the position of the sun. Their shadows were short as they walked back to the Blue Cottage, the memory of Jarrah's song filling the space between them.

Jarrah washed up in his outdoor camping shower and put on a clean shirt while Jules set up lunch on the porch. Chicken salad sandwiches and homemade lemonade, cold and sweet. Sunday afternoon stretched in front of them. Even on Mun'dai, when every day was more or less the same, Sunday afternoon still had its power. Anything could happen on a Sunday afternoon.

"How did you learn to do that?" Jules finished her last crust. "Sing in the whales."

"Passed through bloodlines," Jarrah said. "From an Elder in my mob."

"Your mum or dad?"

"Uncle Charlie. Not a blood relative. A respected community member." Jarrah pushed his empty plate aside. "I never knew my dad, unfortunately."

"Oh?" Jules didn't want to pry but was hoping he'd share more.

"I was born in Maryborough. Dad wasn't in the picture. Mum was just a kid—seventeen."

"So young."

"Too young. She knew the missions were bad places, but someone at church told her they could help with supplies and stuff. So she rocked up, expecting she might get some kid's clothes or something. But those church people lied to Mum. I was taken from her. Neither of us was allowed to leave. That's how I became a part of the Stolen Generation."

Like all Australians, Jules knew about the horrors of a government policy that legalized the removal of Indigenous children from their families, forcing them to live on Christian missions that operated all around the country for decades.

Her throat winched shut. She could barely imagine having her babies taken from her arms with as much care as she and Jarrah had dug out the asparagus ferns earlier that week.

"My mother lived on the same mission, but we were kept apart," Jarrah went on. "No contact with each other or our culture. Men, women, boys, girls, all separated. I still remember eating dinner in the hall. Me on one side, Mum on the other."

Jules was aware of the missions, but she didn't know about the isolation. Her eyes were misting, but she would not cry, compelling Jarrah to console her. "Shocking." She kept her voice and eye contact even. "Inhumane."

The cruelty of her country's history was something Jules found difficult to look at and harder to feel. She thought of herself as a good person—she voted progressive and donated generously and went to all the rallies with bold, hand-painted signs—but sometimes she'd come across a doco on TV with old footage of Indigenous people locked up in chains and she'd switch it off, breathless. Perhaps she was just a performative liberal who'd never understand or do a thing about racism. Hearing Jarrah talk about his past forced her to acknowledge the uncomfortable limits of her own existence, her own place in history. Her own privilege.

"Yeah, rough stuff." Jarrah scrubbed a hand over his eyes. "Messed us both up pretty good. Long story short, Mum moved back to Maryborough, but I ended up in Brisbane, falling in with a bad crowd. Drugs and drink. Hit rock bottom a few times. Then a friend connected me with Uncle Charlie. Still remember our first phone call: *Boy, what the fuck are ya doing? Get back to country before I drag ya back meself.*" Jarrah's chuckle was rueful but affectionate. "I came back to the Bay, and Uncle started teaching me things about our people, our land. Our stories. Our power. Singing in the whales—that was Uncle Charlie. I got sober and did a course in Indigenous Land Management. Completely changed my life. I had no idea how much being on country would be part of my healing. Started as a trainee ranger over on K'Gari in my thirties, worked my way up the ranks. Learned how to be professional. Interact with the public, with all the government people and their lies. Got a reputation for being a good negotiator, which basically just means I don't tell 'em to go to hell when I should. Ended up one of the leads in the native title claim for Mun'dai."

He explained there were two types of native title in Australia: nonexclusive and exclusive. The former was akin to an honorary or symbolic title, guaranteeing few concrete legal rights. K'Gari, the neighboring island, was under nonexclusive, meaning the Butchulla were in a constant struggle with the Queensland Parks and Wildlife Service, the government body who legally co-managed it. But after a decade of work, Mun'dai won exclusive native title, allowing the Indigenous owners full control of their land.

"Now, here I am," he finished. "Chasing tailor. Telling our stories. Talking to you."

Jules crested on empathy and admiration, undershot with something tight and anxious she couldn't pinpoint. She wondered how often Jarrah spoke about this, and to whom. Was it a painful task? Or a liberating one? "What an incredible story. You've been through so much. I don't even know what to say."

"That's not like you, Julia," he teased.

"Are you still in touch with your mother?"

"We reconnected after I got sober. She passed eight years ago."

"I'm sorry."

He scratched the back of his neck. "Never easy between us, sadly. Mum had her demons, too. *Transgenerational trauma*, Julia. I read a book about it. The idea that we carry the pain of our Elders. My bloodlines have a lot of pain. Mum's grandfather—my great-grandfather—was an opium addict. Paid in dope for forced labor, working in a mill, which is what Mum's dad did, too. Cutting down trees, destroying country. Terrible life. Self-medicating was just what our mob knew."

"My father drank a lot, too. But it's different," she hastened to add. "The way grog was used in your communities."

"Poison," he said. "Part of the attempted genocide of Indigenous people."

"You've broken that cycle, though."

"Yeah. Yeah, I have. I also changed my name. It was Blackman in the mission: the name the white people gave us. I changed it to the name of my totem. Milbi: turtle."

"You're taking back your story," Jules suggested.

"Something like that. No real regrets, in the long run. Except for kids, maybe. Never had kids." He took off his hat to rub his forehead. "Would've loved to have been a dad."

"Is that what your mentor program is about?"

He inclined his head. "Yeah, guess so. Never thought of it that way.

You're very lucky, Julia. To have the family you have. I'm glad you were the ones who got stuck here. Could've been a lot worse." Then, in a conspiratorial tone, *"Bachelorette party."*

Jules laughed, but she wondered if her family was inflicting its own set of stresses. Did he hold their initial privileged squabbling against them? He'd have every right to. People felt their perspective was oceanic— mutable and deep—but it was just a grain of sand, tiny and contained.

Jarrah pushed his chair out, gathering up their empty plates. Jules stayed on the verandah, sipping her lemonade, watching a pair of sleek gray dolphins surf the break. She vaguely recalled these introductory conversations with Glen, but they'd been more interested in getting into bed than getting to know each other. In her own way, she'd bumbled through her youth, too, marrying to escape her parents' crushing expectations. She married because, like being demure and respectable, it was what women did.

Jarrah emerged with a plate of Iced VoVos, a classic Aussie biccie. Pink fondant on a rectangular biscuit, a raspberry jam stripe down the middle, all sprinkled with dried coconut. Matty said they looked like something out of a Tim Burton movie.

What would her children think of her I-guess-you'd-call-it-chemistry with Jarrah? Would they be pleased their mother had met someone she liked? No, Jules remembered with a jolt, they'd be furious and scared because she hadn't yet told them their parents had separated.

It still felt like the wrong time.

The conversation lightened into island gossip. Jules made Jarrah chuckle describing Glen and Randall's workouts, and Jarrah entertained Jules with his tale of helping Ludmila learn to fish; Ludmila, in her silk scarf, gutting a whiting on Blinky Beach!

They lingered over the VoVos, neither of them putting an end to the afternoon.

The shadows on the beach started to lengthen as the distance between them shortened. They'd spent the entire day together.

Jules leaned against the side of the Blue Cottage, hands behind her back. "So, you never got married?"

"Came close a few times," Jarrah said, hands in his pockets. "But no. Haven't dated in a while."

"Yeah. Guess we're too old for that," she joked.

"Too old for what?"

"Dating," she said. "Love."

"Nah," he said. "Never too old for love." He hesitated. "But your kids—they still don't know, right?"

"They will."

He edged forward. "Soon?"

Glen wore cologne. Jarrah didn't. His skin smelled earthy and herbaceous, like the rich, complex scent of the Australian bush. "As soon as possible."

Not exactly a lie. Or exactly the truth.

He looked at her with such intent she felt it down to the tips of her fingers. "For what it's worth, you're a very attractive woman, Julia Kelly."

Holy Dooley. It was happening. "You're not half bad yourself."

Jarrah took off his hat, tossed it aside. He sounded nervous, with an undercurrent of humor. "I think I'm about to do something I haven't done in a long time."

Jules's heart was a pinball ricocheting wildly. She wet her lips. "I think I might be about to do that, too."

And with that, Jarrah Milbi stepped forward and kissed her.

It was no movie-magic kiss. It was short and a bit awkward, like two bumper cars with clueless drivers. Yet it was still the single most exciting kiss Jules had ever shared with another human being. Jarrah's lips were warm and lush. He smelled like the earth after rain and he tasted like Iced VoVos.

A barrier between them dissolved. Jules dared to put her hands on his chest. Feel his heart drumming fast beneath the clean cotton of his shirt. Gosh, he was a handsome bugger. Handsome and resilient and hardworking and kind.

Jarrah hooked his pointer finger around Ludmila's ruby necklace. In the late afternoon light, the precious stones glowed like embers. "Beautiful," he murmured, his voice sending delicious chills all the way up her back. "Deadly." Then he leaned in close again.

48

Secret Spot wasn't listed on the map of Mun'dai provided to tourists. The tiny, Mediterranean-style cove was located past the southern end of Blinky Beach, beyond the craggy rocks that offered no pass, or view of it, even in low tide. The secluded bay was only accessible via a hairpin path through the rainforest not suitable for the very young or very old; Liss only revealed the location to those unlikely to sprain an ankle. Ordinarily, that'd be the entire Kelly-Lee party, but given everything, she'd forgotten about the little pocket of paradise.

Amelia laughed out loud when they emerged onto the hidden beach: vanilla sand and a deep gulp of blue. A single red-and-white-striped umbrella had somehow survived the surge. Amelia marveled, "It's like something out of a Visa commercial."

Liss had confirmed with Jarrah that the cove would be safe from crocs, due to the cold water currents the reptiles would stay away from. They'd brought bathing suits, but Amelia arched an eyebrow and suggested they "ditch the cozzies" (take off their swimming costumes) and go "rudie nudie" (skinny dip).

The water was clear as glass. Colorful fish hung suspended above the hermit crabs and sea anemones on the wrinkled ocean floor. Flipping to their backs, the pair floated under a cerulean sky. Stark naked and starfishing, fingertips brushing on the surface of the sea. The sun warmed their bodies, the ocean deliciously cool beneath them. No sound but for the shimmering cicadas and rich chorus of birdsong. Liss's busy mind relaxed, softening to complete peace.

Remember this moment, Liss told herself. *Remember this moment and you will always be happy.*

To keep with the Mediterranean theme, lunch was cheese, bread, olives, and a bottle of white wine. The alcohol made Amelia amorous and soon, her mouth was between Liss's legs. The sharp cries from under the umbrella made two red rosellas take flight, jetting through the trees like twin flames.

They drifted off, lulled by the quiet wash of the turning tide. When Liss woke an hour later, the sun had moved. Part of her calf was burned, blossoming red.

She adjusted the umbrella, admiring the luscious curves of her sleeping lover. Liss was bony, an absence of hips. Amelia's hourglass figure was that of an acoustic guitar. The white sand on her ass-cheek made it look like it'd been dipped in sugar.

A perfect afternoon. If only every day could be like this.

But it couldn't. The sun was edging behind the trees, shadows creeping up the beach like thieves. As badly as Liss wanted to freeze time and stop it from collapsing through her fingers, she couldn't.

> *So Eden sank to grief,*
> *So dawn goes down to day.*
> *Nothing gold can stay.*

The last lines of a Robert Frost poem, likely gleaned from *The Outsiders,* she couldn't be sure.

For so long, each day had been a replica of the last. *Mundane Mun'dai* was scratched on the Cabin's bathroom door. Liss was careful not to take the island for granted, but there was some truth in it. Then Amelia Kelly charmed half a cup of whiskey off her, and the island was no longer predicable. The days felt longer and shorter, the past more prescient, the future more urgent. While it was all a glorious sapphic dream, Liss was back to being worried about what tomorrow would bring.

Nothing gold can stay.

Liss trickled sand over Amelia's feet to rouse her. "Hi."

"Oh." Amelia yawned, showing all her teeth. "Hello. Should we go for another swim?"

Liss braced herself. She'd tiptoed around this topic a few times, but never jumped in feet-first. "Or talk about what's next? For us. Post-island."

Something huge rolled behind Amelia's eyes, a storm barreling up the coast. She huffed a sigh, sitting up. "Baby. Look around. We're in paradise."

"For now," Liss allowed. "But not forever."

"Let's just be in the moment." Amelia's suggestion sounded loving and completely reasonable. "Let's just enjoy this."

Until when? Liss wanted to ask. *And then what?*

Was this rebound sex? Or something more? Was Amelia feeling her heart expand to the size of a planet, too?

But Amelia was already up. "C'mon. Race you in!"

She took off, running toward the water.

Liss stayed seated, wondering who was in the right.

Amelia spun around at the shore, slightly alarmed to not see Liss beside her as always. "I said race you in!"

"I never agreed to that plan!" Liss called back, not a race-you-in type. But she got to her feet because Amelia had a point. Liss did want to live in the moment. She did want to enjoy this. It was still so new—too new to start dissecting it and figuring out its value. They couldn't fight for something that was still forming, right?

A swim was waiting. The most beautiful swim in the most beautiful place with the most beautiful girl in the world.

There was a lot they hadn't talked about.

There was also a lot they hadn't done.

As in, to each other.

And maybe, Liss thought, loping to the shore, that was what she should be focusing on. It was important to keep checking they were sexually compatible. Double-checking. Triple-checking.

"Have you ever had sex with a strap-on?"

Amelia looked up from her phone. They were back at the Cabin on the blue velvet sofa, a few minutes before leaving for dinner at Kooroy. The sun had just set. Their skin was pink and fresh from a shower.

"Yes," Amelia replied. Amending it to: "Well, twice."

Excitement unwound low in Liss's belly. "Did you like it?"

"We had no idea what we were doing, but yes."

"This might be weird." Liss twisted her fingers into her hair, feeling suddenly shy. "But I sort of left Montreal in a hurry and packed a bunch of random stuff . . ."

"You have one? Here?"

"Yup."

"Let's use it! Totally. Omigod, I definitely want you to fuck me with your massive cock."

Liss laughed, pleased but also unsurprised at the instant enthusiasm. "Okay. And maybe you can fuck me, too."

Amelia's eyes got even wider. "I've never done that before. What if I'm no good?"

"There's a learning curve," Liss said, "but I'll tell you what I like."

Amelia sat back in the sofa, regarding Liss as if they'd just agreed to rob a bank. "I'm excited. And nervous. But mostly excited." She squeezed her breasts absentmindedly. Sofia's body obsession was her feet. There wasn't a callus file or Japanese foot scrub she hadn't tried in a never-ending search for baby-soft heels. Amelia's was her boobs. She played with them daily, like a beloved pet. "I always thought I'd have a really big dick if I were a guy."

Liss snorted. "Yeah, I think every hot girl thinks that."

Amelia laughed and whacked her with a throw pillow.

The promise of the strap-on gave the family dinner a palatable frisson, exacerbated by the fact that Jules was serving sausages.

It was a gorgeous evening, clear as a bell. Glen and Randall co-captained moving the raw-edge dining room table to the second-floor balcony. The mood was lively, everyone passing bowls of salad and buttered bread rolls and thick juicy sausages bursting with flavor. Jules had gotten the idea to throw a family talent show in a few days' time, even more fired up than usual. "We're just all so talented, so special," she enthused. "My sister and I used to put on talent shows when we were kids, and so did the girls," she told Liss.

"And what was your talent?" Liss asked Amelia. "Something with batons? Or baton-shaped objects?"

Amelia nudged her under the table, but no one was listening, focused instead on Matty listing out the sisters' past talents: duets and tap-dancing and other things Amelia was flatly refusing to re-create. "No. No, Matty! You know I sound like a cat being strangled when I sing. I refuse to humiliate myself!"

"You've never had a problem with it before." Matty addressed her mother. "Where's all this coming from, Mum?"

"Nowhere! I'm just in a good mood!" Jules leapt to her feet. "Can I get anyone more lemonade? Salad? Jarrah, another sausage?"

"Thanks, Julia." Jarrah held out his plate. "Maybe I can do some of my famous card tricks at your show."

"That's the spirit!" Jules bellowed.

Matty mouthed *Julia* at Amelia, who shrugged, more interested in sawing off the end of Liss's sausage.

"You haven't finished your own," Liss told her, amused.

Amelia put it in her mouth. "It's just the tip."

Liss chuckled, flushing. *Remember this moment*: sun-whipped and loose after a long day at the beach, laughing over a plate of good food with people she cared about. Then Liss noticed Matty watching them, and Liss was reminded of her place.

The Kellys would most likely embrace another queer relationship . . . but this wasn't a relationship. It was an undefined sex thing, forged from the ashes of a savage breakup. Plus, Liss wanted Amelia to tell her family, over her sister guessing and breaking the news as gossip.

"Great sausages, Jules," Liss said, trying to shift Matty's attention away from just how much Amelia's elbow was bumping hers. But Liss could feel Matty's inquisitive journalist eye on them both.

Did she know her younger sister thought of herself as unlovable? Partly because of feelings of inadequacy relating to Matty herself? That usually resulted in people selecting emotionally unavailable partners. Could Matty verify that? If you knew the origins of people's self-hatred, you could guess at the flaws that threatened their relationships. Was Amelia unconsciously self-sabotaging by falling for someone who was flying to a different time zone as soon as they could get off the island?

Jarrah offered Glen the salad. When he failed to notice, Jarrah said his name. Twice.

"I'm good," Glen replied, without making eye contact. "How'd your pitch go, Matty?"

Matty's expression muddied. "Fine."

Liss had assumed Matty was going to do well in her pitch—it sounded like Amelia's sister was a bit of an overachiever—but maybe Liss was wrong.

"We're still—Levi's still—waiting to hear back," Matty added.

"I'm sure you were wonderful, darling. You're always so impressive." Jules said. "Future Supermum of the Year! Gosh, won't it be fun to have a highchair at the table this time next year? A little mouth to feed?"

Matty rolled her eyes. She seemed increasingly ambivalent about having children with her attentive wife and supportive family. Not how Liss would feel in that position. She watched Amelia serve Ludmila and Randall the last of the sausages instead of getting seconds herself. She'd be a great mom. Loving, energetic, naturally selfless and maternal. She'd want to carry, Liss assumed, which suited Liss perfectly. Her mind skipped idly into the future. The two of them painting a nursery, rings on their fourth fingers. Managing a diaper blowout. Pushing a gurgling blonde child on a swing set in a park on a sunny afternoon, pushing them higher and higher—

Liss caught herself with a mortified start. They'd been sleeping together for *ten days*. Ten days wasn't will-you-be-the-mother-of-my-children? Ten days was let's-have-sex-with-a-strap-on. There would never be a gurgling blonde child with Amelia. The thought was more disquieting than Liss anticipated. With the excuse of getting more bread rolls, Liss slipped inside.

The kitchen was a glorious mess, every bowl and utensil evidently used to make the evening's feast. Far more lived-in than was typical. It'd been a treat not to clean up other people's crap for the past month.

The waitlist for the rentals had never been longer. As soon as they finished repairs, they'd likely be full through the end of the year. The idea of staying on, cleaning out a stranger's mess from the Yellow Cottage while Amelia forgot about her in Sydney, made Liss feel angry.

The balcony door slid open.

Matty, holding an empty bottle of tomato sauce. She gave Liss a sharp smile as she inspected the pantry. "You two are looking very cozy."

She didn't need to qualify who. Liss busied herself with breaking open bread rolls. "Yeah, Amelia's a good buddy."

Matty raised her eyebrows in a *is-that-what-they're-calling-it-these-days* way. She wasn't courting Liss's approval, and it was intimidating. "You seem to be spending a lot of time together."

Liss tried to sound vague, slapping butter on rolls. "I wouldn't say a lot of time."

"You're always together." Matty looked at Liss and let out a laugh. "Don't look so freaked out. Obviously I wouldn't care if you guys were . . ." She let the assumption linger.

Liss returned it with the same blank stare she adopted when someone misgendered her. Give people nothing and sometimes things corrected themselves.

But Matty just took a bigger swing, leaning comfortably against the kitchen counter. "So, are you single?"

"Excusez-moi?"

Matty didn't repeat the question; she knew Liss heard her. She was waiting for an answer, as if it was a completely rational enquiry.

Maybe it was. "Well, I had something going on with a swamp wallaby, but he was seeing a dingo, who was totally hung up on a brolga . . ."

Amelia would've burst out laughing. Matty was looking openly critical. Did she not get the joke?

Liss clarified, "Not a lot of options around here."

"Yeah, I get it. You're funny." Matty twisted open a jar of pickles. "My sister likes funny."

Ah. This was an accusation.

"I used to date comedians," Matty added, appraising Liss as if she were a slightly distasteful artwork. "Very sad people."

In another circumstance, Liss would've laughed. "Well, I'm not a comedian."

Matty bit the top off a pickle. "Yes, what do you do when you're not living on a tropical island, escaping crocodiles and tsunamis?"

Liss finished buttering the rolls, keen to escape the Aussie Inquisition. "I'm a social worker."

"Oh, that's cool." Amelia's sister looked abashed, sounding equally surprised and genuine.

"And a musician."

Mouth full of pickle, Matty exploded into a coughing fit.

Amelia liked musicians. Matty must know that. She was red-faced and coughing but also sort of laughing. "How long have—" She tried to wheeze. "How long have you been—"

Liss grabbed the plate and motored back to the table. She and Amelia swung to each other like a vaudeville act: "Are you ready to go?"

Amelia was a half step in front of her, all the way back to the Caretaker Cabin.

"I think Matty suspects," Liss tried. "Something. Everything?"

Amelia shrugged, distracted, yanking her along the sandy track. "So? I want my family to know."

Why didn't Amelia care what her family thought of them being together? Because it had an expiration date? Because it didn't? Or because her attention was focused on the garden of earthly delights waiting for them?

Which Liss was now, happily, able to focus on.

The flesh-colored phallus stuck with cockeyed confidence out of the leather harness Liss buckled herself into. "Does it have a name?" Amelia asked.

Liss tightened one of the straps. "Vlad the Impaler." Half a joke, half not.

Amelia giggled, running her fingers up and down with a respectfully light touch. Sofia treated Vlad with the reverence you'd give an old shoe. Sofia liked the physical sensation of being penetrated, but she didn't like talking about Vlad as if it was real, not even just for fun. "You can't actually come inside me," Sofia had said after Liss suggested otherwise.

"Then I definitely overpaid for this," Liss responded, thinking, *Duh*. But Amelia was into it.

After fooling around for a bit, Liss hovered over Amelia, watching her expression as she gently pushed herself inside. Without the sensation of nerve endings, this exploration was always slightly stunted. But the feeling of being inside a woman in this way still made Liss feel virile, Zeus-like, the anxious motor of her brain finally calming.

Amelia's eyes widened. "Ooh, wow."

"You okay?"

"Yeah, yeah, it's just—you're bigger than James."

A surge of power, like unexpected applause. "That makes me feel . . . amazing."

Amelia laughed softly, wriggling to reposition herself. "Start slow."

"Like this?" Liss rolled her hips back and forth. Tracking the way each movement played on Amelia's face like music.

"Yeah. Yes. Good. Yes. Yes, baby." Her gaze lusted, dropping dreamy deep. "Yes, baby. Fuck me."

Mouth pooling, heart fired, Liss started thrusting.

"Not that hard."

"Sorry." She slowed.

"Harder than that. Faster. Yes. Yes. Yes, baby. *Yes*."

Liss knew what it felt like to be fucked: the sensation of being filled, deeply and completely, right on the border of pleasure and pain. She liked the drama of it and feeling possessed by a lover; the submission could be fun. But that sort of sex would never be enough. If she had to choose, this was her preference. This felt most natural.

They found a rhythm, sinking deeply, easily, into that place beyond thought. That place of unrestrained play.

Amelia shifted to straddle Liss, bucking like a brumby, unrestrained and free. "Fuck me with your hard cock," she hissed, arching her back. "Yeah, baby—ohmigod, you're so huge."

Amelia's perfect breasts bounced like jelly. She was every jock's wet dream, which made Liss feel like the star quarterback. She wasn't aware of the affirmations and instructions tumbling out of her own mouth— she didn't need to be. She'd never felt more comfortable with a new partner.

Remember this *moment*: the hot, horny, former-soap-star-looking blonde, who was also somehow her best friend, riding her until she started to come. Amelia pressed her face into Liss's neck, snorting and snarling. "Oh fuck. I'm gonna come. Oh *fuck*."

Liss slipped her fingers under the harness, swirling her drenched, swollen clit. She came quickly, so hard it hurt, everything contracting and pulsing, shock waves of pleasure that weren't ending, neon, flying, wet wet wet. Their cries bounced off the windows, quivering the panes.

They lay back on the bed, panting. The eight chambers of their hearts pounding in rhythm.

Amelia looked wild-eyed, high. "Fuck, I *really* like you."

Liss was blazing, solar, everything hot and overflowing. "I like you, too."

Not even close to the whole truth.

Liss Chambers knew, as clearly as she knew north from south, day from night, that she'd failed in her mission to protect them both from heartbreak. Because she was falling in love with Amelia Kelly. Deeply, uncontrollably in love, in a way that superseded logic and felt like forever, and she had been, ever since they'd met.

Acknowledging this truth made her feel as expansive as the solar system. The night sky was her skin and the moon, brilliant and powerful and shining so bright, was her heart.

Liss fell asleep with the smell of something sweet lingering in her nostrils. A pineapple fermenting in the fruit bowl, already too ripe.

Nothing gold can stay.

49

Despite Glen and Randall going out longer and later to find the Lady Lushington Boobook, the white bird was proving to be their white whale. They spotted powerful Brahminy Kites and sociable Rainbow Lorikeets. Seussian-named Wompoo Fruit-Doves and a stout Australian Brush-turkey, clucking and grunting as they disturbed it scratching for worms. Close calls with other white-feathered fowls: a Little Corella, a Grey Goshawk. But even though the mysterious bird with the piercing yellow eyes and pinky-red feet remained out of their reach, none of it felt like a waste of time. Randall was reading Glen's copy of *The Last Boobook: Birdlife on Lady Lushington Island,* urging Glen to test him on the Latin names of common species—Randall was competitive and wanted to get every one right. And Randall regularly dropped pearls of wisdom that Glen scooped up and spent hours examining when he was alone. *All feelings are valid* or *A man's happiness comes from his own making.* But perhaps the most valuable of insights came after a monumental encounter with a pair of plump, endangered Black-Breasted Button Quails. After Glen pointed out both birds were female, Randall casually mentioned, "Amelia and Liss seem very happy."

"Yes," Glen agreed blithely, watching the quails flutter off. Penny drop. His voice hitched an octave. "Wait. Whatcha mean?"

Randall blinked. "Aren't they together?"

Glen blinked. "Are they?"

Randall blinked again. "Aren't they?"

"I don't know!" Glen felt feather-ruffled, not so much at the island gossip but that he might be the last to know, as always. He wanted to be more involved in his children's lives. He just didn't know how.

"Sorry." Randall flipped open his bird-watching journal to note the quails. "I thought it was obvious."

A little unexpected, but homosexuality was rife in the animal kingdom, recorded in almost every species. A fifth of all swan couples were gay; every ornithologist knew that! Gay swans would build nests together, defend their territory, even start families. Sure, that sometimes meant one swan in a male couple would mate with an unsuspecting female, then drive her away once she'd laid a clutch of eggs (Glen always felt sorry for this poor scorned swan), but still: swans were monogamous and stuck with one partner for many years. And Liss had saved his daughter's life. Twice. "Well. Good for them. Liss is a good egg." He scratched his head. Matty and Parker. Liss and Amelia. "Mate, is everyone gay?"

"Certainly seems that way," Randall replied, before catching sight of a sulphur-crested cockatoo. "Oh, look: *cacatua galerita.*"

On the afternoon of the talent show, the two men spent an extra hour lingering at the northern end of Blinky Beach, weaving into the thick edges of the bush. As they started to lose the light, they decided it was time to call it a day.

Which meant it was time to hit Randall's weed pen.

Glen had been shocked when Randall first offered. Randall barely drank—he was the healthiest man Glen had ever met. "I don't over-indulge," Randall had explained. "It's relaxing, and calorie-free." Glen hadn't smoked since uni. The first time he tried Randall's pen, he took so small a puff that nothing happened. The second, he took too big a hit and couldn't stop giggling during dinner. Now, he'd figured out how much to have for a lucid, Friday-night sort of mood.

Strolling down Blinky Beach, toward the night's talent show, the talk turned to birds of a different nature. "Debbie Harry," Glen thought aloud, exhaling smoke.

"Ooh, definitely," Randall said. "Had her picture on my bedroom wall, for sure. Something about the eyes. Bedroom eyes."

"Every-room-in-the-house eyes," Glen quipped, and Randall chuck-led. Glen puffed out his chest. He couldn't make jokes like that around his daughters. But here with Randall, what was the harm? Just two mates, talking about girls, having a laugh, like mates do.

Randall took a hit. "Farrah Fawcett."

"Yes, god yes." Glen smiled, remembering the illicit excitement the raunchy seventies pinup would evoke in his pubescent body. "That smile. Those legs. And the really big . . . hair."

Randall laughed again, offering a high five.

Glen went to slap his hand, palm raised. And stopped.

Everything stopped.

There.

Behind Randall, in the trees.

A bird.

A stocky, solid-looking *white bird*.

Glen's heart thrashed with excitement. His skin flushed hot then cold then hot again. He opened his mouth. No words came out, just the tiny, wispy cry of a snuffed candle: *"Ahhhhh . . ."*

Randall followed Glen's gaze. "Holy fuck—"

"Is that it?" Glen squinted. "That's it, right?"

"That's it, that's it, that's *it*," Randall shout-whispered back.

It was *just* too far away to make out the bird with absolute confidence, sitting regally on a high-up tree branch, seemingly oblivious of their presence. But it was the closest thing they'd seen so far. If that wasn't a Lady Lushington Boobook, what was it? "That's the Boobook!"

"That's the goddamn Boobook!" Randall's face was turning red.

"C-Cameras!" Glen spluttered.

They fumbled for their phones. Glen dropped his, rushing to scoop it from the sand, torn between training his gaze on the bird and the thing that'd prove he saw it. His lock screen was a fuzzy mess. "Shit, I don't have my glasses." Glen, like everyone over sixty, hated phones. "What's my passcode?"

"You don't need it to open the camera."

"Really?"

Randall peered at his own screen. "Mine's saying I'm out of storage."

"Shit, shit, *shit*." This might be their one chance. They needed a picture before it flew off. Glen stabbed frantically at his phone until miraculously the camera app opened. He trained it on the owl, just a smudgy white speck in the middle of his screen.

"Are you getting it?" Randall asked, trying to delete photos.

"I'm getting it." Glen started firing off shots. "Oh, I'm getting it!"

The bird swiveled its head left, then right. It spread its wings and silently swooped into the dense bush behind it, Glen still taking pictures until it disappeared.

"Did you get it?" Randall asked.

Glen checked the pictures. Not perfect; could've done better with a good camera and telephoto lens, but surely, *surely* that was the Boobook. "Mate, I got it." He pumped a first in the air, kept it aloft. He'd always wanted to try the gesture. It felt amazing.

"Woo-hoo!" cried Randall.

"Woo-hoo!" Glen echoed.

There *were* Lady Lushington Boobooks on the island. The species wasn't extinct. It had survived. Despite all odds, it was *alive*. Elation rushed into every cell, turning Glen Kelly effervescent with glee. On the empty beach in the fading light, the two men jumped around on the sand, kicking up the water's edge. Laughing deliriously and celebrating like punch-drunk kings.

50

In Jules's cargo shorts and oldest T-shirt, Ludmila scanned the ocean. When she first arrived on Lush, all she saw was water. Now, she saw a landscape: underwater troughs and gullies, affected by the tide, high and turning. The ruffled surface of the water was wind, a sou'easterly, not fish feeding underneath—she could tell the difference as easily as differentiating silk from polyester.

Life was full of twists and twirls. Ludmila could never have anticipated that Australian beach fishing would speak to her soul. Her hair was a loose plait down her back, as relaxed as a long conversation with an old friend.

She found a spot to set up, baited her hook, and cast into the Yves Klein Blue water. The line arced beautifully, like a perfect grand jeté: an elegant split midair. The sea had the restless quality of performers waiting backstage.

That sort of association was happening with increasing frequency. So strange that a deserted beach in the middle of the Pacific was where her old life would choose to return to her.

Ludmila pointed her toes, barefoot into the sand, stretching every muscle in her foot. It felt like locking eyes with an old lover.

The only music was the pulse of the sea and calls of the gulls floating on the breeze. Movement was calling from deep within her muscles, her organs, the blood pumping through her heart.

Ludmila set the rod into the plastic holder, stuck on a 45-degree angle into the sand. She tried not to overthink or doubt. To simply obey the whispered desires of her body.

What did her arm want to do?

Arc up and over her head, drawing a line with her fingertips as graceful as an artist's brush.

What did her legs want to do?

Bend deeply; ah, a plié, as familiar as sunlight.

These movements were a story under her skin that had never disappeared. The words might've faded, becoming less crisp, but they were still there. A dusty book of poetry waiting to be discovered. With enough training and discipline, almost any child can become a dancer. But only those with the gift for the art of storytelling, those with the most sensitive touch, could become a ballerina.

The crash of the tide sounded like applause. The heat of the setting sun, a soloist's spotlight. Ludmila lifted her chin, her arms curved over her head, turning, turning, turning, in the sand.

51

"Babe?"

Matty could almost always pinpoint the meaning of her wife's *babes*.
There was gooey and loving: *Babe? I love you so much.* Short and practical: *Babe? Have you seen my sunglasses?* Insecure: *Babe? Does this top
work?* Wheedling: *Babe? Can you get me a refill while you're up?*

And one of the most common *babes* known to married couples everywhere: the criticism. This was that one. Matty knew as soon as it bolted
out of Parker's mouth. "Babe? *What* are you doing, you can't put a hot
tray there." Parker grabbed the tray with an oven mitt and flung it in
the sink.

Matty had been looking forward to her mum's talent show, largely as
a source of distraction from waiting to hear back about the pitch. Now
she regretted her earlier enthusiasm, specifically volunteering her and
Parker to make lasagna for everyone from the last of the frozen ground
beef. Typically they argued well, able to rise above the heat of their emotions to assess and eliminate the root cause of tension. But they'd been
finding ways to get irritated with each other all day.

Matty had been using a metal tray as a lid for the fry pan, and had
put the tray on a plastic cutting board while she stirred the bubbling
Bolognese sauce. "I can absolutely put a *warm* tray on a cutting board."

Parker blasted it with cold water. "No, you can't."

"Cutting boards are heat resistant."

"No, they're not."

"Omigod, yes they are. Don't treat me like I'm incompetent, because I'm not."

"I know you're not incompetent."

And yet never as competent as Parker herself. "I don't like this side of you. You're not always right."

Parker raised her voice. "I'm just saying it'll burn."

"It was sitting on a fry pan, it wouldn't get hot enough to—fuck it, I'll google it." Matty abandoned the Bolognese to pull out her phone, stabbing *can you put a warm tray on a cutting board?* "God, you're *so* annoying."

Parker laughed humorlessly, giving her a pot-kettle-black look.

Jules swept into the kitchen wearing one of Matty's dresses and lipstick, which she never wore. "Smells great in here, girls!"

Parker returned to the béchamel sauce, and Matty instantly felt guilty. Things with Poppe were clearly not going well, which Parker was being typically tight-lipped about. She'd never been an oversharer, taking on difficulties with a ruthless stoicism Matty was constantly trying to undo. "I'm here to share the burden!" Matty would say, or, "I'm your wife, talk to me!"

Parker rarely did.

They finished assembling the lasagna in silence, then Matty excused herself to shower and change. She put on her most fun dress—a swooshy maxi from the Aussie label Gorman—pairing it with big earrings and plenty of blush. Matty wanted to have a drink and have some fun, keeping everyone happy, including herself.

Returning to the main space, she found the party well underway: jazz on the stereo, snacks set out, Jules pouring "cocktails and mocktails for all!" Matty spotted Jarrah chatting with Parker on the balcony as Ludmila came down from the master looking lithe and graceful in a pair of black leggings and Randall's black cashmere sweater, a fat silk headband scraping her hair off her face. "You look spiffy," Matty told her.

"Thank you. I feel spiffy," Ludmila replied, without a hint of sarcasm.

Possibly their most loving interaction ever.

Glen and Randall were setting up a projector. "Matty," her father commented. "You're in full feather."

Matty preened playfully. "Thanks, Dad." Her father, the odd bird. And ah, here was the swan of the family, beautiful Amelia plating a dozen of her famous iced chocolate brownies, looking fresh and pretty in her flower-print sundress. Matty poured them both a bucket of wine, handing her sister the glass. "So, what's your talent?"

"You're stuffing your face with them." Amelia took a generous gulp, glancing at the stairs leading down to the front door. "You?"

Matty shrugged, chewing her brownie. "Maybe sing something." She licked icing off her thumb. "These are amazing. You should open a bakery."

"I'm sure it's not as easy as I'm-good-at-baking-brownies."

Matty nudged her affectionately. "Not with that attitude, Star Baker. No, seriously: you could open a shop. Start with a pop-up. Parks'll do the business plan, I'll do media strategy."

"I just like doing it for fun."

"You could do it for fun and money and widespread acclaim."

"But I don't want that."

"What do you want?"

Amelia's gaze moseyed back to the first-floor stairs. Poor thing probably thought she was being subtle.

Matty sipped her wine. "Is Liss coming?"

Even her name made Amelia soften and expand, like a pan full of brownies on the rise. She couldn't meet Matty's eye, doing an appalling impression of nonchalant. "I think so. She won't tell me her talent, though."

Matty's mind flipped through sexual innuendo—*Is she crafty? Good at scissoring?*—but before she could settle on one, Amelia faced her. "So, how did the pitch go? Really?"

The buzz from the sugar promptly soured. Matty felt her own pull— to her computer, to see if Levi'd called. They were meant to hear back this week. Still early in New York, but apparently Tom Bacon was an early riser who worked weekends. Even the possibility of her sister hooking up with a woman was a distant second to the phone call that could determine her future.

"I told you it was fine," Matty said. "Should probably go check on Parks."

"Matty." Amelia grabbed her sleeve. "How did it go?"

What could she say? Not the truth. Definitely not the truth. Because the truth was something even Matty herself was grappling with understanding. What it meant. What it could mean. What she wanted it to mean. What that would mean for everyone she loved.

The truth was they *crushed* it. Killed it. Skinned it, stuffed it, mounted its head on the wall. The execs loved the show ideas, but beyond the typical American enthusiasm, they got granular on financial projections. When they started spitballing about a launch strategy, mentioning their excellent relationship with Apple, Matty felt certain they'd get it.

Levi would get it.

"We'll talk about it later," Matty said as their mother clapped her hands to get everyone's attention.

"Okay, gather round," Jules instructed. "The show is about to begin!"

"What's your talent, Mum?" Matty asked, taking a seat on the leather sofa.

"This: I'm MC-ing," Jules said. "Jarrah, you're up first!"

Glen and Randall traded a glance that contained an entire opera.

Jarrah started doing card tricks with a dexterous hand, queens disappearing and reappearing to her mother's shouts of surprise. Matty couldn't get past the look the two men exchanged. Did they not like Jarrah? They'd seemed close ever since the turtle rescue mission. That there might be microdramas playing out between everyone on the island floated through Matty's consciousness and out the other side. She opened her laptop and refreshed her email. No word from Levi.

Jules led everyone in a round of applause, declaring how bloody fantastic Jarrah was. "Absolute cracker! Who's next? Matty, want to give it a burl?"

Matty readied to stand, tossing up between *Chicago* or *Les Mis*.

Her father spoke. "Randall and I will go next."

"Oh, okay," Jules said, as Jarrah took the empty seat next to her.

Glen pressed a clicker. A photo lit up on the wall opposite them. An out-of-focus bird, high up in a tree. Glen sounded like he was about to reveal a wonderful surprise. "I'm sure you've been curious what Randall and I have been up to these past few weeks."

Matty refilled her wine. "We know, Dad. You're working out. It's weird."

"*As well as* working out," Glen said. "I've lost five kilos, by the way."

"And gained muscle," Randall added.

"As well as that," Glen said. "Randall and I have discovered a species of bird thought to be extinct!"

They pointed at the photo like showmen.

Everyone squinted at the picture.

"What is that, hon?" Jules asked, for some reason amending the pet name to: "Glen."

"That," her dad said proudly, "is the Lady Lushington Boobook."

It looked like a splash of white paint. Matty grabbed a handful of nuts from the snacks on the table. "I hope you're not trying for wildlife photography as your talent, Dad, because I have terrible news."

"Matty!" Parker shot her a frown.

"It's a bit . . . smudgy," Amelia hedged.

"Yes, yes, it's a bit out of focus, we know." Randall examined the photo like a doctor displeased with an X-ray.

"*Inconclusive* was the word Dr. Ben Hamburg used," Glen said. "Jules, remember Dr. Gunter Hamburg?"

"No," said Jules.

"He was a mentor; a biologist," Glen said, a little impatiently. "And so is his son: I just heard back from him. He said that while this photograph is not good enough to support my 'claims'—"

"Claims," Randall scoffed. "We saw it! I saw it twice!"

"That if we got clear pictures and ideally a video," Glen went on. "It'd be *big* news, especially in the birding world. I could be interviewed about it. They could do a profile on me in *Birds of a Feather*!"

"You love *Birds of a Feather*," Randall enthused.

"I do. I do love *Birds of a Feather*," Glen said, "and I'm going to rediscover the Lady Lushington Boobook!"

Matty's dad appeared both energized and defensive, as if combating the family's long-held belief he could never do such a thing. But it didn't appear at all conclusive that they'd seen the species in question. Matty looked to Amelia, typically the "That's fantastic, Dad!" child, but she was staring at the empty first-floor stairs like they were leaving on a jet plane. "Awesome, Dad!" Matty supplied. "Onya." She raised her glass in a toast.

"So we all have to be on the lookout." Randall clapped Glen on the back. "At all times!"

Her father started on the basics of bird-watching and how they must all have a fully charged phone or camera on them before Jarrah cut him off. "You'll report all this to the council, right?"

"The council?" Glen repeated, confused.

"The legal custodians of the island." Jules sounded authoritative.

"Because it's not really *your* bird," Jarrah said. "You get that, right, mate?"

Glen looked to Jarrah, then Jules, then back at Jarrah. His cheeks were coloring. "Well, yeah. Yeah, of course."

"Plus, if what you're saying is true," Jarrah went on, "it might not be good for Mun'dai. Government people trampling everything to catch a—What's it called? Boo-boo?"

"Boo*book*," Glen and Randall chorused limply, exchanging a chastened glance.

The quartet began discussing all this, which Matty tuned out, shifting next to her sister. "She might not come," Matty whispered.

Amelia looked alarmed, at either Matty reading her mind or the prospect of that being true. "She'll come. She always comes." And then her sister *blushed*.

Matty laughed, eighty percent sure something was going on, or just about to start.

A flash of blue loping up the stairs from the front door. Liss, in a white T-shirt and black skinny jeans. She was carrying—wait for it— a guitar case.

Amelia inhaled so throatily she started coughing.

Matty upped it to ninety percent. This would explain the gay-film-inspired-cocktails currently on the Barefoot Bar's specials board: *Ma Vie on Rosé. But I'm a Cocktail. Blue Crush Is the Warmest Color.* Someone get U-Haul on speed dial, stat.

Like a shot, her sister was up and over, gesturing at the guitar case in astonished delight. The distraction was enough to bring the ridiculous bird drama to a close.

"Hi, everyone," Liss was saying. "Hi, Jules. Hi, Glen." All very respectful in an I'm-secretly-fingering-your-daughter way. Matty recalled making a similar effort with her mother-in-law in the early days. Things with Ludmila had been easier, lately. Why?

"Yeah, I thought I'd sing something, if anyone was into that?" Liss was saying, overly polite even for a Canadian.

"Of course we would!" Jules shrieked. "Glen, shut that silly projector off. Everyone, sit, sit, sit."

Amelia looked ready to pass out.

"Has she sung for you before?" Matty enquired.

"No." Amelia's eyes were glued on Liss, now tuning up in one of the armchairs. "Never."

"How romantic," Matty murmured. Her little sister was the least musically talented person on the planet—her recurring nightmare since childhood involved an empty stage and expectation of an unlearned song—which meant she treated musicians with reverence bordering on religious. Her sexual Achilles' heel. Matty tried to catch Parker's eye to share the news.

But her wife was staring at her phone, her expression doomed.

Liss strummed a chord. "I haven't played for an audience in a few months, so I might be a bit rusty."

"Go Liss!" Jules hooted, clapping.

"Mum," Amelia muttered.

"No, I love the enthusiasm." Liss smiled at Jules. Despite her own neg, she seemed confident in front of a crowd. "Shout-out to the Kelly family."

Jules punched the air in exhilaration. "Woo!"

Liss strummed a chord. "Okay. Here we go." She counted herself in and began singing in an ethereal, musical voice, *"Salt air, and the rust on your door. I never needed anything mo-ore . . ."*

Possibly familiar as an old Taylor Swift song—Matty wasn't an obsessive like her sister—something airy and sweet, but full of longing, bittersweet. Odd choice for a serenade. Still, diminutive Liss was a surprisingly captivating performer. Glen tapped his toes, Randall chewed his bottom lip in concentration, and Jules tried to sing along, although she didn't know any of the words. But Matty couldn't take her eyes off her sister. Amelia's entire body was vibrating, eyes bugging, hands fisting and unfisting: real cat-in-a-microwave stuff—zero chill. Matty'd been amused by her little sister having a gay moment, but should she be worried? Surely, Amelia couldn't be so far gone she was laying the foundation for a *second* island heartbreak?

Liss was singing about being twisted in bed sheets, August sipping away like a bottle of wine: it was basically a billboard, *Lesbians R Us*. Matty recalled being this into Parker back when they couldn't get through a home-cooked meal without humping each other on the kitchen floor. Now, they were bickering about where you could put a tray.

The song ended to a round of whoops and cheers. Amelia was already restless, staring at Liss like she wanted to devour her.

Liss eye-fucked her right back.

Matty opened her laptop and refreshed her email. Still no word from Levi. She put her mouth against her sister's ear. "How long have you been shtupping the help?"

Amelia swung to her, mouth ajar. Sweetly, completely shocked.

52

Amelia dragged Matty into the Jack-and-Jill bathroom that Parker and her shared with their parents, feeling stunned and exposed and definitely excited that her sister knew the truth. She locked both doors, switched on the fan for white noise, and spun to face Matty. "How did you know?"

Matty looked at her like she was an adorably silly child. "You just told me." She put her laptop on the messy counter and uncapped a lipstick to touch up her lips. "Also, you're staring at each other like rabid dogs—super subtle." Matty met Amelia's eyes in the mirror. "You *were* Middleton-ing Liss at Mum's birthday! That's why you wore those ridiculous swimmers."

"I looked hot in those swimmers," Amelia shot back. "And okay, yes, I was Middleton-ing Liss at Mum's birthday. But I'm not shtupping the help. Don't call her the help!"

"She's the literal definition of the help."

"Well, we're not just shtupping. We're . . ." Describing it was like remembering a warm and glorious dream.

"In love?" Matty barked out a laugh. "Wowie zowie, you really can fall for anyone. It's actually impressive. Your imagination is so powerful you could create a star-crossed romance with this lipstick. That shoe."

"I'm not just— This isn't just— She's special!"

Matty spun away from the mirror to face her. "Wait: Have you been with women before?"

Amelia crossed her arms, feeling a lick of pride. A rare treat to sur-prise her sister. "Yes."

"Really?"

"Yes!"

Matty's face stayed critical. "Who? When? Anyone I know?"

"A few people. After you moved to New York. No."

Someone knocked on the bathroom door.

"Occupied," the sisters chorused.

Matty shook her head in impressed disbelief. "Do Mum and Dad know?"

"No."

"Not even Mum?"

Amelia felt a squeeze of guilt. "I know she'll be fine, big picture, but I know she'll say something about not having a son-in-law or grandkids and ruin the moment for us both." As supportive as Jules was, the sisters weren't *absolutely* certain their mother wouldn't have preferred for Matty to marry a man. "You know what she's like."

Matty acknowledged this with a tip of her head, her gaze glued on Amelia. "And now you're in love with Liss."

"We haven't said anything. But . . . maybe. Yes. I think I love her and I think she loves me." Saying it loud felt so good, so freeing, so *real*.

But her sister failed to join her happiness. Matty's face stayed ques-tioning. "Okay. So, what's the plan for next week?"

"Next week?"

Matty's expression turned incredulous. She spoke slowly and clearly. "We're going home."

Like a bucket of cold water dumped over her head. "*What?*"

"We've been here for five weeks. Guess you lost track of time."

Amelia knew they'd be leaving at the end of April. But she so des-perately did not want anything to change, she'd shoved it right out of her mind. The idea of leaving Liss: well, it didn't even compute. She slid mutely to the bathroom floor.

Matty hitched up her dress, took a seat on the toilet, and started to pee. "What's the plan? Is she going to move to Sydney with you?"

Sydney? "I think she's going back to Montreal."

"Cool. Can you imagine moving to Montreal? A French-speaking city? Where you know no one except her?"

"I haven't really thought about it. Yes. No. Maybe?"

Another knock on the door.

"Occupied!" the sisters yelled.

"Let's say Montreal doesn't work out," Matty went on, still peeing. "How about long distance?"

Never seeing each other, waiting on every text and call. It had been hard enough with James and he was only a short flight away. Montreal was on the other side of the planet. "I'd rather not."

"So, this is a fling." Matty grabbed some toilet paper and wiped. "This isn't love. This is sex with a hottie before you go home to Sydney and restart your life."

Disbelief at the impossible proposition had Amelia's mouth falling open, more certain of her feelings than ever. "But I love her."

Matty was washing her hands. "You love having sex with her. I get it, the whole anime River Phoenix thing is hot. Just don't get attached. *Don't* fall in love. You've already been dumped once on this island. Lest we forget James and the ballroom-dancing dentist."

Amelia's incredulity hardened into defensive anger. "Liss is nothing like James!"

"I'm sure Liss is awesome, that's not the issue. The issue is logistics." Matty dried her hands and folded her arms, looking down at a still-seated Amelia. "Can I be frank?"

"*Now* you're being frank?"

"You are thirty-three. Stop with the die-hard romantic shit and start seeing things clearly. You are responsible for protecting your own heart."

"I know," Amelia whimpered. "I am." But was she?

"Keep it light! Friends who fuck. Have a laugh, have sex, then leave."

Amelia tried to picture having casual sex with Liss then bidding a friendly farewell and trotting back to the Yellow Cottage. No endless snuggling and marathon make-outs and dreaming in each other's arms. It was like trying to imagine her own funeral. "I don't think I can. I don't want to. I want her."

"Well, I don't know what to tell you, Animal!" Her big sister flipped her palms to the sky. "This all ends next week, for better or worse, so you need to figure out a plan before it all hits you on the ferry and she's just a little blue speck on Blinky Beach sadly waving a rainbow flag."

The image was so ludicrously tragic Amelia almost felt like laughing.

Matty plopped down next to her, giving her a side-hug. "Honey. I'm glad you met someone you like. And obviously, I'm taking it as a personal victory she's a she. But not everyone we have feelings for is our forever person. Maybe it's not a love *story*, maybe it's a love . . . tweet. Maybe Liss will be a great friend."

"She's not just a friend. It's not a tweet!" Amelia felt close to sobbing or screaming or both. "I've never felt this way about anyone, ever. She's *everything* to me—"

Someone banged on the bathroom door. "Girls? The other bathroom is—"

"Occupied!" the sisters screeched.

"God, of course one of us would turn this into a lesbian psychodrama." Matty refreshed her email. Her eyes pulsed open. "Shit, it's Levi. He wants me to call."

"But—"

"Sorry. Go talk to Liss." Matty scrambled up and unlocked the door. Jules was waiting outside, legs crossed. "Thank Christ, I'm busting."

Amelia only had a second to compose herself before her mother dashed in, lifted her skirt, and started pissing like a racehorse.

53

The night took on a new urgency. Before talking to her sister, Amelia planned on dragging Liss into the pantry or hall closet or any hot, tight space and showing her just how much she adored being serenaded. But now all she saw were minutes slipping through her fingers like so many grains of sand. She had no appetite for the wedge of lasagna on the plate in her hand. No interest in anything except talking to Liss, with whom her entire family were trying to get their five minutes. Why had she been putting off this conversation? Further proof of her own poor judgment and atrocious relationship skills.

Amelia's nerves were peaking during the final act of the evening: Ludmila. Who, in a moment equally beautiful and bizarre, performed a short ballet routine. She was better than good, moving her limbs with fluid lyricism. The bewilderment on everyone's faces mirrored Amelia's own. She was light-headed with anxiety. As applause broke out at the end of Ludmila's dance, Amelia was rocketed into the future, her and Liss the center of everyone's love and attention, in their hypothetical life together in Sydney. She blinked, and it was gone.

Amelia caught Liss's eye across the room. Even just the sight of her—the delicate curve of her neck, the slight boyish hunch of her shoulders—made Amelia more and more certain.

She couldn't lose Liss. Ever.

Somehow, Amelia made it through the end of the evening and even managed to compliment Ludmila, who looked happier than Amelia had ever seen her, including her daughter's wedding day.

Liss was also energized from performing. All the way back to the Caretaker Cabin, she chatted about how much she enjoyed learning a new song as Amelia's mind whirred.

They showered in the tiny bathroom and got into bed. But when Liss went to tug Amelia close, Amelia stopped her.

"I've been thinking." Amelia tried to sound objective and logical. "About what's next. For us. Post-island."

"Oh." Liss's eyebrows pulsed up in surprise. "Okay."

Amelia tucked her hair behind her ears, channeling a banker or someone equally sensible. "Well, obviously we want to be together—we need to be together. And you've already quit this job, so we're both leaving Lush next week." She checked to see if this was a shock to Liss, too.

It wasn't. "Right."

"Right, so given that, and given long-distance sucks, I think it makes the most sense for you to move to Sydney with me."

Liss's face didn't move. Then she blinked, once, twice. "That makes the *most* sense?"

"Yeah, you move in with me, into my sharehouse. The rent's relatively cheap 'cause it's split between me and four others."

"You have four roommates?"

"Well, five because Kassie's boyfriend, Mikeo, just moved in. He's actually great when you get past the extreme veganism thing. Don't eat sour cream in front of him—made that mistake more than once. Anyway, we're in Bondi Junction, which isn't a walk to the beach but just a quick bus ride with a lot of English backpackers, and have you ever been to Sydney?"

"Nope." It had the short clip of a reality check.

Which only made Amelia double down on the pitch. "It's so beautiful, a world-class city, highly livable! You could get a job—the economy's kind of shit right now, but Australians love live music, and I have some savings. Honestly not much, teacher wages are pretty crap, but we can make it work. Right?"

Liss looked down at their interwoven hands, Amelia squeezing tightly.

Her voice was distressingly gentle. "Amelia. I think it's really sweet you'd want to live together. But I can't move to Sydney."

Amelia's throat tightened. Something inside her heated up, getting slightly frantic. "Right, you'd want to go back to Montreal first, tie up loose ends? Pack? Yeah, that makes sense, of course you can't just come home with me, even though you do have clothes and stuff here and we could just buy whatever you need."

"No, I don't just mean logistically." Liss extracted herself from Amelia's grip and leaned back against the wall, letting out a long, uneven exhale. "When Sof moved to Los Angeles, I was half there, half in Quebec for months. I never officially lived in L.A., but I got a sense of what it might be like to move to someone else's city for them. It sounds romantic, but practically, it's super isolating and really, really hard. Visa stuff gets complicated. Sydney's expensive." Her hazel eyes brimmed with empathy. "I care about you so much, Amelia. More than I can— More than I should. But I can't move to a city I've never even been to, where I know no one except you and your family."

An alarm was going off in Amelia's head; it was all she could do not to wince at the volume. "What if I moved to Montreal?"

Liss let out a strained laugh. "I don't think you'd be happy. For the exact same reasons."

"I'll be happy if I'm with you."

"Maybe in the short-term," Liss allowed. "But long-term, you'd be living somewhere you don't speak the national language, where it's freezing half the year and you hate the cold, and very, very far away from everyone you care about."

"So what? We just break up?"

"Not to put too fine a point on it," Liss spoke delicately, "but we've never even defined this."

Amelia stared in horrified disbelief. "We're together."

"We're sleeping together."

"But aren't you, like, my . . . girlfriend?"

Liss looked stunned. "Am I?"

It suddenly struck Amelia what Liss was getting at. What her reticence meant— What it'd always meant.

She'd gotten it all wrong. Just like James. James, who'd never loved her, who'd never even liked her enough to respect her. A shucked, unstable feeling oozed into Amelia's pores. "You're not . . . *I'm* but you're not . . ."

"What? I'm not what?"

She was too much for Liss. Too much for anyone. Too much to take on, or not enough: both were probably true. Yet again she'd poured her entire being into someone who liked her face and her body but not her mind. Not her heart. Not enough, anyway. Not enough to be together more than a few weeks.

Amelia started snatching up her things.

"What? Amelia, what's happening?"

"God, I'm *such* an idiot. *What* is wrong with me?" Cleanser, cardigan, T-shirt. "*Why* does this keep happening to me?"

"Amelia, baby, what's going on?"

Amelia yanked open the front door and whirled around, her vision blurry with terrified tears. "This is just sex for you. A fling. A *location-ship*."

Liss looked like she'd just suggested Liss was actually in love with the toothbrush Amelia was clutching. "No, Amelia, that's not what's happening."

"You don't care about me, not like I care about you." She could feel herself getting overheated, unable to slow down. *Too much. Too much. Too much.* "Maybe I don't care about you, either! I'm probably just falling in love with you because that's what I do. I'm a love junkie in the ultimate love junkie location with the ultimate love junkie object of affection. How can I not? You're adorable and wonderful and my family loves you and you have a giant heart the size of a badger!"

"I love badgers." Liss's words were faint, stunned. She was staring at Amelia. "Did you just say you're falling in love with me?"

Tears were spilling down Amelia's cheeks. She couldn't keep them in. "I can't help what I feel. I wish I could, but I can't." She should stop talking. She couldn't. "That day at Wonapinga Head, when we did the Great Loop. That's when I knew how I felt about you."

Something was happening behind Liss's eyes. Like a door Amelia hadn't noticed before edging open. Slowly, then all at once. "I knew how I felt about you on Day One."

Amelia blinked tears away, trying to parse the meaning of this. Her heart was still pounding with fear and worry. If Liss let her walk out that door, she didn't know where she could possibly go.

Liss shook her head, moving closer. Her expression was raw, completely unchaperoned. "God, Amelia, isn't it obvious? I love you. I'm in love with you."

Her body rioted with feeling. Amelia dropped her things. "I love you, too."

Liss cupped her face, Amelia's tears running over her fingers. Dizzying, neon-bright emotion fluoresced through her body, obliterating everything, all worry, all doubt, zeroing in on the electric-soft feeling of Liss's mouth touching hers. This kiss, kisses like this: oxygen, sunlight, a standing ovation, an eclipse.

The plan she'd been determined to name and nail down floated out the window, drifting past the sailing sugar gliders, toward the distant moon.

Amelia couldn't get Liss's clothes off fast enough. But something about their connection felt amiss, like a song being sung just off-key. No matter what Amelia tried—sweet words, sexy words, this position, that hair flip—they couldn't get in tune and in the end, Liss didn't come.

"I'm just tired," she said. "It happens."

It just hadn't happened before. All of their firsts so far had been romantic, thrilling experiences. But relationships were also full of other firsts, and Amelia wasn't sure what this first meant.

They curled up under the top sheet, Amelia pressed against Liss's back. Ordinarily, she fell asleep quickly, lulled by the tide of Liss's breathing and the complete contentment of being able to hold her. But Amelia couldn't relax.

They were in love. They'd just said it. That was supposed to be it, the pot of gold at the end of the rainbow. Yet Amelia couldn't shake the troubling idea that their feelings didn't make things easier. Didn't fix all the broken things inside them. Didn't magically solve the problem of what came next.

Liss. Amelia loved the name as much as she loved the person it belonged to: such a languid, luxurious word. One consonant from *kiss*.

But also from *loss*.

Amelia squeezed tighter.

Liss squirmed. "Baby, can you move over?"

Amelia obliged, realizing she was, as always, on Liss's side of the bed.

They ended up with their backs to each other, not touching. Wide awake in the darkness.

54

"You're kidding me." Matty was on the second-floor balcony, staring at Levi in the FaceTime screen on her laptop.

"Nope. Fully funded for the first *three years*!" On the other side of the planet, her friend's eyes were saucers.

Matty's blood felt carbonated, bubbling in her veins. "That's amazing. That's more than we wanted. That's incredible!"

Levi's expression was loaded. "I couldn't have done it without you."

Deep in her gut, Matty knew where this was leading. A prospect that was equally electrifying and petrifying. "I know."

"Matty." Levi sounded absolutely certain. "I don't want to do it without you. You have to come back to New York. You *have* to."

Matty's heart took off, galloping like a dozen brumbies. "But I'm already here. We're leaving next week."

"You wouldn't have helped me if you weren't considering it!" Levi exploded. "This is literally your *dream job*! Once-in-a-lifetime shit! Noisy Brats doesn't work without you, you know that! *Stranded* is a show about *you*."

"I can't." But half of her was already back in New York, striding into their office (Manhattan? No, Brooklyn), takeout coffee in hand, brimming with ideas for the day ahead. The other half was hovering, hands over her eyes, aware that even thinking about this was very, very wrong.

"I'm confused," Levi said. "What did you think was going to happen to *Stranded* if we got it? It's not like we can recast. Look, I love Parker, and I know this is the world's biggest spanner in the works, but Matty: we have to do this. Together."

"Could I, like, start the company with you and get pregnant?" Even as she proposed it, Matty knew it wasn't what she wanted. She'd need to give every second she had for the first three years for the business to have a shot. Start-ups were an extremely tough slog and the learning curve would be steep. Travel for interviews, long hours, and late nights—no.

Matty had to choose.

"Honey." Levi looked dead serious, making him appear older and more powerful than usual. "Just answer this: What do you want to do?"

Matty was churning with every conceivable emotion: guilt, sadness, terror, joy. "I should—"

"No," he interrupted, not unkindly. "Not *should*. Not what you *should* do. What do you *want* to do?"

Matty turned away from the house, facing the horizon. The future. She inhaled a deep, shaky breath summoning all her strength. "I'll go talk to Parker."

Matty searched the entire house for her wife. The parents were all relaxing in their bedrooms, except for Glen, warbling in the shower. Matty finally found Parker huddled in their tiny walk-in closet, staring at her phone. "What are you doing in here?" Then, tentatively, "I heard from Levi."

"Oh yeah . . . ?" Parker's attention was sucked into her phone.

"Parks? Everything okay?"

Parker handed Matty her phone. A Medium piece, by Bhavani Singh. *Poppe's Problem with Pregnant Women, Minorities, and Feminism.* The subhead read *The It Girl Pregnancy Box Company Is a Sham. I Should Know: I Work There.*

"Oh, shit." Matty scrolled through the lengthy piece. Posted fifteen minutes ago, it already had more than a thousand likes. Dozens of comments. Almost all cheering Bhavani on. Coming down hard on Poppe. "What is this? Is this true? What does this mean?"

"It means we've lost a hundred subscriptions in the last hour, which is what we'd usually lose in a week." Parker hauled herself to her feet, taking the phone back off Matty. "It means the *New York Times* is already sniffing around for ex-employees to corroborate Bhavani's story. It means it's a legal and PR nightmare."

Matty followed Parker out of the closet into their bedroom. "Jesus. Did LK break the law?"

"Maybe?" Parker said. "No one wants to go to court—it might turn into a real legal case, it might not. Either way, it's a huge distraction. Total culture wrecker. And it'll look insanely bad to Target." Parker flopped back on the bed and covered her eyes. "Basically, if this snowballs—hashtag cancel culture—we'll get tried in the court of public opinion and we will lose."

"Oh *no*." Matty squeezed Parker's leg, feeling truly terrible for her wife. "Is there anything I can do? Do you want a whiskey or sex or all the brownies? They're really good."

"No." Parker peeked through her fingers. "What'd Levi say?"

"It's not the right time. You should get some rest."

"I'm on EST." Parker sat up. "Did you hear about the pitch?"

"Yes, but now's not the right time."

Parker examined Matty's face. "He didn't get it," she concluded. "Oh, babe, I'm so sorry. After all that work."

"Actually, he did." Matty's voice was the size of a shrimp. "Fully funded for the first three years."

"That's great!" Parker looked confused as to why Matty wasn't happier. "Isn't Levi thrilled?"

"He is. I am, too. We both are."

Matty wondered if the Poppe news would work in her favor. Parker might even be relieved by what she was about to propose. "I guess given everything going on," Matty started, cautious as a cat, "it might be better for you to be back in New York?"

"God, no." Parker groaned. "It'd be a shit show there right now. The best thing for me to do is see this out in Sydney, where I will either be rebuilding Poppe or my own career—almost certainly the latter."

"But isn't this about LK? She's the public figurehead—she'll be the one going down."

"I'm C-suite. We all go down with the ship. Least it'll be easier to be toxic in Sydney; we're not even in the market. Maybe no one will have heard of Poppe." Parker sounded hopeful.

"That sounds like a lot of work. So, maybe we should, um, revisit the baby idea?" Matty tried.

Parker narrowed her eyes. *"What?"* It sounded clean and crisp, a knife being unsheathed.

Matty's head was a mess. She didn't have a plan; she didn't know if this was the right thing to do. But Parker had asked for honesty. So Matty stepped up to the edge, took a deep breath, and jumped off. "It's just—Noisy Brats was always the dream, you know, our dream, Levi's and mine. And I thought I was done with it, I did, truly, but when the chance to pitch again came up, I guess maybe I wasn't? And now that's a possibility, Levi thinks—I think—maybe we should—we *could*—explore, um . . ." Her voice died on the vine.

Parker's mouth was ajar. "You want to go back to New York?"

Matty braced herself. "I just want to discuss the possibility—"

"You don't want to move to Sydney?"

"Noisy Brats isn't in Sydney," Matty tried for light. "But obviously I haven't made any decision."

"Yes, you have." Parker's voice was scarily deep. "You've made a thousand decisions. You decided to give up our apartment, get a new job, get on a plane. All our stuff's in transit. We're already *in* Australia. Which cost us *all* our savings."

"I know."

"It's too late. You're too late."

"I know, but . . ."

"But what?"

It was now or never. "I don't know if I want kids," Matty blurted out.

Parker let out a puff of disbelief. "What are you talking about?"

Matty's throat closed up, her eyes stinging with tears. "I've just had all this time to think about it, really think about it, and I'm not sure if I *need* kids to be happy." Her words started tumbling, unplanned. "I miss New York. I miss the subway and subway rats and dollar pizza and being my own person because I'm *just so scared* that in one year's time I'll wake up in my tiny hometown where it never snows and nothing exciting ever happens and I'll have a baby and Sunday dinners with Mum and Dad and a boring job in marketing and *that's it*. And, Parks, I don't know if that's enough." Matty's cheeks were wet. She was radiating with a giddy, sick relief from admitting a truth she'd been unable to look at, let alone articulate. "I don't know if I can be happy with that life. Not now there's another option. I want to go back to New York. I don't want to get pregnant. I *have* to try. Levi and I—we *have* to try." She was shaking with adrenaline, desperate to convey how monumental this all was. "This is it, Parks. The game-changer, the fucking Big Bang. Noisy Brats: it's *the one*."

The words hung in the air.

Slowly, Parker's face turned murderous. "Are . . . you . . . *kidding me?*"

"Jesus, shut up, my parents are right—"

"Are you fucking kidding me?" Parker raked her hands through her hair. "First LK, now my wife? Anyone else want to screw up my life today?" Her words were stunned. "You want a family, you've always wanted a family, I'm the one that came around!"

"I'm not saying never, I'm just saying I'm confused!"

"Because of a plan you've been making, without me, behind my back!" Parker's eyes were glassy. Alarming: she rarely cried. "What have I been working so hard for? I could've quit this stupid job a million times but I stuck with it because we had a plan and it was paying for that plan. Now what? You don't want kids, you don't want to move, and I've wasted the last five years of my life—the best working years of my life—in a job that'll end up destroying me and my reputation!" She laughed, sounding manic. "This is what a marriage is to you? This is how you want to be married?"

"This isn't about our marriage—"

"Everything is about our marriage, Matty. We're not just dating anymore: you're not single. We're a team—we make decisions as a team."

"I know, that's what we're doing now: talking about the future."

"No, you're telling me about your future that you've already decided."

"That's not true! I'm not saying no to kids. I'm saying, I'm not one hundred percent sure!" Matty said. "Christmas morning in matching PJs sounds great, but so does—I dunno—cooking a turkey for all our friends in a brownstone in Brooklyn we can actually afford. Traveling the world, having awesome careers! If Levi and I do this right, we could sell Noisy Brats in three years for, like, twenty million dollars!"

Parker let out a dark laugh. "Or you go bankrupt in one year and end up with nothing."

"But I *have* to do this," Matty cried, feeling wild with passion. "*Stranded* is all about *me!*"

Her wife went still. "What do you mean?"

She shouldn't have let that slip.

"*Stranded*, your podcast pilot?" Parker went on.

Matty tried to swallow, jittery with nerves. "It sort of ended up being about how I'm stuck here—"

"Uh-huh."

"We're stuck here—"

Parker's eyes narrowed. "Uh-huh."

"And about my decision whether or not to, um, have children." Matty had a realization. "This fight will probably be in it." Should she be getting it on tape?

"Oh, fuck *off.*" Parker stormed toward the bedroom door, yanking it open.

Jules, Glen, Randall, and Ludmila were in the main space, pretending they weren't eavesdropping. For a moment, everyone froze: busted. Then the parents scattered for their bedrooms, leaving the couple alone.

"We had starting a family in our *wedding vows*," Parker hissed.

"I'm not saying never!"

"I have emotions, Matty. I have feelings." Parker was blazing with fury. "You have crossed a line."

Matty had never seen her wife like this. She didn't know this person.

"Hear me, Matty," Parker went on. "I love you. I'm committed to you. I am your partner. We are equals. That's what we agreed to. This—you wanting to change all our plans, like, *all* of them—I did not sign up for this. *I do not want this kind of marriage.*"

For the first time in their history, it didn't feel like a fight about their future. It felt like a fight about whether or not they had one. Shocked and ashamed, Matty gasped for breath. Her instinct was to turn to her wife for comfort.

Parker pointed at the sofa. "You're sleeping out here tonight."

They'd never slept apart because of a fight. Before Matty had a chance to react, Parker was back in their bedroom, slamming the door.

Jules was in her bedroom doorway, watching.

Matty felt a scalding rush of relief, needing her mother's embrace. *"Mum."*

But then she saw tears in her mum's eyes. The unbearable disappointment on her face.

Matty had let her mother down before. Piercing her eyebrow the day before school photos. Bringing an unsanctioned girlfriend to a family reunion. But this was different. Her mother's expression was of someone betrayed, cruelly and cavalierly, by the person they loved most in this world.

"Mum!" Matty moved to her.

Jules flinched as if Matty had struck her. Instead of opening her arms as Matty wanted, Jules swayed back. "You don't want kids?" Her mother's voice was thick and on the brink of tears. "You're not coming home?"

Matty flooded with guilt. She'd tried not to think about her mother's reaction to all this, half convincing herself Jules would be disappointed, not completely devastated. But the look on her mother's face told the heartbreaking truth. Matty's voice was strangled. "I don't know."

"Oh, Matty." It was half a sob. Her mother's hands were shaking, pressing to her lips. Her powerful mum looked so frail. So beaten. "I wanted something to look forward to. I needed it."

"Mum!" Matty cried again, but Jules shrank back, shutting the bedroom door. Behind it, Matty could hear her mother start to weep. Ragged, gut-wrenching sobs. It sliced Matty open, leaving her insides exposed. Only now did she fully comprehend the pain she'd caused the people she loved.

Matty made herself small on the sofa, pulling the too-thin throw blanket around her shoulders. Sleep was miles away; the moonlight was uncomfortably bright. Illuminating every single thing inside the house.

PART THREE

55

Overnight, a strong off-shore wind stirred up the ocean, transforming an ecosystem. Half a mile from the beach, down on the ocean floor, the powerful swell rolled Jarrah's sunken boat. The movement crushed many of the tiny sponges and sea anemones who'd made their home around the underwater structure. This single, unilateral action damaged thousands of tiny living things.

Matty sat on a dawn-cool dune on Mooka Mooka Beach, watching the first rays of sunlight fire the rusted frame of another ship: the Lady Lushington. The colonizer-carrying vessel, shipwrecked on the sand.

The writer Sheila Heti said the egoism of childbearing was like the egoism of colonizing a country. *Both carry the wish of imprinting yourself on the world and making it over in your values and in your image.*

Ambition, ego: two sides of the same shining coin, forever flipping in midair.

As an awkward brace-faced seventh grader, Matty longed to be the powerful and popular school captain. As the powerful and popular school captain, her happiness was pinned on being on the radio. She barely heard the applause while accepting the prize for Best On-Air Talent at a national awards ceremony; her heart was in the Big Apple. The ambitious were never allowed to rest. Success lay just over that next hill. No, the next one. The next one. It didn't matter what anyone else thought about the endless road trip: the ambitious were solo travelers.

But rather than enjoy the spoils of each hard-won achievement, all Matty felt was disappointment she hadn't reached her next milestone. Ashamed and frustrated that she was still so far behind.

There was nothing wrong with ambition. Being driven and enterprising were qualities she admired in other people and in herself. But something was out of balance with how her ambition functioned. It didn't make her happy; it robbed her of happiness. It appraised the things she worked so hard for with pitying disgust, as if to say, *This? You're happy with this?* before revealing another impossibly endless staircase. M. C. Escher, eat your heart out.

Matty recalled a celebratory dinner with Levi the day she made senior producer at Spotify. A goal she worked tirelessly for, after starting as an unpaid intern. They'd spent the entire meal planning Noisy Brats. She couldn't remember where they ate. What they'd ordered.

Last night, she'd told her sister to protect her own heart. Advice Matty was ashamed to realize she wasn't following herself. She needed to protect her own happiness. To be happy, actually happy, with the incredible privilege and fortune she'd been blessed with. With the hard work she put into things. With the astounding life she had. That happiness would never come from career achievements. It would only ever come from within. Matty knew this, intellectually; this wasn't a radical new idea. But she'd never truly understood the vital nature of cultivating inner satisfaction.

Her dad and his bird-watching.

Her mum, pulling weeds from the garden.

Her sister watching everyone moan over her iced chocolate brownies.

These modest, everyday things gave each of them joy. Simple acts of generosity and exploration, of creativity and kindness. Moments of being grounded and present in the physical world.

Ambition told her the most important thing in the world was her work. But she wasn't just a creative.

She was a daughter. A sister. A friend.

A *wife*.

She was a *wife*, and she had failed Parker, the person who loved her and cared for her more than anyone in the world. God, how stupid and selfish could she be? Trying to reverse their plans for yet another moving target in this ridiculous charade of a life? This life wherein she spent too much time feeling miserable with what she didn't have, rather than grateful for what she did? No one's adulthood turned out the way they planned; no one had that much control. The gap between idealism and reality, between one's dreams and limitations, was too great. But she needed to start cultivating true pleasure and real contentment. Accept the choices she'd made and the ones she hadn't. Revel in the simple sweetness of a good laugh or a good deed or a good glass of a wine at the end of a long day. Because if she didn't, the person she'd be harming the most would be herself. And the people whose lives were tied to hers. The people she loved.

Sadness and shame boiled up inside her. Matty wanted to drop her face into her hands and weep, but something about the act felt indulgent and beside the point. Instead, she stared resolutely ahead, tipping her face to the morning sun.

56

When Liss edged into consciousness, something was off. It took a few muzzy seconds to figure it out. Amelia was not barnacled to her back.

Liss used to believe she could only sleep without anyone touching her, but she'd gotten used to drifting off with Amelia curled against her, quietly farting. The lemony light of early morning revealed Amelia on the other side of the bed. A cavern between them.

Last night tumbled back in a joyful, terrifying rush.

Liss had definitely not meant to tell Amelia that she was in love with her. While it was the truth—a cosmically undeniable truth—it was going to make their final few days together absolutely torturous.

As romantic as running off to Sydney sounded, her practical side knew this plan would work for approximately one month. Liss might be able to scrape together enough money for rent and boxed wine, but nothing near enough to save for a house or a wedding or IVF, things that all felt timely and critically important. Things between them were good now, but they were also pure and untested. They'd yet to bore or embarrass or lie to each other. Hurt each other. Change for each other. If things fell apart in Sydney she'd be stuck, a million miles from home, watching Amelia fall for someone else within one week of their breakup. Because that's what Amelia did: fact.

And yet, this: Amelia Kelly loved her. Amelia Kelly, the sweetest, kindest, most wholehearted human she'd ever met. Loved *her*.

And she loved Amelia. Fact.

Liss resolved to dial down the lesbian melodrama from a ten to a three-point-five. Look for a compromise. Something sensible that'd let things move at a slower pace. Amelia clearly wasn't keen on long distance, but that was probably the best solution. In the sober light of morning, they could both afford to be less impulsively romantic, more intelligently rational. No more tearful declarations. To quote Annie Lennox, "No more '*I love yous.*'"

Nothing gold can stay.

Liss rolled over, making Amelia's eyelids flutter.

Her lush mouth curled into an eager, if slightly nervous, smile. "Hi."

"Oh," Liss said, "hello."

Amelia kissed her with morning breath. "I love you."

"Aw. I love you, too." Oh-kay, not exactly a clampdown on impulsive romance. Liss wrenched her gaze from dreamy to wide awake. "How'd you sleep?"

"Good."

Obviously untrue. Their usual ease had a spiky edge. Something was bubbling under Amelia's no-poker-face countenance. Liss asked, "Do you want coffee?" at the same time Amelia blurted, "Do you want kids? Like, with me? Because I'd have kids with you."

"Animal!" Liss half gasped, half laughed. Even for Amelia, this was absolutely insane. "Um, *what?*"

"Too soon?"

"Well, I haven't had coffee and it's been *fifteen days.*"

"But feels more like sixteen, right?" Amelia sat up, gathering the sheets around her. "It's just: we don't have much time, so I think we should lay all our cards on the table."

"Have you *not* been laying your cards on the table? Because all I see are tables overflowing with cards."

"Yeah, I'm honest, I can't keep a secret. I'm just saying, I'm all-in. I wanna get married and have your babies. Well, not technically your babies, a donor's babies, unless you have a cousin or something? Like, he could donate his sperm?"

Liss's jaw was completely unhinged. It took her a long moment to regain control of language. "What's my dad's name? My mom's? Where was I born? What's my star sign? My favorite food?"

"Cup-a-Soup. Also you talk a lot about shrimp dumplings when you're drunk. I don't know your dad's name but his girlfriend calls you Melissa, which you hate, and when you talk about your mum you get a bit sad. I reckon you miss her more than you think. I guess I don't know your birthday, but you seem like a classic water sign. Pisces?"

She was right about everything. Still: "We haven't talked about anything—we haven't figured anything out. We're still getting to know each other!"

"Mum says she knew straightaway with Dad—they got married the first year they met and look how happy they are!"

Liss was out of bed, backing toward the kitchenette. "That was the eighties. You could buy a house for a hundred dollars. Men had bangs."

"I know enough."

Liss had never experienced the feeling of disbelief more acutely than this moment. "You know enough about me to know you'd, what, *parent a child* with me?"

Amelia nodded, looking eerily clear and grounded. "Mm-hmm."

"You don't. You can't."

"I do. I can. Just admit it," Amelia said. "You'd have kids with me."

Liss recalled her fantasy from a family dinner the week before. Two spouses painting a nursery, playing in a park. But that was just a daydream. Her heart was beating so hard it felt like it was fluttering against her top. "Amelia, I'm scared, too. Of this, of what might happen to us. Really, really scared. But this—this isn't how we figure it out. You sound . . ."

"I sound what?"

"I don't know. Desperate."

Amelia narrowed her eyes. "I sound desperate?"

"Talking about kids right now is crazy!"

"Now I'm crazy."

"Kind of, yeah!" Liss rubbed her face, feeling like she was spinning out of control. "Look—I could probably save up enough money to come to Sydney for Christmas."

"Christmas?"

Liss sank onto the bed, trying to think. "Until then, FaceTime. Text. Those vibrators you can program with an app."

Amelia looked dumbfounded. "Christmas is nine months away. No, *no*. No app vibrators. Just answer me honestly. Do you want kids?"

It felt like chatting while skydiving without a parachute. Her ears were roaring, thumping with blood. "Well, I'd . . . I'd want to get married first."

"Me too." Amelia took Liss's hand, her tone on a tightrope between joking and dead serious. "Small wedding, outdoors? Me in a dress, you in a suit?"

"Holy fuck." Liss was up again, backing away. "There's Road Runner and there's you. I'm not like you. I can't move this quick."

"Well, we're going to have to! This time next week, someone else will be in this bed and we'll be—where?"

"I don't know." Liss spun around. "I need coffee. Or air. Or a space-ship to take me back to planet Earth."

"Come here," Amelia said patiently. "Come back here."

And Liss realized as badly as she wanted to hide out on Blinky Beach and avoid the entire conversation, she needed to stay with Amelia and figure this out. So, she came back over and sat on the bed, trying to breathe.

"I'm not saying we should get married right now," Amelia went on, "unless you want to. I'm just trying to get you to see what I already know is true: you're all in. With me. You'd have kids with me. You want to marry me."

Liss's palms were sticky with sweat. "Oh my god."

"Right? *Right?*"

It was like being backed against a wall by a cheerleader with a gun. "Fuck it: yeah, I've thought about it."

Even though it was an honest answer, and even though Amelia's lips were hot and soft as they pressed against her mouth, none of it made Liss feel the bliss she was supposed to be feeling. She just felt more afraid, closer to the end of a gangplank above a pool of thrashing sharks. She couldn't shake the thought that Amelia wasn't acting this way because she genuinely loved her and believed what she was saying. She was saying it because, deep down, she thought she was unlovable and didn't have a plan for them and this was her way of holding Liss close, so close it was hard to breathe. Even as Amelia kissed her, even as she kissed Amelia back, Liss couldn't tell how much of this was real and romantic and wonderful . . . and how much of it was an irrational, fear-driven delusion. "You're crazy."

Amelia laughed against her mouth, delighted, pressing close. "You shouldn't call women crazy."

Liss felt like she might be sick. "You're fucking nuts."

Something was happening. Her pulse was starting to race. Tapping faster and faster, a jog becoming a sprint. Sweat stabbed under her arms. She was on the verge of panting. Liss knew this feeling. This nightmare baring down. A panic attack. She hadn't had one in months. In less than a minute, she'd be prostrate on the floor, gulping for air, sweating and shaking, totally out of control. Panic on panic: Amelia couldn't see her like that. Amelia would never understand. Liss pushed her off, trying in vain to stave off the inevitable.

Amelia's mouth was still open, mid-kiss. She opened her eyes in confusion. "What's wrong?"

"Nothing."

Amelia peered at Liss, readying to protest.

Someone knocked on the front door.

With only seconds to spare, Amelia turned her head away.

57

"Animal?" Matty called from outside the front door. "It's me."

Amelia felt a pinch of annoyance that her sister had interrupted such an emotional moment. They'd basically just proposed to each other. "I'll get her to come back later."

But Liss was already tripping over her feet on the way to the bathroom.

Amelia slipped on one of Liss's T-shirts and found her big sister pacing the balcony. "Hey. We're kind of in the middle of something—Can this wait?"

Matty shook her head. Her red-rimmed eyes flooded with tears. "Parker and I got into a *huge* fight last night."

"Oh no!" She assumed Matty and Parker endured their share of spats, but she'd never heard of a blowout. Amelia took Matty's hand and guided her to the balcony's orange sofa.

"I had to sleep on the *couch*. Super uncomfortable."

Amelia resisted the urge to say, *Yes, I know*. "What happened?"

"Things just spiraled after I told her I wanted to go back to New York to start Noisy Brats with Levi and was having second thoughts about getting pregnant."

Sympathy was replaced with cold shock. Amelia dropped her hand. "What?"

"I'm not going!" Matty cried, eyes wild and feverish. "Nothing's changed, I'm still going to Sydney! It was such a dumb, selfish mistake and now I'm scared she hates me and wants to divorce me, which she probably should because"—she paused to suck in a shaky breath—"*I'm a massive cunt.*" Matty started bawling.

"Oh, honey." Amelia's comfort was automatic, even as her mind stayed racing. "Honey, you're not a cunt."

"I am," Matty howled, a flock of honking geese. "I am a cunt!"

Amelia held her sister as she blubbered about everything she'd done wrong, thought wrong, said wrong, smoothing Matty's hair from her face and murmuring comforting things while she processed what her sibling was saying.

Matty had been having second thoughts about motherhood. Second thoughts about Sydney. Amelia spent months researching places for her and Parker to rent. She'd seen thirty different properties: nights, weekends, before and after teaching, some hours from home, on public transport. Matty moving back to Sydney had been a collective focus for the entire family for months. Becoming an aunt was second only to being a mother herself. But all that, and Matty's family still wasn't more important than her professional aspirations?

What else didn't Amelia know? What else had she gotten wrong?

The instability of the moment made the air shimmer sickly. Where was Liss? She didn't seem like the type to avoid a hard moment: she'd been there through her entire breakup with James-Dale, the fallout for which took place where they were sitting right now. But as Liss herself kept saying, there was still plenty they didn't know about each other. Maybe Liss wasn't as good with hard moments as Amelia needed her to be. She'd been in the bathroom for the past fifteen minutes.

Finally, Matty regained control of her tears and was able to slow her breath.

Amelia tried to focus, summoning empathy alongside confusion, fear, and, despite her best efforts, a flare of anger. "Want to come in for a cuppa?"

"No." Matty wiped her snotty nose on her sleeve. "I need to speak to Parker. Also, there's a storm coming."

"A storm?"

"Yeah, a fucking tropical storm." Matty gestured at the sky. Rather than its typical celestial blue, low clouds hung, the color of bruised fruit. The atmosphere was pregnant with humidity. "We're going to get a shit-ton of rain, even though it's late in the season, apparently. Hashtag climate change." Matty hunted around for a soggy tissue. "How's everything going here?"

Amelia allowed herself the quick pleasure of replaying the morning's uber-romantic events. "Good. Really good."

"So you figured out a plan?"

"No concrete details," Amelia admitted. "But we both said 'I love you.' And we're even talking about kids!"

Matty's expression froze in shock. Then she threw her head back and laughed. "Of course you did. Of course you are!" The tears she was wiping from her eyes were tears of mirth. "Wow—I thought nothing could crack me up right now. Thanks for that."

Amelia crossed her arms, watching her sister head back down the stairs. "You're making fun of me."

"No, never. Okay, I'm going to grovel to my wife. You have to board up the Yellow Cottage—Jarrah's going on about battening down the hatches. Bye, Liss!"

Liss appeared in the doorway, looking flushed, cheeks damp. A tap of irritation: she'd been mindlessly washing her face while Amelia worked through her sister's grief.

"Bye, Matty." Liss raised a hand. "Good luck with the grovel."

Her sister was almost out of sight when she spun around, calling back to the pair. "Oh, I totally forgot. Jarrah's pulled some strings—we've officially got an R-Day."

Rescue Day. In the far distance, a warning growl of thunder. Amelia's heart started throbbing. "When?"

"Monday morning!" Matty called back.

It was Saturday.

"Two days left," Matty underlined, giving Amelia a deliberate look, before heading off down the path.

Two days left to figure out . . . everything. Amelia expected to meet Liss's eyes and find them warm and ready to talk. But back inside the

Cabin, Liss was staring at her phone. "Jesus: Matty's right. They're predicting twelve inches. That's a massive storm."

"Monday." It sounded like a death sentence. "So soon."

Liss wouldn't return her gaze, instead yanking on a pair of jeans, twitchy as a water bug. "I have to find Jarrah."

"But we need to make a plan." Amelia hovered as Liss shoved her feet into sneakers. "Are you coming with me to Sydney? I have to let my roommates know, they might want to charge us more rent, and I have to tell my family, and we should definitely—"

"Amelia, stop, just stop!" Liss scuttled away. "I can't talk about any of this right now."

"We need to!"

"I can't!"

The shout bounced off the windows. Amelia swayed back. She didn't recognize this person. *Or maybe*, a cool voice inside her suggested, *you just haven't met this side of her yet.* The side that ran away when things got hard. She'd run away from Montreal, hadn't she?

Liss gulped a breath, looking unnerved. "Sorry, look, we'll talk later. I really have to find Jarrah."

Amelia watched dumbly as the human she loved ran down the front steps. Unable to get away fast enough. Liquid fear gushed into her body, so hot and fast it felt like lust. "I love you!"

Liss wheeled around, still jogging backward. Her face was as complicated as the weather. "I know," she said, and then she was gone.

Amelia stood alone on the balcony, trying not to feel like a bride who'd just been abandoned at the altar because that was a ridiculous overreaction and completely how she felt.

The ding of her phone was a welcome distraction.

Until she saw the name on the screen.

DO NOT ANSWER ☹ !

James.

58

They were out of eggs. And granola and English muffins. They were even out of coffee filters, meaning Parker was resorting to trying *toilet paper* in an attempt to get a much-needed caffeine boost.

As Parker had predicted, Poppe imploded. The *New York Times* exposé that their crisis comms team gave them twenty-four hours' notice about was on the goddamn front page. *Is Poppe's Bubble About to Burst? Employees past and present of the popular pregnancy subscription box company claim its egalitarian feminist image is an illusion.* Three of LK's ex-assistants were on the record, plus Bhavani and four current employees. The article highlighted the gap between Poppe's official commitment to inclusion versus the lack of diversity in upper management and brand ambassadors. It also teased out the unfeminist practice of creating a corporate culture of working unpaid overtime to keep up with a boss who would, as Bhavani put it, "financially benefit from the company's success in a way employees like us would not. Poppe is about making LK rich and happy. Everyone around her is just a means to that end." The final paragraph was grimly succinct: *Lauren-Kate Cutler built her empire in her image. With its sale to a big-box retailer in question, that strategy may be its downfall.*

Social media was a feeding frenzy fueled by female rage. When a huge lifestyle influencer (@Simone_Says; 1.1 million followers) burned her Poppe box in an Instagram Story, Parker knew the next twenty-four hours would be bursting into metaphorical and literal flames. *Theo and Ben aren't even speaking to me!* LK texted Parker. *Have you heard from Target??*

Parker's lawyer advised her to hold off on responding.

And then, there was her personal life.

Some women tiptoed though the world, afraid their actions would disturb it. Matilda Kelly entered every room to the sound of invisible trumpets. She pursued her goals with the focus of a cat tracking a laser beam and the same underlying threat of feline ferocity. Matty's lack of interest in a work-life balance suited Parker's workaholism, too. Parker never assumed she would become collateral in her wife's ambition.

The irony was, Matty's drive to succeed was one of the things Parker liked most about her.

Now, standing in the kitchen of Kooroy, a pulpy mess of toilet paper and coffee grounds in her hands after having worked damage control the entire night, Parker was feeling a notch above completely dead. It was a surprise when her mother appeared next to her, circling her in her arms, and the first thing she felt was overwhelming *relief*.

"*Rypka.*" A Russian pet name that meant *little fish*. "Let's go for a walk before the rain comes."

59

Jules had never felt so profoundly disappointed in her own child. Matty's desire to return to New York and not make a grandbaby left Jules with crushing sadness and bitter anger. The podcast Jules agreed to be interviewed for turned out to be a sounding board for Matty's maternal doubt: another betrayal. When her eldest daughter blew back into Kooroy mid-morning, frantically looking for Parker, who was on a walk with Ludmila, Jules asked her point-blank what she intended to do. Matty turned the color of a grapefruit and blathered, appearing to walk back her intention to boomerang to New York but "the baby thing is still up in the air. I have to talk to Parks. Which way did they go?"

The baby *thing*.

A knife in her heart.

Jules had to turn away.

To her considerable surprise, she felt a powerful urge to talk to her husband. Glen wasn't as desperate for grandkids as she was, but he was looking forward to having Matty close and could generally be counted on to sit quietly while Jules railed. She finally found him out the back of the house, wrangling a plastic poncho that was fluttering about in the increasingly fresh breeze.

"Can't talk now." He stuck his arm through the hole meant for his head. "Randall and I are doing another sweep for the Boobook before the storm. We've only got two days left!"

Anger yanked Jules under. "For fuck's sake, Glen: no one cares about the bloody Boobook! This actually *matters*."

She expected contrition. Instead, he whirled on her, his face so alive with feeling she barely recognized him. "*I* care, Jules. *I* care about the Boobook. And I don't need your permission to do what *I* want. You've made that *very* clear."

"But our daughter—"

"Can do what she damn well wants! Christ, Jules: When are you going to get it? Our kids are grown—they're leading their own lives! We need to support their choices, not filter them into good or bad based on what suits us. That's probably why Amelia hasn't said anything to you yet!"

"Said anything about what?"

Glen pressed a fist to his mouth, swearing under his breath. "Nothing."

"Said anything about what?" Jules found herself in the bizarre position of hurrying after her husband as he strode away, heading toward the beach. "Said anything about *what?*"

He yanked his arm from her grip. "Open your damn eyes. What do you think it could be?"

The truth landed with a thud. Or maybe, it'd always been there. "She's . . . *with* . . . Liss?"

"Obviously!"

Another gay daughter. How was that possible?

How was that fair?

Another round of coming-out-by-proxy to all her friends who'd probably suspect she'd let her children watch too much *She-Ra*. No strapping son-in-law to clean the gutters and compliment her cooking. Did this mean Amelia wouldn't have kids, either?

Jules floundered through waves of betrayal and shock. "Who else knows? How long's it been going on for? *Why hasn't she told me?*"

"Probably because she knows how judgmental you can be."

Jules flinched like he'd just slapped her. "I'm not judgmental."

He gave her a hard look.

"I'm not! I just have expectations and hopes, like everyone else."

Glen puffed out a frustrated breath. "And your feelings are valid. But your happiness needs to come from *your* choices and *your* life, not the choices and lives of others. The best thing our kids can do for us, the absolute *best* thing, is *let us in*. That's a privilege, Jules. That's a goddamn *privilege*."

Where the bloody hell was this coming from? What'd happened to her emotionally stunted partner who referred to talk therapy as the greatest scam shy of a Ponzi scheme?

"Glen?" she called after his retreating form. "Glen!"

Jules watched, dumbstruck, as he met Randall by the shoreline. They paused to do some sort of peculiar handshake, then bounded up the beach in the graceful way of twin kangaroos.

Lightning flickered in the south. The sky was getting heavier by the minute, the color of a whiskey sour.

Jules set off down the beach, looking for Jarrah.

She found him boarding up a Blue Cottage window that'd cracked in the surge. He and Liss were hammering a piece of plywood into place.

"Julia," he greeted her. "How's everything at Kooroy?"

"Fine. I was, um, hoping to have a word." Jules glanced at Liss, trying very hard not to imagine her in bed with her youngest daughter.

Liss went red, fumbling out something about moving nonperishable food from under the Caretaker Cabin, disappearing inland.

"Everything okay, Julia?"

Jules shook her head, embarrassed to find her eyes filling with tears.

Jarrah's eyes softened with concern, his attention narrowing from the approaching storm to the small, human storm in the woman he cared about. Stepping forward, he wordlessly wrapped her in his arms, pressing his warm lips to her forehead. Even distracted by sadness, it sent a kicky little zing up her back and down between her legs. They'd shared a few more kisses since their first one last week. Each made her heart flip like a fish on the bottom of a boat and reminded her that, yes, she was still extremely interested in sex, thank you very much. But Jarrah had been hesitant to do much more than relatively sweet, chaste kisses unless Jules came clean with her daughters: "It just doesn't feel right till everything's out in the open." Frustratingly moral.

The wind was rising, whistling through the casuarina trees. Jules knew she didn't have much time, so she just let herself talk, blurting out everything: Liss and Amelia's suspected romance, Matty and Parker's fight. The way both children seemed to be making such reckless decisions in their respective love lives. How much she didn't want their futures to end up like hers: one half of a failed marriage. "What Glen just said is right. I know my life can't be based on the lives of others. But becoming a grandmother is all I've wanted, for years. I don't think you can understand unless you're a mother—this *need* I have."

"Say Matty goes back to New York. Say there's no grandkids, at least, not for a few years. What would you do?"

"I don't know!" Jules exclaimed. "I can't even imagine it!"

"Try, Julia. Just try."

Jules blew out a long breath. "Well, I might not stay in the house after Glen moves out. It's too big for one person, and I couldn't afford the mortgage on my own: we refinanced twice to pay for the kids' education."

"So, where would you go? If you could go anywhere?"

"If I could go anywhere . . ." The door to her imagination was stuck. Summoning her courage, she tried giving it a push. "If I could go anywhere . . . I'd go . . . well, I guess I'd go . . . here."

"No permanent residents, sorry."

Jules didn't smile at his joke. "No: here. Queensland. The Bay." She could land at the Shack. She could *live* at the Shack. The door flew open. She stumbled through, into unexpectedly bright light. "If we sold the house in Sydney, I'd have enough to do a reno—put in a new kitchen, fix up the garden. I could do a bit of traveling. I could go to Paris!" She caught herself. "Not that I'd go on my own."

"Didn't you say Ludmila goes to Paris for work?"

"Yes, but she'd never want me to . . . I couldn't just ask if I could . . . Could I?"

Yes, she could. Of course she could.

No more freezing Sydney winters, no more overpriced everything. She could move back home. "That's where I'd go: Queensland."

"Best place in the world." Jarrah brushed some curls out of her face. "You can do anything you want, Julia."

Her growing sense of adventure elbowed out the last remnants of sadness. What she really wanted to do was *him*. More than just a kiss. Jules had sacrificed so much for her family: her time, her energy, her body, and yes, her sexuality. She'd been the woman others needed her to be, always, every damn day. But now, the encroaching storm blew into her an intoxicating desire to claim this moment only for herself, fueled by a thought she'd never once allowed herself to have: to hell with everyone else. "I told the girls about Glen. I told them it was over."

The lie fell from her lips like fruit shaken from a vine.

The wind started to howl, tossing bits of bark.

Jarrah looked surprised. "How'd they take it?"

"Great! I mean: badly. Very badly. At first." The big lie felt strangely insignificant, overpowered by the need to be desired by a good, strong man. Her hands curled around his biceps. Thick and bulging. "But we all talked it out, as a family, and they know the truth. That I'm . . . available. That we're . . . *friends*." She pressed against him, belly to belly, hip to hip.

"Julia." His laugh was nervous, interested. "Steady on."

Jules didn't reply, stroking his skin, gazing at him.

"I have to . . ." Jarrah gulped, eyes losing focus. " . . . The storm."

But his hands were across her back and he was pressing himself against her. She could feel his arousal though his pants, hot, hard heat that shook something loose in her. Lust flooded into every nook and cranny. "Bloody hell, Jarrah," Jules whispered. "Kiss me."

In a blur of movement he had her up against the plywood. Jules let out a gasp of delight. He was so much bigger than Glen, so much stronger. His nose brushed the side of hers, warm breath on her cheek. The smell of him—salt air, green things, growing things—made her woozy. Her eyes fluttered closed and his mouth was on hers. They sank into a kiss. Not a quick, sweet kiss. A real kiss. As lush and hot as the rainforest, different from anything she'd known before.

She fisted the front of his shirt, pulling him close, not close enough. Her body was moving of its own accord; so was his, undulating with her, sending giddy waves of pleasure. The inside of her thigh was pressed to his hip, held there by one strong hand. His other found her breast, the rough pad of his thumb brushing the sensitive center of her nipple. Jules couldn't remember the last time she'd been this turned on. Drowning in sensation, every part of her open for him, needing him. He massaged her breast until her vision blurred and someone was moaning. She could barely tell it was her own voice. Passion overwhelmed Jules until she was no longer a woman, a mother, a sister, a wife. She was pure feeling. A balloon whose string had been cut, tossed by the wind into sweet oblivion.

60

A fresh wind twirled up Blinky Beach, shaking the spinifex, shifting the sand. The island sensed the oncoming storm, its inhabitants moving downwind, underground, seeking shelter. The sugar gliders cozied into their tree hollow. The brumbies sought higher ground, milling under a grove of sturdy blue gums. Seabirds throbbed into the darkening sky, heading away from the gathering wind in the west. There was an aliveness in the air. A preshow buzz.

Parker walked alongside her mother, a woman she felt as if she knew better than anyone else, yet somehow suspected, didn't know at all. "Where did you learn to dance like that?"

Ludmila wrapped her arms around herself, facing the wind as they strolled up the beach. "It's a less interesting question than why I stopped."

"Okay. Why did you stop?"

"Because"—she paused to skim her fingertips down her daughter's cheek—"of you." Ludmila looked to the ocean as one looks to an oracle. "I used to be a dancer. For years, that was all I did."

"You?" Parker couldn't hide her incredulity. She had the disorienting feeling she was meeting her mother for the very first time. "You don't even dance at parties. You didn't even dance at our wedding."

Ludmila lifted her shoulders with smooth grace. "Dancing at parties is not the same as being a ballerina."

"A ballerina?" About as expected as Ludmila announcing she used to be a block of cheese.

"I started taking classes when I was four years old. San Francisco Ballet School. My teacher was from Moscow. We'd just moved to the US— I think my parents thought it was a way I could stay connected to Russia."

Parker hadn't been close to her grandparents. Her friends had Grammys and Pop Pops who showered them with love and lollipops. *Babushka* and *Dedushka* lived in a dark, poky house that smelled like borscht.

"I had a natural talent and I worked hard," Ludmila said. "Even after I started high school, I was dancing, four, five hours a day. When I was fourteen I started being homeschooled."

Impossible on impossible: *"Babushka* homeschooled you?"

"Not very well," Ludmila allowed. "It didn't really matter: at the level I was at, dance was my life." The ballet school was connected to the San Francisco Ballet company. Every student wanted a spot in the company. It was prestigious and paid, a real job. "But highly competitive. Only five or six dancers got offered positions out of the hundreds who auditioned every year. You started as an apprentice: the lowest rank."

"So, you made apprentice?" Parker guessed, trying to keep up.

"Not exactly. When I was eighteen, I danced Odile from *Swan Lake* in my graduation showcase. The Black Swan pas de deux. I'd never felt more beautiful. More alive." A faint smile touched her mother's lips, like just-audible music. "At the end, the artistic director announced I was being offered *soloist* in the company to dance Juliet the following year. Soloist skips two ranks: apprentice and a member of the corps. And, there was a promise that after we did *Romeo & Juliet*, I'd be promoted to principal dancer. That's any dancer's ultimate goal: what I'd been working toward most of my life. But, it never happened."

Parker stopped walking, needing to concentrate on what she was hearing. "Why not?"

"Because five days later, I found out I was pregnant. With you."

Parker shook her head, overwhelmed not just by the story, but the tenderness in her mother's gaze. "But—but you said you met Dad at the gym."

"He was one of the company's physical therapists. We'd been seeing each other, in secret, for a few months. When I told my friends in the school, everyone said to abort the pregnancy. Your father and I were in love, but we were young. I'd just won my dream job, an opportunity thousands of dancers would kill for. I couldn't have both."

"So why did you choose me? Did you always want to be a mother? Was it a moral thing?" Parker had the sense there was an important lesson in all this, the point of which she couldn't yet pin down and name. The gusting wind was fresh against her heated cheeks: Parker had to raise her voice to be heard above it. "I don't understand how you could work so hard for something and then just let it go."

"It wasn't an easy decision."

"Mom!" Parker exclaimed. "I need more."

Ludmila let out a breath. "The day I made soloist was the happiest of my life to date. I remember it being very public: flowers and champagne, people taking my photograph, lots of buzz. A dinner, not that I would've eaten anything. I was crying for days, out of relief, out of shock. It was very . . . big. The day I found out I was pregnant, I was alone, in the dorms, in a bathroom. It was nothing I'd been working toward, completely out of the blue. It was very . . . small." Ludmila's eyes were warm. "I remember feeling very still. Very quiet. All of the noise in my world muted. I wondered what it'd be like to hold a baby. To look into their eyes. How I might see the entire world in them. I felt very big and very small, all at once. Like I was an ant and a planet, at the same time. I'd never felt anything like that. It was bigger than happiness: deeper, more complex. It was true joy."

Parker's skin prickled. There was a familiarity in her mother's words. A feeling she'd never been able to articulate.

"I didn't choose you, *rypka*." Ludmila's steady gaze held Parker's own. "You chose me."

Tears sprung into Parker's eyes. She knew her mother loved her. But she'd never felt the power of that love so profoundly. The lump in her throat tightened her voice. "But I always thought you picked work over motherhood. That motherhood came second."

"I like my work. Not in the same way I loved dancing, but I do enjoy it very much. And I needed to work when you were a baby: your father wasn't making any money, I was the breadwinner. But you came first. I gave up my dream for you, *rypka*. And I would do it again."

The picture of Parker's life had been taken apart and put back together in a way that was still recognizable and, at the same time, fundamentally different. She knew intellectually that motherhood would evolve her relationship with her parents. She didn't know how profound that evolution would be, beginning now, before she was even a mother herself.

If she became a mother at all.

Parker hardened, recalling the pain of her wife's behavior.

Ludmila intuited who had entered Parker's mind. "I'm not saying you and Matilda need to make the same choice," she said. "I have plenty of friends without children who are completely fulfilled. Plenty of friends who are excellent in their professions and average at home, and vice versa. I just felt like it was time you knew the truth. To help you and Matilda decide what you want to do next."

"I don't know if there are next steps," Parker muttered.

Ludmila spoke with finality. "Don't be ridiculous. You are angry and you are tired, but you are married. You must work through. Listen to what's inside. Do what makes you feel like an ant and a planet." She side-eyed her daughter. "She is very good for you, you know."

This was more of a surprise than her mother's secret ballerina past. "Matty?" To put it lightly: "I didn't think you approved."

Ludmila laughed. A big one, from her belly. It sounded a lot like Jules. "I think the Kellys are growing on me."

Affection for her mother billowed. Parker looped her arms around her mom and held her. Let herself be held. Her parents had sacrificed so much to give her a life. And what a good life it had been. Free of suffocating expectations, she'd been free to choose her own path, her own happiness. Her mother had chosen what made her happy. Standing here on Blinky Beach, the wind whipping up new ideas, Parker suspected she knew how to do the same. Even if it didn't look anything like what she—or anyone else—would expect.

The wind knocked them both off-balance. They could see the rain, coming down in sheets in the middle distance. The storm was closer than they thought.

61

Amelia's finger hovered over the Accept button, fighting months of muscle memory. In the days after they'd broken up, she'd prayed James-Dale would contact her with some plausible explanation as to why the whole thing was a complete misunderstanding and would she please marry him after all? In her most desperate moments, she'd wondered if his wife really did want to meet her, if they could share him or—true delirium—become a thrupple. When things with Liss went from zero to a hundred, she'd stopped thinking every ping and trill was her ex reaching out. And just when she'd forgotten all about him, here he was again, like an actor taking one too many curtain calls.

The call rang out.

A voicemail.

She knew she should delete it, and block James-Dale permanently. But as she swiped open her phone to do just that, her brain decided this would be the perfect time to replay Liss backing away from her earlier that morning. *Amelia, stop, just stop! I can't talk about any of this right now.* As if what she was giving Liss was an untreatable disease and not her still-beating heart, fragile as a baby bird.

Listening to the voicemail was the wrong thing to do, she thought, as she pressed Play.

"A-Amelia, it's, um, me."

No rakish flirtation, no sugary pet names. Instead, her ex's gravelly voice sounded scraped raw with remorse.

The familiarity of him split her open.

He paused and let out a rueful chuckle. "I had a whole speech prepared, and now I can't remember a word of it."

A cousin of a smile considered a place on her lips.

"I know you don't have any reason to believe a word of this, but here goes. My wife and I are getting a divorce. I've already moved out, and I'm in Sydney. Because—well, because our marriage wasn't working and hasn't been, for ages. But really because of *you*, Amelia. I lied to you, and I cheated on you, and I'm a complete shit, a complete fucking shit. But I *was* in love with you. I *am* in love with you. I love you, Amelia Kelly. I know this is a lot to lay on you in a fucking voicemail but, look, I do want to marry you, Amelia. That part never—"

The message cut off.

Amelia dropped the phone as if scalded. Her heart was booming so hard and fast she had to flounder to the blue velvet sofa before her knees gave way.

He wanted her. He still wanted her.

Which crystallized the truth in such perfect, angel-song clarity.

I don't want you.

Even if James-Dale crawled over a kilometer of broken glass with ten diamond rings clenched between his teeth, she didn't want anything to do with him ever again.

Because she loved Liss. True love, real love, different from anything she'd ever felt before. Liss was the one inside her, like a photo in a locket, kept there, always. Amelia was deeply and irrevocably in love with Liss Chambers.

James-Dale wanted her and she wanted Liss and Liss wanted to fly back to Montreal without her.

A distant roll of thunder: the storm. She needed to close up the Yellow Cottage as instructed and, more important, get help in figuring out her next move. Matty would be preoccupied with Parker, which left . . . her mother. Jules's reaction might be less than ideal. But when her mum saw how much this meant, how serious this was, surely she wouldn't let her own agenda get in the way. She'd probably be very understanding and happy for Amelia and have great advice! Yes, of course, her warm, wise mother who'd been happily married for almost four decades would have matriarchal, maternal insight that'd shine a light forward. Brilliant new idea: maybe she and Liss could live in Matty and Parker's second bedroom until the baby came! Or even after it was born!

Amelia dressed quickly, throwing her hair into a topknot, kicking her feet into a pair of thongs. Outside, the humid air had the electric feel of a spiraling rumor. The storm was getting closer. Maybe she and Liss would kiss in the rain. Taylor Swift sang about kissing in the rain a lot and it sounded like the height of capital-R Romance. Amelia jogged down the sandy track picturing her and Liss, laughing in love-soaked delight, admitting they couldn't live without each other, kissing in the pouring rain.

Running through the bush toward the Yellow Cottage, Amelia tried to puzzle together the best approach while anticipating the most likely: *Mum! Amazing news! I'm in love! Yes, again. Liss, I'm in love with Liss, but I'm not sure how we can be together forever. Yes, Liss from the island. Jesus, what other Liss would I be talking about? Yes, she's a woman—although everyone knows gender is a construct and binaries are bullshit—but sure, I guess I'm coming out to you. Sixteen days. Yes, you can fall in love in sixteen days, I just told you I have!*

She arrived at the Yellow Cottage panting and flustered, flying around the space like a mini-tornado, shutting up the windows, switching off appliances, trying not to get swept down memory lane: the kitchen bench against which they'd been so distracted making out they'd burned a pan of onions. The bed where they told each other things they hadn't told another soul. The pillow that still smelled like Liss's shampoo. The reality that Amelia would be leaving her sunshiny little nest in forty-eight hours struck her with such desperate sadness she almost broke down, and would have, if there wasn't such an urgent need to enlist her mother in helping figure everything out.

Soon, Amelia was jogging along the beach under a sky swirled with seabirds riding the warm currents of the billowing storm that was starting to make landfall, light rain on her fevered skin. Amelia let out a yell, a battle cry, ready to fight for Liss, ready to do anything! A photo negative of her first day on the island, running the opposite way over the white sand toward the wharf to greet her family.

So much had changed in six weeks.

Her eyes strayed to the long wooden wharf; as she passed the Blue Cottage, she almost didn't look back. But someone had boarded up the front window with plyboard, rendering the sweet abode alien. She tossed a glance over her shoulder.

Two people were pressed against the far side of the house.

She recognized her mother's curls.

Jarrah's dark skin.

Her mother. And Jarrah. In a passionate embrace.

The world warped, slackening at the sides. Amelia stumbled to a stop so fast she almost pitched forward. It took several dazed, breathless seconds for what she was seeing to land as reality.

Jarrah and her mother. Kissing like the world was about to end.

Even from thirty feet away, she could see his hand was on her breast. Her hands grasping his ass. Rocking together.

Her mum was cheating on her dad. Her shy, sweet, devoted father.

Her *mother*. The woman she admired and trusted the most.

Thirty-six years of marriage.

Amelia opened her mouth and screamed.

62

The scream pulled Jules from feverish, giddy heat into an ice-cold reality.

She locked eyes with her daughter. Twin poles of this nightmare moment. Amelia was paralyzed, moonfaced with horror.

Jules pushed herself away from Jarrah. "Amelia, I—"

But Amelia was off, darting up the beach toward Kooroy. Toward Matty. Away from her.

"Wait!" Jules started after her, running in pursuit along the soggy shoreline. Waves smashed at her feet, almost knocking her over. She hadn't run for more than a bus in years and was quickly winded. "Amelia! Stop!"

But she didn't. She didn't want to. The bond that tied them together was stretching farther and farther until finally, it snapped. Her daughter was gone after seeing something that Jules never should've done.

"Julia!" Jarrah was behind her, puffing and confused. "What just happened?"

Cold drops of rain wet her hot face, mixing with her tears. Her Bunnings hat was gone. Jules spun in bewildered circles, suddenly confused as to which way Kooroy was. "Oh no," she whimpered. "Oh no, oh *shit*."

Jarrah was in front of her, both hands on her shoulders. "You said they knew."

The truth was the monster under the bed made real. Impossible, beastly ugliness. "I lied," Jules sobbed. "I'm sorry, I just got caught up in the moment and—"

"What?"

"There's just so much going on and I . . . I . . ."

Jarrah's face was stone. "What did you tell them?"

Jules shook her head, her body heaving with sobs. "I have to go. I have to explain to my girls—"

"What did you tell them?"

"N-nothing. I haven't told them anything."

In Jarrah's eyes, the freshest outrage. "So, you lied to me. Just like you've been lying to your kids."

"I'm sorry!" Jules gasped, swallowed by regret. "I wanted something for myself but it was wrong, I know, and I'm sorry, I'm sorry!"

Jarrah just shook his head in stunned, brutalized surprise. He backed away, dismissing her with a flick of his hand. "Nah, bugger ya." He spun and started walking off.

Jules's entire body was aflame, coursing with the poison of this moment. She wanted to go after him, to explain and apologize and beg for a second chance. But she needed to get to the girls. Guessing that Kooroy was the opposite direction from where Jarrah was going, Jules started to run.

An artery in the sky opened and the rain came down in sheets. The ocean was seething, a wild, angry thing pounding the shore, beating the sand. Jules came to an inlet, rushing deep with water from the bush. She waited between waves, scampering toward the ocean to avoid having to wade through it. Lightning flashed overhead; seconds later, a crack of thunder so loud she pitched forward in fright, falling on her hands and knees. Before she could scramble up, a monster wave crashed around her, drenching her clothes and knocking her off-balance. It rolled her forward, then sucked her back. Coughing and spluttering, Jules scrabbled for purchase on the sand, but the wave was too strong. Suddenly she was in the water, off her feet, summersaulting like flotsam, unable to find the ocean floor. A new sort of terror snatched at Jules: panic. Bicycling her feet, her arms grasping at nothing but angry water.

Kicking hard, Jules burst up like a popped cork. In the roiling sky, a lone bird struggled to fly. Jules felt just as desperate, unprepared to battle the sea. She gasped a half breath, spinning in time to see another huge wave bearing down. It smashed on top of her, tumbling her hard, and she was under again, deeper, churning. Salt water in her eyes, nose, mouth. Running out of breath. She couldn't get out.

No one was coming to save her.

Not her husband or her lover or her children. Not her family.

I'm going to drown.

The thought wasn't frightening. It was a relief.

She'd let her greed overwhelm her, obliterating her values and Jarrah's, the same greed that razed old-growth forests for cheap paper towels. The human race would be extinct in four generations because of the same limitless appetite she'd let direct her hands and heart.

Instead of fighting the ocean, Jules relaxed, releasing herself to the bully, letting them have their way.

In death, there were no more lies. No more disappointment. No more failure or pain or struggle.

The water tossed her like an outgrown toy.

Memories flashed, chipping away at her darkness. The girls as newborns, pink, froggy-faced babies, so sweet and helpless. The early days with Glen, building a bookshelf, a home, a life. Laughing tipsily with her sister on the sunny back patio, then crying together at their parents' funerals. Matty on her wedding day, so happy and proud to be walking up the aisle to Parker. The way Amelia watched Liss at the talent show as the blue-haired knight in shining armor sang so beautifully.

Jules didn't just need to live for her family. She wanted to. They were the ones who colored in the outline of her life, making it full and rich.

Jules kicked again, and again, driven by love and fury and a mother's determination, until she shot out of the water, gasping for air, and there! The shore, barely visible through the sheets of rain. She swam for it, lurched forward on another rocketing wave, her chin grinding into the wet sand. Blood in her mouth, the air hot and cold. Gasping, she clawed at the sand, anchoring herself to the earth until finally, she was out of the water's grip. Spewing up seawater, panting but alive.

The lights of Kooroy glowed up the rain-washed beach.

*

The girls watched dumbly as Ludmila led Jules up the stairs to the master bathroom to shower and change. Ordinarily they'd be all over her like kittens on a mother cat—*Mum, are you okay? Mum, what happened?* But their arms were wrapped tight around their own bodies and their eyes were oddly absent, like smooth, empty bowls. Matty and Amelia together on the couch, Parker flanking them defensively. A trio of accusing women.

"We'll talk when you come down." Matty sounded like a lawyer for the opposition. They hadn't spoken since Matty and Parker's fight the night before.

In the master bathroom, Ludmila helped Jules into dry clothes. "Amelia got here fifteen minutes ago. I haven't said anything."

Jules's teeth were chattering, even in the warm bathroom. "I can't. I can't."

Ludmila caught her gaze, held it. "If I can use a drop dunny, you can do this."

Jules hiccupped a laugh.

Ludmila hugged her. A surprisingly warm, maternal hug.

Jules relaxed into it, letting it reset her strength. "Okay," she said. "Okay."

She descended the stairs from the master feeling like a prisoner on death row. Barely able to look at the girls as she crossed to her bedroom door, dreading having to explain kissing Jarrah to Glen before the awful scene that was coming. "Hon? Can I come in?"

"He's not here," Matty said.

Jules looked to Ludmila in confusion. "I think he's still out with Randall," Ludmila said. "Probably caught in the storm."

Jules's stomach dropped like an anvil. This conversation *had* to happen with Glen by her side. Still a team, still loving parents. And it had to happen at home, in the family room, with cups of herbal tea and tissues at the ready, the girl's favorite casserole in the slow cooker. Not alone in a rental house in the middle of nowhere while a storm raged outside after a near-drowning that left her feeling scraped out and sucked dry. Not like this. Anything but this. "Maybe we should wait. Till he gets back."

"I don't think you have the luxury of calling the shots," Matty said. "You gave that up when you stuck your tongue down Jarrah's throat."

Jules waited for Parker to place a reproaching hand on her wife's shoulder. She didn't. The coolness between the spouses suggested they were still in the middle of their own fight.

"I just think we should wait for Dad," Jules tried again.

"Mum, are you having an affair with Jarrah?" Amelia's question quavered, on the edge of tears.

"No!" Jules moved for her, arms outstretched, desperate for contact.

But her youngest daughter stiffened, her body language clear: *Don't. Touch me.*

Jules paused mid-step, ending up an awkward distance from her two daughters in the middle of the too-big main space. "No, darling. I am not having an affair with Jarrah."

"So, what? You're in an open marriage?" Matty said. "Dad knows?"

Jules almost laughed. "Christ, Matty—c'mon."

But the three women just stared at her.

"I'm not in an open marriage. No one's in an open marriage." Jules glanced again at the stairs to the front door. "If we can just wait for Dad—"

"Does Dad know or not?" Matty asked, louder.

"Have you slept together?" Amelia whispered. "Wait. No, I don't want to know."

Jules said, "Dad and I will explain everything—"

"For fuck's sake, Mum!" Matty exclaimed. "Just tell us the truth!"

"When Dad gets here—"

"Now!"

Jules snapped. "Dad and I are getting a divorce. We're separated."

She half expected one of them to look vindicated—*See, I told you so.* But to her surprise, and horror, the news was clearly a shock to all three.

"What?" Matty bit out.

"Divorced?" A tear slid down Amelia's cheek. "No. No, that's impossible."

"You're separated, now," Parker clarified. "Glen knows about it?"

"Of course he knows," Jules said. "It was a joint decision."

Matty scoffed. "Somehow I doubt that."

Infuriating what a higher standard Jules was held to. Glen wasn't a part of the girl's inner lives, yet instead of being punished for this, they expected less and forgave him more. Their father was never the villain.

"You're getting a divorce?" Amelia started crying in earnest. "You don't love Daddy anymore?"

Jules's heart went off like a bomb. She couldn't get a good breath. "I'll always love Glen. I'm just not in love with him anymore." Even to her ears, the words held as much honest sentiment as a supermarket greeting card.

"But you're Mum and Dad. My mum and dad." Amelia's face was splitting. "You've been married for thirty-six years!"

Jules used to be proud of her long marriage, repeating the length as it grew ever more impressive. Amelia, she'd noticed, did the same. But now it sounded like a ridiculous fetish, a useless spell.

Matty paced and panted like a bull readying to skewer someone. She spun on her mother. "*When* did this happen?"

Bull ants under Jules's skin. Her hands were shaking. "We haven't officially begun anything."

"Dad's still living at home?" Matty asked.

"Yes!" Jules was grateful to answer one question in the positive. "Yes, we're both still at home."

"What's going to happen to the house?" Amelia asked. "Is someone going to move out?"

"*How long have you been separated?*" Matty shouted.

And all at once, Jules realized Glen was right. They should've been honest earlier, as soon as it became clear they weren't getting off the island. Because now the truth was so much worse. Now the truth was a lie.

"These things evolve over time." Jules tap-danced blindly. "There's no hard-and-fast end point."

"End point," Amelia repeated, face wet with tears. "*End point.*"

"Mum." Matty folded her arms. "How. Long."

Jules wilted. "Four months. Or so."

A second shock wave ripped through the trio. Even unflappable Parker looked flapped.

"Four months?" Amelia gaped. "This entire trip?"

"Yep." Matty stared at their mother. "She's been lying to us this entire time."

"As has Glen," Parker pointed out.

"No. Dad wanted to come clean," Jules said. "I thought waiting was better. I see now I was wrong."

"But you called Dad the love of your life on your birthday!" Amelia cried, something Jules did not remember doing. "You sleep in the same bed, you never fight. You're still in love! Maybe you just need a getaway. A therapist. We can fix this. As a family."

"Animal, wake up." Matty addressed her mother, "You realize you've been advertising your happy marriage as one of the reasons for us to move back to Sydney, don't you? All the babysitting Grandma and Granddad will be doing? Not sure if watching you plow through a divorce then start bringing your new partners round to Christmas was what we had in mind. Are you both even staying in Sydney?"

Jules was so thrown, she answered honestly. "I don't know."

Matty laughed, throwing her hands up. "Great. That's just great."

"New partners?" Amelia looked like she might be sick. "Is Jarrah your—oh god—*boyfriend*?"

Jules had been too anxious to cry. Only now did she tear up. "No. He's not my anything."

"So, it's casual?" Matty posited. "That's a health risk, even at your age."

Lightning flashed overhead, followed by a crack of thunder.

"Matty, stop it," Jules snapped.

"Oh, please," Matty said. "After all the shit you said to me when I came out to you."

A hidden blade thrust under her ribs. "I threw you a coming-out party! I invited everyone we knew—I bought you a brand-new dress!"

"I didn't want a new dress, Mum—I wanted to dye my hair green but you said it'd make me look like a brussels sprout. You wanted to control the narrative, like you always do. You also said there was, quote, *'Never a good time for me to tell you something like that.'* You referred to Parker as my *best friend* for the first year. Oh, and that one time at Christmas when you got drunk and said that *two women masturbating each other wasn't actually sex.*"

"Oh yeah," Parker said. "I'd forgotten about that."

"What about Amelia?" Matty pointed at her sister. "If you hadn't been so desperate for a picture-perfect son-in-law, you might've figured out something was really off about James."

"Matty, don't," Amelia wept. "Leave me out of it."

Like a body stripped of its shadow, Jules felt a severing: a part of herself being sheared away. She was a good mother. Better than most. Better than anyone she knew. Her voice shook with grief and, underneath it, rage. "I love you both so much. More than you'll ever know. You're my entire *life*." Jules kneaded her forehead, her head pounding hard. "I'm sorry I lied—I was trying to protect you. But this is an extremely hard moment for me, too."

"You want *sympathy*?" Matty looked amazed. "You've been deceiving us every day since we got here! And now because Animal saw you dry humping Jarrah, we're going through this without Dad to give us his side of the story!"

The front door opened, the sound of the rain momentarily getting louder.

Liss trudged up the stairs, wrangling a busted umbrella, soaked shoes squeaking on the wooden steps. "Wow, it's raining cats and dogs out there. Or what's the Aussie equivalent: kangaroos and koalas—" She was stopped short by Amelia flying into her arms.

Jules watched her younger daughter babble a tearful summary of everything she'd just learned, lurid and shameful in detail. *Separated the whole time. Getting a divorce. Kissing Jarrah on the beach!* From the way Liss was holding Amelia, brushing her hair from her face, listening carefully to every word, Jules could see that once again, Glen was correct.

Amelia and Liss: they just looked right together. They fit.

Her knee-jerk reaction to this partnership, that it was anything other than beautiful and special, sickened her. Jules cast around for something to say, to indicate that Amelia could tell her the truth, right now, right here. "Liss. W-would you like to join us?"

Liss looked at Amelia.

Amelia shook her head, pressing her tearstained face to Liss's neck, whispering something Jules couldn't hear.

"I think we'll head back to the Cabin," Liss said, her arms still protectively around Amelia.

"But, Animal, darling." Jules stepped forward, palms open. "Is there anything you want to tell me first? I'm here: I'm listening." She smiled through her tears, wanting to convey complete acceptance: pure love.

Let me in, Amelia. I know I don't deserve it, but please, *let me in.*

Amelia's eyes went dark with distrust, walled in. "I have nothing to say to you."

The sound of the storm surged as the pair opened the front door to leave.

63

The rain poured around Glen and Randall, soundtracking the typically peaceful bush with a stadium-level roar.

Only ten minutes before, a winged flash of white had lured them off the beach. They'd only scrambled a few minutes into the scrub before it started to rain.

Randall wiped off his brow. "The white whale eludes us again."

Glen pocketed his bird-watching journal so the pages didn't smudge. "Let's go, Ahab."

But they must've gotten turned around because the beach wasn't where it should be. They bush-bashed for ten, twenty minutes. Eucalypts became tall ferns, knitting overhead. Somehow, they were in the rainforest, moss underfoot. The last vestiges of daylight were smothered by rolling yellow-gray clouds dumping an obscene amount of rain. Their phones' flashlights illuminated thick foliage that looked the same in every direction: green, wet, dense, soaked with rain, more rain. Unfortunately neither man had any idea their phones also came with a compass.

"It's got to be this way!" Glen pointed, yelling over the storm.

"That's west!" Randall shouted back. Every piece of clothing was soaked. "We need to go east!"

"That is east!"

"No, *that's* east!"

The wind seemed to be coming from all directions. A gust picked up a tree branch, flung it over their heads. The storm wasn't just getting closer—it was more dangerous than Glen anticipated. They needed to get to shelter.

"Mate, listen to me!" Glen wiped the streaming water from his eyes. "I'm a local!"

Randall looked incredulous. "You live in the suburbs!"

"Yeah: I have a vibe!"

"You don't have a vibe!"

"I do!"

"No, you don't!"

Glen bristled. Randall didn't respect him: he never had. The ripping wind exposed the truth. "It's *this* way." Glen grabbed Randall's shirtsleeve, making him stumble.

Randall pushed him off. "Watch it!"

Dismissal, disregard. He'd been pushed around his entire life. "You wanna go?"

Randall almost laughed. "Go? Go where, Glen?"

In his darkest moments, Glen fantasized about hitting his father. Finally punch back at the man who'd done nothing but mock and taunt his shy, sensitive son. "Come at me!" Glen slapped his chest, sending a spray of water.

"Don't be stupid!"

"Come at me, Randall!" Glen screamed, backing up to give Randall space to take a swing. "C'mon!"

"No!"

"C'mon. *C'mon!*" Glen rushed at Randall, who ducked out of the way. Glen caught his arms, and the pair began a stumbling, sumo-wrestler dance, crashing through the rainforest, both yelling.

"Hit me! Hit me, I'm not afraid!"

"I'm not going to hit you! Glen, just *stop*—"

The ground was no longer underfoot: they were falling. Tumbling down an incline, the world cycling sickly overhead. Glen landed in a pile in the mud, hitting his head hard on a rock. The world dipped black, his ears ringing; a thicker, higher peal than the pouring rain. Slowly, reality came back into focus: a bad situation now worse. With a drunk's loss of gravity, Glen managed to pull himself to his hands and knees. Everything around him was muddy and wet. Painful. A deep scratch on his forearm was already oozing blood. His head was throbbing. Blood in his eyes: another cut on his forehead. Maybe a concussion. Ironically enough, he felt like he'd just got his ass kicked. "Randall?" Glen wheezed, trying to get up. "Mate?"

Nothing. Just rain, relentless rain.

"Randall? Randall!"

Still nothing. Glen was in a small clearing at the bottom of the incline. The vegetation was sparser, but the rain sounded louder, crashing, and booming. Glen whirled in an unsteady circle, squinting through the gray sheets of water, flowing with a new kind of adrenaline. The kind that might find Randall with his neck snapped, his body lifeless. Fear punched through the pain. "Randall! *Randall*!!"

A sound: Was it a shout? Glen pushed his way through a patch of prickly bushes, razor-edged leaves slashing his skin, and suddenly there was the ocean, far below. He was at a cliff's edge. The storm was on top of them, nothing but gray sky and sheets of rain.

"Randall?" Glen shouted. "Mate!"

"Glen!"

The shout came from below. With a pounding heart, Glen peered over the cliff's edge.

A few feet below where Glen was standing, Randall was hanging on to the cliffside. His knuckles were white, his feet were dangling. If Randall lost his grip, like a newborn baby bird falling out of a nest, he'd never survive the drop down to the jagged rocks below.

64

Parker lit the candle on the bedside table and said a quick prayer for her father: *Come home safe, Dad. I love you.* She wasn't usually the candle-and-prayer type—most likely he and Glen were waiting out the storm under a tree somewhere—but still, she worried. The dads had been missing for hours.

A soft knock at the door. Parker stiffened, not yet ready to talk reconciliation with her wife.

"Parker? It's Jules."

"Oh." Parker glanced around the bedroom, ensuring there wasn't a hot pink vibrator or unrecycled glass jar on display. "Come in."

Parker first met Jules over FaceTime. Matty had picked up her mother's call in bed, postcoital. Panicked, Parker had been pulling on a sweatshirt as Matty'd breezily assured her, "She'll love you. She's certainly heard a *lot* about you."

They established what Parker could best describe as a working relationship. Parker kept a running list of things Jules enjoyed—environmentalism, home cooking, hats from home improvement stores—and curated her birthday presents and thought-you'd-find-this-interesting emails accordingly. Jules bawled at their wedding, declaring Parker *her third daughter* in a too-long speech, but Parker suspected Jules still hustled for conversation topics when they were alone. The time on Mun'dai had been the most they'd ever spent together. Jules had rarely heard the wives argue. Let alone fight. And while Parker didn't think Jules should have kept her separation a secret for so long, she understood why Jules did. As her mother-in-law entered the bedroom, Parker had no idea if she was going to get a lecture, an appeal, or an apology.

She stayed where she was, tucked against the pillows, a throw blanket around her legs. "Any word from the guys?"

Jules shook her head.

The two spoke as one. "I'm sure they're fine."

Women forever consoling each other.

Jules took a seat on the end of the bed. "I just want to say I'm sorry about Matty. Her . . . new plan. Obviously, I heard your fight last night."

"I shouldn't have yelled." Parker did regret it. "I'm not usually like that."

"Oh, honey. It's Matty we're talking about. She can be a lot."

Parker let out a surprised laugh. Jules typically sided with her family. But technically, Parker was family, too. Maybe Jules didn't have to be the catch in her relationship with Matty. Maybe she could be an ally. "She has a big personality."

"No idea where she gets that from," Jules quipped, and they both chuckled in understanding.

The candle filled the air with the clean scent of eucalyptus. Outside, the rain sheeted, the ocean a restless gray.

"Can I ask you something?" Jules said. "And, please, if I'm overstepping, just tell me to shut up."

"Okay."

"Did you— Do you—" Jules stumbled. "I mean, we've only ever talked about Matty having a baby. Delivering, I mean. Is that something— Are you—interested in that?"

Jules had never asked explicitly about their relationship. But there was a storm and everything felt upside-down. So Parker was honest. "I had a miscarriage. When I was at business school, when I was still with my boyfriend."

Parker braced herself, expecting Jules's typical hysterics. But her mother-in-law was quiet.

"I was so busy at school, I didn't realize I'd missed a period, and by the time I figured it all out, I was nearly two months along. I wanted kids but a part of me knew it shouldn't be with Kwan. Then less than a week after I found out, I started to bleed. I was at school, in the middle of a presentation."

Parker could still recall the sensation of wetness between her legs. The pain. The intuition that something was frighteningly wrong. She'd finished the presentation then walked calmly to the women's toilets, alone.

"It was really horrible, and scary, and sad, too." Parker bit her lip, assessing whether to tell Jules the full story. In for a penny: "And I never told Kwan."

Jules blinked. "What did he think happened to the baby?"

"No, I hadn't told him I was pregnant yet. So, when I lost it, I don't know, I just thought it would be easier. I'm a private person, I don't like burdening people. The only people I told were my mom—who probably told Dad—a therapist, and Matty. And now you."

"Oh, Parker." Jules leaned over to hug her, misty-eyed.

Parker was surprised to find herself welling up, too. Jules felt soft and warm but strong at the same time.

When they broke apart, Jules was still holding Parker's hand.

Parker wiped her nose with the edge of the blanket. "When Matty and I started talking about kids, I thought maybe it would be safer? If she carried? I know that's illogical, but she seemed so keen. So certain. And I'm not proud of this, but most of our friends assumed Matty would carry, and that was it."

"Sometimes we decide things without ever really making a decision."

Jules went into their shared bathroom, returning with a toilet roll so they could both blow their noses. Usually one of them would offer up a topic before the silence became awkward. But now, they just sat there and the quiet wasn't uncomfortable. It was reverent.

Then Jules spoke. "I had a miscarriage."

Parker's heart squeezed, quickening. "You did?"

"After Matty. Before Amelia. It was a boy."

"Matty never said anything."

"I never told the kids." Jules gave Parker a watery smile. "Guess I don't like burdening people, either."

But it wasn't a burden. It made Parker feel closer to Jules. Not just in this moment. Something had shifted on a molecular level between the two women.

The candle flickered, sending shadows dancing up the wall. The rain was getting harder but inside the bedroom things stayed soft.

65

Too much and not enough.

These were the words branded on Amelia Kelly's tired, bewildered brain.

Was her mother too much for her father? Too forceful, too emotional, too controlling, too political?

Was her father not enough for her mother? Not brave enough, not charismatic enough, not successful or decisive enough?

And had Amelia inherited both these tragic flaws in the DNA lottery? Once the appeal of her beauty wore off, would they forever be the reason her partners lost interest, no matter how hard she worked to make them stay?

"Amelia?"

Liss sounded like she was repeating herself. In her delicate fingers, the Garfield mug, steaming with herbal tea. "Are you sure you don't want Cup-a-Soup? I have exactly one left. Very soothing in times of crisis."

Amelia tried to smile, pulling the duvet around her. Outside the Cabin, the rain roared. "No, thanks." Wait: was rejecting Liss's offer not being adventurous enough? Accommodating enough? The worry made Amelia's chin tremble, but she'd only just gotten her tears under control. Another crying jag would definitely count as too much. Amelia worked hard to roll her emotions back. Her brain hurt. Her heart quivered like a kicked dog.

Liss sat on the end of the bed, knees drawn to her chest. Her question was the compassionate enquiry of a mental health professional. "Do you want to talk about it?"

What Amelia wanted was assurance. That Liss would never leave her, that their love was forever. She knew that was impossible, silly, hopelessly naive. Nothing in life was certain: everything that'd happened in the last six weeks, and especially the last sixty minutes, proved as much. Amelia didn't quite have the self-perception to recognize her Herculean power to love counterbalanced in perfect measure her fear of losing that love. All she felt right now, as the wind rattled the vintage glass panes, was a growing sense of terror that the person sitting on the other end of the bed from her was already slipping away.

Too much. Not enough.

A sip of tea burned the soft flesh of her mouth. "It was just . . . such a shock."

"A huge shock. You had no idea, right?"

"The concept never even crossed my mind." She pressed her fingers into the burning ceramic of the mug, the pleasure of the heat tipping into pain. "They weren't giddy teenagers. But forever means forever. At least, it does in my book."

Liss tipped her head to the side, as if dodging this flaming arrow. "People change. I suppose marriage is about being willing to change with them."

"I'm willing." Too quick; too much. "I mean, that doesn't scare me. Changing with someone. Giving them room to change. Their own personal changing room, built by me."

Liss laughed. The nervous one. "That's very sweet."

A silence spread thick between them. A thousand unsaid words thrashed on its sticky surface.

"Do you want to watch some *Buffy*?" Liss asked at the same time Amelia said, "So, what are we doing?"

"Pardon?" Liss said, even though Amelia knew she'd heard what she'd said.

"What are we doing?" Amelia tried to sound like they were discussing a day trip. "On Monday?"

Liss fiddled with her hair. Her pale skin started to flame. "I do want to talk about this. But you've just been through an extremely traumatic experience and maybe if we relax for a few hours—"

"I don't want to watch television. I want to make a plan."

Liss's breathing quickened, the tendons in her throat jumping. "Okay. What are you thinking?"

Amelia put her tea on the nightstand. Her hands were shaking; it spilled. "What are you thinking?"

Liss's hazel eyes were full of soft regret. "Amelia . . ."

"What? What have I done now?"

"Nothing." Liss appeared taken aback. "You haven't done anything. It's just . . . this situation."

"The situation where we've fallen in love? The situation where we've talked about getting married, having kids?" Amelia tried to laugh. It came out strangled. "I thought that was a good thing."

"It is. Of course it is. But Monday's so soon: I just wish we had more time."

"We could have time in Sydney. Or Montreal. I don't think this is that complicated. We just pick a place."

Liss inhaled fast, like she'd burned herself. "I've already told you I can't move with you to Sydney. I know you're not keen on long distance, but I do think it's our only option right now."

Days, weeks, months apart? With beautiful Liss playing romantically sad songs at Black Dog for heartbroken humans all desperate for rebounds? Where she could easily be living a double life, just like her ex? Past and future anxiety twinned through Amelia's blood, ratcheting up her heartbeat. She scrambled off the bed. "No, that's not an option for me. I can't be apart from you like that. *No long distance.*"

"We can make it work, Animal." Liss was in front of her, clutching her hands. "I promise. It'll give us more time."

"To do what?" Amelia exploded. "We already love each other. We've already figured that part out!"

Liss dropped her hands and backed up. She looked like someone watching their childhood home burn to the ground.

This was it. It was ending.

Again.

Too much.

Not enough.

"Marry me!" The words shot out of Amelia's mouth like a toddler with a gun.

Liss's mouth fell open. *"What?"*

"Marry me! Now, here. On the island, before we leave. Someone can get ordained on the internet. I've got a white dress, you can wear—whatever, I don't care."

Liss was shaking her head in alarm. "Amelia—"

"If we're married we have to be together, we have to figure it out." The words tumbled like marbles bouncing down a flight of stairs. "Married couples don't do long distance, married couples don't fly off to different continents, married couples stay together—"

"Amelia—"

"I love you!" Amelia met Liss's eyes, a mirror of the same fear and confusion she was feeling herself. "I love you and when I leave this island it *has* to be with you." Words flew out of her like hiccups, her emotions hijacking everything. "Whatever it takes. You're my future, you're my everything. So, marry me. Please. Please don't say this is the end, please don't say I'm not enough—"

"Amelia!" Liss cupped her face. "We're not going to get married. Not here. Not like this. Just take a breath. Okay? Breathe with me. In. Out."

Like she was an unhinged lunatic. The complete opposite of a desirable wife.

"No." Amelia pushed her off, scorching with shame. She'd promised herself to be rational and reasonable and here she was begging for a ring like a train wreck reality TV star. *"Fuck.* I just don't understand how any of this is fair. Asshole James still wants to marry me while the person I actually love probably wants me committed. And you're probably right."

Liss blinked, once, like she'd just been flicked in the face. "Still?"

She hadn't meant to mention the voicemail. Amelia turned away to blow her nose.

"James *still* wants to marry you—What does that mean?"

"Nothing. Nothing important."

"Sorry—have you been in touch with James?" Liss's voice sounded like a twisted piece of metal.

"No!" Amelia met Liss's gaze, trying not to look guilty. "He just left me a voicemail."

The wrong thing to admit. Liss's face darkened. "You told me you deleted his number; that you never wanted to speak to him again."

"I don't! And when I listened to the voicemail it just made me realize how much I love *you*."

"You *listened* to the voicemail?" Liss's voice shot up. Her eyes were scarily wide. "So, you haven't deleted his number and you're listening to his voicemails behind my back."

"No! None of this is happening *behind your back*."

"Except that it is." Liss exhaled hard, walking away from her, hands in her hair.

Lightning lit the sky outside. A second later, thunder. The storm was right on top of them.

Amelia cursed herself. Liss was obviously spiraling out over Reggie Richards, the man her ex-girlfriend cheated on her with and ultimately left her for. How many voicemails had Sofia listened to behind Liss's back?

"Liss. Baby. I swear—"

"Give me a second." Her lover sounded uncharacteristically sharp. "I need a minute to process."

"There's nothing to process!"

"Yes, there is!" Liss spun around. "You lied to me!"

"It just happened this morning! And I don't love him, I love you!"

Liss folded her fingers together and pressed them to her mouth. Tears were streaking down both cheeks. "You're right about one thing. Long distance won't work. We'd need to trust each other *completely* and right now. . . I don't."

The thread looped between them was fraying.

"All this stuff about marriage and kids," Liss went on. "It's just *way* too much."

And there it was.

Too much.

Not enough.

The two women stared wordlessly at each other, and it felt like all the memories they'd created over the past few weeks were just fantasies, silly daydreams. Love was an act of imagination and will. As easily as it could be made, it could be unmade.

"Is that it?" Amelia might be dreaming. Might be sick. "Are we really breaking up?"

"This is *exactly* what I didn't want to have happen." Liss's voice was shaking, boiling with pain. "I didn't want to hurt you. And I didn't want you to hurt me. And now both things are happening."

"I literally don't know how I can live without you." Amelia's realization was horrific, like being told she'd need a rare medicine to survive that she did not have access to. "I don't think I can ever be happy knowing I'm not with you. How am I supposed to live like that?" It wasn't rhetorical. It was a genuine enquiry. "No, really: How?"

Liss's wet cheeks shone in the lamplight. But she didn't close the distance between them. She stood in the middle of the Cabin, her arms wrapped only around herself. "I'm—so—sorry."

"Love is a paltry word for what I feel for you." Amelia's grief turned the words to rage. "It's like my heart is exploding out of my chest!"

"I feel the same way! This isn't easy for me, either." Liss tugged at her hair, her fingertips white. "I knew things would end like this. I knew it! That's why I kept trying to protect us both."

"Well, you failed!" Amelia shouted. "All you've done is destroy me, just like you destroyed Gabe. You were right, Liss: you *do* hurt the people closest to you. Every horrible thing you've ever thought about yourself is *true*."

Something behind Liss's eyes crumbled. The light inside her snuffed out.

Her skin paled. Her shoulders started jumping, like she was beginning to hyperventilate. Her forehead shimmered with sweat. Liss took a step backward. "Amelia, go."

Water lashed the windows. "It's pouring!"

"I mean it." Liss gasped, turning away.

"We're in the middle of a *tropical storm*!"

"*Now!*"

"Fine!" Amelia blazed to the front door, flinging it open. Rain gusted inside, sending papers whirling around the room. "You wanna know the worst part? I thought you were the one. I truly believed *you* were my soulmate. And now I'll never believe that about anyone ever again. *Wasted love.*" She slammed the door behind her as hard as she could.

Wind slammed her in the face, knocking the air from her lungs in a gasp. A sick sort of triumph had her laughing—a chemical high of cruelty. She grabbed on to it with both hands. She didn't want to see what would be left behind when it faded away.

66

"Randall!" Glen's voice pitched high in terror. He fell to his knees. "Jesus fuck. Jesus fuckity fuck."

"Glen!" Randall's face was white. Every muscle in his arm was straining, ropey with tendons pulled tight as he clung to the jut of rock. "Help me!"

Glen's mind went static. He'd had close calls before—a car wreck as a teenager, a mid-morning mugging at knifepoint in a sunny Sydney backstreet. Nothing truly life or death. "W-wait here." As if Randall had another option. "I'll get someone—something—"

"No, Glen," Randall wheezed, barely audible above the smash-crash of the ocean below. "Help me. *Now.*"

Randall was bigger than Glen. Heavier than Glen. It was pouring rain. A thousand scenarios flipped fast through his mind. Randall losing his grip, plunging to a certain death. Randall pulling Glen over the edge, both of them somersaulting to the black rocks below. *Two Men Die in Bird-Related Tragedy.* A one-day news story. He'd never get to hold his girls again.

Randall was panting, his face spasming in pain. "Glen!"

Glen was not an action hero. He wasn't any kind of hero. He was a man who enjoyed a perfectly brewed cup of tea and a particularly tricky crossword. But in this moment, at some indeterminate hour in some indeterminate part of the Australian bush, he found himself lowering to his belly. Shimmying through the mud toward a cliff's edge.

Whaddya think you're doing, ya idiot? You can't— You won't—

"No!" Glen spoke over the voice in his head. "I can." He was delirious with fear. "Take my hand."

Randall dared to loosen one hand, take a swipe at Glen's outstretched fingers. Inches away. Randall regained his grip on the cliff, snorting like a bull. Glen shimmied farther forward. Too far and Randall would pull him over. He wasn't sure that wouldn't happen regardless. He wiggled his feet around, managing to wedge his left foot into a crack in the rock behind him, praying it would be strong enough to anchor them both.

"Tell Mila I love her!" Randall's eyes were rolling. "Tell Parker—"

Glen gripped a knobby bit of rock, braced himself, and shot out his other arm again. "C'mon!"

"I can't!"

"You can. You have to!"

"I'm slipping!"

"Take it!"

Randall gritted his teeth. With a sharp cry, he let go of the rock, swinging himself toward Glen's hand. Glen felt contact—skin on skin. Glen squeezed tight. Randall had his wrist; they had each other. Glen's body jerked forward with the weight, even as he jammed his foot farther into the crevice behind him to prevent being pulled over. A second later, the pain. It felt like his limbs were being ripped from his body. Glen screamed.

He needed to pull Randall up.

He wasn't strong enough.

Both men were yelling, screaming, the rain gushing over them, mixing with their tears.

Push! He was twenty-six, watching his young wife scream in a hospital bed, legs in stirrups, her belly the size of a beachball, her face a monstrous contortion. Even then, he loved her. *Push!*

Push through the pain. Push through the fear.

Glen let out a roar and began to pull.

The pain was otherworldly. It lit him up from the inside. It showed him everything. Every time he hadn't spoken up for himself, every desire he'd repressed, every path not taken out of fear and shame exploded inside him, a dizzying Big Bang. He was rising above the mud, the cliff, the rocks, the island. His body shot up like a rocket and out like fireworks and he was as huge as the space between stars, as bright as the colossal moon. He saw the fabric of the universe and understood he was both just a stitch and the entirety of the cloth.

He was pure potential. He was anything he dreamed of. *He was Glen Kelly.*

And he was no longer afraid.

Randall found purchase on the cliff's edge. He was up and over the lip, scrambling to safety. The two men flopped and rolled in the mud, heaving for breath.

Glen's throat was raw from screaming. His body was in agony.

But the rain was starting to relent.

Randall Lee was alive.

And a new Glen had been born.

67

Midnight. A few stars dared to assert themselves through the departing storm clouds.

Amelia fetaled into bed in the Yellow Cottage. She'd been crying so hard for so many hours that when she coughed, she tasted blood.

She'd gotten everything so wrong, ending—oh god—in Amelia tearfully *begging* a horrified Liss to *wife* her. On the day she found out her mum and dad were getting a *divorce*.

Her stomach lurched, sloshing up her throat. She ran to the bathroom, fell to her knees, and threw up.

She obviously wasn't going to sleep anytime soon. And Amelia Kelly wasn't the "suffer in silence" type. When she was done being sick, she rinsed her mouth, slipped on her kimono, and went outside onto the cool, wet sand.

Only one light on at Kooroy. Fortunately, it was the light that mattered.

In the quiet, darkened main space, Matty was snoring on the couch. Amelia paused, feeling a spike of sympathy for her sister, evidently still mired in her own romantic drama. She tiptoed past her sleeping form to quietly knock on her parents' bedroom door. "Mum?"

"Amelia?"

Her father stood by the window, hands behind his back. There was something unfamiliar about his pose. Sort of . . . philosophical. Like she'd just caught him communing with the moon. A white bandage above his eye, another around his arm. "Dad! What happened?"

"Nothing, pet. It'll heal." He seemed different. More at ease in his own body, perhaps. Serene.

She stepped uncertainly inside the bedroom. "Is Mum . . ."

"In the shower." His gaze became concerned. "Sweetheart, what's wrong?"

Amelia pressed her lips together, trying not to cry. "I'll wait till she's out."

She waited for her dear old dad to shuffle off to make some tea or give her some space, reacting to her emotion like it was a piece of clothing he'd be highly embarrassed to wear.

Glen stepped closer. "What's the matter? Is this about Mum and me?"

"No," Amelia said. "I mean, yes, partly. But it's okay, I'll just wait for Mum."

He gave her a look. But it wasn't his usual helpless one, like a man trapped behind glass. "Amelia. I'm not sure if I can solve your problems. But if you want, I'd really love to hear about them."

She was completely taken aback. All at once, Amelia found herself on the bed next to her father, pouring out her story. Befriending the mysterious human with the blue hair and hazel-green eyes. Falling in love on the island, this place of dreams and nightmares, so far from home. How much she liked and respected and admired Liss, how funny and brave and kind she was. Feeling like Liss was the one, the only one, for her.

Her father listened in silence, giving her shoulder the occasional squeeze, until she came to the messy, awful end at the Caretaker Cabin.

"I'll never forgive myself for the things I said." Amelia took an offered tissue to blow her nose. "The way I acted. I'm not saying she's perfect but she *is* the one for me and—" It suddenly struck her what she was confessing to. She looked up at her dad, feeling oddly guilty.

He seemed to understand. "So, Liss is—was—your girlfriend?"

"I don't know," Amelia whimpered. "Yes. No. Do you think Mum'll be upset? She's always banging on about a son-in-law."

"I can't speak for your mother," Glen said. "But I think she regrets that. She regrets a lot of things—so do I. We're both committed to being better parents. Even if we're not still married, you girls are our number one priority." He took her hands, his eye contact sincere and steady. "All I want, Amelia, is to know you. To be a part of your life. To love you, pet. I just want to love you."

"Oh, *Dad*." Amelia was stunned to find herself sobbing in her father's arms—his arms!—as he patted her back and said soothing things. She'd always loved her father but only now did she feel loved *by* him, in a way that felt vulnerable and tender.

"And for what it's worth, sweetheart, I really like Liss," Glen added. "She's a true swan among pigeons."

"Oh, Dad." Amelia pushed him playfully, wiping her eyes. "You're such a dork."

"She is!" Glen protested. "I think you'd make a cracking pair."

"But we're not a pair," Amelia said. "Anymore. I stuffed it all up."

"Well, hang on," Glen said. "The Amelia I know wouldn't give up that easily."

"I'm not giving up," Amelia said, affronted by the idea. "I'll never stop loving her."

"Then do as the common magpie does," said Glen, "and *fight* for her love!"

"How?" Amelia asked. "Chances of me fighting anyone are, as the common fairy wren is, fairly small."

Her father's eyes lit with delight at her use of his bird-world lexicon. Amelia grinned back before adding, "Also, there's no one *to* fight."

"Good point." Glen cocked his head to think aloud. "Let's see. It sounds like you're both backed into your own corners and you're sort of stuck there. But partnerships are about compromise. Creative thinking for workable solutions."

"I guess." Amelia was surprised, even impressed, that her new, post-marriage father could be so wise.

"Maybe there's some way you can keep moving forward that you haven't yet thought of," Glen said. "Sometimes the best solution is right in front of you."

Amelia looked right in front of her. The bedroom, the bathroom door. Through the window, the edge of the bush, and beyond it, Blinky

Beach strewn with seaweed. Washed-silver moonlight glinting on the water. A sprinkle of meditating stars.

The idea arrived without prologue. Imperfect—a compromise—but maybe, possibly, a workable solution. She couldn't make it happen on her own, but perhaps . . . perhaps her dad was right.

"But I don't think she'd even want to speak to me." Amelia pressed the heels of her hands into her eyes, wanting to unsee the memory of their fight.

"Then show her how much you love her," said Glen. "Show her how much she means to you."

"I don't think I'm very good at that," Amelia said. "Unless you count nonconsensual marriage proposals as romance."

A glint lit her father's gaze. Glen snapped his fingers. "I believe that, once again, we can take inspiration from the greatest kingdom of all."

"Oh, Dad." Amelia giggled. "You're not going to suggest something to do with birds, are you?"

"I am," her dad said, entirely unembarrassed. "I absolutely am."

68

Sunlight, a cruel joke. Liss burrowed, wanting to stay in bed, far away from everyone, especially the woman whose name she couldn't conjure without feeling like someone was murdering her soul.

Liss expected to feel like she was being gutted alive, like one of Ludmila's unlucky fish. She expected to feel heartbroken and ashamed, a pool of infinite sadness.

She didn't expect to feel like something was epically, dangerously, *wrong*.

Her phone pinged.

A message.

From Gabe.

His name woke her up like a needle in the arm.

Liss, long time, no email? I was getting used to yr weekly apologies clogging up my inbox. Feel like a bit of a dick for not replying until now. Anyway, heard a rumor you were coming back to Montreal. I'm glad. Things obviously ended pretty badly between us, but I'm doing okay. I'm seeing someone. You'll like her, I think. Hit me up when you're back in town. Sad Sack Sundays isn't as sad without you ☺

She read it once, then again. Waited to feel a ten-ton weight lifting. A rush of adrenaline and pure joy. And while she did feel relieved that Gabe seemed happy . . . she didn't feel how she was expecting to feel.

Liss spent too long in the shower waiting for Gabe's words to click into place and make her whole. Her best friend and her place in his life had just come back to her. Right when she needed it most. It was good, of course it was good. But it wasn't *everything*.

The warm water drummed against the tight muscles in her neck, loosening them bit by bit. Washing away old sweat. Old ideas. A gut-level truth was emerging from deep in her core.

She whipped open the shower curtain.

"Max." The spider was above the bathroom mirror. "Have I done anything right?"

Max's silence was blaring.

It was just so painfully, ridiculously, obvious.

She never should've let Amelia go.

Why didn't she accept Amelia's offer to move to Sydney? It was a world-class city, highly livable! Who cared if they had to live with a few roommates while they figured everything out? That would've been a minor sacrifice to facilitate the *greatest love of her life*. She still had Sofia's engagement ring—that'd cover a deposit for an apartment: Why hadn't she thought of that? Why did she insist Amelia wouldn't like living in Montreal? Because it was *too cold*? What was she, a *cactus*? They could've *bought her a coat*.

Nothing gold could stay, that was true. But ultimately, nothing stayed, good or bad. So maybe the point of the poem wasn't *So don't bother trying to keep it*, but more *So when you find it, treasure it: it's special*.

Someone had slipped a note under the front door. A piece of paper, folded once.

Can we talk? Kooroy at sunset?
—A

And everything Liss had been expecting to feel from Gabe's email smashed into her body like a building collapsing.

69

The storm had shifted the underwater sandbanks in Pigface Bay, creating a new break for the dolphins to surf on Blinky Beach. Change presented new ways of doing things.

Matty sat on the shore, watching the dolphins play, wondering exactly how long Parker was planning on putting her in the doghouse. She'd already apologized, told her to forget everything she'd said—she was absolutely still up for moving to Sydney.

"And kids?" Parker'd asked.

"I like kids," Matty had replied, wishing she didn't sound so meek. She just didn't want to carry a child, as difficult as it was to admit. Not just because it went against her self-conception as a fearless, can-do superwoman. Because she was letting Parker down. Matty had realized she could be happy with or without children. She could be happy without experiencing childbirth. But she couldn't be happy without Parker. Parker was her family and that would never change.

Now, sitting on the beach, she unscrewed the thermos of coffee and sloshed some into her mug, picking out some bits of paper towel from the improvised filter. She fished around her tote for the little jar of half-and-half. No jar: she must've left it on the kitchen counter. That was the sort of thing Parker'd always double-check: *Don't forget your half-and-half, boo boo!* Matty sipped the coffee and grimaced. Life without her wife. Black; bitter.

Someone was coming up the beach. Matty stiffened, squinting in the morning haze: was it her mum? They still hadn't spoken since Jules's big announcement yesterday. Losing her temper out of shock and sadness was yet another thing Matty regretted.

But it wasn't Jules. It was Parker. Holding the jar of half-and-half.

Matty smiled hopefully as Parker handed it over, relieved when she sat next to her on the sand. Not close enough to touch. But close enough to talk. The coffee became rich and creamy: perfect. For a few moments, they watched the dolphins surf the waves, the air around them full of early-morning birdsong.

"I bought a baby wet suit," Parker said.

"I'm sorry?"

"A baby wet suit," Parker repeated. "I read you can't put sunscreen on babies until they're six months, and I figured we'd be at the beach a lot, so I bought a baby wet suit. It's in my suitcase."

"That sounds ridiculously cute," Matty tried. "And practical." A lot like Parker.

Her wife let out a long sigh and faced her. Love and caution in her eyes. "You talked to Levi?"

"I told him I wasn't coming back," Matty told Parker.

"Because you want to move to Sydney?"

"Because I want *you*. You're my whole life, Parks. I don't want to be selfish. I want to be a good wife."

"But would Sydney make you happy?"

"Happy enough."

Parker looked back at the ocean, rolling in and out. In and out. The endless heartbeat of the tide. "I want a baby, Matty."

"I know. We still have options—"

"No, *I* want a baby. I want to have a baby. Me."

Matty wasn't sure she was hearing this correctly. "In your—" Womb? Uterus? Were they the same thing? She circled her hand in the general vicinity of her tummy.

Parker watched wryly. "Tell me you understand the basics of childbirth."

"I understand. Two people bone and nine months later a baby's born in a cabbage and photographed by Anne Geddes."

Parker laughed. A wondrous sound.

"Are you serious?" Matty's skin was lifting, prickling, as if being stroked by tiny fingers. "You want to carry?"

"I'm willing to go back to New York," Parker said, "if the first thing we do—*we*—is start the process of getting me pregnant."

A locked door opening for the very first time. "But I thought— because of your miscarriage, you didn't want to."

"I didn't. But that doesn't make much sense: that's just my fear." Parker looked to Matty, who nodded in surprised agreement, listening. "Not gonna lie," Parker went on. "Your freak-out over all this does not fill me with confidence when it comes to co-parenthood. Part of me thinks you don't want to be a mom because you'd rather be at work. But another part thinks you'd actually be really good at it. I think kids will change your perspective, in a good way."

Matty had the urge to laugh and cry, her breath just out of reach. "I think you're right."

"We start with three years," Parker said. "The first three years with Noisy Brats, then we reassess. I know New York's expensive. But like Fran Lebowitz says, no one can afford to live in New York. Eight million people still do."

Matty was too stunned to chuckle. Something huge and light-colored and sparkling like champagne was rolling through her body. It felt like joy.

"I think this is what I want," Parker said. "I think this is the best way forward for both of us. But have I two conditions."

New York. Babies. Babies in New York! "Okay."

"One: you handle all the logistics for moving back. I mean, *all* of them. And two: you're in. Properly in. No more plans behind my back. If you want to change course, talk to me. But you have to be committed to kids. That's nonnegotiable: I'm not doing this on my own. You don't have to decide now." Parker cocked her head. "But considering we're getting picked up tomorrow, you probably have to decide soon."

The idea felt like finally putting on the right-sized bra after years of it being too tight. A family. With Parker as bio mom. Yes, she'd be away from her mum and dad and Amelia. Yes, it'd be happening over launching a business and that would mean a compromise as to how many hours she could work. But for the very first time, the concept of kids and the future didn't feel complicated and scary. It felt exciting. It felt possible.

Where was home for those who flew far from where they were born? Matty had often wrestled with this question. It was a map that kept changing and getting her lost. But maybe, Matty thought, as she leaned against her wife's shoulder, watching the graceful dolphins surf the rolling waves, the answer lay in the place between them, she and Parker.

Home was the place that they made, together.

70

For the past few days, Liss had been chasing time, alarmed at its pace. Now, the sun crawled overhead.

Inch.

By.

Inch.

Did Amelia want to apologize at Kooroy at sunset, or double-down on her outrage? Smooth things over for a clean break? Or . . . something else?

Liss distracted herself by packing and repacking and re-repacking. To avoid spiraling, she logged into the helpline in the late afternoon, needing to lose herself in the troubles of others.

"Hi, this is Liss?" Wasn't meant to be a question. "How can I help?"

"Good gravy. You sound terrible."

"Ro. H-Hey."

"Oh god. Have you been betting on live eels in West Hollywood again?"

Jesus, did she tell that story to a teenager? They really should vet their volunteers more closely. "Something like that. What's up?"

"Oh-kay. Remember the guy I like?"

"The hot-cool-temperature paradox?"

"I asked the paradox if he wanted to go to a party this rich bitch in our grade is throwing this weekend, and he said . . . no. Because—"

"Oh, man, that sucks." This confirmed everything Liss knew about the life of the romantic loner, the heartbroken heartbreaker: her life. "Yeah, love is hard, y'know? Two people being on the same page at the same time is so *rare*—"

"He said no," Ro interrupted, "because he just wants to hang out one on one. Like, a date? And I am fa-*reak*ing out."

"Oh! Congrats, dude." Liss chuckled at her own dumb assumptions. "That's awesome."

"Right, but what do I do? I've never been on a date. Let alone with a guy. Let alone a bi guy. Let alone the million other things that make us very unlike a straight couple as seen on TV."

Lis settled back in her chair. "But that's what makes it so great," she said. "You're not like anyone else. Neither am I. And when you're queer, you get to create a love story that's never been written before. There's no set expectations of who does what and when: you get to make it up, and, honestly, it's thrilling. And hard. But I've never felt more alive and present and happy than when I'm with"—*Amelia*—"someone whose making it all up with me." Her words came easily, equally heartfelt and true. "Look: being queer in this world is no cakewalk. You and I, we know about prejudice and violence and the things that are scary and tough. But for me, what makes all that shit worth it, is getting to love whoever I want, however I want. It's more than just a right. It's . . . everything."

Silence on the other end.

"Oh, and as far as your date idea goes"—Liss remembered the initial question—"just get drunk. Sorry: no—you're a teenager. Don't do that. Go, um, bowling."

Ro laughed. They sounded a little choked up.

Liss took a moment to let her words sink in. For Ro, and for herself. It felt like Amelia was open to making it all up in a way her ex hadn't. If—or maybe when—Liss continued her exploration of a nonbinary identity, Liss felt certain Amelia would be supportive.

If they ever saw each other again after tonight.

The sun was glowing through the windows. Finally, sunset.

"I have to go," Liss said. "Stay safe out there, okay?"

"You too," Ro said. "Thank you, Liss. You've been a morally question-able counselor and a pretty good friend."

Liss clicked off the call, feeling a wave of something warm and rich. Which disappeared the second she walked out the front door, starting down the sandy track to Kooroy.

71

Many plant species relied on birds and insects to help reproduce—the butterfly or bat that unwittingly handed off pollen in its nuzzling for nectar. But coastal flora used air and ocean currents to spread their pollen and seeds. This always struck Jules as romantic—a love story written on the wind, perhaps? But now the thin breeze on Blinky Beach felt like a warning. As the shadows started lengthening up the beach, she couldn't delay what had to be done any longer. The last sunset on Mun'dai. Her last chance.

On the porch of the Blue Cottage, Jarrah was prying the rain-buckled plywood off the windows. Only the slightest flicker of pain behind his eyes as he gave her a perfunctory nod. "Julia."

Ordinarily she'd fuss about with small talk—*Some storm, huh? How'd everything hold up?*—but it seemed silly to enquire about weatherproofing with someone who'd touched her breast. Her life hadn't equipped her for the kind of honesty Jarrah deserved. "Things got a bit out of hand for us, didn't they?"

He popped a nail out with the back of his hammer. "Ya reckon?"

Jules blew her curls out of her eyes, unsure whether to cross her arms or put her hands on her hips. She wasn't used to admitting she was wrong. What a strange thing to realize. Jules conceived of herself as a selfless, accommodating person. Self-knowledge was like chutney: surprisingly tricky and you couldn't cut any corners to get it right. She sucked in a breath and faced Jarrah head-on. "Yeah, I did the wrong thing. Lying to you was wrong. And I'm sorry. I'm really, really sorry. I wanted what I wanted without much regard for anyone else."

Only now did he look at her. Something about his face made her think of a deserted beach. "You broke my trust, Julia. And I don't trust a lot of people. So, you understand why I can't just say it doesn't matter and pick up where we left off."

"Yes. Of course." Tears blurred her vision. She swatted them away like flies, suffocating in shame.

"Julia." Jarrah put the hammer down and leaned against the outdoor table. "It's okay."

"No, it's not." Her entire body heated up. "It's not because I lied to you, and I like you. I lied to someone I like. What sort of person does that make me?"

"A normal one." He scrubbed a hand through his curls. "The truth can be a tough thing to admit to yourself."

"Why is that?"

He half shrugged. "What we want and what we need can be different things. Or maybe it's just hard to accept how messy we all are."

Jules felt like a plant being uprooted, rising up.

It was easy to love the parts of herself and her family that were, by her definition, good qualities. Loyalty. Generosity. A willingness to sacrifice self for family. It was harder to love the parts rife with contradiction and self-interest, the petty, embarrassing, weak parts. The messy parts. And yet, perhaps, that was the larger project of love. To see the good and the messy and accept both, without judgment. Humans were imperfect. That's what made them human.

And yet there was still so much she could not see. Could not understand, and maybe never would. She was a child of her culture. Part of its story, the good and the ugly. The island held a mirror up to her true self. Jules did and didn't like what it reflected back. But she was determined not to look away.

There was still so much work to be done.

The last rays of sun faded. Dusk. Gosling-soft clouds drowsed over the horizon. The air smelled like Jarrah's skin.

"I have to go. Amelia has a whole thing planned." She gave him a crooked smile and turned to head off.

"Are you still moving to the Bay, Julia?"

The question pulled her up short. "I'm not sure."

Something pliable passed between them. Not forgiveness; not yet. Understanding, perhaps, salted with acceptance.

Jarrah picked up the hammer, twirled it once in his palm. Almost a smile. "Best place in the world."

Joy sparked and caught her in the chest. But she didn't leap in to fan the flames. Jules stood back. "Yes. It is."

72

Liss was used to a cheerful cacophony of sound at Kooroy: Matty warbling *Les Mis* or Glen's jaunty jazz or Jules calling out if anyone wanted a cuppa. Randall brushing past en route to a jog. Ludmila returning home with a shining silver fish. But as Liss approached the front door, no movement—nothing. Had they already left? The boat came early, everyone rushed to the wharf with suitcases and tote bags, no time—or reason—to say goodbye. The thought was so painful, sadness misted behind her eyes.

The front door was closed. Again, unusual; it was typically open to let in the sea breeze. But as Liss went to twist the knob, the door opened from the inside.

Parker, smiling in a strangely formal way. "Liss Chambers? We've been expecting you."

We?

"Hey, Parks. Amelia left a note—"

"Please, follow me to your seat."

Liss trailed Parker up the stairs to the main space, even more on edge. She'd assumed this conversation/confrontation/second breakup would be a private affair. The idea that cool, crisp Parker Lee was somehow privy to all this was deeply troubling and highly embarrassing. A kangaroo court, the Kelly-Lees vs Liss Chambers. Liss steeled herself.

Until she saw the second floor.

Typically, the space was bright and comfortably chaotic; everyone's stuff strewn everywhere, something simmering on the stove, damp swimsuits flung over the balcony.

The second floor was neat as a pin. Everything where it should be. Except for one chair. Sitting on its own in the middle of the space.

Outside, the sky was swirling pink and orange, beginning to darken. But none of the lights inside were on. No one else was around.

Parker, impersonating some sort of *Downton Abbey*–esque footman, indicated Liss should sit.

She obeyed. "But I'm just here to see Amelia?"

But Parker was already heading off.

Liss wiped sweaty palms on her jeans, searching for clues. Fears of the kangaroo court intensified. Perhaps she was the target of a family firing squad. Everyone in military garb, wild potshots from hidden vantage points. Well, she would go down with dignity. She wouldn't deny a thing.

"G'day, love."

Liss yelped.

Jules was at her elbow with Ludmila. Offering her a . . . mug?

"It's not Cup-a-Soup," Amelia's mother whispered.

"But we did our best," Ludmila finished, giving her a bizarrely deliberate smile.

The mug was full of delicate fish soup. Mouthwateringly delicious. Instantly soothing. Possibly, this broth was poisoned. But the first glimmer of another possibility edged into Liss's horizon.

The door to Matty and Parker's bedroom opened. There was Matty, looking, as Glen would say, "in full feather"—bright dress, big earrings. Her expression attempted aloof, but there was a smirk on her lipsticked mouth.

Behind her, Amelia.

Liss's breath hitched hard in her throat. Her beautiful girl was in her sundress, hair loose and woven with native flowers. She looked extremely, painfully nervous.

How could she ever have pushed this angel-creature away?

The two sisters came to stand ten feet from Liss, Matty just behind Amelia. Amelia had something in her hand.

A hairbrush.

A spotlight appeared on Amelia, who winced.

Music roared over the speakers.

Everyone jumped.

"Dad!" Amelia hissed.

Glen was in the kitchen fiddling with a phone. Next to him, Randall aimed one of the bedroom lamps at the two sisters, slightly off-center. Liss caught Glen's eye and shot him a quizzical look.

He gave her a grin and a thumbs-up.

The volume lowered, making the song instantly recognizable.

The strong opening drumroll. The low, throbbing bassline. The jangling guitar line descending and ascending through layers of crashing cymbals and pretty, glittery eighties synths. A lush, dreamy soundscape promising something beautiful and bittersweet.

The best single of the new wave.

The greatest love song of all.

The Cure's "Just Like Heaven" had an overlong opening: forty-nine seconds of instrumental before Robert Smith's off-kilter vox kicked in. Which meant Amelia spent forty-nine seconds turning redder and redder, swaying out of time to the music, looking everywhere but at Liss.

Which just made Liss love her even more.

A flustered Amelia missed the opening, eventually catching up double-time by the end of the first stanza, finally meeting Liss's eye, *"I'll run away with you."*

And Liss just melted. Every last vestige of self-protection washed away like a sandcastle succumbing to the tide. She'd run away with this girl, too. This goofy-sexy girl who kept elbowing her backup-singing sister out of stealing the spotlight—*Matty, get back!*—sometimes singing into the hairbrush, sometimes forgetting to, all while bouncing awkwardly from foot to foot.

Technically, it was terrible. Easily the worst performance Liss had ever seen, and she'd hosted open mic nights. Amelia couldn't hit or hold a note. She messed up the lyrics and fell off the beat. Far from looking like she was enjoying herself, she couldn't stop grimacing and making cringey faces. Yet despite her discomfort, Amelia barreled on, valiantly making eye contact with Liss for the entire bridge and the three precious words inked on her skin, "*Yo-o-ou, soft and only / yo-o-ou, lost and lonely / you, strange as angels.*" It was the sort of thing that'd end up in a cruel viral video. But even before it was over, Liss knew that Amelia's performance would be the best she'd ever have the great fortune of seeing.

Amelia looked surprised when the song ended, then relieved.

Matty grabbed her sister's hand to bow elaborately.

Liss leapt to her feet with a standing ovation, laughing as she clapped, awash with emotion. A chorus of cheers echoed from the kitchen: Jules, Glen, Ludmila, Randall, and Parker, whistling and whooping.

"Don't." Amelia tossed the hairbrush onto the sofa. "God, that was so embarrassing."

"My sister, the star." Matty smooched her cheek before breezing toward Parker, nuzzling in for a kiss.

"Sorry to put you through that." Amelia approached Liss tentatively, cheeks still aglow. "Dad got me all riled up about singing as a form of mating ritual, and I thought maybe I could get it back for you—your favorite song."

"You did." Liss couldn't stop smiling, wanting to touch her, hold her, but aware they weren't alone. "I'll never be able to hear it without thinking of you, so it's mine again. Thank you. But—why?"

Amelia's face was a picture of desperate earnestness. "Because I wanted to show you that . . . Well, as a way of saying that I . . ."

They glanced at the kitchen. Everyone was listening with the sort of excited expectation reserved for wedding guests at the ceremony.

"Guys!" Amelia protested. "Little privacy?"

"Sorry, darling, we're just, um—" Jules picked up a bottle of wine and handed it to Ludmila, who handed it to Randall who handed it to Glen, who put it back on the bench.

"Seriously?" Amelia grabbed Liss's hand, pulling her up the master suite stairs.

As she did, Liss saw Randall hit his weed pen and offer it to Glen, right there in the kitchen. "Dad!" Parker was squawking, "What are you doing?" followed by Matty, "How long have you two been potheads and why haven't you been sharing?"

Liss had to chuckle: Cheech and Chong finally outed themselves.

Upstairs on the suite balcony, the first evening star diamonded in the delicate blue sky. But Liss was only looking into the sweet, worried face of the woman standing opposite her.

"Liss, I'm sorry." Amelia's voice quivered with emotion. "I'm so, so, *so* sorry for saying all those awful things to you. I was just hurt and angry and scared, so scared, of losing you."

"No, Amelia, I'm sorry. I'm the one who should be apologizing to you." Liss took Amelia's hands. Soft and strong, at the same time. "I never should've pushed you away. I never should've let you leave."

"I didn't give you much of a choice. You were right: everything I was proposing—pun unfortunately not intended—was totally bonkers."

"You were just trying to figure out a way for us to be together. While I was too busy focusing on why it wouldn't work." Liss's shame was burnt away by a beautiful certainty as solid as the ground under their feet. "You were right, Amelia. When we leave this island, it *has* to be together. Sydney, Montreal, outer space, the moon: I don't care. As long as it's with you."

Amelia let out a sound of relief, moving close enough for Liss to hold her, their foreheads pressed together. But before Liss could tilt her mouth for a kiss, Amelia spoke in a whisper. "Maybe we don't have to leave."

A tickle of curiosity. Liss pulled back.

"You're right," Amelia said. "Moving to each other's cities is a lot for a first step."

"Well, we can't stay here," Liss said. "I've quit. They're already interviewing for my replacement. As soon as the repairs are done, the whole island will be fully booked out for months."

"And you've always said this is a job for two people. What if . . . I stayed? With you, as a second Caretaker? I talked to Jarrah; he said he'd probably be able to get it approved by the council. Just for a few more months. I'd have to quit my job but that's a risk I'm willing to take. You, and me: here?"

Swims at Secret Spot on their days off. Sunsets at the Barefoot Bar. Someone to laugh with, lean on. Someone to come home to. Someone to grow with. "You'd want to live in the Cabin with me?"

Amelia nodded, eyes fervent. "I know it's a small space, but I'm actually pretty tidy." Half joking, half earnest. "And I can cook."

"Animal." Liss laughed, her blood already fizzing. A new tomorrow unfurled like a treasure map. "You don't have to convince me how incredible you are. I already know."

"So, you'll think about it?"

"I don't need to think about it. Yes."

Joy lit up Amelia's face. "Really?"

"Of course! Amelia, *of course*. I can't imagine my life without you." Living together. Learning about each other. Building something strong and resilient and beautiful. Liss looped her arms around Amelia's neck. "Also, it explains why Max never said goodbye. He knew I'd be back. *We'd* be back."

Amelia laughed, drawing close.

Liss gazed into her eyes and the mysterious galaxies they contained. She would never tire of exploring them. "I love you, Amelia Kelly. I'm yours. So, my answer now, and always, will be *yes*."

"I love you," Amelia whispered, the words prettier than any sunset, sweeter than any love song. "I'm yours, too."

73

"Hurry up, Dad! The boat's almost here!" Matty called, dragging her suitcase up the wharf with the rest of the traveling circus.

"Just a sec!" Glen called, doubling back to Kooroy.

An overcast morning, a touch of melancholy in the lackluster clouds. As if the theater of the island was already over, the audience putting on their coats and filing out into the real world.

Glen retrieved his copy of *The Last Boobook: Birdlife on Lady Lushington Island* from where he'd left it on the second-floor balcony. Lucky to have remembered—it was a keepsake. He already knew this book would have pride of place in his new home in Sydney. The lease Parker and Matty no longer needed, now that they were about-facing back to New York.

"But you can't afford that, Dad." Matty looked alarmed when he proposed it the night before. "Not on your own."

"I'll figure it out," he'd replied, already confident in his plan. "Maybe I'll start a bird-watching club. Charge a few bucks for membership."

Or he'd get a roommate. Pick up some part-time work. His potential was limitless when he stopped clipping his own wings.

The ferry horn sounded. The boat was almost at the wharf. Time to go.

Glen gave the balcony one more glance, bidding a grateful farewell to this avian wonderland.

A blur of white. A soft click: talons on metal.

For a moment, Glen was certain he was dreaming.

Clutching the balcony with its pinky-red feet was a little-known sub-species of the common morepork. Endemic to the island, before they went extinct in the 1970s.

The Lady Lushington Boobook.

The white whale.

Time stood still as man and bird regarded each other.

Up close, Glen could see its feathers weren't the color of clouds, more the color of teeth. It was stocky like a saxophone but majestic like a high F. Perfectly round eyes, the yellow of the sun at high noon. With its cool, unblinking stare, it was easy to see how owls had been connected to wisdom harking back to Ancient Greece. Owls were associated with Athena, goddess of wisdom and war, sitting on her blind side so she could see the whole truth.

Glen's phone was in his pocket. It'd only take a few seconds to take a picture.

But he didn't reach for his device.

Later, he'd tell himself that Jarrah was right: proving the Boobook existed would threaten the island's delicate ecological and spiritual integrity.

But the truth was far simpler. He just wanted to do what birders do. Bear witness to nature. Soak in every glorious second of being present with this magical creature. Its great sagacity. Its ability to survive against all odds.

Glen Kelly didn't need to prove he'd found what he was looking for. He already knew that he had.

74

Earlier that morning, in the liminal place between sleep and awake, Amelia lay cozy-soft in Liss's arms. She wanted to stay in this moment forever, suspended in time. No one would ever leave and nothing would ever change, and she'd be here always, safe and warm with everyone she loved. But then her girlfriend moved underneath her, and reality came into focus.

R-Day.

It wasn't the end of everything. But it was the end of something.

The boat bumped against the wharf. The tanned young captain tossed a loop of rope to Jarrah. The first other human they'd seen in the flesh in six weeks.

Jules threw her arms around Amelia, eyes already wet. "Bye, darling. Oh, I'm going to miss you so much. We *must* FaceTime every night!"

"Maybe not *every* night, Mum," Amelia spoke into her mother's curls. "Maybe every other night."

Jules opened her mouth to protest, then seemed to reconsider. "Yes. Of course. Every other night. Brilliant." She gave Liss an equally tight squeeze. "Bye, my other darling. Take care of each other, won't you?"

"We will," said Liss, slipping Amelia a smile. "And I'm going to hold you to that jam."

"Yes! I'll send it as soon as I'm home!" Jules laughed, kissing them both on the cheek.

Amelia hugged her father. "Bye, Dad."

Typically Glen returned her hugs with arms like iron rods. But now, he held her for a long moment. "Call me anytime, pet. I'm here for you."

"Thanks, Dad." Amelia wiped away a tear—her mother's waterworks were infectious. "Good luck with the move."

Glen looked excited at the prospect, but a pang of sadness prickled Amelia's chest. She wasn't just saying goodbye to her parents. She was saying goodbye to their marriage. She would never get to go back to the home that she knew. It was already gone, and she didn't get to say goodbye. Glen and Jules were being civil but no longer maintaining the fiction they were a couple. Because falling in love didn't always mean forever. As Amelia watched Liss trade inside turtle jokes with Randall and give Parker a hug, she knew that even their love, as pure and true as it felt, wasn't a guarantee.

"Ludmila." Jarrah handed Parker's mother a fishing rod and what looked like a homemade travel case. "So you can go get a fish back in California."

Ludmila accepted the rod with a touched smile. "Thank you very much, Jarrah. I'll be sure to take this on all my travels."

"Where's next?" Liss's hand drifted to Amelia's back, stroking it casually, gently.

How wonderful to be touched like this—like they belonged to each other—in front of her family.

"Paris," Ludmila said, looking at Jules in a strangely expectant way.

Amelia's mother blushed, busying herself with her bags. She'd only given Jarrah a quick hug, the easy chemistry between them muted. But that might be for everyone else's sakes. Amelia suspected there were a lot more changes ahead in her mother's life.

"Randall and I are planning a trip, too." Glen swung his suitcase on board. "The Golden State offers some of the world's best bird-watching. We're going to camp in Joshua Tree. Maybe check out the Pinnacles and hope for a condor!"

Randall's tone was wry. "Prepare yourself for a lot of black-throated sparrows, mate."

The two men exchanged a look and giggled.

Matty and Amelia exchanged an amused smile. "So many same-sex love stories," Matty quipped.

The sound of another engine cut through the morning. A compact silver boat was approaching the wharf, a dark-skinned woman in a baseball cap at the wheel.

Jarrah squinted. "That's Karla, from the local boat shop. What the bloomin' heck's she doin' all the way out here?"

The boat slowed, pulling up to the other side of the old wharf.

"G'day, Karla," Jarrah called.

"G'day, Jarrah," she called back, cutting the engine.

"Nice ride," he said. "Whose boat is that?"

She tossed him a set of keys with a grin. "Yours."

It'd been Randall's idea. Amelia was proud of how quickly her dad, who had every reason to shoot the concept down, agreed to the plan.

Randall clapped Jarrah on the shoulder. "We wanted to say thank you for everything you've done for us these past six weeks."

"Liss connected us to Karla and we all passed round the hat," Glen said. "Karla reckons this is a beaut."

"No way." Jarrah tried to give the keys to Randall, then Glen. "I can't take this."

Neither man took the keys. "It's been a real privilege getting to know you," Randall said.

"Thanks, Randall. Thanks, everyone." Jarrah shook his head, overwhelmed. "Four-stroke outboard, dual console: you could take someone deep-sea fishin' in this thing!"

Glen glanced at Jules and folded his arms. "I did ask Karla about something more suited to *solo* fishing."

"Dad." Amelia elbowed him. It wasn't clear whether Jules and Jarrah would see each other after this trip, but if they did, it was their call to make.

The four parents busied themselves with getting on board the ferry, leaving Matty and Amelia to their goodbyes.

Of all the people leaving, this was the hardest. Because it felt like a true ending between the sisters. The life Amelia had planned for them was never going to happen. In a way, the entire family was flying the Kelly coop.

The sisters hugged until the ferry sounded its horn.

"Call me when you get to the airport," Amelia said, sniffling. "And every five minutes after that."

Matty laughed, blowing her nose into a hankie. "Don't get gay married without me. And don't think it's all over after your first big fight."

"Or the second one," Parker called back from the boat. "Or third."

Amelia giggled. "I won't."

Matty kissed her cheek. "I love you, Animal. You're my everything."

Amelia hugged her one last time. They would always be sisters. Everything else might change. That never would.

Liss and Amelia stood arm in arm as Jarrah unlooped the rope from the wharf and pushed the boat off.

"Bye!" Everyone chorused. "I love you! Stay safe! Goodbye!"

They waved until the faces on the boat became unrecognizable smudges, disappearing into the hazy horizon.

Jarrah hopped in next to Karla, saying something about a test drive. "When I get back, you two can start on laundry. Vacation's over."

Amelia nodded. "You got it, boss."

He pulled off into the bay, carving a V-shaped path through the sapphire water. And then, they were alone.

But they would never be truly alone on the island.

Amelia closed her eyes and inhaled deeply. She wanted to feel everything: sadness and uncertainty. Love and gratitude. The interconnectedness of all living things. The deep magic and wisdom that existed in every seedpod and every fairy wren.

The ending.

And, the beginning.

EPILOGUE

Behind the house that faces the ocean, the leafless milkwort is flowering, dew drops evaporating on blue-purple petals. A baby carpet python slithers soundlessly by the rock shaped like a hamburger, seeking the sun and a lizard or two. In the shadows of a king fern at Wonapinga Head, a lyrebird warbles its liquid song.

Rick, Vyvyan, Neil, and Mike sleep curled up together in the hollow of the Queensland blue gum, dreaming of apple slices. Submerged in the swampy waters of the Lost Lagoon, a saltwater crocodile wonders if the women will ever return. Miles away in the deepest ocean, a three-hundred-pound sea turtle recalls being carried, the feel of human hands forever etched in its memory.

On Mooka Mooka Beach, the tropical storm has dislodged a piece of the Lady Lushington. Now, at full tide, the ocean claims it, rolling the fragment of the colonizer's ship away from Mun'dai. A pelican swoops to land balletic on the new ledge created by its absence, eyeing a school of whiting flickering silver nearby.

It will be a day like every other and unlike any other. It is life on Mun'dai.

When Amelia opens her eyes, Liss is standing a few feet away. The girl she'd build for herself in a lab. Impossibly, hers. Impossibly, here.

Amelia Kelly had come to the island for a fairytale romance. What she ends up with is so much better.

She doesn't know if Liss is the one or her soulmate. She doesn't know if those things exist. What Amelia does know is she wants it to work and she isn't expecting perfection. More than her lover, Liss is also her friend, and that feels important, somehow. That feels different. All Amelia can do is try. Trust. Be willing to go into the dark places in herself. Invite Liss along. Go into her dark places, too.

They won't be alone for long. But right now, it is just the two of them at the end of the old wooden wharf on Blinky Beach, under the gulls that circle and cry overhead.

Liss's eyes are sparkling, sunshine on sea. "Hi."

"Oh." Amelia tugs her close until their lips are just about to touch. "Hello."

ACKNOWLEDGMENTS

I started this book in August 2020 knowing it would be fundamentally different from my pre-pandemic work. Unlike my previous New York–set novels, I needed this story to take me to the place I was unable to go, to the people I was unable to see. Australia. My family. Even though I was quarantining in Brooklyn, my heart was in the Queensland tropics, where I spent school holidays as a child visiting my grandparents, and where my mother currently lives.

I wanted to tell the story we were all living through—disruption to our lives bringing about irrevocable change—but with a hopeful and idyllic rom-com twist. So, an island. Sadly, Mun'dai is fictional (I know, I want to go there, too), but it is geographically modeled off the nearby K'Gari (Fraser Island), a place Mum and I visited the last time I was in Hervey Bay, in 2019. K'Gari is Butchulla land: I figured Mun'dai would be the same. I wanted everything about the island and its history to be as authentic as possible. This was not a feat I approached lightly and there was no way I could do it alone.

Of all the people who helped inspire and shape this novel, I am the most indebted to Luke Barrowcliffe. *Island Time* would not have been possible without this wonderful human. Luke is a Butchulla man, based in Gympie, who runs an Indigenous multimedia company called Goorie Vision. After generously replying to a cold email, we started a conversation that continued over many months. Luke shared his story with me—as an activist, community member, artist, father, and son. There were already a startling amount of parallels between Jarrah and Luke—Luke helped enrich and deepen them. From the cleansing ceremony to the creation myths, from the houses' designs to the names of significant landmarks, Luke helped bring the Indigenous past and present of Mun'dai to glorious life. Learning from Luke and sharing his story was an emotionally, intellectually, and culturally enriching experience that I'll never forget. Luke, thank you for sharing your heart and your history with me, and my readers. I really hope I did a good job.

I discovered "singing in the whales" via Cherissma Blackman-Costelloe, LLB, a First Nations Educator in Laws, Culture/s, and issues impacting Survival (Humane & Environmental). Thank you for sharing this moving ritual and sacred words with me.

It was an honor to interview Michelle Deshong, of the Kuku Yulanji nation, as part of my research. Butchulla Elder and artist Karen Hall was also kind enough to answer my endless questions.

As always, I'm supremely grateful for my rock star literary agent, Allison Hunter, of Trellis Literary Management, and her smart assistant, Natalie Edwards. I'm so glad I'm not doing all this alone.

I bow down to my powerhouse editor, Emily Bestler; associate editor, Lara Jones; publicist, Megan Rudloff; marketer, Katelyn Phillips; production editor, Sonja Singleton; design director Dana Sloan; cover designer Sarah Horgan; map illustrator Alexis Seabrook; marketing director Karlyn Hixson; deputy director of publicity Lisa Sciambra; vice president/director of backlist Suzanne Donahue; associate publisher of Atria, Dana Trocker; senior vice president and publisher of Atria, Libby McGuire; and everyone at Atria/Simon & Schuster who helped make this island dream a book reality.

Sarah Cypher is the developmental editor I recommend to every author. Thank you for sharing your incredible gifts with me.

Big thanks to my screen agents, Jason Richman and Addison Duffy of UTA. Also to Gail Gilchriest for an important early chat; volcanologist Emma Liu; Connor Beaton of ManTalks for invaluable insight into Glen Kelly; Lauren Letta for all the COO/Poppe stuff; Liz Dinerstein for Ludmila's design background; Madison Keesler of the San Francisco Ballet; and early reader Melissa Epifano.

Thanks to author pals Hannah Orenstein and Kate Spencer for such beautiful early blurbs.

Bookstagram, I adore you and support you in getting paid for the incredible work that you do.

While the pandemic took a lot from me, it also gave me the clarity that I want to tell queer love stories, which I've never put front and center despite being, to quote K Stew, "like, so gay, dude." I'm grateful to queer creators, especially queer writers, for their work in inspiring this refocusing.

This book is dedicated to my family, the Clarks, especially my mum, Jayne (wearer of Bunnings hats, maker of jams), my father, Ken (listener of jazz, reader of words), and my brother, Will (catcher of all the fish). Extra love for my sister-in-law, Louise, and niece, Evie-Peevie. I miss you more than words can express.

Thank you to my lovely in-laws, the Ratowskys, who are nothing like the Lees!

My goofy-sexy wife, Lindsay Ratowsky, is the magical beating heart of my own love story. I love you, boo boo. You're my favorite.

This book made a dark time unbelievably bright for me. I've never loved working on a project more: it was a privilege and a true career highlight. I hope *Island Time* was likewise pleasurable for you and so, finally, thank you for being a reader.